The Weight of Dark Love!

Karina Vega

Karina Vega

Book Cover by [AI designed and generated by Karina Vega]

Illustrations by [AI designed and generated by Karina Vega]

Dedication

To the broken part within you...

Author's note

Hello dear reader,

I write darker romance that can be upsetting and disturbing. My books and the characters within them aren't for the faint of heart.

Elijah Dominion and Monica Puscasu are not your typical couple — they are the very embodiment of obsession, possession, and psychopathy. *The Weight of Dark Love* is an intense dark romance with graphic and explicit content. Please proceed with care and awareness of your triggers.

This book includes the following triggers:

- Extreme possessiveness and obsessive territoriality (graphic claiming, fixation, violent threats).
- Rough, primal sex with dominant and possessive behaviour.
- Breath play (choking / gagging).
- Deep-throating with limited breathing breaks.
- Impact play (slapping, biting, nipple/breast play).
- Marking / bodily fluid play.

- Restraint, teasing, edging, and mutual surrender.
- Intense verbal dominance and primal claiming.
- Vocal possessiveness and territorial threats ("I'll kill anyone who looks at you").
- Highly explicit sexual language with dark psychological undertones.
- Detailed torture descriptions, including tools.
- Manipulation and psychological control.

Note on intimacy: This story includes elements of light BDSM (toys, restraint, breath play), but it is not a BDSM romance. These acts are expressions of Elijah and Monica's obsessive, psychopathic bond rather than negotiated kink dynamics.

Both Elijah and Monica are unapologetically psychopathic with true Machiavellian traits. This is not a redemption arc. This is not a fade to grey. Their journey is about embracing who they are — unhinged, relentless, and devoted.

This book is recommended **18+ only**.

The Weight of Dark Love is the conclusion of **Dominion Series I**, and the series must be read in order.

For more about my work, visit www.karinavega.com

From my heart to yours,
Karina V.

Blurbs

Monica

I need to see the beauty in what society deems perfect.

My life has been a performance, a carefully crafted mask, a well-rehearsed deception, a game played for survival. They don't *see me*. They see what I allow them to, the image they need to believe.

Because if they ever saw the real me, they'd run. They'd scream.

I thought I was alone. Destined to exist as a ghost among the living, bound by the rules of a world that has no space for someone like me.

But then I saw him.

And in his eyes, I found the one thing I never thought I'd have.

Recognition.

I've spent my entire life suppressing my shadow, burying my truth beneath layers of control. But now, faced with someone like him, someone who shouldn't exist, yet does, a question lingers, clawing at the edges of my sanity...

How can I step into the light, when I was never meant to be seen?

And how can I not, when for the first time... I'm not alone?

Elijah

I've never hidden what I am. There's no need.

Fear is a language I speak fluently, and power always bends to those who embrace their nature instead of denying it.

I was born into the Bratva, raised in blood and violence, forged into something more than human.

I never questioned my place in the world—because there was no equal. I was the anomaly. The one.

Until *her.*

For the first time, everything makes sense. Because I'm not alone. Because now, there are two of us.

Nothing worth having comes easy. To claim something truly valuable, you fight, crawl, steal—whatever it takes—until it's yours.

And what she is to me, what I feel for her, it's not love. It's not obsession.

It's the very definition of reality.

I see the beauty in what the world calls imperfect.

But to me, she's the only perfection that's ever existed.

She doesn't understand yet.

There's nothing I wouldn't do for her. Legal or illegal. Pleasure or pain. In the light, or in the darkness.

She is everything.

My first. My last.

My light. My darkness.

My final breath.

Without her, there is nothing left. No reason to breathe.

Contents

Chapter One

Monica

It's like any other day. I wake at 4 a.m., take my coffee black and my shower cold. By six, I'm at the shop. Routine. Repetition. Nothing new.

If my life had a color, it'd be beige. A flavor? Cheap, synthetic vanilla. One word? Boring.

I'm a busy woman. Forty-two. A daughter who's twenty-two. A business to run. A charity to manage. A husband. An appearance to maintain.

On paper, it looks full. In reality, it's all too predictable. And quietly, it feels empty. I guess hiding my entire life would do that to a person.

Since I was a small child, I knew I wasn't like other people. I could feel it, something inside me that didn't match the world around me, even if I couldn't name it then. Over time, it became clearer. I am different.

School and anything academic wasn't difficult. It was pointless. A complete waste of time. I could do the work with my eyes closed, but only mathematics, science and physics held my interest.

The reason I became a florist is because I wanted to do something for myself, not something I was pushed into. And by that, I mean by my parents, to please them or the society around me.

They forced this mask on me. I won't give them my last breath of sanity as well.

They can all go and get fucked, for all I care.

I'm not sure what my parents wanted from me, but one thing is for certain, no one liked a girl who preferred numbers to people. So I was mostly alone throughout my childhood and in school, not to mention my teenage years.

The whole social aspect of life was a mystery at first. It took years to observe, to decode, to mimic what was expected of me in certain situations.

They became learned behaviour. But I got there in the end.

My mask was formed to perfection. Now I fit into this damned society like a glove. No one would suspect who lurks around them, the real person behind the smile, the polite remarks and the courteous gestures.

People don't want the truth. Not really. They definitely don't want my thoughts or real opinions.

I learned that early, thanks to my upbringing. Tried it once, earned myself beating after beating so severe I couldn't sit straight for days.

So thank you very much, but no thank you.

I adapted. I learned to hide in plain sight. It's my power now.

By the time this fire, this need, rose up inside me, I made the mistake of sharing it once. Just once. With my mother.

She was beyond mortified by my... what did she call it?

Ah, yes. Dark thoughts.

That was the moment I understood. There's no saving this. No fixing me.

Who I am — what I am — isn't meant for the spotlight. It's something to control. To contain.

So I learned... to hide.

I hide in plain sight.

Somehow, I see patterns. Events. The probability of things unfolding a certain way, it's inevitable for me. I don't force my mind to do it. My brain just works that way. Naturally.

It sees through people. Strips them bare. Past their masks, straight to their ugliest, rawest selves, as if they're offering it up for inspection.

And I've always wanted to drag that truth out. To force them, to look inside them.

To see what they really are.

That hunger's been with me for as long as I can remember.

The problem is... people don't want to see themselves. Not truly.

They prefer their bubbles, ignorance, self-loathing, pity, pride, narcissistic selves.

On and on.

And always — always — everyone thinks they're the good guy. The righteous one.

Everyone else is bad. Dirty. Twisted.

It's fascinating, really. Watching from a distance.

Analysing.

Laughing to myself at what humanity actually is.

I see how easily I could manipulate everyone around me.

The hunger to unmask, to punish, to hurt — gruesomely — is like a thirst I've never allowed myself to taste.

But it's there. Always.

And I know, no one could ever understand what I really need.

This isn't a want. It's a need.

A gnawing thing inside me. Constant. Consuming.

Still, I know better.

I can never show my true self, in my natural form, to anyone.

I have perfected my mask so well that I exude an aura of serene tranquillity.

My outward demeanour is a mask of calmness that belies the tempest raging within.

When I was finally old enough to understand myself — to recognise why I felt the way I did — Angela arrived. My daughter.

And just like that, everything had to be buried even deeper.

The darkness. The hunger.

My psychopathic instincts were forced into the background, locked in a labyrinth of shadows and deception.

Hidden beneath a carefully constructed calm.

Society's expectations taught me that I needed a man to raise my child — even if I never truly cared for the idea.

My mother couldn't bear the shame of me being a single mother before twenty.

We were a religious family. Catholic to the bone, where appearances meant everything.

In truth, it was all bullshit — and we all knew it.

So I found myself pregnant with a husband who, like all men, was boring, beige and fake vanilla.

At least we came to an understanding from the beginning. I realised I didn't need to give in to my tendencies and dispose of him once I was out of my parents reach.

We reached a mutual agreement — a façade of a marriage, and that was the extent of it.

He escaped his family, and I escaped mine by moving to England. Neither of our families could mess up our lives any further.

The moment I gave birth to my daughter and looked at her for the first time, I felt something unfamiliar.

It wasn't dark.

It wasn't flat. It wasn't indifference. It wasn't like any of my other needs.

It was possessiveness.

For the first time, I understood my version of love.

I named her Angela — after the angel she is.

There's no doubt in my mind, if what happened to me hadn't happened, my life would've taken a very different path.

I would've become an assassin.

Truly.

I despise people, and I wouldn't feel a thing ending the lives of the shit-fuckers who walk around thinking they're better than everyone else.

Life is simple.

It's black and white.

Grey is rare. But people cling to it, because admitting the darkness inside themselves? That's too much for ordinary people to accept.

I don't have that problem.

I like that I feel nothing.

I love knowing I could kill in a hundred ways.

Slow or quick.

Merciful or brutal.

With precision. With chaos.

In silence. Or through screams.

I could break a body, shatter a mind, erase a soul — and feel nothing.

No hesitation.

No regret.

Just the cold, simple thrill of control.

It's who I am.

So why the hell would I hide from myself?

I have to suppress it, for them.

But never for myself.

I accept who I am. What I am.

Society could never accept me for who I am. My family doesn't love me — never even cared about me.

But I do.

I accept it all as a gift. A rare inheritance.

Because that's exactly what it is.

Supreme genes.

In the mirror, I don't see a monster.

I see a master. A predator wrapped in silk. A phantom moving unseen among the weak.

I've embraced the truth of my nature — not with shame, not with hesitation, but with the cold satisfaction of knowing exactly what I am.

The darkness in my veins isn't a curse.

It's power.

I'm not burdened by guilt or conscience.

I don't waste time on self-loathing or doubt.

I am liberated, unshackled from the illusion of morality.

I move through the world with a clarity most will never know about themselves.

Their minds are clouded with emotion, hesitation, fear.

Mine is not.

I am a psychopath. Calculated. Precise. Free.

And the fact that I can wear a mask so flawlessly that not even my husband or daughter sees the truth?

That is the ultimate proof of my power.

I am a master of deception, a queen of control, and my strength lies in the fact that no one suspects a thing.

Angela is the only thing that matters in my world, the only anomaly that's ever stirred any kind of emotion.

Then there's the charity. A convenient distraction.

It does some good in the community, and perhaps, in the world.

Once I settled with Dan and we got married, I realised it wouldn't end badly for him.

I could fantasise about hurting him without needing to act on it.

I didn't have to kill or torture him, and that realisation was a relief.

It meant hiding in plain sight beside him would be easier.

I could focus on what truly mattered... raising Angela.

Over time, I learned more about myself, peeling back layers of forced civility, understanding the depths of my own mind.

And with every revelation, I saw just how lucky I was compared to the neurotypical masses trapped by emotions, ruled by impulses they can't control.

I am not like them. I never was.

And that is my greatest advantage.

I was in my thirties when I was finally diagnosed with Asperger's Syndrome.

It meant nothing to me. Just a label for what I had always known, a name for the way my mind worked, nothing more.

What mattered was the realisation that if I wanted to exist unnoticed, I had to refine my control even further.

I needed to sharpen my mind — to use it as both weapon and cage, containing the darkness within while perfecting the performance of social etiquette.

I opened my charity for children with ASD (Autism Spectrum Disorder) and the families navigating it.

We provide therapeutic support, psychological and psychiatric care, as well as medical and artistic programs.

I built it with my grandfather's inheritance — every cent going into its foundation.

The rest came from Dan's and my savings over the years.

So now I help children who are hiding, just like I am.

We work with over forty families, and I know there's a boy among them who is just like me.

Given the right support, he will find his way.

He will learn to navigate the world as I have.

One day, he will make a great businessman — cold, strategic, untouchable — or some kind of doctor.

A CEO runs the charity. Keeping my distance is necessary. Close proximity could become a problem down the line — and only a fool allows themselves to be blinded by a title.

Power is about control, not visibility.

As I said, my life is boring.

But it makes sense for me.

From every angle, it serves its purpose.

"Hi, Mum. I'm back!"

Angela's sweet voice cuts through the air, pulling me from my thoughts.

What time is it? I've been stuck in this damn fridge, cleaning flowers and foliage for the past three hours.

Sometimes, I wonder why I bother. Angela is twenty-two. She doesn't need me the way she once did.

So why the fuck am I still enduring this, when I could just retire and live off Dan's earnings?

I could hire someone. Make them do this tedious shit while I watch.

"Hi, my darling! How are you? Did you have coffee yet? Do you need me to get some coffee and maybe a pastry?" I ask Angela, my tone light, easy.

The fact that my heart warms whenever I see her is still a mystery to me.

In all my years, I've never met someone I didn't want to hurt in some way — except for her.

Is this what other people feel?

This absence of calculation — this strange desire to protect rather than control?

I don't want to manipulate her. I don't want to break her, bend her, push her.

I am painfully aware of how much of myself I reveal to her, careful to let her see just enough, but never too much.

She is my daughter. She should know me... to a degree.

But my words are always measured. My presence carefully calibrated, so she never has reason to fear me.

That is my greatest fear — that one day, Angela will see me for what I am.

That she will look at me and her heart will quiver with fear, recognising the cold, calculating nature beneath my mask.

That will never happen. I won't allow it. I'll make sure of it.

I will never manipulate my daughter.

But my husband is fair game.

With him, I do as I please, shaping his words to serve my purpose.

Think of it like a business transaction.

He gets his wins. And I most definitely get my own.

"No. I missed breakfast and dinner. This mock trial for finals is stressing me out. I think I lost at least ten years of my life," Angela says, plopping onto an upside-down bucket with a dramatic sigh.

"Oh, my darling! Look at my daughter, the big lawyer, beating herself up and sitting on a bucket," I say, biting back laughter at her exaggerated distress.

Neurotypical people are endlessly amusing.

So much weight placed on something so light.

"Mum, it is not funny! *State vs. James Thompson* is a big case! I was lucky my professor chose me as Lead Defence Attorney. This mark is thirty per cent of my final score. This is serious. Stop laughing, Mum!"

Angela is up from her bucket now, her voice rising as I struggle to keep my laughter in check.

Her frustration over something so small is adorable.

"I'm sorry, my darling. I'm just trying to distract you, to make you laugh," I say, smoothing my expression into something softer.

"You're going to be a great lawyer, but your greatest asset is your determination.

I have no doubt you're researching every possible way to shift the perspective, to turn the light in a different direction.

Do you think he's guilty?"

"Fuck yes! Sorry, Mum," she blurts out, quickly lowering her head, scrambling to find a more professional way to express what's already written all over her face.

"So what's the problem? Are you having trouble defending someone who's guilty?"

This is the moment I've been dreading.

Is my daughter truly mine — or is she too pure?

The anticipation coils around me like a vice, tightening with every second of silence.

The weight of her next words lingers in the air, casting a shadow over my confidence, exposing something raw within me.

My mind races. Calculating. Bracing for the impact of her unfiltered thoughts.

This moment will either draw us closer, or start building a wall between us.

I won't force myself onto my daughter.

If my true nature is too much for her, if she recoils from what I am, I'll step back.

Silently. Without hesitation.

But then, she speaks.

"No."

That single word is like a hug to my soul.

She is mine.

My daughter is mine.

She may not be exactly like me, but there is no doubt now, she is most definitely my daughter.

"I'm going to get some coffee and a pastry. Let's take a break, then we can finish cleaning the fridge together," I say, my voice even, though satisfaction thrums beneath my skin.

By the time I return with the coffee and pastry, Angela has just finished a colourful arrangement for Jake and Jack Consulting.

"Nice! Did they give you a budget to work with this week?"

"No, not really. He just keeps saying to do whatever I want because *everything I make is beautiful — just like me.*"

Angela rolls her eyes, her voice dripping with disgust.

"I feel like throwing up every time I see Jake. Can we drop them as clients?"

She makes puppy dog eyes at me, silently pleading to be spared another unfortunate encounter with Jake.

"Sure, my baby. I'll even cut off his balls for you if you want," I say with a smile, already picturing my knife slick with blood.

Or maybe scissors would be better. My flower pliers could use some bloodstains.

The thought settles something deep inside me — calming the restless edge as I picture his screams, the warm drip of blood coating metal.

"But what do I always say? What's your biggest strength?"

"My brain," she mutters, her expression sour.

She sighs, then grabs a coffee and a croissant.

"I still think he's a dick."

"If your brain is the strongest part of you, don't let trash take up space in it."

I take a sip of my coffee, watching her.

"I love you. Now go deliver their arrangement. We have a very busy day ahead, my darling."

The next hour passes as I process orders from Interflora, Teleflora and Bloomerx.

I prefer working with international companies, it minimises my exposure to imbeciles.

Or at least, that's what I tell myself.

Clearly, Jake is the exception I've not managed to shake off for the past six months.

Angela is right.

I need to drop them.

I'll work something out, pass them off to another florist who would kill for their business.

Let them deal with his nauseating compliments.

Floristry has never been about money or people.

If anything, dealing with people is the worst part of my job.

What I love is the scent.

The moment I unlock the shop in the morning and the fresh, crisp aroma of flowers and foliage engulfs me — drowning out the world.

I love the colours, the textures, the way I can shape something beautiful from nothing.

It's the closest I'll ever come to being an artist — not that I care for the title.

People romanticise flowers.

They see each blossom as a symbol of love, hope, and the endless cycle of renewal.

They fixate on the light — blind to the truth.

Flowers are not just delicate. They are strong.

They wound, they poison, they suffocate.

Beauty does not mean innocence.

I feel sorry for them.

They will never see life in its truest form — the perfect balance of beauty and ugliness, pain and happiness, darkness and light.

Chapter Two

Monica

A few hours later I was lost in thought when Angela stomped into the shop, her movements sharp, radiating frustration. Instinct kicked in instantly, that a familiar, simmering urge to control and correct. I forced it down as always. What else can I do?

"My darling, what happened?" My voice stayed steady, measured, calm.

Angela's face twisted with anger.

"I hate him, Mum! What the fuck is wrong with him? Every time I'm there, he just stops everything and stares. At my breasts, my arse, like I'm something he owns. And the way he talks, the slimy little remarks! Ugh! Mum, I actually dry-heaved today."

As I process everything without letting my mask slip, an SUV pulls up behind our car and something in the air shifts. I can't put my finger on it, but something is different.

If it's Jake, he's mine!

Something always felt off about him, but then again, most people are annoying by nature.

If I applied that standard too strictly, I wouldn't be able to work with anyone.

The doorbell rings and a tall, handsome man strides into the shop, commanding attention as if he owns the place.

His lean frame, towering yet poised, carries an air of quiet confidence. Strength radiates from him, drawing eyes to his striking presence. But it's his ocean-blue eyes that hold the real pull, a mesmerising depth that could fool the unwary.

This might be interesting.

His sharp features soften with the faintest hint of a smile, the kind that might make someone believe he is the perfect man. Laid-back. Effortless. That is, if they don't look too closely.

His posture is too stiff. His hands tremble, barely noticeable, but there. The charming smile does not reach his eyes.

He is nervous as hell.

And if he is here for Angela, he's in for a surprise. If he thinks he can try something while she is next to me, he will regret it. I might not be able to kill as my nature demands, but after what happened to me before we moved here—what changed everything—I started Krav Maga. I needed to know I could protect myself and her at all costs. If he comes after her, he will regret it. I will make sure of it.

My gaze shifts to Angela. I keep my voice steady and gentle.

"My darling, go to the back and take a moment to compose yourself. Once I've dealt with this man, we'll figure out a way to cancel their contract. Is that okay?"

Without another word, she turns and disappears into the fridge room.

I adjust my mask with the grace of a hundred celestial beings and offer the man a smooth smile.

"Hi, can I help you with something?"

"Thank you. I'm just browsing for a moment. I'll let you know."

He turns, deliberately presenting his back to me.

Interesting.

I'm not buying this act for a second.

Who is he, and why is he after Angela?

I analyse him discreetly, careful not to trigger an attack, because if he is what I'm assuming, I want this to run smoothly and not escalate into a fight.

He's definitely armed.

At least two guns. Two knives, judging by the way he holds himself.

His posture screams military training—controlled, precise—but there's no doubt he's nervous.

His eyes stay locked on the gladiolus display, his back still to me.

I don't think he's a threat.

But there's only one way to be sure. I need to let him do what he came here to do, and then act on it.

"The delivery went well, Mum. They loved the colour scheme I used this week, and they asked if I could make an arrangement for his home and deliver it later today."

I glance at Angela. She's doing her best to appear professional and calm, but I see the shift, the subtle change in her posture.

Disgust flickers into something else... interest, the moment she locks eyes on him.

My gaze moves to the man.

Panic rolls off him in waves.

Oh...

Is he into Angela? Do they know each other?

He doesn't seem to understand what he's feeling. His muscles are tight, his hands trembling just that bit more. The conflict within him is radiating off him in waves.

Right...

"I'm sure he loved the last arrangement you delivered. Did he give you a budget or a theme?" I ask, keeping my tone light.

"Not really. He just said to make something I'm happy with."

As the words leave Angela's mouth, the man turns to face us so fast, his movements so uncoordinated he's almost tripping over a vase, his urgency a perfect match for the panic rolling off him.

Right...

Jealousy... you sweet, sweet thing.

Nothing grabs a man's attention faster!

Angela doesn't seem to notice the danger in him. She's too caught up in the smooth lines of his face, the crystal-clear ocean-blue eyes that have her mesmerised.

"Excuse me, could you please help me?"

And there it is.

Desperation. That honey-sweet taste.

I almost chuckle at his reaction.

He's making a real effort to look only at Angela — like I don't exist.

"How can I help you?"

Angela is completely oblivious when a man makes a move on her. It's almost adorable how out of touch she is with it.

Right! Let's see how this plays out. Maybe I can remove the death threat hanging over this man's head.

"Angela, I will arrange some flowers outside if you need me."

I grab the first bucket of flowers within reach and step outside, giving them space.

As I pass the man, I make a point of meeting his eyes, letting my most discreet 'I will kill you slowly' look settle on him.

Not overtly violent. Just a promise.

I've perfected it over the years.

It works wonders on difficult clients, and men who think they can outmaneuver me in negotiations.

The moment I step outside, I feel it again.

Something is catastrophically wrong.

Something just feels different. Out of place.

It's visceral, an icy chill that coils through my veins, numbing me with uncertainty.

But there's something else. A sense of familiarity.

What is it?

I keep my hands busy, arranging the flowers, adjusting the outside display just enough to look occupied.

All the while, I listen in on their conversation.

"*I noticed you looking at the gladiolus. Would you like something along those lines?*" I hear on Angela's voice, calm and professional, while I keep working the flowers.

"*Not quite, but thank you for noticing. I'm a blank canvas. Feel free to suggest anything that comes to mind.*"

Well, fuck.

That's a terrible line, but at least he's managing to get the words out.

Judging by his panicked posture, I'd say that's an achievement. I am almost proud of him.

The thought makes me chuckle out loud. At that moment, the car window rolls down, and I meet the gaze of a man with white and grey hair, a short white and grey beard, and dark blue eyes.

His features are sharp, sculpted with an air of wealth and elegance.

But it's his eyes that hold me still.

They carry the weight of untold wisdom and experience, their mere presence demanding submission.

That's when I realise.

His eyes are dead. Hollow. Void of emotion.

And he doesn't care to hide it.

I smile.

He does not react. His face remains a perfect blank, untouched by human sentiment. But I can feel it. The weight of his attention, the way we are analysing each other, dissecting without a single word.

An invisible thread has pulled at me, tugging me outside the shop. Something deeper than logic. A *recognition* that defies explanation.

Without words, my mind sharpens, attuned to the energy shifting between us. I felt his presence before I even saw him. Catastrophic, all-consuming.

His darkness called to me.

For a split second, something flickers in his eyes.

Gone as fast as it appeared.

Then the window rises, signalling the end of our "conversation."

Fuck you, Mr Santa.

If you think I'm some common woman who'll run back inside just because you tried to intimidate me, you're fucking mistaken.

I'm not that person.

"I like it. How many should I put in an arrangement if I'm trying to impress someone?"

Oh, this boy is killing me.

Just ask her for her number and get out of my shop. How hard can it be?

I glance inside to check if his posture has changed.

"*Criminal law. I absolutely love it. I love the psychology of it, and I love the cause-and-effect element to it.*"

Oh dear.

Angela takes after someone else, because she is absolutely the serial killer of hot vibes.

I glance at the man and catch the shift. His posture tightens, turning defensive.

Right. Not military. Criminal.

This conversation needs to wrap up.

"*Interesting. What made you study this?*"

He tries to steady himself, to appear unaffected. He really is trying not to put Angela off.

But it's too late.

I'm on to him. And this needs to end.

From the car, I feel the fury rolling off Santa like a tidal wave, and I couldn't give a shit. If he hasn't figured out what's happening here, then he's not who I thought.

Though I'd be very surprised if I misread him.

That is my cue to step in and protect my child from a criminal.

He's not good for her, and he needs to learn that sooner rather than later.

"I'm just going to the back to clean up, Angela. Could you come and help me once you are done with the gentleman?" I say as I pass them, my tone smooth, casual.

I step into the fridge and turn to the cameras, watching the shop and the car in the front.

I have a monumental problem.

I think there are two of us.

Chapter Three

Elijah

I sit in the car, calculating and recalculating the next steps of the day. Planning. Assessing. Optimising. Efficiency is absolute, both for myself and my team. There is no margin for error.

Then I hear it.

A laugh.

It's melodic, unfamiliar.

It stops me mid-thought, seizing my attention with an authority I would never allow.

Unacceptable.

Yet I am listening.

At first, I'm so stunned by my reaction that I do nothing. The sound has paralysed me.

It feels like a violation, sharp and unwelcome.

This is an intrusion—unexpected, unnatural.

An explosion in a black hole. Like a meteorite colliding with Earth and eradicating all life.

Something has penetrated my world without permission, without warning.

It shatters the order I have built, plunging me into an abyss of uncertainty.

Unacceptable. An intrusion that demands consequences.

And yet, I cannot ignore it.

It demands my attention as if my next move, my response, will determine the fate of humanity itself.

I open my eyes and take in my surroundings. Every detail registers, analysed and stored.

The woman stands next to my car, pretending to arrange flowers. But she's not arranging anything. She keeps touching the same flower, again and again, a motion too deliberate to be innocent.

A distraction. A cover.

The car window rolls down by itself.

For a brief second, it almost feels as if I willed it to move with my sheer interest in this woman.

My eyes lock onto her, and the world blurs at the edges. Everything else fades into irrelevance.

Time slows, each detail of her seared into my memory with unnatural clarity. The absence of makeup. The sweet curve of her lips, concealing something far darker. And her eyes—dead, cold, holding secrets too vast for the ordinary mind to comprehend.

The contrast is undeniable. A paradox in human form.

A shockwave pulses through me. An anomaly. A critical error in the system I've spent my entire life perfecting.

I do not lose control in any aspect of my life, yet here I am.

She is like me.

Whoever she is, she is like me.

And in that moment, my world shifts.

Irrevocably.

Nothing will ever be the same again. I know it in my soul, something changed forever.

I am a person of few words.

Even if I were not, even if words flowed from me as rivers carve their path, I would still have none for this creature.

They escape me.

The sheer violation of her existence renders me incapable of holding her gaze for more than a moment. My mind, trained for precision and control, stalls.

Unacceptable. Where was she until now?

I roll the window up, ending this encounter.

In forty-three years, nothing prepared me for this. No initiation. No contingency plan for something like this.

She has violently invaded my existence.

And that is not something I will allow to pass easily.

It would take a simple message to Sofia for her to compile a full report and send it to me in minutes. The tablet next to me would hold everything there is to know about this creature and that young girl.

I warned Dominic, that little shit, that the girl who sang her heart out off-key does not belong in our world. That he should stay the fuck away.

I run my business and my staff with precision. I do not dictate who they date, who they fuck, or who they marry. That is their decision. But if I disapprove, for any reason, I remove them.

No one is indispensable.

And I'd hate to cut Dominic off over some woman.

He's efficient. And funny.

There are days when he even makes me laugh—internally, of course.

And who wouldn't appreciate a perfectly timed joke—in the middle of negotiations or even torture?

I have never been lucky with women, but luck has nothing to do with it.

I cannot stand most people. The opposite sex is no exception. In fact, they are even worse.

The only reason I have ever touched a woman is to satisfy a physical need. Nothing more.

They understand this from the start. So do I, the moment I send them a hefty gift for their services and erase them from my life.

At no point have I ever felt like I was missing something.

I've never envied those who have someone.

It has never mattered.

Love is overrated.

Irrational.

A biological illusion, crafted to ensure survival and reproduction.

It tricks the brain with a cocktail of chemicals—dopamine for the rush, oxytocin for attachment, serotonin to stabilise moods. A chemical haze masking reality behind temporary euphoria.

This so-called love breeds dependency, blinds people to flaws, sets them up for inevitable disappointment.

They idealise. They cling.

And when the illusion shatters, they are left with nothing but disillusionment.

Love is fleeting. Unreliable.

A construct driven by evolutionary imperatives, not some profound, enduring truth.

So why the fuck would I want it for myself? I think to myself as I open the file that Sofia just sent over with the details of the shop's owner.

Name: Monica Puscasu

Date of Birth: 27 July 1982

Place of Birth: Botoșani, Romania

Parents: Catrinca and Teodor Ionescu

Business Ownership:

- Owns a flower shop: *Beautiful Things*
- Last year's gross income: $202,000

Other Interests:

- Silent partner in *Little Steps*, a charity for children with ASD

Family:

- Daughter: Angela Josephine Puscasu
- Husband: Dan Puscasu

The tablet screen goes black as I lock it and drop it onto the seat beside me.

Husband!

She is married?

My creature is married?

Monica. Romanian.

Is this some kind of sick joke?

Is she connected to Bogdan? Did he orchestrate this? Did he plant this encounter, sitting behind his screens, laughing now?

I feel it. Control slipping. Fracturing under the weight of something foreign.

Doubt.

Panic.

Only once before have I experienced these feelings, and the ones responsible for provoking them within me are long gone.

Dead.

In the most horrific way I could conceive at the time.

An avalanche of questions and uncertainties flood my mind at once, disrupting the order I have spent a lifetime perfecting.

Every breath is a calculated effort.

Each heartbeat pounds with the rhythmic certainty of impending catastrophe.

The air grows heavy, thick with something suffocating.

Dread coils around me, dark and relentless, casting a shadow that has no place in my world.

This is not acceptable!

This is not *me*.

And yet, the shadow of disaster lingers.

As Dominic enters the car and sits beside me, my attention shifts to him.

The tablet, holding information about the creature, rests on the seat between us, and just his nearness awakens something primal inside me.

A beast.

Animalistic.

Possessive.

Every instinct in me screams to protect her.

What is happening to me?

This isn't something I've ever experienced. Nothing has ever mattered beyond my coding, my team, and my empire.

They're all I've ever needed, all I've ever prioritised.

None of them has ever triggered this.

Yet the overwhelming urge to guard a creature I've never even spoken to defies every core logic of my being.

"Monica is off limits."

The words leave my mouth before I can stop them, low and edged with a threat I didn't intend.

Yet it's there. Undeniable.

Even I'm surprised by it.

"Monica? Who, the old lady? She'd be easy..."

I do not think.

Before I can calculate or even think, something buried deep within me lunges.

Possession.

Primal.

Absolute.

My hand shoots out, fingers digging into Dominic's throat, crushing his Adam's apple with all my force. My movements are swift, precise, brutal.

Somewhere in the depths of my mind, logic whispers—*this is Dominic.*

He respects me. He listens. He obeys.

But the thing inside me—the defective beast—screams louder.

This creature is mine!

To protect.

To possess.

To dominate.

And I can't bring myself to loosen my grip.

"This is the only time I'll repeat myself. Monica is off limits."

My voice is calm, just above a whisper. Measured. Cold.

I make sure there's no trace of emotion. No sign of the turmoil clawing beneath the surface.

Dominic doesn't need to know. No one does.

"You do not make a move against her. You do not make a move on her. You do not mention her. You do not even think of her. Monica is absolutely off limits. For everyone."

I keep my grip on his throat for a few more seconds, forcing myself to breathe, to pull back from the red-hot fury clouding my vision.

Logic fights the beast inside me.

Rationality claws at instinct.

This is not who I am.

And yet, I struggle to let go.

"Boss, I didn't mean any disrespect," Dominic quickly says as I let go of his throat.

"I understand where I stand on the matter now." Dominic's broken voice pulls me back to the present completely.

"The discussion is over," I say, moving back to my seat.

"Have a look at the device. I asked Sofia to send you everything on Angela Josephine Puscasu," I say, my voice calm and measured. Control settles back into place.

My mind slows, recalibrates.

"Thank you."

"Be careful. It's all in or nothing. Do not make contact unless you're certain." I pause, ensuring the weight of my words lands. "I don't want to clean up after you."

This creature bewilders me.

With a single laugh, a mere second of her gaze, she shatters my world with the force of a meteorite.

Unacceptable. This needs to have repercussions.

I will learn everything there is to know about her.

I will dissect this anomaly, rule out this absurd notion of protectiveness.

It's nothing more than a bug in the system. A minor glitch in the process.

It cannot be anything more.

It simply cannot be something precious.

Husband: Dan Puscasu.

The words loop in my mind, poisoning every thought, corroding my control as we arrive at the Barrow.

As soon as we step out of the elevator, Sofia and Dominic are arguing — voices sharp, cutting — but their words don't register.

My mind doesn't process them.

My mind doesn't process anything except the corrupted script playing on repeat.

The code ceases. Logic halts.

Only her husband's name remains.

A broken, sick record — dragging me into the darkest corners of my own personal torment.

Husband: Dan Puscasu.

Husband: Dan Puscasu.

Husband: Dan Puscasu.

She is married.

She is fucking married!

As I make my way to my office, I force myself to regulate my breathing — to steady my mind against the torment of feeling something for the first time in so long.

She exists.

And she's married?!

She's not mine. She belongs to someone else.

And there's fuck all I can do about it!

I sit at my desk and log into my device. All six screens come to life at once, flooding the room with data.

The familiar glow brings the tranquility I am desperate for, the order I am dying to reclaim.

Applications launch in sequence. Surveillance feeds. The dark web. My emails. Encrypted communications.

For three minutes, I work.

Three minutes pass before the itch starts. Before the relentless need for knowledge about her takes hold.

The creature.

The moment it does, there is no ignoring it.

Tiny, relentless ants crawl beneath my skin and through my mind, itching, demanding.

To *know*. To *learn*. To *dominate*. To *possess*.

Before I do something irrational, I open TrackMate, one of the first applications I designed over fifteen years ago.

A tool built for tracking and control.

Precision. Efficiency.

I tap into the street cameras near her shop, fingers steady, mind sharp.

The feed connects.

And then, she comes into focus.

The creature.

Loading a large flower arrangement into that dreadfully colourful car of hers.

Something about the arrangement looks off, not quite right. But I'm not an expert. Not on flowers and certainly not on women.

And yet, here I am, tracking her.

A creature who should mean nothing.

An anomaly I've yet to eradicate, slow down, or even understand.

And that *is* a problem.

"How did the session go?"

Buddy's deep voice registers for the first time, dragging me back to reality.

"Dominic has all the details. Feel free to catch up with him," I say, my tone leaving no room for discussion.

He studies me for a second before turning and leaving.

The soft click of the door settles into the silence, and only then do I realise. I dismissed him completely.

This side of me—one I never knew existed—was protecting Monica again, just now.

Why?

Why am I trying to hide her? What exactly am I protecting her from?

To the outside world, I am nothing more than a business tycoon in IT.

Even if I engaged her somehow, she would never see the darkness surrounding me.

I spend the next three hours extracting every piece of information I can find on her.

School records. Teacher and psychologist notes. Documented concerns from her parents.

Financials and legal filings for the charity.

On paper, she is a silent partner. In reality, she is deeply involved, operating in the background, careful to keep her name from the spotlight.

She does not want to be seen.

That, in itself, is remarkable.

The first piece of information that starts to make sense is her diagnosis.

She was thirty-one when she was diagnosed with Asperger's Syndrome.

"Clever little creature," I murmur to myself, a rare smile tugging at my lips.

I wonder if her family and the people around her ever realised she was more intelligent than them.

Or did she *hide*?

Dr R. Nair
10 September 1998

The subject, a sixteen-year-old adolescent, presents with a history of violent outbursts and defiant behaviour, often perceived by authority figures and peers as inherently aggressive and problematic.

However, a deeper examination reveals a complex interplay of environmental, emotional, and psychological factors contributing to these actions. The teenager has experienced significant trauma and neglect, leading to deep-seated feelings of abandonment and mistrust.

Her aggression appears to be a maladaptive coping mechanism—self-protection in an unpredictable and often hostile world.

With appropriate therapeutic interventions focusing on trust-building, emotional regulation, and resilience, along with an assessment to rule out antisocial tendencies, there is potential for significant behavioural improvement, as well as a redefined sense of self.

"Neglect," I murmur to myself.

I know that feeling too well. And yet, all these so-called specialists failed to recognise what she really was. They didn't see the brilliance beneath the surface.

Instead, they handed her tools to mask — to pass as neurotypical.

Hilarious.

I read and analyse all the reports — until one stops my entire world.

Dr. S. Subodh
8 March 2001

The subject, a 19-year-old adolescent with a documented history of antisocial behaviour and psychopathic tendencies, has recently endured significant sexual trauma. This event has further complicated her psychological profile, intensifying existing traits such as impaired emotional regulation and episodic violent outbursts towards family members.

The subject refuses to disclose the identity of the assaulter or file a police complaint.

Of particular concern in our last session was the subject's information processing, specifically, her highly detailed and premeditated descriptions of violent acts against the assaulter.

While it is not uncommon for victims of sexual assault to experience violent ideation towards their assailant, the subject's level of detail and methodical planning appear markedly outside normative post-trauma response patterns.

Multiple tranquillisers were prescribed, and the subject was referred to a psychiatrist for ongoing assessment and management.

A pain unlike anything I've ever known engulfs my chest.

The revelation strikes like a lightning bolt, searing through me with an unbearable force.

Words could never contain it.

The thought of her enduring something so horrific fills me with a rage I can't rationalise, a sorrow I don't want to acknowledge.

Each imagined detail of her suffering twists like a dagger in my chest — sharp and relentless.

The sensation is suffocating. Consuming.

Helplessness.

Guilt.

Emotions I don't feel. Emotions I'm not supposed to have — overwhelm me from all angles, demanding my last breath.

Yet they're here — clawing at the edges of my mind, demanding everything from me.

I should've protected her.

I should break them.

Ruin them in the most sinister way imaginable.

Anyone who caused her harm — anyone who touched her — should know suffering beyond comprehension.

The world around me dims, my thoughts locked in a cycle of anguish, rage, and something deeper.

Something closer to grief.

It's insufferable!

Unacceptable!

"What the fuck did they do to you?! What the fuck are you doing to me?!"

This creature! She's disrupted everything!

She's breaking my reality.

If I ever believed I was beyond feeling, beyond despair — I was wrong.

She did this.

She demanded my attention.

She provoked this chaos within me — without my permission.

Heat spreads through my body, an unrelenting fury consuming every inch of me.

I lock my device, stand, and make my way to the top level of the building. My penthouse.

The lights flicker on automatically as I step out of the elevator, but I barely register them.

A deep, guttural growl rumbles from my chest.

The thought of her—of what she endured—sets my blood on fire. My body cannot contain it.

Where the fuck was I when someone touched what is mine?

Because she is mine!

The moment she took her first breath into this world she became mine!

She just does not know it yet. And what is mine, I will have at all costs.

The question surfaces, unbidden, just as my fist slams into the wall with full force.

Pain jolts through my knuckles, sharp and grounding. And only then do I realise what I just asked myself.

"What the fuck am I doing? She is nothing to me." Well, she *should be* nothing to you, my logic self reminds me.

I exhale sharply, pacing.

"You haven't even spoken to the woman, Elijah. What the fuck is this avalanche of feelings and reactions?"

I make my way to the freezer, pull out an ice pack, and press it against my knuckles. The cold bites into my skin, grounding me.

She might not even be like me.

She could be a fucking fraud. A wannabe faking her way through life, manipulating psychological profiling, and cheating her IQ tests.

For all I know, she has not a single loyal cell in her body.

And yet, here I am, worked up over nothing.

Rationality and logic slowly take hold, forcing some order back into my mind.

The pressure eases as I begin to form a plan. One that will accomplish three objectives:

1. *Eliminate* the distraction.

2. *Assess* the creature and rule out any possibility of fraud.

3. *Determine* if she is truly like me.

I exhale, the weight in my chest settling into something steadier.

"I'm going to pay you a visit tomorrow, Monica."

Let's see who you are, and what you're made of.

Chapter Four

Monica

"That won't be a problem. We'll leave the arrangement here on the floor and invoice you tonight.

As for your attention toward my daughter, do yourself a favour and pack away that joke of a dick you keep waving around.

With that, the best you could manage is to tickle a woman, never satisfy one.

You'd probably hurt yourself in the process.

So, as I said, be kind to yourself."

The memory of dropping off the floral arrangement at Jake's house replays in my mind on a loop, each detail fuelling the violent urge clawing at my control.

Every fibre of my being screams to turn back, to walk into that house, stab him slowly, then pour acid into the incisions — watching as he writhes, agonising, begging me to end it.

What the fuck was this slimy motherfucker thinking?

He made a move on my daughter?!

I'm coming back after I drop off Angela.

And I'm ending his pathetic existence.

Fuck the consequences.

Fuck prison.

I would gladly go to jail if it meant this piece of shit never breathes the same air as Angela again.

Fuck!

My mind races with torture scenarios, each one more brutal than the last, each one a way to ensure I get away with it.

My blood burns.

My hands burn.

My face and head burn with the need to kill, to end him in the most grotesque way imaginable for daring to think he could touch what is mine.

Who the fuck does he think he is?

I hate these slimy, entitled pricks who think that money and a presentable face make them untouchable — that they can take whatever they want, whoever they want, without consequence, as if consequences are just rumours—never a reality.

Fuck them all. Fuck him.

I'm coming back to finish him off.

"I cannot believe what just happened. You were out of this world, amazing! Mum, the tongue on you!"

Angela's excited voice reaches me as if from a tunnel — distant, echoing — yet she's right next to me in the car.

I barely register her words.

My body is transforming.

Every molecule shifting, sharpening, preparing for the inevitable kill.

I realise I'm losing control — fast.

My mask is slipping, barely holding. I cannot detonate in front of Angela.

I need to protect her.

At all costs.

My entire life, I never felt like I had anything of true importance.

Never owned anything real.

Nothing ever mattered.

Until the moment I gave birth to my baby girl.

The first time I looked at her, I felt something — for the first time in my life.

I finally had something of value.

Angela was mine.

Not her father's. Not the world's. Mine alone.

No one — not him, not anyone — could take her from me.

She would forever be mine.

Call it love. Possessiveness. Obsession.

Whatever label the experts want to slap on it.

I know the truth: there is no limit when it comes to my daughter.

I take a breath, forcing words past the fire threatening to consume me.

"Shhhh, my darling. I need a minute to think and calm down. I might turn this car around and skin him alive. Give me until we reach your apartment to settle myself. Please."

I'm surprised by how calm my voice sounds when inside, a volcano is erupting.

Deep within me, a fury simmers—dark, consuming, unstoppable.

A potent blend of rage and something deeper.

Something primal, swirling like a raging inferno.

Every breath feeds the fire, stoking it higher, hotter.

The drive to hurt him — to ruin him — is relentless. Obscene. Grotesque.

I can already see it.

And it is glorious.

I need to finish him.

Every part of me is calling for the kill. Screaming for it.

But Angela would know.

She would see me—*truly* see me.

She would look at me like I'm someone else. Like I'm a monster.

She would stop visiting me in prison. She would be ashamed of me. She would erase me from her life, pretend I didn't exist.

Something inside me cracks.

The thought alone shoves me over the edge into a panic so raw, so unfamiliar, it terrifies me.

I cannot lose her.

I cannot lose her.

I simply cannot lose her.

As we approach her apartment building, the cry of desperation pounds through my head. A relentless siren of dread that leaves an acid taste in my mouth.

I *cannot* lose her.

"Mum, are you okay?"

I turn to her, startled out of my thoughts, and smile, the perfect image of calm.

"Of course, I'm fine."

I deepen my smile, throwing in a wink for effect.

"Don't get me wrong, he's clearly a dick. Did you see the courage in him, strutting around like that thing he calls a cock is worth anyone's attention? What a joke," I say, laughing as if the whole situation is beneath me. My mask is back, flawless, seamless, exactly as she needs to see it.

"I'm more concerned about you," I continue, shifting the focus. "We're definitely dropping them as clients tonight. The moment I get home, I'll email him and his brother, and they're gone. I don't give a fuck about the money, their complaints, or if they bad-mouth me in the industry. They are out of our lives."

I let my tone sharpen, letting the outrage land just right for her, for the illusion that I am truly okay.

And it is true. I don't care about the money. I don't care about their reputations or what they say about me.

I care that they came after my daughter.

And I care that I might not be able to torture and kill him without serious repercussions from Angela.

So, yes — I do care.

Just in my own way.

"It's all good, Mum. Fuck 'em!" Angela says, then starts laughing. "I'll call you tomorrow, okay?"

"Not a problem, my darling. Rest up and forget all about that imbecile. Focus on your studies and your exam, and let me know if you need anything," I say, infusing as much warmth into my voice as I can manage.

"If I get any ridiculously big orders, I'll call you to help, but otherwise, don't worry about the shop. I won't bother you unless it's on fire," I add, bursting into laughter.

"Oh, don't remind me of that ridiculous mock trial. I've already had a bad enough night, Mum." Angela pulls a disgusted face, which makes me chuckle.

"Anyway, talk tomorrow. Bye."

The moment the car door closes and I pull away from her apartment building, my fury erupts—violent, unrestrained, the force of a tornado tearing through me.

Panic claws at me. The terror of losing Angela at war with the insatiable need to torture and kill.

The clash is unbearable.

Tidal waves of emotion crash over me, drowning reason, crushing control, and suffocating logic beneath sheer, unrelenting rage.

Thoughts collide, frantic and chaotic, each one more desperate than the last—racing, spiralling, as if trying to outrun an invisible threat closing in.

But there is no escape.

Not from *this*.

The pressure builds to unbearable levels, an invisible vice tightening around my chest, squeezing the air from my lungs.

My thoughts grow heavy, clouded, and suffocated beneath the weight of it all.

Each breath is a battle against something unseen, something relentless—pushing me closer to the edge of my endurance.

I need to *purge* it.

Or today will be the day I kill.

Chapter Five

Monica

The pressure is eating me alive, burning me from the inside out. It needs to hurt somewhere.

I cannot lose Angela. No matter what.

I cannot kill that fucker without losing her.

Fuck my life!

Something has to give.

Dan could take my fury, he has once before, I think, as my memory takes me to the beginning of my marriage.

After I fell pregnant, my parents insisted I marry Dan to avoid the shame of being a single mum.

What a fucking joke.

But I had to listen. So I married him.

We had sex once and I felt more disgusted than anything else.

The second time he came to me, I told him fuck no.

He didn't like that. He tried to manhandle me.

Something inside me snapped.

I punched him—hard.

The shock on his face was almost comical.

Before he could react, before he could even think, I grabbed a vase and knocked him out cold.

By the time he came to, he was zip-tied to a chair.

And I was sitting across from him.

Waiting.

When his eyes met mine, I just held his gaze.

No mask. No pretence.

I didn't move. I didn't speak. I just looked.

He was the first—the only—one I had ever shown even a fraction of my true self to.

And I let him see.

Time stopped being a metric, turning into something loose and insignificant. A suggestion rather than a rule.

Then, it warped.

Stretching, compressing, bending around us like a living thing.

He gasped for air, caught in the suffocating grip of something he couldn't understand. Panic clawed at him, twisting its way into his bones.

Rationality slipped through his fingers like sand, leaving only one primal instinct—flee.

Escape.

Find safety.

But there was nowhere to go.

Nothing to run from.

Nothing except me.

And that was enough.

His face twisted as raw, unfiltered terror took hold, panic flooding his features at what was about to come.

"It seems we need to clarify a few things," I say, my tone calm, controlled.

The steadiness of it startles him further.

"I am not your ordinary woman. And you will learn that moving forward."

The corner of my mouth lifts into a slow, provocative smirk.

"If you think you can manhandle me or worse, force yourself onto me, I won't kill you."

I pause, letting the words sink in.

"I will fight back. And not only that... when you go to sleep, I'll put the kettle on, make myself a nice cup of tea..."

I tilt my head slightly. My smile widens.

"And the rest of the boiling water? That goes straight on your dick."

I watch the meaning settle in his bones, his breath catching in his throat.

"You will never be safe next to me. And by the time I'm finished with you, motherfucker, you'll be the one running from me."

I smile fully now, my expression bright, almost sweet.

Then I wink.

"So tell me, Dan. Do you really want to force me to have sex with you?"

I pause, tilting my head again, letting my disgust sink into every syllable.

"Because let me tell you something—this marriage is a fucking joke."

I watch his expression shift.

"At no point—not once—in our so-called sex session, if you even want to call it that, did you manage to arouse me. Not even close."

I scoff, my tone laced with venom.

"You're a selfish bastard with zero idea how to please a woman. So fuck no! I will never sleep with you again if I can help it."

Disgust drips from my voice like poison, deliberate and unrelenting.

"You know what? I am fucking pissed."

I take a slow breath, letting the anger settle into something colder.

"And I think you need a lesson, to make sure my point lands. So you never even think about trying this shit with me again."

I stand, looking down at him, drinking in the disbelief written across his face.

His jaw clenches, his muscles coil with tension, his body betraying what he refuses to say.

He is panicking.

Good.

He opens his mouth, the words spilling out in a rush, desperate and uneven.

"Monica, please! I'm sorry. I didn't think you'd take it seriously."

His voice wavers, desperation creeping in.

"I was just joking! Can't you take a joke?" He swallows hard, eyes darting, searching for a way out.

"Why are you so difficult?"

I burst out laughing, full-bodied, unrestrained.

His shoulders relax. His body eases.

He starts laughing too, convinced he has reeled me in, that his pathetic attempt at blame-shifting has worked.

"You are a sweet, sweet man, Dan," I say, my tone warm, dripping with false affection.

I see it, the shift in his eyes. He thinks he has won. That I will soften, that I will fold, let him walk all over me.

Pity.

"The only problem," I continue, my voice still light, almost teasing, "is that I am not like other people."

I let that sink in, watching as the realisation creeps across his face.

"All this manipulative bullshit? I see it coming a mile away."

I lean in slightly. Just enough for him to feel the shift in power.

"I know what you're doing, Dan." My voice drops, smooth, precise.

"Because I see emotions. I don't feel them."

I let the silence hang for a moment, my words lingering in the air before I turn away.

I walk to the kitchen, my movements unhurried, deliberate.

A knife. Scissors. Salt. Two large kitchen towels.

I gather each item carefully, gathering them in my hands with quiet precision.

Then, I head to the laundry room.

A bucket. Ice-cold water.

I fill it, watching the water settle into stillness, sharp and unforgiving.

Then, I walk back to the bedroom.

Calm. Measured. Smiling as I step inside.

I set everything down in front of his fallen chair, my gaze never leaving him.

"Oh! My darling, have you been busy?"

I try to lift him, but the fucker weighs a ton.

I sigh, irritation flickering through me.

"Help me, or I'll hurt you beyond repair," I snap, my voice edged with annoyance.

He scrambles, pushing with his legs, helping me right the chair.

The moment he's up, I don't hesitate.

"You stupid fuck!"

I punch him square in the nose.

His head snaps back, his breath hitching in shock. He starts to wiggle, trying to loosen himself, to flop back onto the ground.

I don't let him.

I drive my fist into his throat.

A satisfying thud.

His air vanishes, replaced by frantic, choking gasps. He convulses, his body racked with a desperate coughing fit.

I watch. Unmoved.

I let the silence stretch, his coughing echoing through the room before I speak again, my voice sweet and dripping with venom.

"We are going to have fun," I say sweetly, my tone laced with mock affection.

"And you, my darling husband, are about to learn some manners and the true nature of our relationship."

"Monica, seriously, this is not funny! Stop this right now!" he screams, his voice cracking with desperation.

I tilt my head, watching him.

"Let it all out, husband," I say sweetly.

"All the screams. All the pain. All the panic."

I smile, my eyes never leaving his.

I let the tension hang in the air, his panic feeding my calm before I speak again.

"Let me see you in your true form."

He thrashes, his body jerking, legs pushing, kicking, fighting.

Pathetic.

"There, there, my darling husband," I murmur, my voice smooth, almost soothing.

"I told you we'd be having fun today."

I trail my fingers along the edge of the table, unhurried.

"And now, we finally get to know each other's true form."

Reaching down, I pick up the knife.

Then the salt.

And smile wider.

The memory dissolves as the road stretches before me once again, reality sliding back into place.

That was the moment I established the nature of our relationship. At no point would this be a real marriage, that his role was just to cover me so no one would bother me again with this nonsense of marriage, and in return, I wouldn't murder him in some creatively gruesome way. He escapes his family, and I escape mine, but at no point would this ever be more than a façade.

Over the years, we refined the perfect mask — me, the perfect wife, and him, the respectable husband with the right tone in public.

No, I think to myself. Dan cannot be on the receiving end of my outburst today. At the end of the day, he is too close to my daughter for comfort, and she might catch sight of me hurting him. So whatever I do, I need to rein in the anger and release it somewhere else.

I turn the car and make my way to the one place I know I can let it all out — where no one will look at me the wrong way.

Bet Ke'ev.

This isn't a studio. It really is a place where we're supposed to be learning Krav Maga — but we all took it to a new level of fighting. You don't walk out the same as you came in — if you even walk out at all.

For twenty-three years, this has been my coping mechanism — my way of managing the condition — and the violence inside me that never fucking sleeps.

I might not be able to kill, I think, as anticipation boils in my veins.

But I can hurt.

And I can enjoy it. To its fullest. The thought carries me forward as I reach the door.

The moment I open the door, my eyes find him...

Kai.

I know.

I just know.

Tonight, there are no restraints. No masks.

Tonight, I can come out and play in all my marvellous glory.

Well — not quite.

I cannot kill.

But I *can* hurt.

And for now... That'll have to do.

The decision settles over me like ice, steadying my pulse as I step closer.

I step closer, slow and deliberate, letting the silence stretch between us.

My eyes trail over him, drinking in every inch.

Then, in a whisper barely audible, I ask...

"Are you ready to play?"

Chapter Six

Elijah

My entire life was very structured, very predictable.

Well, to me it is.

It's a sequence of events that I have perfected since an early age, when I realised I am different and there is no one out there like me.

Life is easy. Identify patterns, design optimisations, implement steps, adjust, implement a fix, result.

On repeat. All day, every day, regardless of the situation, person, outcome.

My system works, and it got me to where I am today — not only enjoying the fruits of my labour, but enabling me to set the stage for any outcome I desire, manipulate any situation and any person into what I need for a particular time or task.

My entire life, I felt suffocated to speak to people.

Yes, I do not like people, enjoy their company, or even allow them in my vicinity if I can help it.

But what makes me feel suffocated is how flat everyone is.

How simple, almost unrealistic tasks they struggle with — and for some absurd reason, they need support with.

Not to mention all of those irrational things called feelings.

I do not understand why people use that word to justify their stupidity.

I've never understood why people are so fond of these feelings when they are irrational, illogical, and drive people to do the most idiotic things in the world.

I understand, from a logical point of view, that everyone needs someone, and that is why I allowed myself to have Buddy and Sofia.

It's not about feelings — it's about logic. I understand the human need for belonging, just as I understand hunger or sleep.

But I don't feel it.

I am not quite sure if I do have those needs of belonging within me, but I do know that even if I feel suffocated speaking to them, I can tolerate their presence around me.

Still, even in my detachment, I recognise this: there is something about the moment someone finds their equal.

When you find something truly remarkable, and one can mirror themselves into it.

It's that moment where a simple and clear NO morphs into a YES—without your permission or approval.

And it becomes so clear, so firm, that there is no possibility to change it, because the decision was made at the cellular level.

And that is that.

Understand my bewilderment at what is happening around me and within me for finding something remarkable.

How is she even alive?

How am I going to make room for this creature in my life?

How am I going to deal with having feelings?

Because whether I want them or not, they're coming.

I can see the pattern, and I can see the cliff, and in both situations there is no control within reach. For a man who thrives on precision, this chaos is intolerable.

How am I going to fight this pull to dominate her?

What the fuck am I going to do?

The following day at 7:30 a.m., I am sitting alone in my car, watching *her*.

The creature moves around her shop, fussing over details with practised efficiency.

I cannot recall the last time I drove alone—or the last time I wasn't accompanied by one of my men.

Yet here I am.

This pull, this unbearable need to see her, has become too aggressive in my subconscious to ignore.

And my possessive beast will not allow anyone in my organisation to know about her. Not yet.

These feelings, these reactions, must be analysed. Understood. Dissected.

I do not make contact unless I am certain.

I spent hours last night dissecting every detail of her life, searching for cracks, for deception, for any evidence that she is not what I think she is.

That we are not the same.

I came up empty-handed.

And now, here I am.

Still watching her.

Still learning about her.

Still pulled toward her with a force I cannot rationalise.

This thing she has awakened in me—*this hunger*—it will demand satisfaction soon.

And if I do not find a way to control it, to control her...

It will grow into something irrational.

As I step out of the car, the pull toward her is magnetic, an irresistible force I cannot fully comprehend.

The moment she glances in my direction, every subtle movement she makes, every shift in her presence compels me to step closer.

I keep my stride firm, my presence commanding — ensuring I can be near her without betraying the war raging inside me.

She ignites something in me.

A fire.

A force I do not yet understand—equal parts admiration and longing tearing at my very core.

I am captivated.

By the way she moves, by the depth in those black eyes.

By the way she exists.

And it is... *unacceptable*.

Her face is free of makeup again.

Yet somehow, she is the most beautiful woman I have ever seen.

As I step closer, I realise she is shorter than me—but not by much.

Unusual.

At six feet tall, I am used to people looking up at me.

But this creature?

She *does not.*

If anything, she looks *down at me*—disregarding our height entirely, establishing her dominance without a single word. It unsettles me in ways I cannot name.

The pull toward her is not just physical. It is deeper.

Primal.

Consuming.

A force that eclipses reason itself, demanding possession, demanding control. An undeniable connection that feels both exhilarating and inevitable, as if proximity to her is the only way I could survive.

She begins analysing me.

Her gaze moves slowly—deliberately—starting at my shoes and travelling upwards, taking in everything.

Not just my clothes.

Me.

It is as if she is reading me, peeling back layers, seeing my darkest thoughts, my deepest secrets, uncovering them with nothing but a look.

And then, with unsettling precision, her stare locks onto mine.

Provocation radiates from her.

A dare.

A silent challenge to see who will break first, who will submit—who will establish themselves as the alpha between us. Her challenge leaves no room for retreat. The beast within me—the one I barely shackled last night—bursts free.

And before I even process it, this primal instinct takes over and my hand is suddenly at her throat, pinning her against the wall.

Squeezing.

Just enough to let her feel my strength.

But not enough to hurt her.

Not yet.

"It seems we need to set some ground rules," she says, her voice calm.

Her gaze locks onto mine, unwavering.

"I *am not* your ordinary woman," she continues, her tone measured, absolute.

"And I *will not* allow you to treat me as such."

Her words hang in the air for a heartbeat before something brushes against my cock, sudden and deliberate.

A flicker of surprise lashes through me.

What the fuck?

A sudden pressure, a firm squeeze on one of my balls.

My body registers it before my mind does.

I start to move back, instinct taking over.

But whatever it is, it's not letting go.

"You may think you're stronger than me," she murmurs, her voice unshaken.

"But I'm happy to *educate* you, *boy.*"

Her grip tightens ever so slightly.

"If you don't want to lose one of your balls at the hands of my pliers," she continues, her expression infuriatingly calm.

"I suggest you kindly remove your hand from around my neck."

Her words settle between us, razor-sharp. Then... she smiles. And winks.

She knows. She's figured it out. She's realised there are two of us.

A sound reverberates around me, low and raw, vibrating through my chest. Then I realise—it's coming from me.

I am *laughing*. Not a chuckle. Not a measured exhale of amusement. But a full-bodied laugh, tearing out of me with force.

Oh! **I've found her!**

This creature — this woman — she is *mine!* She has me by my balls. And she *called* me *boy.*

The sheer audacity of it — of her — makes my laughter deepen, pushing past the edges of control. I cannot remember the last time I laughed out loud.

But this woman... this amazing creature... has made me laugh.

There is no doubt.

She *is* my match.

Monica is just like me... Brilliant. Strong. Cunning. Beautiful. Majestic. Graceful.

She is the epitome of the supreme woman. Hiding in plain sight.

Far too superior for ordinary minds to comprehend, too elusive for them to recognise unless she allows them to see her true nature.

But she has *exposed herself* to me.

Interesting...

I release her and step back, my gaze locked onto hers. Those black eyes pull me in—consuming me. The beast within me, the one she has awakened, settles.

If it recognises her as its match, then it can breathe. It can rest at her mercy. Because now, it is no longer alone.

Each interaction with her is a symphony of precision—every shift in energy a calculated note, each unspoken word another movement in a composition neither of us wrote, yet both of us feel.

And as I watch her, I realise she might be just as confused as I am.

Just as caught in this maelstrom as I am.

Just as unprepared.

And that? That makes her *mine.*

"Your guy will stay away from Angela."

The moment her voice cuts through the air, something shifts—something irreversible. She made a request... more of a demand.

It is as if she has sealed our fate together, intertwining our lives with an unbreakable bond.

From this point forward, our paths are linked.

Irrevocably.

Not by choice, not by circumstance, but by something greater. A force neither of us fully understand. An unspoken truth that exists between us, beneath the surface.

Whether in the light or in the dark, we are the same.

Even without physical touch, her presence lingers — like a whispered promise, a silent reminder that some connections defy logic, that some bonds *exist* beyond reason itself.

I take one last look into her powerful, dark eyes. Then, without a word, I turn and walk out the door.

"We'll see."

Chapter Seven

Monica

A week passed.

And Santa hasn't graced me with his presence.

Stupid fuck.

Who does he think he is?

Striding into my life, demanding authority—thinking he's my equal?

The courage. The audacity of that man.

With each passing day, my frustration simmers—volatile, on the edge of boiling over.

He stormed in, intruded without hesitation—then vanished.

And now?

Now, I'm left with the aftermath of his presence.

I just know he's digging.

Unravelling my past, pulling apart every shadow, hunting down my skeletons as we speak.

I exhale sharply, my nails tapping against the counter.

Fuck you, Santa!

This past week has been just lovely. Not.

Angela buried herself in study, stressing over that rubbish assessment at Uni.

Yesterday, she sent me a newsletter about her performance in the mock trial.

I laughed.

She tries so hard, when she's already one of the most intelligent people there.

It's cute. And concerning.

But I learned early on—she has to live *her life*.

I can advise from the background, but her choices, her mistakes, are hers to make.

As long as she's safe, I don't interfere.

Not directly. But no matter what I do, his words keep circling back, dragging my thoughts to him.

"We'll see."

His words play in my mind for the thousandth time.

Like fuck we'll see, Santa.

I'll cut your balls off next time if you didn't get my first memo.

Fuck my life.

Forty-two years. It took me forty-two years to find someone like me.

And he's fucking Santa?!

Seriously?

Sometimes, *I hate my life.*

Jake and Jack, those miserable little shits, have been badmouthing me all over town.

I lost two more clients this past week.

Delightful. Just delightful.

Moments like this make me wish I'd just give in to my violent nature completely.

Cut Jake into pieces and bury him in my flower garden.

Let him rot under something beautiful.

These fuckers deserve to suffer.

For all the shit they pull, for thinking they'll always get away with it.

The sharp ring of the door chime snaps me back to reality.

I glance up from my device.

And there he is.

Santa.

He strides into my shop with purpose, every step deliberate, calculated.

There's a mystery to him, an enigma that pulls people in — while keeping them at arm's length.

What I've learned about him so far is that he's a man of few words.

But when he does speak, his voice demands attention.

He doesn't reveal much. Yet everything about him communicates more than words ever could.

Especially those eyes.

They hold a deadly truth I recognise.

And no matter how I try to rationalise it...

I still think he might be like me.

I wonder what he'd do if I called him *boy* again.

Or, even better...

If I called him Santa out loud.

I tilt my head, a slow smirk forming.

"Good morning, *Santa.* Fancy seeing you here."

My smile widens, my voice dripping with sweetness.

Let's see what he does now.

An undeniable aura of confidence and intimidation surrounds him. An unspoken power that seems to radiate from his very being.

Even in silence, he commands respect — effortlessly, without trying.

His quiet nature doesn't diminish his presence. If anything, it sharpens it.

It makes him more aware, more dangerous, as if, by not wasting time on small talk, he sees more, observes more.

It's obvious.

You either keep up with him...

Or you get left behind.

Simple as that.

Then, just as effortlessly, he graces me with a smile and takes a seat on the chair beside the counter.

It takes me a moment to realise what he's doing.

His gestures feel familiar, *too familiar*, like we've been friends for a lifetime, and he has the liberty of just sitting next to me as if it's nothing.

He settles into the space beside me with unnerving ease, his presence both comforting and disconcerting.

As though the boundaries between us have already dissolved.

Leaving behind something unspoken.

Something that feels both natural — and bewildering.

"It seems you're confused about something, *Santa.*"

I pause, watching, waiting to see how he reacts to the name.

His eyes narrow slightly, a flicker of amusement flashing across his face before he smooths it away.

The tension between us thickens, the pull snapping back to life — like a vengeful force, ready to consume us both.

Perfect!

This moment of discomfort is exactly what I intended.

A small victory in our ongoing battle of wits.

He leans back in his seat, casual, his arms crossing over his chest as he locks his gaze onto me.

Waiting.

For my next move.

"The North Pole is that *way*," I say, pointing at the door, my lips curling into my first real smile in days.

I almost burst out laughing.

Because—*fuck if I care*—but that was a smart-ass remark to throw at someone as intimidating as this man.

And I enjoyed it.

Just like before, that sound wraps around me, like a warm hug to my soul, erasing pain in its wake and promising things I never knew I wanted.

It's the second time I've heard him laugh out loud.

And if he's like me, then he isn't supposed to.

People like us don't experience emotions like the rest of the neurotypical world.

Yet...

Despite his detachment, there's a depth to him.

A quiet intensity that betrays his stoic exterior.

His silence speaks volumes.

Every unspoken word is loaded with meaning.

It's as if he exists on a plane beyond mortal emotions, his very presence a reminder of how fleeting human feelings really are. And I don't care for it.

And the more I provoke him...

The more he reacts.

The more he processes me.

And the more I observe him...

The more certain I become.

He is like me.

Without a doubt.

From his relaxed posture and carefree laughter, it's clear... he knows.

He knows *who* I am.

He knows *what* I am.

And he's come to the same conclusion as me.

Yet, somehow, I am at a disadvantage.

Because, by the looks of it... he knows everything.

And I don't even know his name.

His confidence is unsettling, a stark contrast to my own uncertainty.

Every note of his laughter, every casual movement, only highlights the imbalance between us.

It makes me acutely aware of the gaps in my knowledge.

His familiarity feels almost intrusive, like he has stepped ahead in a game that we are both playing.

I need to level the playing field.

I tilt my head, smirking.

"Right! Pliers time, Santa?"

I let the words linger...

Then wink.

"Good morning, Monica. I'd like to spend a few moments with you, if that's alright."

His voice is calm, measured, each word carefully chosen.

There's class in the way he speaks. A quiet assurance that exudes control, professionalism —*power.*

His tone is steady, reassuring, every syllable deliberate.

He carries himself with an undeniable authority, one that makes refusal feel impossible.

Yet, his approach is gentle.

Almost courteous.

It's disarming.

Something about him is compelling, a blend of sophistication and genuine interest that catches me off guard.

His gaze never wavers.

Unhurried. Patient.

It makes me feel both at ease — and acutely aware of the weight of this interaction.

"I assume you know everything about me."

I meet his gaze, unflinching, waiting.

A sincere smile is all I get in return.

No denial. Just the most sincere answer a man like him can give.

"This places me at a disadvantage," I continue, my tone cold, precise.

"I don't even know your name."

The edge in my voice leaves no room for negotiation.

A clear message.

I am not pleased.

"*Elijah Dominion.*"

His name rolls off his tongue with the same quiet authority he carries himself with.

I tilt my head.

"What do you do for a living, Elijah?"

"I work in IT."

I let the silence stretch between us for a second before pressing further.

"And what do you do besides IT, Elijah?"

He tilts his head slightly, offering me another one of those infuriatingly composed smiles.

The kind that tells me he won't be as open as I expected.

We sit in silence, locked in a wordless battle of wills.

Seconds stretch into minutes.

A test. A challenge once again.

I don't lose in these situations. So I take control, again. I establish my dominance. And I make it clear.

This is my game. And *I* set the rules.

"Right. Please, correct me if I'm wrong."

I keep my voice steady, controlled.

"You know my name. My family. My business. My charity. My school."

I pause, letting the weight of my next words settle between us.

"Perhaps even some *personal* information you shouldn't know."

I stop and watch him, studying his reaction.

His face remains composed. Unshaken.

But there's a flicker of acknowledgment in his eyes.

A slight, almost imperceptible smile at the corner of his lips.

As if he's amused by my bold confrontation.

His calm doesn't falter.

If anything, I sense something else lurking beneath it — a hint of respect for my directness.

The silence stretches, thick with unspoken tension.

I wait.

For him to confirm or deny.

For him to decide how he wants to play this game.

"As I said, your knowledge puts me at a disadvantage."

I hold his gaze, unwavering.

"Therefore, I see only two outcomes. One, you level the playing field. Or two, you go back to your North Pole and never look back."

My words are deliberate, laced with a challenge I know *he* understands.

I watch him closely, searching for a crack in his composure.

But as expected, he remains unshaken.

Still, there's something there. A flicker of interest in his eyes.

He leans forward slightly, considering my words, and for a moment, he holds my gaze.

A test neither of us intends to lose.

"I work in IT," he says smoothly. "I'm the head of Quantum Gate Cybersecurity. We have a vast portfolio of software and apps, both in cybersecurity and beyond."

He pauses, watching me, analysing.

Waiting for a reaction.

But there's no surprise here.

From the moment I saw him, I knew, he's highly intelligent. Wealthy. Powerful.

This only confirms what I already suspected.

Yet the casual way he reveals it, like it's nothing, like it shouldn't impress, adds another layer to his enigma.

I nod, acknowledging his words, but my mind is already racing.

Reassessing.

Because I know this isn't everything.

And if he wants to be anywhere near me, he'll need to come clean.

"And?"

My tone is firm, demanding.

He bursts out laughing.

Again.

I stare at him, unbelieving.

What the fuck is so funny?

I narrow my eyes.

"*Santa*, are you having a stroke?"

His laughter fades, and then...

He looks at *me*.

As if I'm made of something untouchable.

Something as pure as light.

I don't remember anyone ever looking at me like this.

His gaze is intense yet gentle, filled with something I can't quite name — something dangerously close to reverence.

Admiration.

It takes my breath away.

As if he's looking straight through me.

Not at my mask, not at the persona I wear so well.

But at me.

Seeing something beautiful, something unique. Something he wasn't sure even existed.

The moment feels surreal.

A connection so deep, so unspoken, it defies logic.

For the first time, I feel truly *seen*.

Valued.

The warmth of his gaze wraps around me, comforting, affirming.

"It's just Elijah."

His voice is smooth, sweet, but deliberate.

"There's no need for pet names yet."

A slow, knowing smirk.

"I wouldn't want to scare you away."

Then...

He winks.

Holy fuck!

He lets the moment breathe, calm and deliberate.

"I also inherited a drug business from my family."

His voice remains unbothered, as if he's discussing the weather.

"But my main focus is cybersecurity."

He leans back slightly, assessing me as he continues.

"I developed EmberWall when I was 25 years old. It's the backbone of my operations."

His tone is factual, steady.

"One of the top three firewalls in the world. Used primarily by enterprise-level, Tier 1 and Tier 2 businesses."

"A precise system, guaranteed to protect our clients from external threats."

He pauses.

For too long.

I narrow my eyes, making it clear I know he's holding back.

His lips curve slightly, then he gives me what I'm waiting for.

"However," he continues, his voice perfectly measured.

"As part of the firewall, we install a virus, one that collects sensitive information."

He watches me, waiting for a reaction.

"We store that data, then we sell it on the black market."

His words land heavy between us, settling like a blade placed deliberately on the table.

"This," he finishes, unblinking. "Is what I do for a living. In a nutshell."

I can see him studying me, measuring my reaction to his confession.

The realisation settles within me.

I was right about him.

And that knowledge brings me a strange sense of peace.

He is intelligent. Cunning.

Probably ruthless. Probably violent.

The fire inside me ignites, burning hotter, higher.

There's a thrill in knowing my instincts were dead on and right on point.

A sharp, cutting validation that makes my mind clearer, my focus sharper.

His intelligence and potential for ruthlessness don't just confirm what I already suspected.

They make him even more intriguing.

Even more dangerous.

Our eyes meet again. And the connection between us charges. A blend of challenge and attraction. An undeniable pull, humming between us like a wire stretched too tight.

The moment is electric with possibility.

And this time...

It's my turn to laugh.

"And?"

My laughter fades, but my challenge remains.

"And..." he repeats after me.

For the first time, his eyes soften. Warmth flickers in his gaze, a shift so subtle yet so profound that it unravels something deep inside me.

Something breaks. Not in a way that weakens. But in a way that rebuilds.

It is only the second time in my life that I feel it.

That I *have* something.

Something *real*.

He watches me, his stare unwavering, filled with something too deep to name.

Something unspoken.

It's not admiration. It's possessiveness. It's obsession.

It's *recognition*.

As if he's whispering to me without words, telling me *he knows* we are the same.

As if he sees a *future* I haven't yet dared to picture.

A silent promise lingers between us.

Unwavering devotion.

An unspoken reverence for the connection that already exists.

"The rest," he finally says, voice low, measured. "I think you've already figured out."

Then he smiles.

And lowers his head, hands resting on his knees.

It's not submission.

But it is *something*.

A quiet acknowledgment.

And not for a second since I first saw him did I ever think, that he would bow to anything.

Or anyone.

My mind is cluttered with emotions I can't quite pinpoint.

And to be honest. I don't care for them. It's a cocktail of panic, excitement, anxiety, nervousness, attraction.

And did I mention pain?

Each feeling collides into the next, a chaotic swirl tearing through me. Leaving me questioning myself for the first time in my life.

It's overwhelming.

A tidal wave I can't control.

Yet, beneath the confusion, there's something else.

A thrill.

A sharp, dangerous exhilaration that keeps me on edge. That makes every moment with him feel electric.

All-consuming.

And I have never felt anything like it before. I'm not sure if this feeling business is for me. It's... a lot.

"So, you can sit here and tell me you're involved in some kind of mafia. That you play both sides when it comes to cybersecurity. But I'm the one who has to speak up about something I may or may not have already figured out on my own?"

My voice comes out steady, demanding, the opposite of the pain and panic clawing inside me.

Is this how neurotypical people feel all the time?

Fucking hell.

It's not pleasant.

It's terrifying.

I don't care for it.

And I can already feel myself calculating escape routes.

Options... Ways to get the fuck away from this situation as fast as possible.

Part of me wants to run.

To fight.

To claw my way out of this moment before it devours me.

The pliers are in my pocket.

I could fight.

But another part of me, a louder, more insistent part – screams at me to stop – to stay.

Because I have something.

For the second time in my life, I have another thing in this world.

This man.

Whoever he is...

He is like me.

"Monica, Monica... You're not going to make this easy for me, are you?"

He lifts his gaze, locking onto mine.

And those eyes. Deadly power. The kind of look that could give anyone a heart attack. Or, in my case, creep his way into my mind, my soul, my subconscious.

"I waited for you my entire life. I was sure I was alone. And now here you are, demanding I say it. That I call you for what you truly are. That you are... *The same as me.* You can hide all you want. From your family, from your friends, from everyone around you. But you can't hide from me. Because I *see* you. I know you. I can predict your next move, your next words. And how you're about to swear, tell me to fuck off, and stop thinking too much of myself."

I try to glare at him.

To give him my best disgusted look. To show him exactly how dare he speak to me like this.

But part of me is... impressed. Because he's right.

That is exactly what I was about to say.

Well... almost. He missed the part about the pliers.

"And yes," he says smoothly, amusement playing on his lips. "I'm aware you have your pliers in your apron pocket."

My breath stills.

Before I can react, he winks.

"And now you're thinking, *'What the fuck.'*"

Then, that laugh. That fucking laugh.

A sound that unsettles me, that promises something... something I haven't quite deciphered yet.

"Monica, please understand. All this fight or flight? I'm experiencing it with you. Right now. You and me both. That's why I hesitated for a week. If this is how neurotypical people feel all the time, no wonder they're all over the place." He exhales sharply. "I don't care for it."

It's my turn to laugh. And when it comes, it rips out of me, loud, raw, unapologetic.

The tension that has been coiling between us finally snaps, giving way to something else.

Something undeniable.

Because now, we both know.

We are the same.

And we are one for the other.

In this strange, shared moment of honesty and vulnerability. The barriers between us dissolve. Replaced by something stronger. A connection neither of us can ignore.

It's all out in the open now.

For better or worse... We found each other.

I soften my features. And for the first time, I look at him without my mask. Without reservation.

Just *me*.

In my true form.

The gesture makes me feel exposed — vulnerable in a way I have never allowed before. And worse, it scares me. Because for the first time in my life, I care what a man thinks of me.

Elijah has awakened something inside me — something I don't recognise, something I don't want to name.

And it unsettles me.

Yet the call to show him my true self, it's like sand crying for rain. Like a volcano aching to erupt after thousands of years. A force that is bigger than me.

A force that demands I expose myself to an inevitable truth that can no longer be denied.

"There she is." His voice is steady, full of something I don't want to name.

He stands, holding my gaze. Unflinching.

"You are *a remarkable creature*." His words land heavier than I expect.

"Why are you hiding?"

The question stuns me.

I stare at him for a few seconds, my mind scrambling, trying to piece together a response.

Something diplomatic.

Something detached.

Something that lets me slip my mask back on, with a beautiful, professional excuse.

"Don't you dare, Monica!"

His voice cuts through my thoughts, sharp and absolute.

"I can see what you're doing, and it won't work with me."

His gaze holds me captive, filled with something I don't know how to handle.

"I already saw you. Even with your masks on. So for all that is true in this world... Don't hide from me."

He looks at me as if I am the most precious thing he has ever laid his eyes on.

Like I am undeniable.

The sincerity in his eyes is disarming, making it impossible to slip back into my façade.

In that moment... I feel *truly* seen.

And the fear of being exposed is overshadowed by something stronger.

The comfort of his unwavering acceptance.

His words settle inside me, a plea not laced with weakness, but with truth.

A truth that demands to be acknowledged.

And for the first time, I feel the pull.

To let go.

To trust in the connection we share.

"Not everyone was lucky like you. Born into a family that sees violence as a virtue, where manipulation and power aren't sins but achievements. I was born and raised in a world where all of this is a straight path to prison, where being like us makes you the worst of the worst. Where logic, loyalty, and respect aren't the foundation of a person's being — they're just rumours, whispers people speak of but never live by. You ask me why I hide? I hide because I know the light was never meant for me."

He takes a step closer, then leans in.

The moment I register the movement, I step back, hands up, defensive stance.

"Elijah, no."

Just because he sees me, doesn't mean he can do whatever the fuck he wants.

We might be the same, but that doesn't mean I belong to him.

I straighten, shifting into my most dominant, confident posture.

Then I rake my gaze over him.

Up and down.

A deliberate move. One designed to make him self-aware.

To remind him who I am.

"We might be the same. And I might not need to hide from you. But don't mistake that for acceptance of your presence in my life." My voice is cold. Professional.

Fuck! I'm pleased with myself for sounding so dismissive.

"I might not process emotions like others, but understand this. If I ever feel you're a threat, I'll kill you. Without a second thought. Without a single ounce of remorse."

A beat of silence.

Then...

"I expect nothing else," his response is so calm and collected, completely at odds with the death threat I just delivered.

"Let me state the obvious, so you know exactly where you stand, Elijah. I don't want misunderstandings. I don't know what the fuck is happening inside me, but I do know it can't lead to anything." I hold his gaze, steady. "If you're looking for a wet hole, I'm not the one. I am a married woman. Even if I don't love him. Even if I never will, my loyalty is with him."

My tone is calm, clear, and precise.

"Loyalty and respect, until the day one of us dies."

I narrow my eyes.

"So don't think for a second that I would leave him like he's nothing, just because you graced me with your presence."

He takes a step back.

The warmth in his expression shifts, not disappearing, but hardening into something more serious.

Something contemplative.

The weight of my words settles between us, thick in the air, wrapping around the moment like a suffocating fog.

His eyes, still filled with acceptance, now hold something else.

Respect.

A deep, unwavering respect for the boundary I've just set.

For a moment, we stand in silence.

Letting it sink in.

Letting it matter.

Then, slowly, he nods. A quiet acknowledgment.

There's something in his gaze... Not quite sadness. Something quieter. Something heavier. But beneath it, there's a newfound resolve.

"I understand." His voice is soft but steady.

Sincere.

He turns, moving towards the door.

But just before he steps out, he pauses.

Glances back at me.

And in a voice just above a whisper, he leaves me with one final promise.

"I won't cross that line."

A beat of silence.

"Just *don't hide* from me, Monica."

Then he's gone.

And the shop feels different.

Chapter Eight

Elijah

It's been two days since I last saw the creature in person, and I've come to a pivotal realisation: her power over me is absolute.

All these emotions I've only ever observed in others surged through me when we spoke — and it was suffocating.

There is nothing like it.

My body took over my mind, and I was left behind for the first time in my life when I leaned in to pull her into my arms.

I couldn't believe I had initiated physical touch.

Even when I had sex, it was a mere transaction of needs — nothing more, nothing less.

All my partners knew it.

No kissing. No touching. No intimacy.

It was as transactional as it could get.

A mere physical need. Satisfied.

And then there is her — and the power she wields over me by simply existing.

My body is screaming to touch her again.

To feel her in my arms.

To feel my hand around her delicate neck.

Part of me wants to break that beautiful body — then put it back together in the most intimate way imaginable.

And I don't do that.

I don't do needs.

I don't do feelings.

And yet here I am, completely losing myself in this void — of feelings, and needs, and contrary thoughts.

I'm searching for the logic in my reactions. For the pattern. For the process. For any familiar element, in a last, desperate effort to understand myself around this creature.

The second pivotal realisation I've come to is this: I can only tolerate short encounters with her.

Anything longer, and I might accidentally attack her.

And I'm certain she wouldn't take kindly to being forced in any way.

So I'm reduced to this strange version of myself — stalking her every movement.

Watching.

Pacing.

Analysing.

Forming plans.

Tracking patterns of behaviour.

If I gave into these feelings consuming me now, I would take her. Force her to be with me. Force her to accept me. Give her no choice.

Ensure she could only breathe me from that day onward.

That thought brings a smile to my face. A sweet taste in my mouth. And warmth in my chest.

Yes.

I should just take her...

One problem.

The moment she pushed me away and explained her reasoning, was the moment I knew, without a doubt, she is mine.

Forever.

There's no stopping this. Even if either of us wanted to stop — I would never allow it.

She is mine.

She was created for me.

She is my creature.

Not only is she like me — she thinks like me. She sees the world like I do.

Her soul, as dark and twisted as it is, calls to mine. And I'm going to answer that call. With everything I am. Without hesitation.

I am torn between this desperate need to see her, to speak to her, to breathe in her vicinity — and this horrendous flood of emotions consuming me.

I don't like it.

I don't care for it.

And if I could pull them out of my chest, I would.

But I can't extract and dispose of these intrusive sensations running through my body, so I'm stuck.

For the first time in my life... between a rock and a hard place.

Twenty minutes later, I'm in the car with Vasile, my bodyguard and driver, followed by two other vehicles.

I assigned two cars with guards to Monica the first day I saw her.

Something in me was already aware of the significance of her presence in my life, and I couldn't bring myself to leave her unguarded, not for a second.

She is my creature.

Mine to protect.

Mine to possess.

Mine to conquer.

A part of me is beyond irritated that she's going home to her husband, while I'm left watching her from afar like a common stalker.

I may be a stalker — but I am not common.

For her to wield this kind of power over me, to the point I can't even focus on my work without watching her for hours each morning and through the day, is not something I ever imagined allowing.

But this thirst to see her, to be near her, it's all-consuming.

And it must be addressed regularly, there will be consequences.

So what if she doesn't love him?

So what if she said she never will?

He is allowed in her vicinity, and that alone is punishable by death.

With everything in me, I suppress the images, the idea of them living like a family, because if I let it surface for even a millisecond, the rage would be unstoppable.

She is not his.

She is mine!

We've bugged and hacked all her devices. Every location she travels. She is completely engulfed in my world now.

I know her schedule. I know her orders. Her shopping habits.

When she leaves. When she returns.

I know her entire day—down to the millisecond.

And it still isn't enough.

The only place I haven't entered is her home.

Not because we can't enter, but because I don't trust myself to be anywhere near it.

My entire life, I've only killed out of necessity.

Yes, I have the need to kill.

As does my creature.

But unlike her, I've mastered control over the urges. Maybe it's because I have time, or the right people to unleash it on.

Every kill I've made, was calculated.

Justified.

Deserved.

Her home, specifically, her husband... that's where the line blurs.

If I ever stood in front of him, I would kill him.

Without hesitation.

Because the fury that she is not mine is feral—a craving to end a life, just so I can start one with her.

And it's her logic—her loyalty—that drives me insane.

Every time I think about her devotion...

I lose my fucking mind.

Like some unhinged teenager desperate to fuck someone into oblivion.

I want her.

I need her.

She will be mine.

At all cost—she will be mine.

The car stops in front of the shop, and I spot the two surveillance vehicles assigned to her.

I don't even need to ask for a report—my phone pings with incoming texts.

It could be their efficiency. Or it could be because I've demanded updates every thirty minutes.

We may never know.

Regardless, the report is what I expect.

Routine. Predictable. Comforting.

And even though I know this is her business, she is expected to interact with people, every single person who enters her shop, places an online order, or walks past her in a shopping centre is thoroughly checked.

And disposed of, if needed.

Last week, two fuckers at the shopping centre looked at her.

Criminal records.

By nightfall, they were gone.

Erased.

No trace left that could ever connect them to her.

She will forever be safe.

There is no reality—none—in which peace of any kind can exist in this world if she is not in it.

She is mine to protect.

And she will never be alone again.

Case in point: she will receive two more vehicles.

Fully staffed with guards.

Watching over her.

I step into the shop, and that dreaded ding from the door sensor announces my arrival.

I've never hated a sound more than I do in this moment.

She's not in the front. She's in the back room, or the fridge, as she calls it.

She's most definitely seen me on the cameras, the same ones I tapped into when I started watching her. But now, it's her turn to watch me.

A smile plays on my lips.

She's adorable for doing this.

And I wouldn't be surprised if she'd install cameras all over my apartment, if I ever gave her the chance.

An idea forms in my mind. Perhaps I should install the cameras myself and give her access, so she can stalk me anytime she wants. It's only fair.

And this way, she might see all the glorious things I offer, things no one else ever could.

I can nurture, feed, and grow every dark desire she has. I can support them, build them, indulge them—until every one of her needs is completely satisfied.

But again... I cannot just take her, no matter how much I want to.

She wants to be loyal.

And above all...

I respect that.

When that word—alongside her action—left her lips, I knew that was the moment everything changed. From that point on, I lived for her.

There is no business.

No friends.

No life beyond this.

There is only my creature.

I take a seat in the same chair next to the counter, stretch my legs, close my eyes, and wait.

And I wait a long time.

The longer I wait, the more amused I become.

She's too adorable—I could devour her completely. Scenarios start to flood my mind, each one more vivid than the last, where I do exactly that.

And the longer I sit here, the more creative I get. And I savour every second of it.

"Santa!"

Her voice is joyful, and I take a second to finish planning what I would do to her body one day. Then I open my eyes, and sure enough, she's standing there, the most contagious smile on her face.

The only problem? She's wearing her mask.

It breaks something in me to see such a phenomenal creature hide. *Who the fuck dared to push her into this box?*

I raise a brow and hold her gaze, saying nothing.

Then—she lets the mask fall.

And I witness the most beautiful transformation.

From a beautiful woman into a magnificent creature—one who could destroy or conquer anything and everything.

"Lisichka."

The pet name escapes me in a breathy exhale, because again, I am transfixed—caught in a paradise crafted solely for me when I look into those dark eyes and see my creature.

She is magnificent.

We just sit there, transported into a world of our own, drowning in each other's gaze. She is so beautiful, and these warm feelings grip my chest with such force it physically hurts—but at the same time, it's the best pain I've ever experienced.

Part of me wants to keep my distance and respect her boundaries, but another part of me—the more dominant part—is urging me to grab her and steal her for myself, no matter the cost.

I want her.

And I will have her.

I just need to live by my own rules, and to do that, I must learn to control one more part of my nature: the part that must respect her loyalty.

"Having fun, Santa?" she says in a playful tone, daring me to react.

I've noticed this about her—she isn't quiet. She's daring, cunning, and beautiful in her manipulation. Every word, every gesture pulls me further into her orbit.

I just smile, absorbing her beauty for myself, letting her provoke every feeling inside and out.

She walks past me and, not so discreetly, stomps on my foot with all her might.

A deep laugh bursts out of me, because fuck me, this woman only needs to exist in my proximity and I'm melting in front of her.

She stomped on my foot.

How fucking hilarious is that?

"I'm sorry about that," she feigns innocence. "You have very long legs. Maybe you want to pack them up and go back to the North Pole?"

She provokes me some more—with her words, with her glare, with her very existence.

I hold her gaze and relish the fact that she is her true self around me.

I asked for one thing, and she granted it.

An inexplicable sensation forms within me, and it's so consuming I have to force myself to stay composed.

I want to jump on her. I want to make her mine.

She is mine, for fuck's sake!

As I stare into her beautiful dark eyes, my mind traces every line of her face and neck. I revel in absorbing her—even from afar—because I am seeing the truest version of her. And I am the only one who can see her in her entirety.

But she is not mine...

So I need to stop this, before I lose complete control.

"I missed you." Three words, but the weight of them is unspeakable. There was no stopping them.

She's completely taken aback by my admission, and she sighs.

I know she feels it now.

I know she's as confused by these feelings as I am.

And I can only admire the strength it takes for her to keep her distance... even when she knows she is mine.

"This is me, Monica, matching your pace. Following your lead. Giving you the space—and the respect—you deserve. But understand something. I know exactly where you belong."

And with that everything shifts.

The silence belongs to her now. She's the one quiet, analysing, processing.

And I'm the one laying it bare.

"The fact that you're still with your husband doesn't say you don't want me. It tells me you know what loyalty means. And that? That's rare as hell. I waited 43 years for you, Lisichka. I can wait a little longer, for you to catch up to what we already are."

There. My truth is out.

I'm not fucking going anywhere!

And no one, not her or anyone else, will make me let go of the woman who was made for me.

She is mine.

And in time...

She'll understand.

Her place is by my side.

"This is inevitable. Just as I know the sun will rise tomorrow and just as I know my heart only beats for you, I know you were made for me. It's a fact." I say it with all the authority I possess, studying her reaction. "That's the one truth nothing can touch."

I pause and let the words have their true weight between us. This is final. Nothing will change that.

"For years, I believed I was too different for anyone to be like me. But I was wrong. You're like me. Exactly like me. This world was never meant to contain us. It was meant to kneel before us."

She didn't expect that, it's written all over her face. Good. Now she knows exactly where I stand, where I see our future, and where she belongs. Permanently. She has the data now. It's hers to analyse, refine if necessary, then execute. Or, as the neurotypicals would say—make it happen.

"So I'm going to give you time. Space. Care. Protection. Everything, until you take your place." I stand. Calm. Centred.

"Take all the time you need. I'm not going anywhere."

Then I turn and walk out of the shop.

Chapter Nine

Monica

I didn't sleep at all last night.

I understand where Elijah is coming from. I understand his logic. I even know he's right.

His words are haunting me like I'm dragging a heavy rock behind me. It's strapped to me, and no matter how hard I pull, it doesn't budge. Its weight is crushing.

I get all of that. I understand it, as unpleasant as it is. I understand my feelings. I don't want them. They feel intrusive. Disturbing. But from a logical perspective, I can see what's happening around me, and inside me.

Still, my loyalty stands with Dan. Not out of love, but out of our escape together.

And I don't want Elijah to think that I'd never consider *this*—whatever *this* is between him and I— because I'm in love with my husband.

He needs to know what I have with Dan isn't real. It's not a marriage. It's an arrangement. A contract of convenience. That's all.

As twisted as my thoughts are, and as far as I'm willing to go in the dark, cheating isn't one of the things I would ever do.

I am who I am, and I know what I am.

And for a very long time, well until my daughter was born, there wasn't a single person on this earth who cared about me. Let alone loved me.

My parents. My family. The family I was born into.

The ones meant to love, protect, and nurture me. They were cruel. Vindictive. Downright evil when it came to me.

It didn't matter what I did, or how I did it. It was never enough.

There was never peace in that house. It was like they went out of their way to look for things I'd done wrong. And they always found something.

I was never good enough.

The mental abuse. The physical abuse. The constant torment—it was unbearable. Even for someone like me.

I had to escape. Somehow. Anyhow. I needed to get out.

So when I found myself pregnant, I swore they would never see my baby.

Because to me, this baby wasn't just mine. She was only mine.

I refused to tell anyone what had happened to me.

I erased my assaulter from the equation.

Angela is mine and mine alone.

No one will ever be able to change that.

I still remember that day.

I walked into the apartment, and as always, the smell of borscht hit me at the doorway.

I can still see it, my mum rushing into the kitchen threshold, wiping her hands on the corner of her apron, looking me over like she always did. Scanning everything. Ready to strike with her disgust and disapproval.

When she noticed the blood on my legs and clothes, she lunged at me. Fast. Like this was the moment she'd been waiting for an excuse to unleash all her hatred at once.

By the time my father stepped into the hallway, I was already curled up on the floor.

There was no way for him to see the blood from where I was.

But that didn't stop him.

He kicked at me like he didn't need a reason. Like the violence was already in him, waiting.

By the time they were done, I had three broken ribs, four bruised ones, two broken fingers, and more.

At the emergency department, they said I'd had one of my violent episodes. That I'd exploded. That I'd attacked them.

They said they'd supported me through my worst. That when I started to hurt them, they pulled back.

Because deep down, I didn't want to hurt them and they knew that.

Even now, it disgusts me.

Not one fucking soul on this earth believed me when I said they were hurting me.

So I gave up.

Eventually, I just took it.

And took it.

Until I found my way out.

I knew Dan in passing. He lived a few buildings down from us in the same apartment block. I didn't really mingle with him growing up—I didn't mingle with anyone—but that's beside the point.

When my parents put him forward and said I had to marry him because I was a filthy slut for sleeping around, I exploded. Like a bomb. Right in front of them. As always, they both jumped on me.

But this time, I pushed back. Because there was a baby inside me, and I wasn't going to let them hurt it.

In the chaos, I accidentally smacked my mum.

And we all froze.

In that moment, I saw it differently.

Dan wasn't another shackle. He was my ticket out of their grasp.

So I agreed.

After we got married, it took no effort to convince him to move to England. He was more than eager. Later, he let it slip, his parents were abusive shitheads too, so he wanted distance. Out of sight, out of mind.

He didn't push himself on me at the start.

We didn't even know each other.

But at least he had the decency not to expect sex straight away.

The first time we had sex was after we settled in.

He made the first move. I let him. By then, I was free. Free of my family, free of the pain. And that freedom came through him.

But I didn't feel like I owed him anything.

Truth is, I just wanted to see if I could feel something.

I didn't.

I felt the physical part.

But not the emotional. Not the intimacy.

No orgasm. No pleasure. No attraction.

Just mechanics. Cold. Transactional. Empty.

That heart-to-heart we had after the second time he tried to have sex led to something useful.

It forced a real discussion. And something shifted between us.

We have... well, it's not quite... or at least I don't think it is...

But we have an open relationship.

And by open, I mean him.

He's allowed to meet his needs, discreetly.

As long as there's no shame, no public awareness, and—most importantly—Angela never finds out.

I don't care. Not one bit.

I understand the physiology.

We all have physical needs. They need to be satisfied. It's that simple.

People who don't understand the body's chemistry might argue with me.

But I've done my research. I know I'm right.

As for me?

I have beautiful toys. And I take very good care of myself. I love my body in every way I deserve to be loved and cherished.

And again—I don't care what anyone thinks about that. Most people hate their bodies.

I chose to love mine.

I know which one of us is at peace and satisfied.

Even so, I know.

I can feel it, deep in my core.

One day, I'll be by Elijah's side.

It's like that feeling in the air when spring is approaching.

You know there are still some cold, shitty days ahead.

But soon enough, spring will come.

And the air will be full of the sweet scent of flowers breaking into bloom, soft and unstoppable.

It will warm everyone's hearts. Even mine.

Dan could've been a shithead. He could've been abusive, especially in those first few years.

He could've left after I hurt him. He could've done a million things.

But he didn't.

He chose to stay. For over twenty years.

Yes, he's comfortable in this situation. So am I.

Yes, I manipulated things so he'd stay. But I've always believed this—and I know it's true: A man stays because he wants to. Not because someone makes him.

A man who wants to leave will take the first opportunity to run. And Dan didn't run.

Feelings or no feelings. Real marriage or not.

My loyalty stays with the man who got me out of that hell.

It's 3 a.m. when I finally give up and get out of bed.

Dan and I have never shared a bedroom—not a single day of our marriage—so it's easy to just start my routine and get on with it.

Just after 4 a.m., I'm out the door, and one of the SUVs my beloved Santa put on me visibly shakes.

I giggle to myself. I scared the poor boys awake. I love it!

Patterns. People don't realise how attached they get to them.

I count—one, two, three, four SUVs.

What the fuck?! What the hell is wrong with him? I have neighbours.

They stand out like a fucking panda on a beach.

Oh, Santa...

Next time I see you, I'm stepping on both your feet and—accidentally, on purpose—kicking you in the balls.

Then I see it.

One of the street cameras turns toward me.

Surely not. Right?

I smile at it. My most plastic, professional smile.

And I stare into it like I'm staring into Elijah's eyes.

Sure enough, my phone pings.

Unknown number

Good morning, Lisichka.⊠
Are you alright?⊠
Why are you up so early?

Are you kidding me right now?!

I look up from the phone, and another SUV shakes.

Now I'm just mad.

Clearly, these idiots are sleeping on the job.

Unknown number

Talk to me.

I think about letting him sweat.

But then I realise it'll be more fun to have a go at him.

What can I say? I'm sentimental like that.

Monica

Who is this? I'm blocking you.

Unknown number

...

Don't you dare.

Monica

Blocking now

I go to block him, and my screen glitches in my hand.

What the fuck?

I raise my head slowly and stare straight into the camera.

Then I lift my middle finger.

Whatever voodoo shit he's pulling with my device—it's not cool.

And he'll pay for it.

Monica

You just lost the privilege of one SUV.

Move.

Unknown number

...

Monica

Stop this shit with the ... What are you five?

Also your guys are sleeping on the job.

I slip my phone into my pocket for a second—just to free up my hands.

Then I lift both middle fingers to the camera.

Now. I mouth.

One of the SUVs pulls out of the car park and takes off.

My phone dings. I ignore it.

It dings again. I keep ignoring it.

Then it dings a few times in a row.

I pick it up, put it on silent, take out my keys, and head to the shop.

By the time I get to the shop, it's still dark outside.

Because hey, why wouldn't I torture myself some more with this place?

But again—it's mine.

It's my shop. Why wouldn't I keep it if I want it?

The moment I park and look at the front doors, I see it.

Spray-painted in graffiti, all over the glass:

"Filthy cunt."

Well, that's just rude. Not because they called me a cunt. But because they called me filthy.

What the fuck is wrong with people? When did this become acceptable?

Since that incident with Jake, I've been getting all sorts of rubbish. Complaints. Clients leaving. Handwritten crap left in the shop. I've been pushing it to the back burner. Because I know I can't give in to my tendencies and accidentally hurt someone.

All of this started when I dumped Jack and Jake. It has to be connected.

The third time Santa came to the shop, I told him straight. *If his boy wants to be with my girl, he needs to prove his worth in blood.* And take care of that fuckhead Jake.

Santa said it was handled. But this nonsense is still happening.

My phone vibrates for the millionth time in my bag. And sure enough, it's the same Unknown number calling me.

"You can tinga-linga my phone and stop me from blocking you, but you can't guard a simple shop from vandalism?" I say flat.

"Are you okay? I'm on my way now." He says in a panicked voice.

"No, you're not. Stop the car and do a U-turn."

"Lisichka..."

His voice is low. Threatening.

I'm not impressed of any of this.

"If I can't call you Santa, you can't call me Lisichka. Understood?"

He grunts softly into the phone, then sighs.

One of his cars—and I'd bet anything it's his—pulls up behind mine and cuts the engine.

In all my time at this shop, I've never seen a Bentley on this street.

Fancy.

It has to be his.

"I needed to see you." His voice is calm. Controlled. But there's something in it. Just a flicker beneath the surface.

"I needed to see with my own eyes that you were well."

"Are you in the car behind me?" I ask.

Silence.

"You're acting like a child."

Nothing. No response.

A few minutes pass.

I just stand there, staring at the car.

The windows are too tinted for me to see inside.

When I've had enough, I lift my middle finger again. I go to end the call. Then his voice comes through in a rush.

"Don't hang up!"

I want to defy him. I really do. But something in me, something as panicked as his voice, won't let me end this call.

I want to talk to him. I want to be near him.

"I just want to talk to you, Lisichka. That's all. I needed to make sure you're alright. And to assure you, whoever did this will die today. From now on, I'll have our men at every location you own. It was an oversight on my part, not guarding what's yours. I take full responsibility for that mistake. It won't happen again."

Our man?

It doesn't escape me how easily that came out of his mouth. How naturally he called his men ours.

I could make a joke out of it. But it feels honest. More than anything, I see it for what it is.

He's like me. And he's definitely feeling the weight of his mistake.

"And you'd better never forget it again," I say, my voice laced with mischief.

Then I let the mask slip. And I look straight at him.

He audibly inhales through the phone.

I'm speechless.

Breathless.

Completely taken aback by the way he always reacts to me—the real me.

I've never seen myself as beautiful. Not even behind my most perfect mask.

And yet he sees the real me as someone who takes his breath away.

I don't know what to do.

I feel exposed. Vulnerable.

And the only thing that comes to mind is to make a joke.

So I do what I do best when it comes to him.

I slowly, gently lift my middle finger again—holding what I think is his gaze.

He bursts out laughing. So hard I hear it through the phone, and from the car before me.

"Okay, you had your fun. Now leave."

"No need. I wrapped up all my work this past week and handed everything over to my second-in-command. From now on, I'll be out here, guarding you myself."

I freeze, because that was the last thing I thought I would hear from him. *What?!*

"Don't you have, you know, some information to steal? Or a drug logistics problem to sort out? Or maybe some human trafficking to negotiate?"

I throw in the last one just to see what he'll say. Let's see how he handles that.

"Also, roll down your window. Let's talk like adults."

The window lowers. He looks displeased as hell. I pocket my phone and play indifferent.

"Monica, I am not a good man. You know that. I know that. I've done terrible, despicable things, by some people's standards. But I would never—listen to me, because I will only say this once—I would never deal in human trafficking. I wouldn't even work with people who move in that world. Because there are limits, even in this darkness. And those who think of themselves as gods, who think they can submit other humans to that, they are the worst of the worst. So no, Monica. I do not have any human trafficking problems to deal with."

His tone is so sharp, I don't even feel like joking after that little outburst.

A psychopath with principles. I like it.

I know there's more I could get out of him.

But that window into his past—it's not opening today.

He needs to process this. Just as much as I do.

"There'll be a team here in five minutes to clean the graffiti."

"They called me dirty. No—actually, filthy. Not cool."

He just smiles. But it's that smile. The smile of a psychopath right before he strikes.

"You're not doing a very good job stalking me," I say, batting my lashes at him. "Someone beat you to it," I add. "Not to mention your guys are sleeping on the job."

Then I burst out laughing at the look on his face visibly horrified, like I actually kicked him in the balls.

I need to do this more often. Hit him where it hurts. Let's see:

Balls, check.

Ego, check.

Stalking skills? Check.

This is going to be fun.

"I will leave for a while to deal with this situation personally. Vasile will remain with you as extra."

"Oh my. You cannot even deliver on the first promise to guard me yourself. You are dropping the ball big time," I tease so more.

His laughter explodes out of him, rich and deep, like medicine to a dying person. And it does terrible things to my insides. But for some reason, I can't get enough of it.

This teasing game, these cheeky remarks, I've never had anything like it in my life.

But with Elijah, everything feels... *natural.*

Effortless. Fitting.

His laughter fades.

Then he extends his hand toward me, a quiet offer to hold mine.

And everything in me screams in opposite directions.

It's confusing. Loud. Overwhelming.

I know if I make physical contact, it might be too much.

Too much for me.

That said, every part of me wants to touch him.

It's this need—buried beneath my skin.

It's the kind of hunger that lives in the blood, at a molecular level—like I was made to need his touch, whether I want it or not.

As if he's an essential part of my being.

The moment the tips of our fingers touch...

I can't even describe the depth, the impact, the magnitude.

It's not like a current ran through me.

Not just a spark.

It feels like connection. *Real* connection.

Like I've actually linked to another person.

I'm so stunned that only the tips of my fingers are resting in his palm, but my whole body, my whole mind, is aware of every collision of sensation right there at that point of contact.

I don't dare take his hand.

I don't even dare breathe.

I just stare—bewildered—at the place where we're joined.

Relishing every feeling my body is suddenly creating.

Then a car pulls up next to us.

The horn blares.

And just like that, the moment is dead.

I pull away quickly.

My eyes find Elijah and in his gaze, I see my feelings reflected back.

And I can't believe it.

Me.

Feeling.

Processing emotion.

Processing *this.*

"Hello. Sorry about the doors. I'm here to fix everything up for you." The handyman says it with a laid-back attitude and an even more laid-back pair of pants. He walks up and shakes my hand without even asking. He just grabs my arm, takes my hand, and shakes it like we're old mates.

A deep growl rumbles from the car behind me, low and dangerous, like an angry bear.

I don't even have to look. I know Elijah is already picturing tearing this guy's arm clean off. And the thing is—I get it. If someone touched Elijah like that, I'd be ready to rip their arm off too.

Wait. *What?!*

That thought is so out of place, it sobers me up, cuts right through the chaos. All the feelings, the situation, the stimulation, everything colliding inside me, and jealousy is what pulls me back to centre?

Jealousy? Really? Me?

Well, that's new. And dangerous. Because without a doubt, I know I'd dismember any woman who so much as tries to touch Elijah.

Wow!

That's mind-blowing. To realise—*actually realise*—that I'd hurt someone just for touching him.

Well... That's eye-opening.

"If you value your life, don't touch me again," I say, clear and calm. "No offence, but the guy in the car might have a problem with it." I smile at the surprise on his face.

"Sure thing," he replies quickly. "I'll just get to it now." And off he goes, rushing to clean the filthy remark off my doors.

"Your guys are slacking," I say, turning to Elijah with my mischievous smile.

"They're not slacking, Lisichka. The car moved because I went at them a bit."

He gives me a look and I know there's more to it. By "a bit," he probably told the lead to smack every one of them.

"You broke pattern. And I might... or might not... have panicked a little."

Right. He panicked because I broke pattern.

"You're a child. You know that, right?" I smile at the face he makes.

"I act childish with you," he says quietly. "Because you see what I see, you think how I think. But to everyone else, I'm always the smartest person in the room."

He inhales and holds my gaze for a long second.

"With you... I don't even know what I am." There's so much sincerity in his gaze, it's almost disarming. Remarkable, even.

"This is a lot, Lisichka. My entire being wants to jump on you. And I'm really scared I might hurt you if I give in to what's inside."

He's right. This is a lot.

One major positive. We both feel the weight of it with the same intensity.

We stand there for a few minutes, taking each other in.

Letting his words sink in with all their depth and gravity.

"Off you go, Santa."

"Santa, hmm?"

He raises an eyebrow at me.

"I'm sure you can do better than that, Lisichka."

"What does it mean?"

He smiles, and it's not just any smile. It's the most sincere one he's given me so far. His whole face changes. His eyes soften, beautiful in a way that catches me off guard. A small dimple appears on his left cheek.

"It means little fox. Because that's what you are. Cunning. Intelligent. And made perfectly for me."

Lisichka.

His perfect little fox.

Chapter Ten

Elijah

It's becoming harder and harder not to be in her presence.

Over the past week, I've wrapped up every urgent deal I had across the globe and handed full authority to Buddy for the rest.

Because the moment I touched her, I knew—there's nothing more important under the sun than her. And whatever this thing is between us.

From now on, my full attention is on her. That's final.

My businesses can self-manage or perish. I don't care.

Because I found her.

The creature made for me.

The one that fits perfectly.

She's not just a woman.

She is *the* woman.

She knows her strength. But she doesn't yet understand her power.

And she *definitely* doesn't know the power she holds next to me—what she could become with me.

Most of all, I don't think she understands the power she has over *me*.

I'll bring her into the light. Or rather—I'll bring her into my darkness, where she belongs. Where she can flourish. Where her true potential can shine with the full brilliance of who she is.

She's hidden in plain sight long enough.

It's time the world sees her.

Knows her. Fears her. Admires her.

She is magnificent in every way. And every time I see a trace of her mask it's like someone reaches into my chest and squeezes my heart.

Something that tremendous should never be shackled by ordinary human expectations.

I understand. I really do.

We were born into different worlds. But her beauty—her power—it's a crime against humanity to keep it hidden.

I texted Buddy, told him to find whoever committed such an abomination against my creature, and bring them to the Barrow. We're going to have a discussion.

I haven't told Buddy about her yet, or the fact that I'm stepping back. I'm not concerned. None of my men would ever say no to me. Buddy owes me his life. Many of them do. In my world, my word is law. Everything I say is carried out with precision.

It's not just fear—though I know they fear me. It's respect. Loyalty. The kind I've nurtured over years of action. Too many leaders think if they sing a good song, people will follow. But if you don't follow up with action? It's only a matter of time before good people leave, once they realise you're full of shit. That's not a leader. That's a manager.

And I'm not just a leader.

I'm the head of leaders.

I've made sure all my men are looked after. Most of them have millions in the bank. The ones I knew could handle the real work—they climbed the ladder. Now they're in my UBT, or one rank below.

It's not for everyone.

I don't force anyone to do what they don't want to do, what is not in their nature.

But they all know—if I wanted to, I could destroy their lives effortlessly. But that's a different story.

I value respect and loyalty above all.

To me.

And to each other.

Simple rules.

If they don't follow them, they're out. No matter who they are.

Am I judge, jury, and executioner?

Yes. I am.

And they all know it.

Now that I'm almost at the Barrow, my headquoters in London, the pleasant aroma of my creature is fading. What's left is the not-so-pleasant part of my psyche.

Yes—some of us thirst for blood.

Some don't.

Some of us manipulate everyone and everything.

Some are psychopaths without the intelligence to pull it off, just narcissism or violence with no direction.

There are as many variations of us as grains of sand on a beach.

And yet, two grains are exactly the same.

And someone was stupid enough to pick on *my* grain.

Unlucky for him, this grain is a genius. This grain is Machiavellian. Narcissistic. Calculated. And thirsty for blood.

Unfortunately for him—it's his blood I'll be washing my hands in today, for what he dared to do to my creature.

Dominic

Apologies, Elijah. Something came up, and I dropped by the flower shop.

I am planning to buy all the flowers for my angel. I am here with her mum now.

"Oh, Dominic," I say, calm and cold.

One of my men is driving me to the Barrow. Vasile stayed behind to watch over Monica. The sound of my voice, the driver checks the rearview mirror. Quickly, alarmed.

If I was eager to kill before that text, now I want to add Dominic to the list of people I'll slaughter today. The only reason he won't die right now is simple—he's with my creature's daughter. If I touch him, Angela will be affected. Which means Monica will be affected. And I can't have that.

Whatever's coming for him will come in time. And I will remember this slip-up—when the time is right.

Elijah

Be very careful, Dominic. Your life depends on this. Next time you speak to Monica, I need to know about it the moment the thought comes into your mind.

Dominic

Understood.

"The kid's in one of the conference rooms," Buddy says, calm and collected as I step out of the elevator.

"He was pretty surprised we picked him up. As you requested, we didn't make it obvious he's in trouble—just told him it was a business meeting."

"Thank you."

"Do we need to move him to one of the other rooms?" Buddy asks, likely reading my body language. After all, he's known me the longest. He already senses this won't end well for the man lounging in one of our see-through boardrooms.

We have special rooms at the Barrow for more intimate discussions—but I deliberately told Buddy to place him in a glass boardroom.

To give him a sense of safety.

Confidence.

Tranquillity.

What can I say? I like to play with my prey.

And I'm definitely going to enjoy playing with this imbecile—for what he's done.

"What do we know about him?"

"He's a low-level enquiry agent," Buddy replies. "Jack and Jake use him from time to time."

"This is connected to Dominic's little fun?" I ask, my voice edged with disbelief. That fool's been dead for days. How is this only coming to light now?

"As I understand it, he had his fun with Jake, and it's been resolved. However, what I gathered is that Jake took it very personally when Monica..."

The moment Buddy says her name, I glare at him. Murder and terror written so clearly on my face, it silences him instantly.

He's not allowed to speak of her.

None of them are.

She is only mine.

She is fucking *mine!*

And no one will take her from me.

My breathing picks up.

My hands start to shake—from the sheer force of restraining myself from tearing Buddy's face off for daring to say her name without my permission.

We stand in silence. While in my mind, I kill him. In every brutal, horrendous way I can think of. When I'm done—when my subconscious is satisfied he's suffered enough—I look him up and down. I try to level my voice, to sound like my usual cold, collected self—but what comes out is raw. So raw, it sounds unhinged even to my ears.

"You will never say her name again without permission."

Buddy just nods. He knows better than to say a word when I'm like this.

I've never reached this level of rage before. Not even close.

I can feel it. I'm losing control.

This is Buddy, of all people. And I still can't tolerate him saying her name.

No one can be trusted when it comes to the creature, my mind whispers. *She is only yours. And everyone needs to know that.*

I turn to him.

"She is off limits to all of you. She is mine. And mine alone. No one comes near her without my permission."

He nods again and lowers his gaze and posture, a clear sign of submission.

If I was angry before, and rightfully so, for what this insignificant creature did, then Dominic's idiocy has made it absolute. He went to Lisichka. Without permission. Without even a text.

That alone would warrant punishment.

But this, this string of events, it's layered. Built. Loaded. And now the weight of it has broken something in me.

Possession has turned to obsession.

And obsession?

It has given way to instinct. Primal. Violent. Unstoppable.

I've crossed a threshold.

There is no logic left. Only her. And the blood that must be spilled to protect what's mine.

"Good morning, Brandan. How are you this wonderful morning?" I speak in my usual cold, professional tone as I take a seat across from him.

He's a joke.

His clothes are disheveled.

His features, the same.

And he didn't even have the decency to sit up straight, despite the setting.

He's seated in a boardroom with actual gold on the walls, and yet this prick is slouched back like he's at some pub, waiting for his mates, arms behind his head, posture screaming disrespect.

"Good morning. And you are?" he says, dismissive as ever.

Oh, seriously. A little manners wouldn't kill him. I can't with this kid.

"Pardon me," I reply, still polite and professional. "I seem to have forgotten to introduce myself."

As I speak, I watch Buddy move into position behind me.

Smart man.

He knows better than to get caught in the crossfire. Seems he still remembers the old days. When he had to physically hold me back while I tore through anything in front of me.

"My name is Elijah Dominion. I'm the head of this organisation."

I pause briefly, studying his reaction.

His eyes widen, already excited at the idea of speaking with someone like me.

Oh, he'll be speaking all right.

"It's come to our attention that you possess a particular set of skills we may find useful. Would you mind providing more detail? Tell us a bit about yourself."

The excited look on his face is almost comical.

Normally, I'd offer a few compliments, make some remarks about their mediocre achievements, just enough to put them at ease. Maybe even hint at a possible collaboration, how valuable their skills might be to my organisation.

Anything to plant the seed.

Doubt. Hope. Illusion.

Whatever it takes to get them to where I need them to be.

This fool didn't even need a compliment. His two brain cells lit up the moment I mentioned we knew about him. How pathetic.

"Sure thing," he says, practically buzzing.

His expression is transfixed, like he's already counting the money he thinks he'll get from us.

It never ceases to amaze me the sheer amount of stupidity people can carry within themselves. I sit there for a solid ten minutes, listening to him babble about his painfully mediocre achievements, boasting like he's just won a Nobel Prize. All the while, I have to nod. Smile. Make encouraging noises like I'm actually impressed.

It's torture.

Pure and utter torture.

"I'm your go-to guy for all your needs, Mrs Dopinion."

Did this imbecile just butcher my surname?

Buddy flinches beside me sensing, correctly, that this might very well be the day that I kill someone in this room.

Because in my world, mispronouncing my name is punishable by death.

"It's Dominion," I say, with a small smile.

"That's what I said," he laughs.

I shake my head inwardly at the audacity. He just corrected me. In my own office. I very much doubt he's good for anything beyond confirming one thing: that his actions came from Jack and Jake.

"Yes, of course."

I turn to Buddy. It's written all over his face, he already knows this is going to be fun for me.

"Who recommended the gentleman again?" Time to shift the conversation toward Jack and Jake, and confirm what I already suspect.

"Jack and... "

"Oh, yes!" the man interrupts Buddy, as if cutting someone off mid-sentence is perfectly acceptable in an interview. "My pal! I love that guy. He throws me all sorts of jobs here and there. He definitely gave me a good recommendation after the last job I just did for him."

There you go, you stupid imbecile. Keep talking. Tell me more.

"Tell us about your last job for them."

"I probably shouldn't tell you this," he says, lowering his voice like we're sharing a secret, "but I really want to work with you. I reckon I'll make loads of cash from you rich people."

Buddy just shakes his head in disbelief. That this man—Brandan, I think his name is—could say something that inappropriate. Out loud. To us.

We sit there, listening, as he walks us through the past week, every childish, pathetic little way he tormented Monica. And then, as if he hasn't said enough, he lands the final nail in his own coffin.

He tells us about the graffiti.

As the words leave his mouth and I turn to tell Buddy to move him to one of our interrogation rooms at the Barrow, I feel the floor vibrate slightly.

Then, the sound hits us.

A bomb.

A fucking bomb. At the Barrow.

Fucking hell. I need to get to Monica!

I need to get to Monica!

In a flash, I'm on my feet.

"Move the prick to one of the secure rooms!" I yell over my shoulder as I run for the security centre.

It's empty.

No sign of Hunter. No sign of Sofia.

I call Monica—no answer.

She probably still has the damn thing on silent from earlier.

For fuck's sake!

I call Sofia. No answer.

Hunter. No answer.

It'll have to wait.

If they've hit us here, this attack might be bigger than just the Barrow.

And if they've gone after her—if they've gone after my creature—nothing else matters.

"What do you need me to do?" Buddy's voice is crisp—clear, steady, and ready for instructions.

"Status."

One word.

He knows what it means.

Buddy's in charge now while I confirm what's happening with Monica.

The P1 emergency protocol has just been activated. Hunter's already on it, by the looks of it.

I tap into the surveillance feeds around her shop and in her shop, desperate to get eyes on her.

Four minutes since the explosion. In my soul, it feels like eternity.

It's been just over an hour since I was near my Lisichka, and I feel like something is being ripped out of me.

A desperate, physical need to be near her.

As if she's carrying my oxygen with her.

Something inside me is dying—slow, brutal agony.

And I can't move.

I can't deal with anything except her.

These thoughts—intrusive, dangerous—invade my mind like poison.

What if she's hurt?

If I thought I could hyperfocus before—this is something else.

This is tunnel vision. Absolute. Consuming.

My mind is screaming.

My skin itches. My fingers are flying across the keyboard.

And I can't find her.

I can't fucking find her!

Everything goes red.

I freeze.

I can't find her.

I can't breathe.

I can't think.

All I see is red.

Hot rivers of blood pouring behind my eyes.

The sound—the smell—it's all there. Too loud. Too sharp. Too real.

This is my personal brand of hell.

I can't find her!

I can't fucking find her!

Something happened...

A hand lands on my shoulder. And in that single touch—I realise I was screaming.

The sound was real. Even if the vision wasn't.

I completely blacked out.

"She was in the bathroom," Buddy's calm voice cuts through the fog.

"Look." He points to one of the screens. And sure enough—my creature is walking through the shop like nothing happened.

She's fine.

She's safe.

And then I see him.

Dominic.

Why the fuck is Dominic just sitting there?

The fool's paralysed. Just standing there. Doing nothing.

"It's from Bogdan," Buddy says. His voice registers like it's underwater. "The bomb, he's behind the attack."

I hear the words. I understand them. But I can't break free from the tunnel vision.

All I can think about is getting to Monica.

Getting her to safety, at any cost.

Elijah

Get Monica out now! Panic room City Hall.

Dominic! Get Monica out now!

I'm going to kill you.

"I'm going to kill Dominic." My voice is calm now. Too calm.

I still can't believe I was screaming.

The last time I screamed... was after my family was killed.

Shit!

This woman has broken me into pieces. And I don't even bother trying to rationalise what's happening to me—because, quite frankly, it doesn't matter.

All of me belongs to her.

Every part.

She can do with me whatever she wants.

If she asked me to die, I'd happily die for her.

At least then, I wouldn't be dying at the hands of a moron.

I try to call her again.

Nothing.

I check the cameras. She's there, just talking to Dominic.

Calm. Casual.

As if nothing happened.

Talking. To that fool.

Elijah

Lisichka, listen to me, baby. Please. I beg you, please leave with my men.
There was an attack. You need to get to safety. Now.

I know you're mad, and I'll make it up to you—but please, I'm begging you—get to City Hall. Now.

I watch as she finally pulls the phone from her pocket and reads the messages.

My Queen

So besides being a bad stalker, you're a bad keeper too?

What am I going to do with you…?

I look at the screen and she's smiling.

Of course she is.

Leave it to my creature to be all sunshine and rainbows... while there's an attack happening.

Elijah

Get to safety. That's all I ask.⊠
After that, I'm yours to do with as you wish.

My Queen

You say that like I actually want anything to do with you.

Elijah

Please, Lisichka.⊠
Please let Dominic take you to City Hall.⊠
I can't fucking breathe right now.

My Queen

Panic much?

Elijah

Sure as fuck I'm panicking, woman.⊠
If anything happens to you, the world ends.⊠
If you die, I die with you.

She pauses.

Then looks straight into the security camera in her shop, holding my gaze. She nods once, then turns to speak with Dominic.

There's a lot of chaos to deal with right now. A full-scale clusterfuck. But none of that matters.

All that matters is getting to Monica.

And silencing the screaming in my mind.

"Did you find anything?" Sofia asks, breathless. She was frontline for the blast. Not sure why she was at Level 1, but she was—and by the look of her, it's more than just her exterior that's shaken.

"Yes. The bomb was a gift from Bogdan," I say, my tone flat and stern.

"Well, that's just great. How come the building didn't collapse?"

"Hmm," I grunt. As much as I want to at least sound polite to my daughter, all I want is to leave. To run to my creature. To see her, touch her, make sure she's truly fine.

And that fucker Dominic... He better not have done something stupid. Like touch her. Stand too close. Breathe next to her. Or today will be the day I collect for his mistake.

"When we built this place, we reinforced the building's structural integrity—especially around the emergency exits. Everyone was out and on their way home within twenty minutes of the P1 evacuation being activated." Buddy steps in, offering Sofia some reassurance.

"So... the building can't be brought down?" Her surprise is almost comical.

But I don't need any of this.

What I need is to end this conversation, and leave.

Now!

"It can," I say, fingers still flying across the keyboard, "but it would take a nuclear bomb."

"What Buddy's saying is, we didn't spare a cent when we built this place. I wanted my legacy to withstand human stupidity. We prepared for a lot of scenarios. If anyone comes at us, they'll need one hell of a bomb to bring this building down."

This place cost triple what any similar facility would.

And while I don't like people in general—and avoid contact as much as possible—I value good employees.

And as I've said before, every single one of them understands *respect and loyalty.*

My Queen

We're leaving now.

"We need to leave," I say, standing, my phone in hand.

"We're heading to the panic room at City Hall." I don't wait for a reply, I'm already moving. Storming to one of the hidden emergency exits in my office, with Buddy running to keep up behind me.

My Queen

My daughter?

Elijah

I checked on her before I left the office.
She's with Aleksey Maetney.

Dominic was smart enough to put her on the P1 protocol list.
Probably saved her life.

My Queen

Who is this person?
And why didn't *you* put her on the list?

Elijah

Alec's also in the UBT. You can trust him.

Dominic beat me to it.
When I added you to the list,
I intended to include your daughter too.
But she was already there.

He has it bad.

I lower my phone, my mind still spinning. I need to get to Lisichka at all costs.

"Elijah, is everything okay?"

I don't answer. Because if I do, I have two choices:

Lie — something I've never done to my friend.

Or tell him about *my creature.*

And neither of those options is acceptable right now.

So I say nothing.

"Let me come with you," he offers. "I can drive, if you like."

There are plenty of my men waiting in the car park next to the emergency elevator.

When we built this place, I designed it to be a masterpiece of architectural precision, and more importantly, equipped it with multiple escape routes in case of an attack. I never thought I'd be using this elevator, the one hidden behind a false wall in my office. But here we are.

Buddy's talking to me, but I'm completely disconnected from reality, and his words are not registering at all right now.

The only thing that matters now is getting to my creature. At all costs!

"If you're coming with me, you need to keep your eyes to yourself at all times. You don't have permission to even look at what's mine." My voice is cold. Threatening.

Buddy nods and takes the seat beside me as I tell the driver to head for City Hall—using the tunnel we built when we designed the building. Six minutes later, we're back above ground, entering the private car park attached to the City Hall arm I bought off officials years ago.

Only a fool thinks good times will last forever.

And I'm no fool.

If someone comes after me—after what's mine—there will be no place on Earth where they can hide.

Bogdan...

I've entertained his little cat-and-mouse game for a while now.

I didn't think he had the nerve to come after me directly.

But here we are.

And here I am, taking the stairs two at a time, desperate to catch a glimpse of my creature. Then I hear it—the crash of fists and shouts. Fighting.

I round the corner and see it. Dominic brawling with Alec.

Seriously?

Now?

"Dominic. Alec."

My voice crashes into the room like a gunshot, and everything stops. Everyone freezes.

My eyes are already on her.

My Lisichka.

She's standing against the wall, her daughter beside her, a subtle smile tugging at her lips. Not amused. Calculating. She's analysing every person in this room, every movement, every reaction, and she's enjoying what she sees.

She's stunning.

Not just in beauty, but in how completely in control she is even when the room is in complete chaos.

It hits me all over again.

She's real.

She's here.

She's mine.

And I'd burn this world to ash to make sure it stays that way. Nothing else matters than her.

I want to run to her. Rip the distance between us to shreds.

Tear the clothes off her body and fall to my knees.

Out of surrender.

Out of hunger.

My body aches with it.

Skin crawling. Hands shaking.

I need her.

Need to touch her, taste her, lose myself in her until I've carved her into my bones. Worship every inch until I've devoured her completely and then wake the next day starving to start again, like I hadn't already taken every part of her for myself.

Her pull is a gravitational force.

Her scent is in the air, mine, sweet, dangerous, and it's driving me fucking insane.

I need to be near her. Just stand next to her.

Breathe her in. Own the moment. Claim the space.

Then our eyes lock.

She holds my gaze for a second, then shakes her head—barely.

Subtle. Calculated. Absolute.

Whatever she sees in my eyes, it's not something for others to witness. Not for her daughter to see.

And she's right.

What's in me now... is not meant for anyone else.

"My office."

Two words. Barely controlled.

I need to get away from her. Now! Before I do something that will tear everything apart and cross the line with her.

If I stay one second longer, I'll take her.

Claim her.

Force the truth of us onto her body before her mind is ready to accept it.

And I know—I know—she won't forgive that.

So I walk to the office.

Because if I don't, I will ruin the one thing that matters more than my own life.

I sit behind the desk while Dominic and Alec start blabbering their petty dislike for each other.

I want to scream! Not because of the chaos, not even because we're in the middle of a P1 protocol. But because this need is ripping through me, consuming every part of me, demanding I go to Monica, take her in my arms, and devour her.

Every cell in my body is aching for her.

I've never felt such a desperate craving to be near someone, to breathe the air they exhale, to feel their skin against mine.

I register the noise in the room. I see Buddy step in to handle it. I know I need to shut this shit down.

But my entire existence is spiralling, lost in a storm of need and fire, because I'm not next to her.

"Dominic, there is a time and place when we settle matters between ourselves. This was not the time." Buddy's voice truly registers for the first time. "There are people out there who didn't know Alec's past, and it was not for you to divulge it. Even worse, what you said—and how you said it—made your brother feel less than what he is. You are in the wrong here."

Buddy's judgment lands like law. Good. Let him deal with the noise, I can't think past the fact that she's still not beside me.

Dominic starts blabbering again, and I've had enough of this nonsense. I rise to my feet, finished entertaining the circus.

"You're in the wrong, Dominic. And you will fix your mistake." Calm. Collected. Cutthroat.

Let that echo. Let it be the end of it—because I have better things to do than babysit bruised egos. I need to get back to my creature.

I step back into the conference room, eyes scanning like a predator until panic claws at my chest.

Where is she?

Fuck!

Then I see her. Back turned. Sitting on the couch. Watching fucking TV like my world isn't imploding every second I'm not near her.

I need a drink. I might need a doctor. At this rate, my heart's going to give out. I pour one drink, then another. The burn in my throat barely registers. It's the burn in my chest I can't silence.

I need rules.

Boundaries.

Anything.

How do you draw lines around a heart that's sprinting toward someone like it has no brakes?

I lean on the bar, drink in hand, staring at her.

My Lisichka. What the fuck am I going to do with you?

She stands. Moves to the bar beside me, calm and unhurried, pretending to fix herself a drink.

We don't speak.

Not at first.

We just stand there.

Side by side.

Drenched in each other's presence.

No words.

Just breath, heat, and the weight of everything unspoken pressing between us.

"You okay?" she asks, her voice soft—warm, even.

I turn to her. Her mask is off. All I see is her. Real, unguarded, stunning in a way that short-circuits my thoughts.

My head spins, at war with itself.

And my cock—the traitorous bastard—decides to join in, hardening like it has a mind of its own, dragging all reason down with it.

It's the first time she's spoken to me like this. No games. No barbs. No teasing. Just concern. Real and disarming.

"No," I say, honest and bare.

She holds my gaze, searching, studying. Trying to read between the cracks I've never let anyone see.

"Is it the explosion?" she asks, still calm. Gentle. Controlled.

"No," I answer, just as calm. Just as controlled.

But the war inside me is anything but.

She studies me a moment longer, like she's trying to decode the truth behind my eyes. Whatever she sees makes her flinch, just a flicker, but enough.

She breaks eye contact. Turns away.

She pours herself a drink with slow, deliberate movements. Says nothing.

And that silence? It screams.

"It was the first time in my life I blacked out. What are you doing to me, Lisichka?"

My voice is soft. Wrecked. Raw. Vulnerable.

There's a tremble in my body I can't control, it starts in my hands, humming beneath my skin.

I'm unravelling.

For the first time in my life... I don't know what I'm doing.

She slides her hand down the bar, closer to mine.

She doesn't touch me — not quite — but it's the first time she's ever reached for me.

And I'll take it.

Whatever she's willing to give, no matter how small, I'll take it.

Gladly. Hungrily. Without pride or protest.

"You didn't see this coming? That would surprise me. Who did it?" Her voice is sharp, skeptical. She doesn't let anything slide.

"I test my people regularly," I say, tone even, controlled. "Loyalty, respect, discipline — all of it. I'll leave money, access, drugs, even sensitive information just to see who takes the bait."

I pause. "One of them did. A Romanian. Took something that wasn't his."

"Wait a second. He took something from you... and you let him?" Her eyes narrows, watching me. Calculating.

Then she lands the punch.

"You let him take it. Why?"

The question is too quick, too precise. A smirk pulls at the corner of my mouth before I can stop it.

She sees it. She knows.

“You were bored.” Her voice is flat, amused. “I told you, you’re a child sometimes.”

I smirk, only because she got there faster than anyone ever has.

“They needed direction,” I say, voice calm, calculated. “So I gave them an enemy.”

I let the words hang just long enough.

“Nothing unites like shared hatred. While they rallied the troops, I cleaned my house.”

A shrug. Almost casual.

“It’s efficient. Elegant. Even entertaining.”

“Except he just threw a bomb at you. Was that part of your entertainment plan too?”

"Your daughter is so much like you," I say, watching Angela as she talks to Dominic on the couch, taking in every subtle shift of her posture.

"Don’t change the subject. And get your eyes off my daughter."

"Yes. There was chatter about a bomb on the dark web, but no specifics — no location, no clear target. I made the mistake of thinking Bogdan didn’t have the resources to pull something like this off. He doesn’t. Which means someone helped him. And now, I need to flush out who."

"Why haven’t you killed this guy yet? I doubt you don’t know where he is."

Her voice is clipped, annoyed. She's not wrong.

"Lisichka..." I turn to face her, a slow smile tugging at the corner of my mouth. "I was bored out of my mind before you showed up. I had to entertain myself somehow. You should’ve seen my team—scrambling to track crumbs. It was almost... cute."

My tone drops, cold and final.

"But after today? He's finished."

"You were bored?" she scoffs, pure disbelief in her tone. "Pick up knitting, you fool."

A laugh explodes out of me before I can stop it—loud, sharp, real. I try to mask it with a fake sneeze, but it's useless.

She's outrageous.

She's brilliant.

She's terrifying.

And she's mine.

Holly shit, I'm so far gone. I'm in big trouble here.

I look at her and I swear I feel gravity pulling from her direction.

Every second I breathe next to her is borrowed time before I break and do something irreversible.

"Lisichka, I really have a problem."

She doesn't even look at me. Just stirs her drink and says, "Yeah, it's called common sense. Seems like a chronic condition for you."

I stare at her, completely undone.

"No baby, I mean it." My voice is lower now, raw around the edges.

"I'm losing my mind over you." I take a moment to let that sink in.

"I'm at war with myself." I swallow hard. My voice drops low. Honest. Unfiltered.

"I live by loyalty, respect, and control. I built an empire on discipline. But now?" I shake my head, barely able to meet her gaze.

"My brain's failing me, Lisichka. For the first time in my life, it's second place. My instincts—my needs—they're all screaming for you. I'm intoxicated. I can't think straight."

She studies me. Calm. Calculating. I think she is the only one in this world that understands what is within me.

"I need help," I whisper.

"Give me a rule, a boundary—something—because if you don't, I swear I'll take you. Rip you out of this world and lock you inside mine."

Her eyes drop to my lips.

That one look is all it takes.

My blood floods south. My vision blurs. I feel lightheaded.

I want to kiss her.

Not out of lust. Out of need.

To taste her. To breathe her in.

To survive.

She drops her gaze, turns, and walks back to the couch.

Fucking damn it!

Maybe I said too much. Maybe I scared her.

Maybe she's just as lost as I am... and I just pushed her deeper into her own abyss.

This is harder than I ever imagined.

I built an empire. Crushed souls. Moved kings like pawns.

And here I am—stuck, breathless, defeated—because the woman who was made for me just turned her back and walked away.

There's no manual for this.

No logic. No control.

Only her.

Only... her.

Chapter Eleven

Monica

Goddammit! He's making this so unbelievably hard. Why can't he just keep that big mouth shut?

Him asking me how to stop his feelings? That's not helpful. Not even close. What the hell am I supposed to say? I don't *do* feelings. Me and emotions don't belong in the same sentence.

Well... we didn't.

Until him.

Now everything's upside down. I feel... suffocated. But in the best way possible. That doesn't even make sense—to me or my own goddamn thoughts.

Let me break this down.

I like his presence. I like how sharp he is. I like how cunning he is. I even like how stupidly silly he can be with his people. I like that he takes care of his people. I like how he looks—smooth and dangerous and hot—and the way my body reacts to him like it's never belonged to me in the first place.

But most of all? I like this *thing* inside me when I think of him.

It's not what I feel for other people. It's not even what I feel for Angela.

It's different.

It's new.

I don't know what to call it, or how to explain it. It's like... the moment he enters my mind, everything else falls quiet. The noise stops. The chaos settles. And what's left is this feeling—a mix of safety, comfort, hunger, excitement.

And this desperate, goddamn *need* to touch him. To be near him.

No idea what it is. No idea what people would even call it.

I wouldn't say it's love—that would be absurd.

And I'm pretty sure it's not something you can eat.

That last thought actually makes me chuckle as I sit down next to Angela on the couch.

A few minutes later, we're in the car, heading to the shop so I can pick up my car.

I want to drive.

Honestly, I doubt anyone's coming after me.

It's not like Elijah's out here guarding me himself, so there's no way this Bogdan prick would pick up on whatever's going on between us — not enough to realise my true worth in Elijah's eyes.

I'm so bloody tired. Physically, emotionally — the whole lot. At least tomorrow I don't have to stress about anything to do with the shop. Dominic bought all the flowers, and one of the boys delivered them straight to Angela's place. I'm happy for her. The guy's absolutely head over heels — kissing the damn floor she walks on. Sure, he's a criminal. And yeah, he's intense — and by intense, I mean holy hell he's full-on — but it's clear as day he loves my daughter with everything he's got.

A few days ago, when we had that heart-to-heart about love, me and Angela, how it sneaks up when you least expect it and shakes your whole damn life off its foundation, I was talking about me. I didn't expect this. Whatever's happening to me, it doesn't feel real. It *shouldn't* be real.

From a logical, intellectual point of view, I'm still sceptical. I keep trying to make sense of it — looking for reasons, clues, anything to explain what the hell this is. But if I stop thinking, if I let logic fall away, like Elijah said, and just listen to my body, to my instincts, it's simple. It's a no-brainer.

I want Elijah.

Every part of me wants him.

Every part of me *longs* for him.

He said he's afraid I won't survive him if he gives in to whatever's inside him. Well, mate I promise you this much: you'll have the scars to remember me by. And probably an icepack on your cock for a good while too.

But none of that matters, because I can't think like that. I don't even know what I'm doing, let alone how to advise him.

What kind of lunatic lays all that at my feet and then asks me for advice? Moron!

Me. Me, of all people!

I don't have a fucking clue what I'm doing — not with emotions, and definitely not with him.

But the worst part?

I want to take him up on it.

I want to wreck him. Worship him. Make him mine.

And it terrifies the hell out of me.

What he's offering.

What future that means.

And what my life would be... without my mask.

My whole body was on fire while he was saying it. The way he worried about me, offered himself up like some twisted, beautiful sacrifice — it was so goddamn hot I nearly combusted on the spot.

Who does that?! He basically told me I could do whatever I want with him. Oh, have mercy on my panties... I'm getting worked up all over again just thinking about it.

I'm still lost in my spiraling thoughts when I turn the corner onto our street. The rhythm of my mind slows, and real life creeps back in—there's our house at the end of the block, familiar and grounding. Dan's car is in the driveway. He steps out, casual as ever, and heads toward the front door.

I'm about five houses away when he opens the front door to our house, and then, everything disappears.

A flash. A thunderous boom. My ears ring as the shockwave hits me.

I slam on the brakes by instinct, frozen as debris fills the sky, some of it raining down onto the hood of my car. Smoke. Fire. Screams in the distance.

My neighbours are pouring into the street, phones out, faces twisted in horror.

I don't move. I can't. I just sit there in the middle of the road, staring at the wreckage of what used to be my life as it burns to the ground in front of me.

I am not scared of what just happened. I am not excited either, as I was in the shop at the news of the first explosion. Perhaps I lack the skills to process fear or traumatic events as well.

Hearing someone coming after Elijah excited me. Not because there is any chance of someone actually hurting him—because I know there is not. That much is clear. What excited me was the fact I would have a front-row seat to observe the events unfolding.

I love it.

I analysed so many different people at City Hall, and I could not wait to see what Elijah would do in retribution.

But this... this is my life going up in flames.

The life I built with my own two hands.

I don't feel a loss for things. It's just... blank. Like my brain knows I should care, but there's a delay in the signal or maybe it's not coming at all. Knowing myself, it will never come.

Elijah said he knew about the first bomb. Did he know about this second one? He seemed panicked out of his mind trying to get me to safety. I try to piece it all together when someone suddenly yanks open my car door.

At first, I'm just annoyed. *What's his problem?*

Then he grabs my arm and shoulder and starts pulling—hard. I'm not budging. The damn seatbelt's locked, so all he's doing is yanking me like he's on a mission to rip my arm clean out of its socket.

Finally, he seems to realise it's not working. Without a word, he pulls a knife from his combat pants and slices through the belt in one smooth motion.

Now, I should probably be panicking. Maybe screaming. But the only thought in my head is *how sharp is that knife?* Seriously—clean cut, no hesitation. I start wondering where he gets it sharpened, and if I can pick up that skill myself. That would be useful.

I'm dragged violently to an SUV, and that's when I realise—he's one of Elijah's men.

What a fool.

I roll my eyes at his back. Seriously, he could have just asked me to come with him. Now I'll have to explain this to the authorities, to my neighbours, and—least pleasant of all—to Angela.

Elijah can be such a dumbass.

He could've simply asked.

When the guy shoves me into the back seat, I pull out my phone, expecting at least a missed call or a message from him so I can give Elijah a piece of my mind.

Nothing.

Oh, wait—there's one text. And an email. From the CEO of the charity.

Kane

Good evening, Monica,

I emailed you earlier today to inform you that we've received a significant donation. Our accounts had been frozen for the past few days while the bank completed all the necessary approvals, given the size of the amount.

Quantum Gate Cybersecurity has donated one billion dollars to the charity. I still can't believe such a level of generosity.

Perhaps we could collaborate on crafting a thank-you message to the company. The entire team is incredibly excited.

Speak soon.

"Motherfucker!" I yell inside the car, and all the goons turn to stare.

I glare back, forcing myself to shove my real self down again.

That slimy bastard just killed my mask—then tried to bribe me with his fucking money.

I told him I wouldn't leave Dan.

And what did he do?

He killed him.

And now he's trying to pay me off, like I'm some common woman with a price tag.

As if his billions could buy my forgiveness, or worse, my silence.

Oh, he has no idea what he's unleashed.

Whatever this thing is between us, whatever he's awakened in me, it's nothing compared to the fury his betrayal just ignited.

Today, Elijah will bleed.

Chapter Twelve

Elijah

Goddamn it. I knew it. I fucking knew it! Knew in my gut I should've chained her to me.

It was only a matter of time before some idiot tried to use her as leverage.

And now look.

Fuck!

I'm putting a tracker on her. I don't give a shit what she says. I don't care that she's already surrounded by guards, that I have surveillance on every location she steps foot in. It's not enough. It'll never be enough!

Because right now?

There's no air in my lungs because of her.

Only terror.

Only panic.

My mind races through scenarios—useless.

Logic is dead.

This isn't strategy. This is survival.

Hers.

Mine.

One of my men called me the second it happened. Told me they reached her seconds after the explosion. That she's safe. But they're missing the point. This wasn't an attempt to kidnap her. They tried to kill her.

To erase the one reason I even bother breathing.

They tried to obliterate my world.

My Lisichka.

And for that? For even daring to attempt it? The world will bleed.

If she's gone—if she's even scratched—there is no line I won't cross, no hell I won't unleash.

Because she's not just mine.

She is everything.

Even if the world hasn't realised it yet, it will.

They'll all kneel.

To her.

To their Queen.

And I'm standing here, useless, in a goddamn carpark.

Eyes glued to a flickering dot on my phone, watching her get closer. Every second is a razor to my chest.

I hear the screech of tyres before I even see them.

They're driving like maniacs.

If a single hair on her head is out of place, they die.

By my hand.

Today.

The first car pulls in. Not her.

She's in the second one, completely in the middle protected by my man. I know it in my gut, my man would not fail me.

I don't wait for it to stop.

I'm already moving, yanking the door open and a boot slams square into my chest. It sends me flying back. My phone hits the ground. My instincts kick in.

What the fuck?!

Before I can recover, she's on me—one arm tight around my neck, anchoring my head forward, while the other holds a blade in reverse grip, the spine of the knife pressed firm against her forearm and the edge kissing my throat.

Her mask is off.

She is terrifying.

She is magnificent.

More than I imagined.

She shoves me backwards until my spine smacks against the wall—and I let her.

"I thought we understood each other, Elijah," her tone is calm and confident, completely at odds with her actions and it sends my head spinning in pleasure.

Fuck, this creature is extraordinary.

"You are not allowed to touch what is mine," she continues. The truth in her eyes, of who she really is, what she really is, is fully on display. I have no doubt that if I slip up now she will kill me.

Plain and simple.

No remorse.

From the corner of my eye, I catch movement—one of my men raising a gun toward her. Panic punches through me, raw and immediate. I twist the blade from her grip and drive it into his eye in one brutal motion. He's dead before his knees even buckle.

I slide the knife right back into her hand, resting it against her arm, exactly as she had it. Like nothing happened.

“Please continue, Lisichka,” I say, voice calm. “Don't mind him. He's already dead.”

She is taken aback by my actions. I can see it clear as day. I can feel the coldness of the blade on my neck and a small trickle of blood starting to pour out.

"This does not concern any of you," I say over Monica's shoulder. "Leave!"

The authoritarian tone I deliver shuts down the room, yet some of them start babbling and I've had enough of their stupidity.

"Leave! If she wants my life, I will gladly give it to her. But if I see any of you in the next ten seconds, you'll die today."

My voice is cold. Measured. Deadly.

One by one, they all leave and then it's just me and my Lisichka. I meant it. If she wants my life, I will give it to her. There is nothing worth living for if she is not by my side.

"Did you know?"

"Yes."

She does not need to elaborate because I know what she is referring to.

Did I know that there might be a second bomb?

"And you let it happen?"

"Yes."

She presses the blade harder, and now I am bleeding. Bleeding or not, I am in complete awe of this woman. She is everything that I thought she would be when she came out from her hiding.

"Why?"

"There are always bad things happening, Lisichka. Murder, attacks, bombs, rape—all sorts of despicable things going on in the world right now as we speak. Just as there are so many beautiful things happening at this very moment. I intervene, but not always, because there is a balance of good and evil that needs to be maintained. Is the balance always accurate? No. But if I intervene, then I'm changing everything to my own will..."

"Cut the crap, Elijah!" she snaps, cutting me off. "I'm not interested in your existential justifications or your warped sense of balance."

She kicks me hard in the balls, and it takes everything in me not to double over, because the woman really landed one on my cock.

"Hey..." I say shortly, trying to recover and mask the pain I'm in. I grunt, wincing. "Don't do that. We might need my cock for later."

"You won't be needing your cock for anything, because I might cut it off."

Her words slice cleaner than the blade in her hand.

"Why?!" Her voice is so sharp and cold.

"What do you want me to say? I knew an attack was coming. I knew bombs were involved. I didn't know the location. I have many properties. I suspected something about you. But in my desperation, I thought they'd try to take you from me—not kill you. What they tried has already signed their death certificate in blood. I'll have Bogdan in the next few days."

"Why?!"

I take a slow breath, steadying the chaos inside me.

"Because you're not his."

My eyes lock on hers, unflinching.

"You're mine."

Her hand trembles on the blade. I feel the shift in her body—the hesitation, the recognition. So I press forward, voice low, lethal, and raw.

"You were made for me, Lisichka. You know it. You feel it—same way I do. Stop running from it. You're not built to belong to anyone else. You belong at my side. Always have."

I lean into the pain of her blade—an offering. My surrender. My vow.

"You can lie to the world. You can hide behind your mask. But don't lie to me. You are not meant for shadows. You are meant to be seen. All of you. All the fire. All the power. All the strength.

With me, you don't have to pretend to be less than what you are. I see you—all of you—and I accept every dark, brilliant part of you. You don't scare me. You undo me. And I'd burn the whole world if it meant keeping you."

Her eyes are glassing over, her body trembling, she's barely holding it together.

She wants this. Just as much as I do.

She's not fighting me... she's fighting herself.

And she's losing.

"And who the fuck do you think you are—to ask me, take me, or force me into the light?!" she roars, her voice sharp enough to cut through steel.

"I am who I choose to be! I'm not hiding from myself—I'm hiding from *them*! Whether I stay in the shadows or step into the light, it's my choice. Mine! Not yours, you arrogant, delusional motherfucker!"

And with that, she twists the blade in her grip and cracks me across the forehead with the hilt—no hesitation, no mercy.

Fuck, that hurts!

She steps back, panting, the knife resting in her hand by her side.

There's something monstrous in her expression—and it's stunning. Beautiful, dangerous, absolute, like drawn from the depths of her true self.

She's mad—clearly and unrestrainedly mad.

And rightfully so.

But I think I'm cracking her armour, and she's finally beginning to understand what she could be in the light.

"It is not up to you. It is up to me," she spits out, disgust dripping from every word.

"Don't come anywhere near me again. I don't want to see you."

She continues, throws the knife to the ground, and starts walking toward the exit.

"That will never happen, Lisichka. I will never go away. You know that."

"Yes, you will listen. I know where to hurt you."

She turns and faces me, her gaze ice-cold and lethal.

"If I see your face again, I'll hurt myself."

FUCKING HELL!!!

GODDAMN IT!!!

Panic punches through me like a blade to the gut.

My thoughts splinter. I can't breathe. I can't think.

She's tearing me apart without even raising her voice.

She's smart. So smart.

And cruel in the most perfect way.

She found the one place I'm weakest and drove the knife straight through.

True to her nature, she twisted the moment with surgical precision—turned herself into a weapon I can't fight back against.

The battle's lost, and we both fucking know it.

FUCKING HELL, THIS CREATURE!

"You're not safe!" I try to reason with her as I sprint forward and grab her shoulder. She flinches, and in that split second, I press the tracker into her skin.

"Ouch! What was that?"

"What was what? Let me see." I turn her slightly—and freeze.

There's a massive bruise on her shoulder.

For a second, I forget how to breathe. Rage overtakes me.

"What happened?"

"Your goon manhandled me."

I did this?

My team is an extension of me.

So I did this.

"Which one?" I manage to get out, my voice tight with fury.

"The one you helped wink wider," she says, turning on her heel and walking away.

"You are not safe, Lisichka," I try one more time, pleading with her.

"They just struck. They failed. Now they're regrouping." She turns slightly, her eyes cutting through me. "Save your stories for someone not playing at your level, boy."

Goddamn, this woman is phenomenal!

She saw straight through all my manipulation—effortlessly—and still turned the tables in her favour.

For a woman like this, I'd be a fool not to bend the knee and worship her.

Chapter Thirteen

Elijah

Two months later

About that bending of the knee to worship the woman who was made for me?

I'm all for it.

There's just one major problem.

She is fucking brilliant in her revenge, and she's been driving me insane for the past two months.

After that night, after her ultimatum to stay away—well, I did what she asked. Partially.

But I did it.

She doesn't see me.

But I'm always here.

Watching over her every second of every day.

She moved into her daughter's apartment after the funeral—Angela moved in with Dominic—and that worked perfectly for me.

I'm actually extremely grateful to Bogdan for blowing her house to smithereens, a fact I may have mentioned after we captured him.

I couldn't stand that building or what it represented.

She didn't have a marriage. She had a mask.

A mask I so kindly helped her remove.

And now?

She's furious.

And she's intelligent.

Which means she's making me pay for it. Every. Single. Day.

I'm on the brink of madness, and I swear to the heavens—she knows it.

I bought every apartment in the building. Every single one.

Now she's got an army of my men watching over her, whether she likes it or not.

The entire floor above hers? Empty. Sealed. Reinforced. No one's getting in—or out.

The floor below? Same deal. Except for one unit. Mine. Right under hers.

It's small. Cramped. Miserable. Uncomfortable. I hate it.

But it keeps me close.

Keeps her safe.

That's all that matters.

And I swear she knows I'm here.

She makes it her mission to drive me insane every fucking day.

It's not enough that she's taking her sweet time admitting that her place is by my side. She knows it as much as I do.

This is her power play—a deliberate game to make sure I understand the hold she has over me.

And she has it.

All of it.

Piles of it. Mountains of it.

I feel like a caged animal in heat, pacing, growling, coming undone—on the edge of madness, every single day.

The first time she started to undress—ever so casually while walking into the bedroom—I grunted so loudly I'm sure she heard me.

Because she just burst out laughing... and then continued the torture until she was completely naked.

I was stunned. Transfixed. Drawn into a world where only her beauty exists.

It was surreal.

The surveillance caught it all. And all my imaginings of how she looked naked were nothing compared to the devastating reality.

Dominic had bugged Angela's apartment when he was stalking her, and once again, it worked out perfectly for me.

She walked right into another location where I know every second of her every day.

When I bought the building and accessed the full surveillance feed, I found his user account still logged in.

I confronted him—said nothing, just looked at him—and he understood.

One glance. That was all it took.

He deleted the account on the spot, in front of me.

Smart man. He knew I was seconds away from killing him.

I got so paranoid that someone might break into the feed that I configured an entirely separate firewall just for her—a fortress of protection for every camera, every feed tied to her every location.

Her phone, her laptop, every smart device she touches, including her car, are now under my firewall, under my protection.

But one thought keeps plaguing me, scraping my sanity raw... *What if the tracker fails? What if I lose track of her?*

The possibility is eating me alive from the inside out.

I can't afford even a moment of not knowing where she is.

I need to know her every move. Her every breath.

I am simply consumed by her existence.

And I cannot lose her.

My every thought, my every breath, my entire existence revolve around this creature—and she knows it.

I might have allowed her to be free.

I might have even outsmarted her in that regard—because I didn't directly kill her husband. I just allowed it to happen.

I did outsmart her, and she does not like that.

She is surely taking her vengeance to another level, because she is cruel, cunning, and perfect in every respect.

Including how she is tormenting me beyond any limits.

I've never been in the apartment myself—I fear she'd recognise my scent. But I've left things at her door on several occasions. Every time I left a present—like a $100K necklace, a million-dollar bracelet, flowers, or even dinner when I knew she'd skipped breakfast and lunch—she would simply open the bin and toss it in. No hesitation. No questions. No emotion. Just pure, heartless perfection.

I renovated her apartment after Angela moved out. It looked spectacular.

She was so furious that she wrote a note and stuck it to the door: "*Stop this nonsense or I will burn it all to the ground!*"

Then she began pushing furniture out of the apartment.

It's truly fascinating how minimalist she is. Her kitchen has one table, a single chair, two sets of cutlery and plates, and a small plant. There's a modest couch and coffee table, and an average-sized TV.

The bedroom? Just the bed, a bedside table, and a walk-in wardrobe. The bathroom contains only towels and a few body care products.

It's completely fascinating how she lives so simply—when everything inside her is monumental.

The day she brought out a dildo so massive it had to be at least thirty inches, I jumped to my feet so fast I made myself dizzy. I was ready to storm in, rip it out of her hands, and remind her exactly who she belongs to.

She smirked directly into one of the cameras—as if she knew it was there. I'm fairly certain she doesn't know the exact placement of the surveillance inside the apartment... but with her? I could be wrong.

And the day she first used a vibrator? Right there. Right in front of me and my cameras.

I grunted so loudly when she started, she actually paused, smiled again, then kept going—pushing herself to the edge, lost in pleasure, until she climaxed while I watched.

I don't even remember taking my cock out, but by the time she was moaning in pleasure, driving me insane with her voice, her fingers, her fucking toys—I was right there with her.

I jerked so violently, I was sure I'd hurt myself—but I could not stop because what was before me was too intoxicating, too consuming, not to join in.

When her climax hit—those little spasming jerks racking her body—hot cum exploded out of me, splattering all over the keyboard and screens.

And I knew, right then and there, **she'd won the war.**

One day, I will cover her in my cum—mark her, drown her in my scent. And she'll wear all of it.

It doesn't help that just seeing her now hurts like fuck—so much worse than I ever imagined.

Some days, I swear I'm on the brink of death from the sheer, savage ache in my balls. Not blue balls—this is something darker. Deeper. A vicious, throbbing punishment that won't stop.

I've been jerking off for two goddamn months, and having her this close, this untouchable, is unbearable.

She's establishing her dominance over me with every silent breath—and I can feel myself snapping, second by second.

I would give in. I really would.

I'm past the point of pride or power.

I am completely and utterly undone by my creature, and I would surrender and beg.

The only problem? I know it wouldn't help.

She wants me to suffer. She wants me in this much pain.

She wants me destroyed for forcing her out of her world.

And she won't stop tormenting me until she's seen me broken beyond repair.

Fuck. My. Life.

Then there's that imbecile, Hunter, who—with all of two brain cells—thought he could claim my daughter. How dare he?!

The real problem is that Sofia actually likes him, even if she can't look past her trauma and give in to her attraction.

I wanted to kill him and end it the moment she said no, but then she started begging on his behalf, and now I'm stuck with him in a warehouse, watching him take a toll on my men.

At this point, I'm not even sure who's suffering more—him or my team—but I'm almost at my limit.

Not to mention, my nights are pure hell.

I barely sleep—because even when I close my eyes, I'm listening to Lisichka sleep.

On one side, she snores—and I think it's adorable.

I installed a top-of-the-line surround system in my room, and every night, the moment she goes to bed, I follow.

I crank the sound to maximum, just in case there's even a whisper of danger so I can leap in and protect her.

The sound of her breathing—and that cute-as-hell snore—is like the song of angels to my ears.

I stopped sending her presents because she found the perfect way to punish me for it.

It all ended after I sent another fat donation to her charity—thinking I'd softened her somehow.

Instead, she came home like a storm—slamming the door, eyes blazing straight into one of the cameras.

And in that moment, I knew.

I'd fucked up.

I was going to regret it.

She disappeared into her bedroom.

No tantrum. No note. Just silence—and I swear that's worse.

She went into her room, stripped naked under the doona, threw her clothes on the floor, then started watching porn and using her toys.

No performance. No teasing. Just pleasure—raw and selfish and entirely for herself.

And I got nothing. Not a glance. Not a sound. Not a goddamn moan meant for me.

I was gutted.

Talk about blue balls—and the real threat of bursting a nut.

That was the cruellest thing she could've done to me.

And she did it with a smile on her face.

I learned my lesson and stopped sending her things after that.

A week later, she used the showerhead—and held eye contact with the camera the entire time.

I'd done well to remember my place.

And she rewarded me for it.

The power she has over me is unreal.

And as much as some part of my mind screams that I should fight it—to reclaim my dominance—I don't care.

I'd gladly give it all to her.

All my money. All my power. All my influence.

My life.

Just to have her by my side.

Days are not much better.

She wakes us up early and follows a very specific routine every single day—and I love that about her.

She's closed the shop now, choosing instead to be more active with the charity—probably because she doesn't trust the CEO not to dip into the funds, now that the donation sum is so large.

I don't blame her.

I looked into the guy myself. On the surface, he's an outstanding citizen. But underneath, he's tangled up in some shady business with the Italians—the kind of mess I don't want Lisichka anywhere near.

Her instincts, as always, are spot on.

She was right not to trust him.

So the moment she's out the door, I follow her through the surveillance cameras until she gets to her car—then I sprint to one of our own and trail her like a shadow.

We move as a convoy, silent and invisible, protecting her every step of the way.

She spends her days at the charity, then goes shopping for groceries or meets up with Angela.

Then she comes back to the apartment.

Then repeat.

Until my sanity finally leaves the building—and I explode.

I see the end for me approaching. I feel it in my entire body—the pull, the ache, the need to be near her. To breathe the air she breathes out.

I would give it to her. Whatever it is she's after—I'd hand it over without hesitation.

I just don't know what it is.

And if it's my sanity she wants... then she's about to get that, too.

Chapter Fourteen

Monica

My daughter is getting married. She's getting married to the love of her life, and I could not be happier for them both. Well, I'm happy for her. For him? I already told him I'd chop him into small pieces if he ever hurts my daughter in any way.

I expected him to laugh it off, but he didn't. He looked terrified.

He might be on to me—and I don't like that.

Elijah might have said something to him, but I doubt it, because something tells me Elijah might be as possessive of me as I am of him.

And I haven't told anyone about this thing that's between us.

Regardless, my baby is getting married, and today is the wedding day, so Angela is spending her day with me until the ceremony begins.

I am so happy and excited for our day together. It's been a while since it was just the two of us.

Well, there are all the helpers running around us getting everything ready, but in my heart, it's just me and my daughter.

My. Daughter.

She was the centre of my life from the moment I knew she was inside me, growing, and I knew with every fibre of my being that I would be a better mother than my own.

No matter what.

No matter the pain.

No matter the sacrifice.

I knew I would protect this baby with everything in me.

And now she is going to start her own life, and I hope with everything in me again that I did not fail her in some way, and she is as prepared for this as she can be.

"You okay, Mum?" Angela's soft voice and kind presence pull me out of my doubts.

"Of course, my darling," I smile at her. "Are you nervous?"

"Not really. But this Brenda lady is driving me insane," she says in an exasperated voice.

Brenda, true to her role as wedding coordinator, is as bossy as they come and has pushed for her vision to take place at times—not necessarily what Angela wanted for herself.

Dominic was desperate to marry her as soon as possible, probably scared she might change her mind, but was supportive of waiting until after our loss.

He does not know anything about how things were in our marriage and he sincerely mourned with Angela for what happened.

I'll give Elijah that respect.

At least he is not a chatterbox going around talking about things he should not be sharing with others.

My life is mine, and who I decide to let in is entirely up to me and me alone.

At least he got that much.

"We're at the end bit of things. It's going to be okay, love," I say and pat her on the back reassuringly. "Or we can always kill her after this if she has really got on your nerves."

Angela bursts out laughing at that, and I join in—because she thinks I'm joking, when in reality, I mean it wholeheartedly.

If she corrects me one more time—that at this level of class, things should be done this way or that way—she might not make the reception herself.

But again, this day is not about me and my need to make Brenda bleed.

It's about my angel getting married and being happy with her partner.

"Do we have some time to eat something, or do you think she'll come and tell us off for taking a break?"

I walk to the fridge, pull out the sandwich platter, and wink at Angela.

"Let's go." I continue, and then make my way sneakily to what is now my bedroom. I walk into the closet and close the door behind Angela.

She bursts out laughing at my antics and sits on the floor with me, platter balancing on our legs.

"This is crazy," she says, taking a big mouthful of the chicken sandwich.

"Should she not fear us? Why are we hiding? Also, I like it—this is hilarious." She laughs and talks with her mouth full. The laughter fades, leaving behind a softness I haven't felt in a long time.

I miss her so much. I miss this carefree version of her. I miss being silly with my daughter. I miss her company so much.

Damn it!

"I missed you," I finally say and take one of the sandwiches myself.

She looks at me with those big eyes of hers, a mirror of mine, and there is so much sincerity and vulnerability in her gaze.

I didn't want to make things awkward, but I also wanted her to know how much she means to me—and how much I miss her company.

"I'm sorry, Mum. I truly didn't mean to be so distant. It's just been a lot."

"My darling, don't apologise. It's not needed. This is part of life—you finding someone and wanting to spend your time with them. It's perfectly normal and acceptable. If you were clinging to me, then we'd have a problem."

"Actually... I wanted to talk to you about something. You remember how you told me about love a few months ago? How it just happens when you least expect it, and how it's unapologetic, raw, and terrifying sometimes?"

Her voice is small as she plays around with her food instead of eating it.

I remember the conversation—she held me hostage because she was terrified of what Dominic ignited in her.

"I'm not sure if those were my exact words, but okay—continue."

"I wanted to ask you... did you love Dad?" she says in a small voice, her gaze down, not daring to meet my eyes.

Fucking hell. Out of all the questions in the world, I really did not expect this.

If I tell her the truth, it might be too harsh for her—but again, she's not a child anymore.

If I lie to her... well, I don't want to lie. I don't have anything to be ashamed of, nothing I need to hide.

"I don't think I did."

My tone matches hers, because I know it was really hard for her to ask that question.

"What is this all about?"

"I'm not sure. I was just thinking about how you and Dad were, and how you never shared a bedroom or showed any affection towards each other.

I found out—I think in primary school—that parents normally sleep in the same bed, but you two never did.

I never questioned it, or the fact that you were never even warm to each other. Then again, a lot of parents in my class weren't warm to each other either."

She takes a big breath in, trying to steady herself. Then she meets my gaze—and there's so much pain and doubt in her eyes that it throws me off for a second.

"What I'm getting at is... will my marriage become like this after a while? I'm just scared. And I don't want a marriage like yours, Mum. I'm sorry, that sounded harsh—but it's true. I love Dominic, and I am terrified that one day my marriage will become cold and distant like yours with Dad."

Oh, my poor baby.

I had no idea that I'd led her to believe that a normal marriage would look like mine with Dan.

"No, my darling. You and Dominic are different."

I lean over and pat her hand.

"My marriage with your dad was completely different from what you'll have with Dominic. I never told you this because I didn't realise thoughts like this were roaming in your mind, but our marriage was arranged. I didn't really know your dad before we got married."

The pure shock on her face says it all.

She didn't expect this—and why would she?

We were great at pretending everything was all right.

"Your grandparents arranged it all, and we got married."

"Just like that?!" she squeaks, quite loudly.

"Shhh!" I whisper-yell. "That bridezilla will find us. Wait... you should be the bridezilla. What should we call her? Never mind."

I burst into laughter at Angela's surprised face.

"Yes. I married your dad because my parents arranged it."

"Is that why we never visited them?" she says, just above a whisper, lowering her gaze again.

"It's one of the reasons. They are not good people, Angela. You are the best thing that ever happened to me, and I didn't want their filth to ever touch you. So I kept you all to myself."

Her gaze meets mine once more, and she most definitely did not expect me to be this sincere.

"Listen, my darling. I truly am sorry for not giving you a better example of marriage. I'm truly sorry I never connected with your dad—and that you picked up on that. I'm sorry you learned what a successful marriage looks like from school or wherever, and not from me. I was so focused on being a good mum to you, to protect and love you, that I didn't even see that you might look at my marriage and think I'd failed at it."

My voice is trembling now, because I did fail her.

"I'm sorry."

I failed so badly I didn't even realise that this was an area where I should've provided support or guidance.

"It was an arranged marriage. Nothing more. Nothing less."

I reach for her hand, and she lets me take it in mine, and I gently pat the back of it.

"I'm sorry I didn't give you a better example of a marriage. It's just... not within me."

She stays there for a long moment, considering my words—and then she strikes again.

"Were you happy?"

"I was, and I am, happy with you. In my marriage... I'm not sure if happy is the correct word. We came to an agreement very early on in our marriage, and we stuck to it. And we let the years go by within our bubble—and it worked for us."

"Hmmm." She regards me again for a moment.

"Listen, Angela. If I had good advice about marriage, I would offer it to you. However, I know your situation is completely different from mine—because Dominic worships the ground you walk on. The poor guy is beyond in love with you, and when a man loves like that, there is no limit to what he would do for you. Your marriage will be nothing like mine, because at no point was there any form of love between me and your dad. It's nothing alike—and it will not become anything like it."

She sighs and meets my gaze again, conflict still playing in her eyes.

"Is that what's happening with you and Elijah?"

It's like the entire air was sucked out of the closet, and I was sucker-punched hard.

This was the last question in the world I was expecting from her.

I cannot speak. I cannot think.

I just stay there, mortified—looking into my daughter's eyes, holding her hand, and trying to decipher where she picked up on this.

"I'm sorry?" I say in a strangled voice, and I cannot believe my voice is betraying my torment.

"Is that what's happening with you and Elijah? Is this how he loves you?"

FUCKING HELL!

GODDAMN IT!

What the actual hell am I going to say to her?

Oh my God. What is happening?!

Why is she asking these questions?!

"Breathe, Mum. You look like you're about to have a heart attack."

"If I say I don't want to talk about it, will you drop it?" I manage to say in a small voice.

She studies me for a moment, then she nods.

"Yes and no, actually. I'm not sure what's going on with you two, and quite frankly, I understand it's none of my business. What I do want to say—and then I'll drop it—is that I want you to be happy. Or whatever form of happy you can be. If that happiness comes from Elijah or someone else, I want you to go for it. I want you to pick yourself, Mum. I want you to be happy. No matter what. Pick yourself."

I didn't even realise that tears were gathering in my eyes until one sneaky bastard rolled down my cheek.

Pick myself.

I raised an amazing woman.

A caring, amazing woman whom I could not be more proud of.

I hug her tightly to my chest and say nothing more—because there is nothing more to say.

I failed her, and she still saw the best in me.

I failed her, and she still accepted me.

I failed her, and she still wants me to find my happiness.

Chapter Fifteen

Elijah

Dominic is driving me insane.

Well, he drives me insane on most days, but today—today is an especially shit day for him and his anxiety, because it's his wedding day.

Unfortunately for him, he's all out of jokes, apparently, and all that's left is his intense craziness that might or might not grant him a bullet from me.

I know. I know. I can't shoot him without making things even worse with my creature.

But so help me God, if he doesn't lay off the panic and constant mumbling, I might give him a tranquilliser and knock his sorry arse out until he needs to say "*I do.*"

"I think I should have just stolen her. What if she changes her mind and makes a run for it? What if she doesn't—and then realises she can do so much better? What if she comes and says no instead of yes? Holy shit, she's going to say no in front of everyone, then she'll make a run for it," he says in a panicked voice, hand running through his hair while the hairstylist flinches at the motion.

"What the fuck am I going to do?"

He is borderline hysterical now, and there's still half an hour to go until we need to go to the altar and wait for Angela.

"You look tense," I say in my signature cold tone. "Is something the matter?"

He turns to me, and he's barely holding back from snapping.

It's hilarious as hell, and I would laugh—internally, as usual—at his antics, if I weren't slowly dying inside from the constant torment Lisichka has put me through for the past few months.

I am a defeated man, and we both know it.

For the past week, she's been extra sinister in her revenge—playing with her toys every day, in all sorts of positions.

And there's only so much I can take before I lose my mind completely.

She knows I'm the Best Man, same as she is the Matron of Honour, and her vengeance has been without mercy.

Every time she starts rubbing her breasts or playing with herself, I start swearing like a madman—and she just laughs.

I'm sure now she can hear me, and all of this—every teasing movement, every look, every act—is on purpose.

She's trying to break me.

And it's working.

I'm so sick and tired of jerking off when all I want is to sink my cock into her.

And believe me—the moment she gives in, I will take my pound of flesh from her.

She will scream, she will beg—and there will be nothing left but me at the end of it all.

And what I'm going to do to that body—no toy or person will ever be able to undo it.

Dominic's grunt pulls me back from my very visual, very disturbing image of my creature using a vibrator this morning—as she screamed the building down.

I am beyond blue balls, jerking off to her undoing me, or even fantasising about all the depraved things I'm going to do to her.

This has to stop!

It really has to stop!

I'm not sure how much more of this I can take before I just take her—whether she wants it or not—and trap her in my house until she gives in to us.

"You got your woman. I'm not sure what more you want."

"You would have got your woman as well if you'd known some boundaries." The moment his words come out, he makes a face of shock, because he knows how badly he just fucked up.

I stand, towering over him, and hold his gaze, letting him see the real danger he's in.

"Congratulations, Dominic. This is your wedding present. You get to keep your life."

He audibly swallows at my words—delivered matter-of-factly, completely lacking any emotion.

"I was planning to gift you one of my estates, but clearly your life is more valuable to you at this point."

I turn and leave, completely ignoring his apologies as I walk out.

I make my way to the ceremony hall and stand in my designated spot, next to where Dominic will arrive in a few minutes.

I look down the aisle, and I know that in just moments, I will face the hardest thing I've faced so far in my life.

My Lisichka will walk down that aisle—and she won't walk towards me.

She might not even look at me.

And if I don't steal her by the end of the day, it will be a miracle.

Sure enough, twenty minutes later, everyone is standing while the music plays and the flower girls make their way towards us.

The moment Lisichka turns the corner and starts walking towards me, it's like an out-of-body experience.

There's no more gravity holding me down—I am floating, melting away at her beauty.

She's always been beautiful.

But now? After being kept from her for so long—only to see her like this?

It shatters something fundamental and brutal inside me.

No warning. No mercy.

Just one look at her in that dress and I'm broken into a thousand jagged, bleeding pieces.

It's not longing.

It's not desire.

It's pain.

Raw, guttural, primal pain—the kind that drags your soul out through your ribcage and leaves you gasping.

And underneath that pain, pulsing through it like a second heartbeat, is the *need.*

The need to be with her.

To touch her.

To ground myself in her skin.

To claim her.

To own every breath she lets go of.

Everything in me is screaming...

Go to her.

Take her.

Breathe her in.

I lower my gaze before I do something stupid—before I tear down that aisle and drag her to me.

I force myself to breathe, to endure.

When I raise my eyes again, Dominic is tearing up like a baby as Angela walks slowly down the aisle.

She turns to her mum to give her the flowers, and I hear her whisper, *"My God, Mum, the way he looks at you."* To which my Lisichka just tells her to ignore me.

Ignore me, she should.

Or better—avoid me at *all* costs.

Because one way or another, her mum will be mine.

I'm done playing this game with her.

She broke me—and she knows it.

Whatever else she wants from me, she'll have to voice it today.

Put me out of my misery.

It has to end today.

It must end today.

Or I'll take things into my own hands again.

When the ceremony is over, she's supposed to walk by my side—but the moment I move next to her, she steps on my foot so hard I involuntarily let out a small sound of pain.

She just smiles, and for the first time, meets my eyes for a brief second.

Whatever she sees in my eyes knocks her back. She takes a step away, her smile vanishing, before she turns and makes her way down the aisle and out of sight.

I want to chase her.

To corner her.

To force her to give in to what's between us.

Except the last time I hurried things with her—it got me into this mess.

So I take a deep breath and make my own way to the reception bar and order a drink.

The moment the burning sensation hits the back of my throat, it hits me: getting drunk over how I feel might not be the best idea.

What the fuck has happened to my life?

What has this creature—this woman—reduced me to?

I used to plan. Prepare. Manipulate.

I used to adjust to every situation, every conversation, every outcome—so that everything worked in my favour.

And now?

Now I just do things.

Just act—without thinking—because clearly, my entire mind is indefinitely occupied by her.

Her being.

Her essence.

Her power over me.

Before I know it, people are dancing, enjoying themselves—while I'm still at the bar, contemplating my drink.

At least I had the common sense to only have two, even if all I want is to put a stop to the pain and agony within me.

Even if it's only for a little while.

I'm not sure how long I've been sitting here, and I'm fairly sure a few women have come up to talk to me.

But they don't exist.

No one exists except my Lisichka.

None of the people here even register—except her.

I look up from my drink—and Dominic is dancing with Lisichka.

And just like that, I feel like I've combusted into flames, because all I can see is red-hot fury, directed straight at Dominic.

"Please don't kill my husband. It's far too early to become a widow," a soft voice says from beside me.

That's when it registers—Angela is sitting beside me, a big smile on her face.

"Hi. I'm Angela. We've never formally met."

She extends her hand, and I take it in mine—noticing how small and delicate she is compared to her mum.

"Also, please stop sending daggers towards my husband. It kind of scares me."

Her voice is shaking, but she holds my gaze.

Brave. Just like her mum.

Not too intimidated to stand her ground against the apex predator wearing a tailored suit.

"It's lovely to meet you, Angela."

I try to sound approachable, but by the look on her face, she's not buying it—she still looks terrified of me.

"Would you like to dance?"

I'm completely surprised by her question.

I tilt my head and study her for a moment.

She flinches under my scrutiny, and I realise I'm going about this all wrong.

If there's one person I need in my corner right now, it's this little creature.

Maybe she can talk some sense into her Machiavellian mother.

"Sure."

My voice—short, cold, calculated.

I stand and I tower over her like a mountain over a valley.

We make our way to the dance floor, and she places her hand in mine, resting the other on my shoulder.

I leave plenty of room between us as I take her hand and rest the other on her upper back.

This is as uncomfortable as a root canal treatment without any painkillers.

I do not like to be touched—in any way, shape, or form.

And if she knew me at all, she would have never initiated this absurdity of a request.

"You look very scary," she says, holding my gaze.

"I'm sorry you feel that way."

"Even so, if you hurt my mum, I will find a way to hurt you back."

She delivers the jab so calmly—then smiles.

Oh my.

I did not expect that at all.

Maybe there's more of my creature in this little girl than I initially estimated.

How fascinating.

She is most definitely not like us, but even so, she's not afraid to voice her opinion.

The corner of my mouth lifts because her statement is just adorable.

"Understood. I expect nothing less."

We dance for a few more seconds, then Dominic spins Monica—and at the same time, he gently turns Angela.

In that seamless, swirling moment, we end up swapping partners.

And just like that, Lisichka is in front of me.

She freezes.

I freeze.

For a heartbeat, we stare at each other and the world stops breathing.

Then I grab her.

I don't think. I don't breathe. I just act.

I drag her flush against me, her body crashing into mine like it belongs there.

Her hands land on my chest, startled. She tries to pull away, but I can't let her go. I won't!

One arm locks around her waist, the other around her shoulders, caging her in completely.

There's no space. No escape. Nothing but us.

The feel of her—real, solid, warm—brings me back to life.

I've been starving for this. For her. For the one thing I can't have.

My pulse is in my throat. My head. My cock.

I want to sink into her. Bite her. Bury myself so deep she forgets where she ends and I begin.

She broke me...

Before she can stab me with more of her words, my voice cracks open, the plea tearing straight from my soul.

"Lisichka... please."

Chapter Sixteen

Monica

Goddamn it, this man. Fucking hell.

I'm trying—really trying—to keep away from him.

But wherever I go, however I try, he's there.

Always there.

And now he's pleading, like his life depends on it, his body wrapping around mine with such terrifying ease it shouldn't even be possible.

I can feel him—shivering under my hands, his heart a chaotic drumbeat, a warning to everyone of the danger if he loses control completely.

I know he means it.

I know I struck where it hurts the most.

I know he's losing his mind—if all the muttered curses and guttural sounds I've been hearing from him lately are anything to go by.

It's one thing to suspect it.

It's something else entirely to see him break—right in front of me.

He did this to himself.

He should've never forced my hand like that—and now he knows I won't stand for it.

He either accepts me as his equal... and my dominance over him, or this twisted little game we've been playing ends.

His hands are pressing me so hard into him that it's like he's trying to mould our bodies together—right here, right now.

His breath fans against my neck, and his shivers ripple straight through me, echoing in my own bones.

His breathing is erratic—just like mine.

And when he begs again...

As much as I want to push him away, I can't.

Something inside me cracks at the sight of him like this.

So raw.

So undone.

And it ruins me.

"Lisichka, please..."

He cuts himself off and buries his face in the crook of my neck.

I can't. I just can't with this man.

I move my hands around him and hug him back.

The moment my arms wrap around him, he starts trembling—truly trembling—at my touch.

And I genuinely don't know how to react to that.

I pull my head back, trying to meet his gaze.

And when our eyes lock...

He's broken.

Truly broken.

I knew I was hurting him.

But I didn't realise I was destroying him.

I say nothing.

Because there's nothing to say.

"Your hands on me feel like life itself, Lisichka," his voice is breaking—throaty, raw.

And that's when it truly hits me.

I didn't realise he'd become *this* version of himself.

Didn't realise he had surrendered—*completely*.

I won.

I pull back a little further, but he barely allows any space between us.

Then I place my palm on his stubbled cheek and he leans into my touch.

I've wanted this.

To feel his skin on mine, like this, since the first time I saw him.

Something within me has been calling to him—to *his touch*—so loudly that I was only lying to myself thinking I could stop it.

But this... *this* can't be stopped.

As much as a storm can't hold itself back...

As much as waves cannot stop crashing into rocky shores...

I—no, *we*—can't stop what's happening between us.

It's inevitable.

As inevitable as the Earth circling the sun.

Only now I do see it clearly.

He is the Earth.

Circling around *me*.

And *I* am his sun.

"You are more than what you just compared yourself to," he whispers—so close to my lips, I can taste his words.

"You are life itself to me, *my Queen*."

I try to pull back to study his gaze, but he quickly cups the back of my neck and rests his forehead against mine.

I am completely and utterly losing myself in him—in his very existence.

His embrace feels like coming home. Like slipping back into reality and fulfilling something that's always been missing inside me.

My entire being is flooded—with emotions, sensations, and unfamiliar truths I can't yet name.

But one thing is certain...

I'm choosing *myself*.

"I want to kiss you, Lisichka," he says, his voice trembling—raw with sincerity.

"But I don't know what I'm doing. I've never kissed anyone before... and it might not be any good."

He finishes with a sigh, as if bracing himself for rejection.

"You muppet." The moment the words leave my mouth, he bursts into laughter—so loudly and genuine, his entire body shakes with it.

He squeezes me to his chest so tightly it almost hurts... but I can't bring myself to say a word. His laughter wraps around me, pulling me deeper into his warmth, into him.

And I swear—the entire room freezes at the sound.

What the hell is wrong with them?

It's just a laugh.

"What, do you have any experience?" he asks through laughter.

"No."

"Didn't think so."

He leans in and presses a kiss to my forehead.

"Before you, I couldn't even stand human touch. Now... I'm completely addicted to you."

I have no comeback to that. How is he making this so easy for himself? How is he navigating these emotions with such ease while I'm barely holding myself together?

As if he can sense the storm inside me, he pulls me flush against his chest again.

His lips trail along my neck, soft and slow, until they reach my ear.

"Don't do that," he whispers. "Please stop running."

"You're my entire life. And even if you need time to figure out these feelings... we can navigate them together."

"Why are you so good at this?" I whisper, pain threading through my voice.

It's not fair.

"I'm not," he says softly.

"I gave up trying to understand any of it a while ago... and just surrendered to it. It's madness—overwhelming, dizzying—to feel this much, all at once. But I'd still embrace every single bit of it... because it's all from you. And I know—I can't live without you."

I rest my head on his chest, and we dance like that—slowly, intimately—to what I now realise is actually an upbeat song.

We're completely out of rhythm, dancing the wrong way.

Elijah doesn't seem to care.

And, quite frankly, neither do I.

We stay like that for what feels like forever, just existing in each other's arms.

No pressure. No games. Just us.

I chose myself.

I stepped into the light—with him.

And he claimed me as his, publicly.

There's no turning back now.

Chapter Seventeen

Elijah

Goddamn this woman, she'll be the end of me, and I don't mind it one bit.

She is finally mine. Every cell in my body screams it. My arms tremble around her. I don't care. I don't want to stop. I know she knows she's won. I am completely, utterly hers. She holds the real power now.

What she doesn't know yet is what's coming once we arrive at my estate. She might rule the world—me included—but once the bedroom doors close, I will rule everything. And she will take it all. Everything I give her. Anything I give her.

My cock has been hard for what feels like more than an hour, and I fear something might happen to my brain from lack of blood flow. So I gently tug at her hand, pulling away as we make our way to one of the SUVs waiting for me.

I don't need to explain anything to her. What's happened. What's coming. She knows I claimed her publicly now, and in my world, that's as good as a blood oath. No one has ever seen me with anyone before, and no one in their right mind would dare come after her now.

I help her into the back seat, and once inside, I place her hand on my leg—and immediately regret it. My cock flinches at the mere proximity of her hand to it. I'm already dizzy from the blood deprivation, so I move her hand to my chest, over my heart, and turn to face her.

It seems so small. So stupid. But I just want to take her in—record every line, every freckle, every gesture. Everything she's willing to give me.

I've studied her for so long, stalking her every second, memorising every movement, every habit. And still—it's not enough.

I want more.

I *need* more.

She's staring straight ahead, completely ignoring me. Or at least pretending to.

"You're staring, and it's a bit creepy."

"Is it really?" My voice settles, and for the first time in my life, I notice it's *warm*.

Fuck. I've never had that tone with anyone—but somehow, she pulled it out of me.

"No, not really. I just felt like it's something people would say."

"What would you say, Lisichka?"

She takes a moment. Then she turns her gaze to me—and blows my mind open.

There's absolutely, irrevocably no emotion in her eyes.

She's her true self with me. And I feel like dropping to my knees right here, right now, just to worship her.

"I would say... go for it. I don't give a damn. I know I want to study you, so I assume you want to do the same."

A small laugh escapes me, and I lift her hand to my mouth, kissing the back of it. She feels soft, feminine, fragile—but even in this simple gesture, just feeling her skin on mine, I'm reminded of the power she holds over me.

This woman could really kill me—and I'd let her.

I start kissing more—one finger at a time—then I feel myself losing all reason to the sensations she stirs in me. I take one finger and swirl my tongue around it, sucking, kissing, nipping. I take the next and work my way with small nips and licks, and that's when she lets out a moan.

I freeze.

I've heard her moan and climax through my surveillance system, but nothing could've prepared me for this.

Both my mind and my cock are in complete agreement: she's the one in danger right now.

"Oh, stop it, you big bad wolf. I'm not scared of you. Remember I don't have feelings? Well, I do have some now—because of you—but fear isn't one of them."

Her tone is so dismissive, it's almost amusing. She doesn't realise that if I unleash all of me on her, she might get hurt.

"Are you sure about that?"

"Please. There's nothing you can do that I can't handle, iubire scumpă."

The last of my restraints snaps the moment she calls me by my pet name. I'm pretty sure she just called me her sweet love—and if I thought I understood what I felt for her, it's nothing compared to what just exploded in me when I realised she's given in to *us* just as much as I've given in to her.

The car isn't even fully stopped when I open the door, grab her hand, and throw her over my shoulder. The next second, I'm running into the house at full speed with a very noisy Lisichka hanging off me.

My bedroom is too far from the entrance — I know I'm not going to last that long. I take a hard left into my office and slam the door shut behind us.

The moment I put her down in front of me, she knows she might be in trouble. She takes a deep breath, still holding my gaze, not backing down an inch.

I'm onto her in seconds — kissing her, crushing my mouth to hers, sucking her lip, her tongue, her very existence.

The more I feel her on me, the more deranged I become. Every restraint, every shred of control, fades into the background.

She thinks she won't be afraid of me after this.

I hope not.

Because there's *no escaping me.*

I grab the top of her dress and tear it apart in one go. Her breasts bounce free, brushing the back of my hand, and a guttural, animalistic sound escapes me.

Our breath is mingling, our tongues dancing, exploring each other. For every stroke I give, she gives me more.

I rip her bra off with one forceful pull, and she yelps into my mouth.

The moment her breasts are bare between us, I pull back for air and look at her.

The look in her eyes mirrors mine.

Hunger.

Desperation.

Destruction.

Need.

I look down—and I feel like my legs will give out beneath me.

Goddamn it!

Fucking hell!

She has the most beautiful, full breasts with big, engorged nipples, begging for me to bite, suck, and tease them.

So I do just that.

I take both of her breasts and push them together, burying my face in the valley between them. I start licking, sucking, and biting with the desperation of a madman—suffocating on her warmth, her taste, her feel.

But even if I die right now, smothered between her breasts, it would be the best fucking way to go.

Her hands roam my shoulders, my back, then move around to the front of my belt.

I know I need to stop her because if she touches my cock right now, I'll come so fast it'll be pathetic.

I'm already hanging on by a thread, clinging desperately to reality.

So I bite down—hard—on one breast. She yelps, and I suck the spot into my mouth, circling it with my tongue until she moans.

I shift fast, capturing the other breast, catching her off guard.

I kiss, lick, and bite my way across her chest—walking her backward with each maddening stroke.

Her back hits my desk.

She's trapped now.

And I'll have my pound of flesh tonight.

I pull back and look at my handiwork—at the perfect marks blooming across her breasts.

My cock twitches in approval. Soon, there'll be more than just marks.

Her dress is barely clinging to her shoulders now. Her bra long gone, discarded when I tore it off. The only thing covering her now is a pair of nearly see-through knickers that only make my mouth water even more.

In one motion, I shove everything off my desk. Monitors, keyboard, papers—everything crashes to the floor.

The moment it's clear, I lean in and kiss her deeply.

She gives in to my touch, and the dance of our tongues is pure heaven to me.

I gently slide her dress off, letting it fall in a soft heap to the floor.

My hands move to her back, down to her arse, and I pull her into me—hard—trapping her there.

She yelps into my mouth, and then...

She bites me. *Hard.*

So hard, I taste the blood she's drawn.

If it's my blood, my mind, or my very soul she wants—she can have it all.

My fingers slip beneath the waistband of her underwear, teasing the soft hair at the edge of her pussy.

She's soaked—soaked for me, wet and ready for everything I want to give her.

Whatever restraint I had left is obliterated.

I rip away the last piece of fabric between us, and it gives with a satisfying snap.

I want to unleash all of me on her.

I want to see how much she can take.

I want to see how compatible we are in our truest form, when nothing's left between us.

So I do just that.

I gently lower her onto my desk and take in the sight of her—completely naked—for the first time.

Her cheeks are flushed.

Her breathing erratic.

Her breasts are swollen, red from my bites.

Her stomach is flat, dotted with freckles and delicious little imperfections.

The valley of her pelvis curves down to her centre—wet, pink, and dripping for me.

When I lift her legs and rest her heels on the edge of the desk, her thighs part.

And her pussy opens up for me—glorious, glistening, and begging.

"Fuck me!"

The scream tears out of me as I brace one hand on the edge of the desk, head bowed, trying to catch my breath.

Fucking hell—this woman is going to kill me.

"That's the idea," she says, laughing... at my reaction, at my unravelling, at the fact that she knows exactly what she's doing to me.

I look up at her—and for the first time, I see it.

Genuine laughter...

Not a smirk. Not a tease.

But a real, unguarded laugh that reaches her eyes and reshapes them into soft crescents, her smile so wide it knocks the breath clean out of me.

It guts me. Completely.

My cock is painfully hard, every vein pulsing with wild, untamed blood—demanding I lose myself in her. But I can't. Not yet.

So I hold back. Just enough.

I reach for the remnants of her dress, tearing it into strips with precision. She watches me—silent, curious, waiting.

I take her right hand, kiss it, and place it over my chest.

"This is yours," I say, eyes locked on hers.

My heart.

I bind her wrist to the desk.

I move to the other side. Kiss her left hand. Place it on my temple.

"This is yours."

My mind.

Another tie. Another offering.

Then I move lower. Her skin is hot under my mouth. Her breath is quick. Her legs are already trembling. Her body is art, every inch a weapon forged to ruin me. And I want that ruin.

I lift one foot and kiss the arch, then guide it to my cock.

"This is yours," I tell her.

My body.

Her foot twitches against me, and I nearly lose control.

I kiss her knee, then tie her leg to the desk.

When I lift her second foot to my lips, I hold it there.

"Even my last breath is yours," I murmur against her skin.

My life.

I let her foot drop gently to rest against the edge of the desk before I fasten her in place.

I stand back and look at her—completely naked, bound, and at my mercy.

But we both know the truth.

She might be the one tied to the desk...

But I'm the one undone.

Because with the *vow* I just made, with everything I gave her—my heart, my mind, my body, my life—I've shackled myself to her far more than any rope ever could.

She has all the power now.

And I wouldn't have it any other way.

The look in her eyes says it all.

Not fear. Not hesitation.

Devotion.

Surrender.

Not to me—but to *us.*

I come beside her and look down into her eyes.

She's devastating. Intoxicating. Mine.

Every nerve ending in my body pulses with raw anticipation for what's about to happen.

"My Queen," I murmur, voice low and rough, "I'm scared I might hurt you. We need a safe word—something, anything—to stop me if it gets too much."

Her laughter crashes into me like a wave—warm, disarming, and beautiful in a way that wrecks me from the inside out.

Goddamn, this woman is undoing every last thread of who I was.

"You really think I'd let you tie me up if I was scared of you?"

Her voice is calm. Certain. Unshakable.

"If I thought—even for a second—you could hurt me, I wouldn't be here. Don't forget... we're the same."

She lifts her chin, gaze blazing with a dare.

"So even if *you* fear yourself right now, *I don't*. I want this. I *need* this. And I want to see all of you. Every glorious, brutal, beautiful piece."

A beat.

"Don't hold back, iubire scumpă. Give me everything."

My hands are trembling as I play with her breasts, struggling to undress with one hand.

I've never hated wearing a three-piece suit—until this moment.

Fucking hell!

I change tactics, lower my mouth to her breasts, and free both hands to deal with these goddamn buttons.

The moment my shirt drops to the floor, she inhales sharply—probably not expecting all the tattoos.

I pause.

Her gaze travels over me, wide and reverent.

She's in awe.

Of *me*.

That look alone nearly finishes me.

I flick my tongue over the tip of her nipple, slow and deliberate, and when she moans, heavens help me, I nearly explode in my pants.

I move across her chest, kissing the valley between her breasts, tasting her like she's the only air I've ever needed.

She shivers beneath me. Her body flinches slightly when I pass over bruised skin—but I can't stop.

I won't.

I need to mark her.

To leave my scent on her skin.

I need to know what it's like to have her impaled on my cock—to finally, irrevocably, make her mine.

The moment I free my cock, I completely misjudge the distance to her tied hand.

When it springs loose from my boxers, her fingers accidentally brush the length of my shaft.

Lightning.

A full-body surge.

Like she just injected pure voltage straight into my bloodstream.

"Bloody hell, woman!"

The words rip out of me as I jerk back, panting.

I glance down—and fuck me, no wonder I've been light-headed.

He's flushed dark red, almost purple, thick veins bulging across the shaft, the crown gleaming with pre-cum.

Pulsing. Demanding. Desperate.

"If you're not planning to open wide while I lose my cum all over that pretty face of yours in the next few seconds, I strongly suggest you keep your hands to yourself."

I meet her gaze, my breath a goddamn storm.

"I'm hanging by a thread here. Whatever I am right now—it's more beast than man. And I don't want to hurt you."

She just laughs—unbothered, fearless—and then tilts her head, opens her mouth, and locks her eyes on mine.

A dare. A promise. A challenge.

"Oh, don't you worry—you'll be drinking my cum for the rest of your days. But not before I get to tease you first. There's no fucking way I'm finishing before you."

I move across and kiss her, our tongues clashing in a war for dominance.

She might be the one tied to the desk, but she owns me just by existing.

When we finally break for air, I reach for her pussy, and her wetness swallows my fingers completely.

I bring them up, letting her see her own arousal glistening on my skin, and I smile at the truth written across her body.

I might be losing my mind slowly... but so is she.

I move between her legs, lean in, and inhale deeply.

Her scent hits me like a drug.

Earthy. Sweet. Clean. Powerful. Her.

It's everything.

Intoxicating in a way that should scare me—but it doesn't.

It just makes me hungrier.

I want—no, I need—my scent all over her.

I need to cover this body with my scent, and mark it as mine.

And she wants it too. She aches for it.

Even before I touch her with my mouth, I know—this is going to end me.

The moment my tongue meets her wetness and I get my first full taste of her...

Every sense will overload. Every boundary will break.

If I didn't know what to do with the emotions and needs she's already pulled out of me... this?

This will shatter me.

And I don't even want to contain it.

I want to surrender to it—to her—and savour every fucking second.

So I wrap my arms around her legs and pull her into my face, as close as humanly possible, and start licking and sucking at everything in front of me.

I have no idea what I'm doing.

There wasn't a single moment in my life where I imagined myself down here, eating pussy but here I am, on my knees, worshipping my Queen like the starving man she made me.

I start with long strokes of my tongue, from her entrance to the edge of her folds.

She moans at the first touch—loud, unrestrained, wild.

I don't ease her in. I don't give her time to breathe. I want to ruin her with my mouth, just as she ruined me.

I do it again. Then again.

Her body starts to tremble. Her sounds get messier, sharper.

Then I latch onto her clit—rolling it between my lips, teasing and circling until she's panting and moaning, her hips rocking in perfect sync with every movement of my mouth.

I can feel it building in her the tension, the edge, her climax rushing towards her at alarming speed.

She's so close her body starts this sweet shiver.

So I bite her.

Hard.

Right at the mound of her pussy.

She yelps in protest and tries to kick, body jolting between pleasure and shock.

Before she can do any serious damage, I latch onto her thigh and start kissing up and down the soft flesh, shoving two fingers deep into her pussy.

She rewards me with that delicious moan again, and I know, we're back in pleasure territory.

It's not just arousal—it's ownership.

Her body responds to me like it was made for this.

For me.

For us.

I kiss closer. And closer.

To where she needs me.

Slowly. Deliberately.

While I thrust my fingers shallow, steady strokes inside her slick heat.

I pause.

Just for a beat.

Just long enough to drag her to the very edge of despair.

And before she can protest... I curl my fingers inside her and latch onto her clit, trapping it between my tongue and lips.

Then I lose it.

I start lapping at her like a madman—relentless, not letting her catch her breath for even a second, all the while fingering her sweet spot into oblivion.

Her hips are moving so erratically now—so desperate, so wild—that it's getting harder to pin her down with just one hand.

So I let go of her clit for a breath, just one, and bite her thigh, sharp, punishing.

Before she even has a chance to cry out, I'm back on her clit.

But this time, I don't lap.

I keep it in my mouth.

And I grind it mercilessly between my tongue and lips.

"Holy fuck!" she screams, her back arching hard off the desk.

"Iubire, I'm about to explode—my pussy's actually on fire!"

Fuck!

If I thought I was losing my mind—she's completely gone.

Coming apart right there in front of me.

I turn my head and softly bite one of her pussy lips, then slide in a third finger and start fucking her—harder, faster, ruthless—giving her exactly what she needs in this moment.

The second my mouth lands on her clit again and I start sucking—deep, tight, merciless—she screams.

Not a moan. Not a cry.

A full, guttural scream of pleasure, ripping through the walls of my office and straight into my mind, my heart, my fucking cock.

I've heard her climax before, while I was stalking her.

But this...

This is nothing like what I've seen.

Nothing like anything I've ever survived.

I shift my hand, rubbing in tight, savage circles instead of thrusting and her walls start spasming around my fingers in erratic waves.

She's shaking. Screaming. Coming undone.

And every sound is carving into me like a *fucking brand.*

I keep lapping and sucking at her clit until I feel her completely let go.

There's so much wetness pouring out of her—a filthy, addictive sound fills the air, mingling with her moans and screams.

Her whole body is shaking now—trembling with pleasure so intense her voice cuts out, leaving her in staggered silence as her body takes over her mind.

Goddamn. She's gone. She's not thinking. She's just feeling.

Desperate for a taste of her cum, I move my fingers to her clit and drive my tongue inside her.

Her scent—earthy, primal, pure fucking sex—floods every nerve ending, hijacks my senses, and takes over my reality.

I lap at her release with a hunger that feels like death and rebirth, heaven and hell.

Like this is the real meal I've waited my whole life for.

I lick and suck at her entrance, trying—desperately, hopelessly—to drink her dry.

It's not enough!

I need more!

I want more!

I start lapping at her entire cunt, frantic, starving, unhinged.

Then I suck my fingers clean, trying to cling to the taste that's already fading.

Then I dive back in—tongue-fucking her like a man unraveling at the seams.

Then I suck her again, not caring how raw she is.

I want more!

Goddamn it, give me more!

Please... fucking give me more!

I understand now... I've completely lost control.

But I don't care.

Fucking hell, this woman has changed me.

That scent of hers—it's not just intoxicating, it's... consuming.

This is not lust—it's *obsession.* Dependency. A need so fundamental that it rewrites who I am.

A voice screams inside my head: *More...*

I want more!

Give me more!

I stand back, desperate, scanning every inch of her body for any lingering trace of her cum.

Then I see it—a slow trickle down the curve of her arse, pooling slightly on the desk.

And before I can rationalise what I'm doing, I'm lapping it up, my tongue dragging fast and frantic over her back entrance.

I kiss and suck her arse cheeks, then lift her hips and lick the mess off the desk, moaning into her skin.

Her sounds—those shocked, breathless moans—mirror my own confusion.

Even I didn't expect this.

I knew I'd have no limits with her.

But I didn't know I'd become this desperate for her cum.

My cock is pulsing.

Throbbing with a need that's beyond pain.

And I know exactly where to put him at ease.

I climb over her, moving fast—frantic, desperate.

Now I'm facing that soaked cunt again, and she's face-to-face with my cock.

As if he was made for this.

To rest on her lips.

To live in her mouth.

To belong to her.

The crown of my cock finds its place—right there on her lips, aching for entry.

And I start again.

Burying my face in her addictive, dripping pussy—because I can't stop.

I won't stop.

"Iubire... oh!"

A guttural moan cuts through her words.

"Wait."

I pause immediately, my face still buried in her cunt, inhaling her deeply, grounding myself in her scent.

I can sense her cunt—feel it calling me—and I know I'll drink her in again soon, even if it's the last thing I ever do.

"I've never given head," she says quietly. "I've never done any of this. I'm not sure how good I'll be."

The raw sincerity in her voice grabs hold of something deep inside me.

I pull back from her cunt, shift until my eyes lock on hers, not because I want to stop, but because she matters more than my hunger.

"Lisichka... I've never done any of this either. All my sex before this, it was transactional. Mechanical. Nothing more. I'm right here with you. Learning you. Surrendering to this hunger inside me. Doing whatever I can... to taste more of you."

I don't even finish the sentence, because her tongue is on the crown of my cock.

And something in my mind snaps.

"Holy fuck, Lisichka! That feels amazing—fuuuuuck!"

I can't even think straight.

Every ounce of my focus is locked onto her mouth and the relentless pulse of pleasure tearing through my cock.

The moment she takes the crown between her lips and sucks—slow, careful, intentional—it takes everything I have not to lose control and come right there.

"Holy fuck, Lisichka... fucking hell, your mouth feels like heaven on my cock."

She laughs while sucking me, and the vibration of it makes my head spin.

I know I'm seconds away from covering her in my cum, so I move fast.

My hands slide behind her arse and I lift her slightly, just enough to change the angle.

It gives me better depth, the perfect position to tongue-fuck her... and I take it.

I start rolling my tongue over her sweet spot—faster, deeper, rougher.

That's when I realise—my chin, more specifically my beard—is grinding against her clit in sync with every motion.

She moans.

Low. Broken. Needy.

And she licks my shaft up and down with the same desperation I'm burying in her cunt.

When I move back to her tight little back hole, I roll slow, teasing circles over it with my tongue.

Then I shift back to her clit, licking with force, while one of my thumbs keeps teasing her arse. Soft, relentless pressure that makes her gasp against my cock.

I start fucking her mouth...

And she lets me.

She gives me everything—full surrender. Complete control.

My mind snaps from reality.

There's nothing left but this.

Her body. My need. The way we burn each other alive.

I thrust into her mouth harder now, my hips rolling as my chin continues to grind against her clit—adding pressure, friction, heat—while I bury my cock deep into her throat.

She gags.

Beautifully. Deliciously.

Each time I take her breath away, her throat tightens around me—strangling my cock in the most perfect way.

I'm seconds away from rewarding her with my cum.

But no matter how deep I thrust into her throat, no matter how hard I suck or how desperately I lick her cunt...

She just takes it.

Every last fucking bit of it.

Like she was made for this.

Made for me. Designed for my ruin.

She moans, thrusting and stretching beneath me—her body moving with the same madness that's taken hold of me.

She's gone. We both are.

I can feel it—she's seconds away from detonation.

So I latch onto her clit and suck her hard, deep, while I plunge my fingers back into her soaked cunt—driving her sweet spot into oblivion.

She screams her pleasure around my cock.

A guttural, body-breaking sound.

Her back arches off the desk again, moulding into me like her body knows exactly where it belongs.

The vibrations around my cock are maddening—tight, wet, overwhelming.

But what truly ends me—what snaps the last thread of restraint, is the renewed gush of cum coating my fingers.

I don't even think.

I drop to her cunt again and devour her, lapping and sucking like she's my only salvation.

I need every last drop. I need to drown in her.

I want her soaked across my face, in my mouth, etched into my soul.

I want to drink it all.

And when I feel her start spasming around my tongue again—trembling, pulsing, breaking—I start fucking her mouth with brutal, unrelenting thrusts.

I'm gone.

I'm ready to empty myself.

All of me.

Into her.

"Lisichka... I'm about to come, baby," I groan into her cunt, breathless.

"You can swallow me—but don't swallow all my cum. I want to see it in your mouth... and dripping down your face, baby."

She nods eagerly around my cock—not letting go for a single second since I started fucking her face.

I latch back onto her cunt and just like that, my filthy promise makes her gush again, violently, beautifully.

I can't get enough.

I will *never* get enough.

There's nothing more addictive in this world than this woman... and her pussy.

I start thrusting wildly now.

Fucking her mouth like a madman, tongue-fucking her cunt like I'm trying to live inside her.

She moans again, and I can feel her spiralling into another orgasm.

Her walls are spasming, tight and rhythmic, gripping my tongue.

And her throat—damn, her throat—is opening up even more for me, like she wants to take everything I've got.

I thrust one final time... then bury myself deep in her throat as my mind explodes in ecstasy.

Hot ripples of cum shoot out of me without mercy, my hips pressing even harder against her as the release overtakes me.

My balls are drawn tight, my shaft and the crown of my cock hypersensitive—almost too much—but I don't pull out.

I let my body take over, surrendering completely as shards of pleasure explode through my skull with every shot I pump into her throat.

Even as the tremors begin to ease, I stay buried inside her.

She keeps sucking.

Eager. Devoted. Insatiable.

Draining me of every last drop.

And through it all...

No matter how deep I pushed her. No matter how much I took.

She never tapped out.

She never said it was too much.

She took all of me.

Because she is me. My mirror. My madness.

My hands are shaking as the final wave subsides.

I pull back slowly, finally easing out of her mouth.

Then I stand.

And look down at her.

She smiles.

That fucking exquisite, infectious, *real* smile of hers.

Then she opens her mouth.

And there it is.

My cum. In her beautiful mouth.

An animalistic roar tears out of me before I even know what my body is doing.

Something primal.

Something dark.

Something deep inside me snaps and claims her in that moment—as *irrevocably mine.*

I slide two fingers into her mouth, press them down on her tongue, and watch—*transfixed*—as my cum drips down her throat and disappears from sight.

There's no way to explain this feeling.

It's not rational.

It's not intellectual.

It's not even human.

It's the knowledge that she has me inside of her... just as I have her inside of me.

Her cum inside of *me.*

My cum inside of *her.*

This satisfaction... it lives in the part of me that no one ever tamed.

She's reduced me to the most barbaric, feral version of myself.

The one that needs to see her coated in my cum to feel whole.

When I spot some cum still clinging to her lips and chin, I don't hesitate. I swipe it across her face, rubbing it in like a branding, like a mark no one else will ever wear.

She starts to dart her tongue out, ready to lick it... but I stop her.

"No, my Queen. By the time I'm finished with you, you'll be completely covered in my cum. Your scent will be mine... and mine will be yours—from this moment forward."

And with that, I devour her mouth again, tasting myself and her in our kiss.

It's maddening.

Filthy.

Primal.

Because no matter how much I push her. No matter how far I take her... She only demands more.

When I finally pull back for air, I don't go far.

I start kissing her face—every inch of it.

Her beautiful, ruined face.

The face of a woman *no longer hiding* anything.

The face that shows me her true self and the pleasure I gave her.

I reach over and take one of her nipples between my forefinger and thumb, pulling *hard*.

Before she can cry out in pain, I smother the sound with a kiss—swallowing her gasp, her shock, her everything—then bite down on her lip, hard.

She starts laughing into my mouth, and that delicious, reckless sound makes my cock twitch back to life.

I reach for the other nipple and twist them both at once—rough, merciless.

This time, the sound I trap with my mouth isn't pain.

It's pleasure.

A deep, guttural moan as she arches her back, offering more of herself to me—more of her breasts, more of her surrender, more of her wildness.

Holy fuck!

She's as desperate for pain and pleasure as I am to give it to her.

I start playing with her breasts as I deepen the kiss, letting my hands roam. The moment she relaxes into my touch, I yank hard on her nipples and slap her breasts, sharp and punishing.

Each time, she rewards me with a cry of pleasure, a moan curling around our kiss while her tongue dances wildly with mine.

I'm completely hard now—throbbing, feral, savage with need.

I pull back for air and glance down.

Sure enough, my cock is swollen, flushed, looking downright angry with need.

She turns her head, and there it is.

My cock, mere inches from her greedy, wicked mouth.

That smile.

That goddamn smile.

It says it all.

She wants this. Every filthy, unrelenting part of it.

And fuck if that doesn't turn me on even more.

"Don't look at me like that, Lisichka. I'm just a mere mortal in front of you. One look from you, and I'd drop to my knees."

She laughs again, and I'm completely undone by this carefree version of her. So much so, I don't realise what she's doing until it's too late—she's stretching, reaching, taking me into her mouth again.

The moment I feel that wet, hot heat around me, I moan so loud it echoes off the walls.

"Fuuuuuck!"

Cock is what she wants? Cock is what she'll get!

I slide my palm behind her head and start fucking her mouth again, watching her beautiful face as she takes me. She hollows her cheeks, sucking deep, and I thrust harder, rougher—then lock my hand in place, holding her down on my cock.

I don't give her room to move. Or breathe. Or think.

She raises her eyes to mine, and the moment our gazes lock, I feel my cock jerk deep in her throat of its own. I don't ease out. I don't let go. I don't move. I hold her there, letting her choke on me again and again, feeding her more of my length with every gag.

Her eyes water, her face flushes red, but still—I don't pull back.

And when the next gag wracks her body, I push all the way in. I bottom out, my balls resting against her chin.

It's obscene.

It's erotic.

It's completely unhinged.

Her face is a mess of spit, tears, and heat—and it's the most feral, soul-ruining thing I've ever seen. She's destroying me, breaking me down into nothing but need and nerve endings.

This isn't just sex. It's war. It's worship. It's complete madness.

And I'm fucking gone—lost in her.

I pull back slightly, and she whimpers in protest—that delicious, desperate sound that makes my cock throb harder. I smile down at her, at her eagerness to choke on me again.

I wipe a tear from her eye and let her take a quick breath, just enough to keep her dancing on the edge of control.

Then I start fucking her throat again—deep, brutal, unrelenting.

My thrusts are raw. My movements unhinged.

Every time she gags, I hold her there, face trapped against me, until she's completely suffocating on my cock. Her teeth graze the base of my cock, drool spilling down her face, mixing with her tears—tears of pure pleasure.

And still, she moans around me. Still, she sucks and takes me deeper, even hungrier.

Holy fuck!

Her reaction to my touch is beyond anything I could've imagined. I was scared to unleash this hunger on her... but she's meeting me thrust for thrust, moan for moan, demanding more of me at every turn.

I trap her on my cock again as I reach over and slap her breast—hard.

She yelps around me, and the sound is pure pleasure, vibrating through my length and driving me insane. Every sensation she gives me, every sound she makes, feeds the beast clawing inside me.

I reach between her legs, and the moment my fingers brush her cunt, I freeze.

She's soaked again. Dripping.

And I'm missing out on tasting every drop of that delicious cunt. I want more—I want to drink her until I forget my own fucking name.

Before I can move, she starts bobbing her head, taking control, fucking herself on my cock like she was made for it.

And fuck, I love it.

I love how she's claiming whatever she wants from me—like it's hers by right.

She comes up for air—just a second—then zeroes in on the crown of my cock, wrapping those perfect lips around the most sensitive part of me.

And just like that, I'm gone again, a guttural growl tearing from my throat, at the need to empty myself in her again. I would gladly give her all my cum, until there is no more of me to give.

"I'm going to eat your cunt again... and then I'm going to fuck you."

My voice is low, rough—completely feral.

"I might take your pussy, or I might take your arse. I haven't decided. But if you want something specific... tell me. And that's exactly what I'll give you."

Then I crash my mouth into hers, tasting the mix of her and me still slick on her lips.

She's mine.

And she should taste like me—like *us*.

When I pull back for air, I take a second to study her, waiting for a reaction.

All she does is smile and wink.

Goddamn it, this woman... she's beyond anything I ever imagined. Beyond dreams. Beyond my power of control.

I kneel between her legs, desperate to worship her more and more. Just give me more!

My body moves on instinct, the need for her burning hot through my veins.

The first taste knocks me back on my arse—again—because she tastes like sin and magic, and everything in between.

I bury my face in her cunt, as deep as I can get, licking and tongue-fucking her over and over until I'm dizzy from her scent, the lack of oxygen, and the unbearable throbbing of my cock.

When she starts to spasm around my tongue, I know without a doubt—it's her cunt I'm taking next.

I keep lapping, prolonging her orgasm, teasing her sensitive nub with the tip of my tongue until she cries out that she is too sensitive and locks her legs around my head, trembling.

She's wrecked, and I'm completely addicted.

I stand and look down at her pink, glistening pussy, and I know.

The scent of us—sharp, musky, raw—hangs thick in the air as I pull back, licking the last of her off my lips. Her thighs tremble beneath my hands, slick and hot.

This is it.

The moment of no return.

I've already given up my entire life for this woman, surrendered everything I was, because somewhere deep in my soul, I know...

We are one.

In every way. In all the ways that matter.

And now... we're about to seal that truth—body and soul, *fully united.*

I grip my cock and run it slowly up and down her soaked pussy, coating myself in her arousal. When I circle her clit with the swollen crown, her body arches, and she loses herself in pleasure all over again.

I look up—and she's watching me with that same raw hunger I feel in every cell of my body. We both know what's coming. What it means. This moment... the one where our bodies stop being separate things and finally become one—in the truest, most primal way.

The second she smiles at me, everything inside me breaks. I stop teasing and start pressing forward.

The head of my cock meets resistance—tight, wet, gripping me like a vise—and it steals the air from my lungs.

Fuuuuuuck!

I've barely breached her, and already it feels like she's trying to swallow me whole.

"Fucking hell, baby. You're strangling me," I growl, a deep moan escaping as her tightness clamps around me. Every muscle in my body is screaming—*break her, mark her, make her mine. Break her in pain and pleasure.*

She doesn't say a word, so I lean forward and pinch one of her nipples hard as I press in another inch. When she starts to roll her hips in response, something in me *snaps.* If I don't bury myself inside her now, I'm going to lose my goddamn mind.

I grip her arse with both hands, lifting her, angling her, trying to open her up more for me. When she's spread as wide as she can go, I press her knees back and down, giving myself full, unforgiving access. I glance down—and there it is. The tip of my cock, swallowed in her tight cunt. My gut tells me this is it. This is as far as she can stretch, as much as she can take.

I wait for one more breath. Hers. Mine.

Then I thrust.

All the way in.

Until my balls smack against her arse.

She cries out—pain, pleasure, shock—and her head jerks up, eyes searching for mine.

"Stay with me, Lisichka," I murmur in that comforting voice only she's ever brought out of me. "By the end of the night, you'll love my cock more than I do."

She clenches around me, her walls still tight with pain, strangling my cock to the point of madness.

I don't thrust. I roll my hips instead—slow, controlled. Deep.

With each roll, she begins to loosen, her body learning mine. Her moans shift—less pain, more pleasure. More need.

She's taking me.

I glance down and see myself buried completely inside her. The sight alone makes my cock jolt like it's got a mind of its own—because maybe it does, when it comes to her.

She's so exquisite like this. Opened up entirely for me, my cock buried deep in her cunt, and her perfect clit practically begging for attention.

Seeing her cunt like this, full of my cock, her clit crying out for me, takes my breath away. I'm completely mesmerised. With one hand, I lift its hood to reveal the swollen, sensitive bud—engorged, glistening, and completely mine.

I spit directly on it, watching as it coats her skin. Then I start rubbing—up and down—with my thumb and forefinger. Gently. Then with more purpose. All while continuing to roll my hips into her.

The moans spilling from her lips are desperate, uncontrollable—like a siren song of pleasure dragging me into madness.

And then I hear it—that shift in her voice, that sharp cry of rising bliss.

I've got her.

I can do whatever I want now with her cunt and she will take it all and demand more.

I switch to deep, unrelenting thrusts mid-moan, and she cries out from the sheer force of it.

As a reward for her reaction, I press harder on her clit, rubbing in firm, tight circles. When her cries build again—spiralling toward release—I give her a sharp slap on her clit, and she gasps, her body jolting with the mix of pain and pleasure.

The moment our eyes lock, she's screaming murder with her gaze—rage, lust, desperation—and I just laugh. I know this edging, as maddening as it is, will have her blacking out from pleasure soon enough.

I spit on her clit again and resume rolling her hood between my fingers in slow, teasing motions until the swollen bud is throbbing, crying for me.

My thrusts are deep, unrelenting, and every time I pull out, I roll my hips just right—dragging my cock along her sweet spot, giving it the perfect grind. She's wailing within minutes.

And when I hear it—when she starts to break—I spit again on her clit, pull the hood taut, press, and roll her swollen bud until she detonates.

Her scream of pleasure is so guttural, so primal, it tears through me—and there's no restraining my own release. She squeezes my girth so tight it borders on pain, on madness, and I pound into her harder, faster, consumed.

The first shot of cum crashes through me like a violent wave, so overwhelming it blinds me. All I see is white. I shake my head, trying to ground myself as more of me spills into her, and I'm fighting to remember how to breathe.

My greedy little Queen starts rolling her hips, meeting me thrust for thrust, demanding every last drop of me into her cunt. When I finally catch my breath and my vision clears, I look down at where we're joined—her perfect pussy red, swollen, and glistening with my cum.

I pull out, fist my shaft, and stroke myself, needing to give her every last drop.

The final spurts land on her mound, and a slow, white trickle begins to slide out of her, dripping from her cunt—and it undoes me all over again.

"Fucking hell, Lisichka. That wasn't fucking, baby," I say, my voice soft and disbelieving. "That was *mating*. There's no other way to describe it. You sealed yourself into me, woman, and there's no saving me now."

The words fall from me raw and full of something I've never let anyone hear... vulnerability.

I watch, transfixed, as my cum mingles with hers and begins to drip, trailing down to her arse, pooling beneath her.

I'm frozen in place, caught in a moment of impossible peace—a kind of happiness I never believed a man like me could have.

But looking at her now, tied up and spent, yet still so greedy for everything I give her, I know the truth.

She's my safe place.

She's my salvation.

Without hesitation instinct takes over. I latch onto her cunt again and start tongue-fucking her.

She tastes divine.

Her cum mixed with mine, is the most intoxicating thing I've ever known, and the more I roll the tip of my tongue over her sweet spot, the louder she screams in pleasure.

I slide my fingers inside her, pushing our cum back into her while still devouring her with my mouth. Her walls are soft, hot, and so fucking addictive—I want to stay buried here, face-first in her, until the day I die.

Only... I think she might be sore by now. Maybe she needs to breathe, to process what just happened between us—just as much as I do.

I press a final gentle kiss to her clit and rise to my full height.

The moment our eyes meet, it hits me—clear as day. She didn't expect all of this. Neither did I. She's sore, sated, and—dare I say it—*happy.*

I turn and pull one of the curtains from the window. As I move to untie her, I press soft kisses to every spot I touch along the way. Draping the curtain over my back, I look down at her waiting form—and I'm completely taken by surprise at how submissive she still is beneath my dominance.

This isn't an ordinary woman. And yet, she trusted me with her entire being.

And now... she's waiting for more.

I settle between her legs, and sure enough, my cock is still semi-hard—the perfect plug to keep our cum inside her. I catch what's just spilled out with the tip of my cock and push it gently back in. She instinctively locks her legs around me, and I smile at her.

There's no need for words between us. We both know exactly what this is and exactly where we stand now.

I slide my hands beneath her and lift her into my arms. The weight of her against me is perfect—soft skin, sweat-slicked, legs trembling. She melts into me, arms wrapped around my neck, head resting on my shoulder—rolling her hips gently on my cock. If she keeps this up, I'll be fully hard again in seconds. But she doesn't seem to care. She keeps grinding slowly, then starts licking and sucking at my neck.

She's fucking intoxicating.

And I want to fuck her again so badly... but we need to get to the bedroom. I need more space.

I cover her completely with the curtain, making sure not a single part of her is visible—not even her head.

She is mine!

All mine!

No one gets to see what belongs to me. If anyone dares look at her, I'll rip their fucking eyes out without a second thought.

I move to the door and open it. Cool air from the hallway brushes against her bare shoulder, and I see red blooming on her neck where I bit her.

I know the guards are stationed at the end of the corridor, and the overwhelming, all-consuming urge to kill them where they stand—for simply existing near my Queen—flares in my chest like a desperate need for air.

She stops kissing my neck and pulls back to look into my eyes. Then, as if she knows exactly what she's doing, she starts bouncing on my cock—slow, deliberate, calculated.

I'm fully hard again. Because of her. Because this woman was made to undo me.

"Don't kill them," she whispers against my lips. "Focus on me," she breathes, then flicks her tongue across my bottom lip.

"Tell them to go away... and focus on me."

The power she has over me—the power I willingly, eagerly gave her—shouldn't exist.

Yet it does.

And she has it.

Because just like that, the bloodthirst in my mind fades, and all I can see now is her.

Bent. Begging. Moaning.

My Queen.

And the filthy things I'll do to her once we get to our bedroom.

"Leave!" I roar, my voice echoing through the corridor with a menacing finality.

"Sir?" one of the imbeciles dares to call back, footsteps approaching like a death wish.

"Fucking leave if you value your life!" I bark, and the steps halt.

"I don't want to see a single soul in the West Wing for the foreseeable future. Anyone who so much as breathes in this direction will be executed on the spot."

I pause. My voice drops to something darker. Crueller.

I turn my head slowly, rage pulsing in my temples.

"If I see even a shadow of any of you near this wing again, I will rip your fucking spine out and mount it as a warning."

Silence.

Then the sound of retreating boots.

Good. They may be stupid, but they're not suicidal.

But the second she breathes against my skin, the fury collapses—folding into something deeper. Something darker. Something only she can tame.

Lisichka hides her laughter in the crook of my neck, and her hot, ticklish breaths make me want to start biting her all over again.

When the last sounds from the hallway fade away, I turn my full attention back to the menacing, addictive woman in my arms.

I lift her arse so only the tip of my cock remains inside her, kiss the breast now perfectly in my face, and then bite down—hard—as I let her drop completely onto my cock in a brutal thrust. The scream of pain and pleasure that rips out of her is absolute unhinged madness to my mind.

But I know I need more room to give her what she craves—to give in to the darkness gnawing at my insides.

I cover her completely again and take off running, full speed, with her cradled against me. The moment we reach our bedroom, I kick the door shut behind us, then pull back just enough for our eyes to meet. Without a word, I turn her around, pin her to the door, and lower one of her wrapped legs to the floor.

Silence greets us. Just her breath against my neck and the thundering promise in my veins. We're finally here.

"Welcome home, my Queen," I say, my voice soft, warm in that way only she created within me.

This is it...

The moment I completely break apart for her.

I destroy what's left of myself, just to be inside her.

I start thrusting, deep, hard, fucking her with the kind of madness that leaves nothing behind.

Brutal. Complete. Final.

The world outside the bedroom ceases to exist.

Chapter Eighteen

Monica

WHAT. THE. FUCK. JUST. HAPPENED. TO. ME?!

Holy hell!

If *that's* what sex is supposed to feel like? No wonder people lose their damn minds over it. No wonder they lie, cheat, beg, *kill* for it.

Holy fuck!

I cannot believe that actually happened.

I'm speechless.

Shaking...

Wrecked...

And not just physically.

My mind is... I don't even know where my mind is.

What the hell did he do to me?!

Chapter Nineteen

Elijah

HOLY. SHIT.

What just happened?!

Holy hell!

This is beyond anything I ever expected. Beyond anything I could've dreamed of.

I am completely—utterly—consumed by my Queen.

And rightfully so.

I called her a *creature* because she sucked the very *existence* out of me... and left behind this barbaric, raw version of myself.

I'm trying to gather my senses—my conscious and subconscious torn to shreds—because she *obliterated* it all.

There's nothing left inside me but Lisichka and my hunger to devour her again.

But I know she's sore now.

I know I'm sore.

And there's this feeling inside me...

I'm not sure what it is or what to call it.

It's not fear.

It's something else.

All I know is—I completely lost control of myself.

And now, there's only her.

There's no doubt in my mind about that.

What just happened between us—the way we're compatible on every plane... the way I took her, dominated her... was the perfect match to how she gave in, submitted, and wanted more.

It surprised us both—her submission and my savage dominance.

I knew I might attack her... but I didn't realise it would go that far.

That feeling inside me—it has to come from that.

I know she needs time to process what happened.

She needs to understand—just like I do—where we stand now.

But for now, we both need time to feel it.

To process all the sensations our bodies created by being with each other.

My entire body is buzzing with energy—and if she were in front of me right now, I'd take my fill again.

I've decorated her body with my mark, bites, cum.

There's only a little of her left to finish off, and then she'll be entirely covered in me.

I'm not sure if this is a kink… or if it's borderline deranged by "normal" standards.

But that doesn't matter.

The only thing that matters is this:

Me and her—we're not like the others. In any way, shape or form.

Fucking her proved it again how different we are from everyone else. Yet somehow, we are completely reflecting one another.

Completely compatible.

Perfectly made for each other.

It's been twenty minutes since I tied her to my bed, covered her, and left her to rest—to gather her thoughts after what just happened.

All the sensations.

All the feeling.

All the desperation for more.

It caught us both completely off guard.

But her submission?

That…

That was something else.

I know she's as dominating as I am, so for her to let go like that—fully trust me, without a hint of hesitation—it has to be sending her mind into panic. No doubt.

As much as it broke me to give her space, because she doesn't know it yet. This is the *only* time I will ever give her space—I had to step back and let her process.

So I came back to my office.

Poured myself a drink. A large one.

And seriously considered putting an ice pack on my balls for a few minutes before going back in to fuck the living hell out of her.

The only problem... I can't bring myself to move.

Because the entire room still smells of her. Of us. Of what just happened here. And it's driving me fucking insane.

I swirl the ice in my glass again, take a long sip, and close my eyes.

Images of Lisichka—moaning, rocking on my cock—invade my mind so vividly it's making me dizzier than the drink.

Fucking hell.

This woman is really going to kill me.

"So... Angela's mum?"

I'm so startled by Buddy's voice invading my mind, I jump to my feet so fast he takes a step back.

"Easy. It's just me," he says, calm, like he's trying to reassure me.

"What do you want?"

My voice is sharp. Clipped. Cold, as if I'm speaking to an enemy, not my closest friend.

"I thought I'd check on you."

He pauses.

"You laughed. Publicly."

"It's none of your concern."

He studies me for a second.

This isn't how we speak to each other.

He would never dare speak to me like this, even if he felt inside what I'm feeling now.

But still... this is most definitely out of character. Even for me.

This is borderline emotional—not cold, not distant—and he's definitely picked up on it.

His eyes travel around the room... then settle on my desk, across from where I am sitting.

Then they drop lower.

"Is she still alive...?" he asks, halfheartedly.

What?!

My eyes follow the same path his just did.

That's when I notice the shreds of her dress still on the floor... and next to them, dried patches of blood.

I lunge at Buddy with everything I have—punching, kicking like a man possessed.

Because that's exactly what I am.

This is what she's reduced me to.

This is not my friend in front of me anymore. He's just a man who saw part of my Lisichka—and he must die.

Red-hot fury invades my mind, and the only thing satisfying my thirst to kill are the cuts gathering fast across his face, blood pouring out like tears.

No one is allowed to see what's mine!

She is mine!

Mine!

No one will take her from me!

No one will see her!

She's only mine!

Buddy tries to block my punches, but more are landing true than he can keep up with.

The more my mind spirals out of control, the more I hit him to kill.

I have to protect what's mine.

At all costs!

She is mine, goddamn it!

I ram my knee into his stomach with full force. The impact sends him crashing down, gasping, landing hard on his knees.

I reach for one of the secret compartments in my desk and pull out a gun to execute him.

I press the barrel to his temple—ready to defend what's mine.

He's not pleading.

He's not crying or screaming.

He's just sitting there, looking at me.

And the moment our eyes lock...

I see it.

It's the same look he had when I first found him.

The look of someone who knows they're going to die—and has already accepted it.

Same as back then...

I have a gun to his head.

And he's simply okay with me taking his life.

Because to him, death holds the same value as life.

And just like then...

I know *his life is worth more.*

I take a deep breath in—for the first time since he came into the office.

This is my friend.

This is Buddy.

He wouldn't try to hurt me.

He wouldn't try to take my reason to live.

I pull the gun from his temple and really look at him—my friend, kneeling before me.

He wouldn't harm Lisichka.

He knows she's mine.

And the world knows it now.

"She's upstairs."

I offer him my hand, pulling him to his feet.

"Tied."

Then I turn back to look at the blood—really look at it.

What's going on?

I licked her body clean—I would've noticed blood on her. Right?

Was I so completely out of control... I didn't even see it?

As I look around and gather her dress, what's left of it, I stare at the torn fabric.

And sure enough... it's dried blood on the floor.

What the actual fuck?!

What have I done?!

"It's from your toe," Buddy says in that signature calm voice of his.

"Even if... by the look of the room and her clothes, it looks like you tore her apart."

I turn so fast, murder in my eyes, that he takes a step back and lifts his hands in surrender.

"I'm not sure what's going on, Elijah. If you need me or my advice, I'm here."

"SHE'S MINE!"

I roar at the top of my lungs, ready to attack him again.

He keeps his position, not moving an inch, probably trying not to trigger me again.

"And the world knows it now," he confirms, calm as ever.

I take a moment to let the words settle in my mind.

And the world knows it now.

Yes. Yes, it does.

The world also knows how powerful I am.

But that's not enough.

I need to marry her—to erase any trace of delusion that someone else could even breathe in her direction.

I need to chain her to me.

Marry her. Claim her. Lock it in blood.

I'll drag her down that aisle if it comes to it.

But she is mine! Forever!

And soon, the world will know that too.

"Are you feeling well?"

He's still holding my gaze while I try to settle myself.

He hasn't seen me like this since I annihilated every last motherfucker responsible for killing my family over twenty years ago.

I understand his confusion at my state—but this is different.

This is *much* worse.

Because if I painted the streets of Moscow with the blood of the man who ordered the massacre, then what I'm willing to do for my Queen... Is far worse than that.

"Elijah..."

I shake my head, take another deep breath, and look at my friend of over twenty years, and tell him the truth.

"I'm not sure."

We've built an empire together, one that spans the globe.

And in all that time, he's never once heard me doubt myself.

Not in any way.

Not in any shape or form.

Everything I've done until now has been logical.

Planned.

Manipulated.

Enforced.

Or broken into submission.

But *this*...

This is something else entirely.

I don't even know what it is.

It's...

Feelings.

We stand there for a moment, then I pass him and sink back onto the lounge, finishing off my drink.

When I let out a long sigh, he walks to the bar, pours two more drinks, and hands me one.

I gesture for him to take a seat.

We drink in silence.

And I like it.

One of the best things about Buddy is that he doesn't push.

He knows I always have a plan.

And a backup.

And a backup to the backup.

And a person to manipulate after that.

And so on.

Until the job's done.

Fuck knows I have no clue what I'm doing right now.

I'm running on pure, unhinged instinct—and it's roaring at me to execute my friend... then go fuck my woman in his blood.

Even I know that's a bit too unhinged.

So it has to be the wrong decision.

"I can't even explain it."

He watches me as I swirl the ice in my glass again.

"I feel..."

The word lands awkwardly, *foreign*— too soft, like it doesn't belong in my mouth.

My voice isn't commanding.

It isn't authoritative.

Not this time.

It's barely above a whisper.

By the look on his face, I'm not sure what shocks him more—what I said, or how I said it.

Raw. Quiet. Unarmed.

"Oh..."

I take another sip.

Then swirl the ice again. The sound is louder now. Or maybe it's just heightened senses in this moment, amplifying everything around me.

"As I said... I can't even explain it."

"Is she okay?"

I lift my gaze to his—and the scream of murder in my eyes comes so fast, he flinches back in his seat.

"Hey. Hey," he says, hands up, tone defensive.

"You don't need to try to kill me every time I speak of her."

"She. Is. Mine."

He blinks, staring at me like he doesn't recognise what he's seeing.

"Elijah... this doesn't sound like you."

"SHE! IS! MINE! MOTHERFUCKER!" I roar, slamming my drink down so hard the glass nearly shatters.

"AND NO ONE CAN TAKE HER FROM ME!"

I'm panting now—chest heaving, fists clenched—battling the wild, feral creature she's made me... and the man who still knows Buddy.

He doesn't flinch this time.

"No one will, Elijah," he says calmly. "I'll work with you. I'll make damn sure no one ever comes near her."

It doesn't escape me—whatever's left of my mind since my Queen stole it—that he deliberately moved into my corner. That he hasn't said her name again. He wants me to see he's not a threat.

Smart bastard.

"I don't understand what's happening to me, Buddy."

My voice is quieter now. Ragged. Unstable. "I feel on fire. Like I could kill everyone just to protect her... and keep her all to myself."

He doesn't speak right away. Just watches me like I'm a live weapon. Probably weighing his next words carefully, knowing how close I am to the edge.

"That sounds reasonable... for a man like you." His words are calm, composed, steady. Typical of the man I call my friend.

His answer catches me off guard.

I didn't expect that.

I expected him to tell me to calm the hell down.

"Elaborate," I say, my voice cold, authoritative once more.

"You said you have feelings, right? That's completely uncharted territory for you."

I must make a face, because he lifts his hands slightly, in surrender.

"Hang on—just hear me out. I've known you for so many years. I've been your shadow that entire time. And in all those years, I've never seen you show even a shred of emotion. Not to me. Not to Sofia. And we're the closest thing you have to family."

He pauses, watching me.

"So for you to feel something, that means there's complete chaos inside you right now. And knowing you... that's dangerous."

"You're stating facts. Not helpful. Get to the point."

My voice is colder than usual—clinical, cutting. I don't need his analysis. I need clarity.

"That is my point," he says evenly. "This is all new for you. You're trying to protect what's yours. Maybe... this is your new normal."

Damn right I want to protect what's mine.

I also want to cage what's mine.

Because it's *only* mine.

"Perhaps," he adds carefully, "you're just a tad over the line into possessive. But who am I to judge?"

"You are no one to judge," I snap, standing abruptly, towering over him.

He doesn't move. Just sits there looking up at me, lips twitching.

"Are you... are you smiling?" Disbelief laces my voice. He full-on starts laughing, right in my face.

I clench my fists, looking down, trying to breathe through the fresh avalanche of desire to see his blood pouring at my feet.

That's when I see it.

"Fuck! My toe!"

Holy hell.

My nail is ripped off.

What the actual fuck?!

I glance at the dried blood next to my desk.

Oh. That's what he meant earlier.

Of course it wasn't from Lisichka—I licked her entire body, here and in our bedroom.

Even unhinged, feral, and half out of my mind, I would've protected her if she was bleeding.

"Yep," he says between chuckles, wiping his eyes. "Your toe, Elijah. Whatever primal ritual took place in here left shredded clothes, I'm sure unholy sounds echoing through the walls—and a fucking toenail sacrificed to the gods of madness. And by the look on your face, you didn't even notice your own body was bleeding for her, screaming in pain."

He's completely right.

I ripped my nail clean off while fucking her and didn't even register the pain.

Fucking hell. I knew I lost control—but this? This is a whole new level.

"I think you're in love," he says.

I raise my gaze to him. Now he's just pissing me off.

"You think?" My voice is flat, dismissive, bored.

"Wow. You're not even going to deny it?"

"I want to kill you now for boring me to death, Buddy. If you don't have anything useful to say, fuck off. I need to go back."

She's had enough time to process. I'm coming back for more.

"I'd say 'be yourself,' but I'm not sure that's the best idea right now."

"You're completely useless right now. Fuck off." And with that, I storm out of the office and into the hall.

Then I stop.

Maybe she's hungry.

Am I?

I don't even know anymore. My body's buzzing under my skin—tight fists, clenched jaw, pressure building behind my eyes like I might snap.

What the fuck is she doing to me?

My senses are misfiring. Twisted. Completely off axis.

I try to think—really think—but there's only silence in my mind.

No logic. No plan.

Only her. And the constant, burning need for more.

Always her.

I look up the stairs—and it's like I can hear her hum. Like she's whispering to me, feeding this unhinged need.

She's pulling me. Calling me.

I want more.

Give me more.

Let me mark you again. Keep you again.

Chain you to me so you never leave.

She's in my blood.

And I just want more of her.

Fucking hell. It's like I'm enchanted, because this can't be healthy.

Still, she needs her energy if I'm going to attack and feed on her again. And I will the moment I am back up there.

So I make my way to the kitchen and start pulling out anything and everything I can find in the cupboard, fridge, doesn't matter. If it looks remotely edible, it goes on the tray.

I power walk back to our room, heart pounding, and leave the tray by the door.

Hunger or not...

I need to see her. I need to taste her. I need to know she doesn't hate me now.

I grip the door handle, my breath caught in my throat.

Please don't look at me differently.

Please still be mine.

I push the door open...

And I feel my knees giving out beneath me.

Chapter Twenty

Monica

God, his bed is comfortable. I thought I would get cold after a while being tied up like this, naked under the duvet, but no. If anything, I had a little nap, because he has been gone for a while.

I would say I cannot believe he tied me up again before he left, except I can completely understand it, and I was expecting it.

He is a tad bit obsessed at this stage and scared shitless that I will make a run for it. All things considered, after everything I put him through these past few months, I expected nothing less.

I do appreciate him giving me a second to process this, because what I cannot believe is that I submitted to him.

Me!

Me!

I submitted!

To him!

If anything, I was expecting it to be the other way around and for me to rip him apart.

But nope. It was all so natural and fitting—nothing that happened felt out of place for me.

Again, if I think from a point of view of what is expected of me to feel in a situation like this, I should be appalled, shocked, crying myself into a panic attack for all the depraved, filthy, deranged things he has done to me.

That being said, I'm in the open now. I don't need to hide and pretend other people's reactions, feelings, and speech are my own.

I'm in the light now. I can be myself in my truest form.

And my truest form enjoyed the fuck out of that.

It was dirty and extreme, powerful and unhinged, raw and depraved, and the entire time, I wanted more.

I might have been the one tied up, but he was the one breaking.

I might have been the one submissive, but he was the one completely losing control in me.

So everyone can have their opinion, if they knew about what has happened, but as far as I am concerned... I want more.

A shiver of excitement travels through my entire body, and involuntarily, I pull at my bound hands.

Who would have known I enjoy being tied up?

Crazy!

Crazy, I tell you!

I am giggling to myself at the absurdity of my findings. The expectation and the intent I had of myself in contrast to what I truly love now that I am free.

The best part of it all... I am not afraid.

At all!

I cannot wait to explore more with Elijah, to discover new things, to push the limits and find our boundaries together.

It's crazy what my mind is creating—what I want to do to him, or what I want him to do to me.

Also, holy hell, his kink of drinking me dry?!

Fucking hot!

Seriously!

I did not expect him to be so into that, but I am enjoying the hell out of it.

I can feel myself getting worked up again as all of these filthy, depraved things invade my mind, overlapping with images of what he's already done to me.

Noise from outside the door pulls me back to the present, and I know he is seconds away from fulfilling my most unhinged, dirty desires.

All I have to do... is ask.

The moment the door opens and he sees me lying on the bed, waiting for him, I smile.

The moment our eyes meet and he sees the smile on my face, he grips the doorframe, as if his legs are no longer keeping him up.

We don't say a word to each other—we just take each other in, and that is more than enough for us.

The look in his eyes is so... so emotional, even.

For others, it might be nothing.

But for someone like Elijah and I, who are completely incapable of feeling things, this... whatever this is—it's more than love, physical, lust, or even rational thought.

And we both know the real value of finding each other.

"My Queen..." his voice is so small, and it trails off as if he does not even dare to speak to me. Then he lowers his head, as if he is bowing to me.

Holy hell! I understand people think they know love, they know devotion, loyalty, and respect.

All the while, what I have with Elijah—the way we fit together—is nothing I've ever known, or even expected us to share.

Everything feels so effortless, fitting and justifiable that one might argue even feelings are now explainable between us.

The moment he looks at me again, I smile wider, then wink at him.

"Come, iubire scumpă."

The way he spread his cum over me—rubbing it into my skin with deliberate intent, claiming me with every drop—felt like a ritual.

Possessive.

Like he wasn't just inside me, but on me.

As if even my pores now belonged to him.

And holy hell... I loved every second of it.

I loved how he marked me.

How he needed to possess everything about me—even my pores.

How I let him.

No. I didn't just let him.

I wanted more.

"If I untie you, can you swear to me you're not going to make a run for it?"

His voice is so small and sweet.

It did not go unnoticed how his tone changed today, and something inside me tells me this is not something anyone else has the privilege to see in Elijah.

This is mine.

This is my version of him.

And no one has access to him.

This is all for me.

All mine for the taking.

I burst out laughing, because, to me, that was hilarious.

But when I see he's not joining in—when he lowers his head into the valley between my breasts once more, as if trying to claim even my heartbeat—I feel his pain.

I think I need to do some damage control here.

I knew I would hurt him with my distance this past few months, and yes, he needed it—because he was very naughty for how he pushed me out in the open.

That being said, seeing him like this breaks something inside of me.

Truly...

"Iubire scumpă," I say, prompting him to look at me.

"I'm yours. I'm not going anywhere."

He sees the truth in my eyes, stands, and starts to unbind my wrists, kissing the spot where I was tied.

It's been a while in this position, and this delicious pain runs through my arms, reminding me of my newfound delicious kink.

It's truly crazy to think of myself as a sub, but fuck me backwards all the way to Tuesday—I fucking loved it.

And if he wants to tie me all up, I would probably be okay with that... and still ask for more.

Shit! That thought is really extreme, even for me.

But the moment Elijah comes into the picture, it's only... peace and pleasure, and crazy hot fucking.

That last bit bursts another laugh out of me, and he just studies me as he finishes untying my ankles.

I lift myself to my knees in front of him, and I wince at the pain between my legs.

It is delicious... but it also hurts like a motherfucker.

"Oh shit! Lisichka, please let me look."

He gently guides me to the edge of the bed and lays me on my back, moving between my legs.

"Oh fuck," his voice is a mix of awe and fear.

"I don't like the sound of that," I quickly bite back. "What have you done down there?"

"Alex?"

"Yes, Elijah?"

A soft chime sounded, and a voice—smooth, calm, unmistakably clear—filled the room.

I stand so fast when this male voice comes out of nowhere and desperately try to cover myself.

"What the actual fuck, Elijah?! If you think I'm into any type of threesome or some shit like that, you are sorely mistaken, boy!"

I pour as much venom into my tone and words as humanly possible.

What the hell is going on?!

"For the record, no one and nothing is allowed to even breathe in your direction, my Queen."

He pulls me to his chest, and I take a deep breath in.

Yep. That sounds more like the unhinged Elijah I know.

"Alex, this is our Queen. Her name is Monica Dominion. I call her Lisichka, and the world will call her their Queen."

Wait... What? *Dominion?*

WTF?!

“Good evening, my Queen," the man replies in a calm, friendly tone.

"Memorise her voice and give her the same security access and account privileges as mine."

"Confirming Global Admin?"

"Confirmed," Elijah continues as he breathes me in.

I have no idea what he is doing, but he seems so at ease holding me to his chest and peppering kisses on my shoulder.

Clearly, there is no reason to panic.

Perhaps it's some type of call?

"Please introduce yourself to her," Elijah instructs Alex.

"Certainly, Elijah."

There was no cold monotone, no artificial stiffness.

He's intelligent. Measured. Polite, but not servile.

“My name is *Alex*. Elijah has granted you Global Admin Access to the system. I manage all layers of security, logistics, and internal support for him—and now, for you as well.”

A brief pause. The voice softened, just slightly.

“I do not feel, but I understand. And if you ever need assistance—be it protection, information, or even silence—I am here.”

Then, as if already anticipating my next question...

“You are safe.”

"Holy shit, what was that, Elijah?!" I push at his chest with all my might.

What the actual hell was that?!

He laughs—and it's so genuine and warm, very much not like the big bad wolf I'm in desperate need of.

"Alex is exceptional. I designed him a while back, and I'm constantly working to improve his potential. I couldn't love him more. He's intelligent, adaptable, and always there. As he said... you are truly safe now."

"He's some type of AI?" I pull a face at him, disbelieving. "Also... *him*?"

"He's more than just an AI. You'll get to know him better. Just know—you are always safe."

He leans in and kisses my forehead, then gently guides me onto my back again.

"Alex, I slept with my Queen and her pussy is all red and swollen. What do I do?"

I lift my head again, unsure if I should laugh or call him a muppet again.

WTF?! He is asking an AI what to do with my sore pussy?

Really?!

"What? People Google this shit every day. Alex is far superior to Google, please."

Elijah's tone is so defensive of this AI, as if it were a real person.

"I'm terribly sorry to hear that you're in pain, my Queen. Perhaps running her a hot bath and applying some ointment could assist with the discomfort."

The voice is so considerate, friendly, and sounds so genuinely concerned for my well-being that you wouldn't think for a second it's not a real person.

"If not that, you can always lay off all the hardcore sex, Elijah."

Elijah bursts out laughing so hard.

He's really enjoying the joke—and quite frankly, it was a good joke.

How is it doing this?

"Great. Thanks, Alex."

He lowers his head and kisses my pussy gently, then takes a deep breath in.

"You still smell of us. It's truly maddening, Lisichka."

He lifts and bites my knee, and a shiver of excitement runs through me.

My entire body is decorated in bites and bruises, alongside all the crinkles from the cum on me.

I am truly claimed.

"Let's go to the bathroom and let me take care of you."

"If you think your giant cock will get anywhere near my pussy right now, you are sorely mistaken."

My tone is teasing, but it does carry some truth to it.

I am sore—deliciously sore—but sore, nevertheless.

The moment he lifts me and I wrap my legs around him again, a new pain shoots through my core.

Damn it.

My body wrapped around him sends my senses into overload, and as much as I want to say no—I'm sore—I want so much more of him.

But I can't have more.

I shouldn't have more of him right now.

With every step he takes, I feel my will breaking, and my desire for more of him is winning.

The moment I glance over his shoulder, and unlike before, actually have time to take everything in, his bedroom is magnificent.

Beyond magnificent.

It's elegant and sophisticated.

Classy, showcasing old-money richness.

The entire room is perfectly aligned, every item placed with almost obsessive precision.

Everything is dressed in shades of black, white, and gold.

There isn't a single trace of any other colour—total control.

The furniture is handcrafted, each piece bearing exquisite detail, the kind that whispers of private ateliers and artisans flown in just for him.

And then I notice it. Discreet, yet unmistakable—his initials, engraved in gold on the edge of the bedside table, on the drawer handles, even along the base of the mirror.

A quiet flex.

A signature only someone like Elijah would dare leave everywhere without apology.

Every decorative piece screams wealth, class, and restraint wrapped in indulgence.

Then we step into the bathroom, and I forget how to breathe.

The room opens to a floor-to-ceiling window that frames the ocean like a living painting.

Beyond it: three cascading pools, layered into the cliffside.

Built into the rocks, they give the illusion of floating—serene, surreal, majestic.

It's beyond magnificent.

And the way Elijah moves—calm, confident, holding me to his chest as if I weigh nothing, it's his way of telling me without words... *You are the most precious thing in this space.*

It's a lot to take in.

His care is disarming my defences.

The sheer opulence of this bathroom is intimidating as hell, and the ocean view—those floating pools blending into the sea— it's overwhelmingly beautiful.

As I said, I'm not even sure where to look.

It's just... a lot to take in at once.

The bathroom itself is wrapped in slabs of black marble, each cut in immense, seamless pieces, with elegant white veining running like lightning through stone. The walls, floor, and counters gleam under the soft glow of recessed lighting, each surface so polished it reflects back fragments of gold and shadow.

All the furniture is sleek and sculptural, modern minimalism with old-money refinement, and of course, black.

Every accessory gleams in brushed gold, understated but intentional. The fixtures, the mirror frame, even the trim around the monogrammed towels. E.D.—engraved discreetly like a whisper of ownership.

Even the bathtub is a statement: matte black, freestanding, curved like it belongs in a design museum. It radiates quiet power.

The space breathes with tranquillity, elegance, and precision.

A room designed not just for use, but for worship.

Of him. Of his taste. Of control.

I've never seen a bathroom like this in my life—not even in magazines.

It doesn't feel like a bathroom. It feels like a private temple.

And he's holding me like I'm the more valuable thing he has ever touched.

"Fuck! I just realised this tub is way too big," he says in a frustrated tone as he steps into the tub. "You are not allowed to move from next to me." His tone is sharp, controlling. He clears his throat, then sighs. "My sincere apologies, Lisichka. Please forgive me."

He pulls me to his chest, and his heartbeat is drumming so fast it's ready to jump out of him.

He's slightly trembling, and something tells me it's not the temperature in the bathroom.

It's *me*.

Somehow, I'm the one doing this to him.

Because once again, I'm the one completely naked while he stands fully dressed in front of me—yet he's the one breaking apart.

And that fact alone?

It excites me.

This power play he does.

This dominance, always held just at the edge—never too far.

Always watching me.

Always adapting.

It's... endearing, I would say.

The big bad wolf, endearing.

Who would have thought?

"I just want you. I need you next to me."

His voice is a whisper of hope in my ear, and I know he's just battling his own underlying feelings—trying to make the most of the hand that was dealt to us both.

Psychopaths having feelings... well... what do you expect?

Of course we're both navigating uncharted territory now, trying not to cause too much damage to the other.

I say nothing.

There really is nothing to say.

I just rock my hips again—and sure enough, he's rock fucking hard.

I reach for him, kiss him, and then bite his bottom lip—hard.

A feral sound escapes his lips.

"Baby... please. You're sore. I saw your pussy. I really don't think I should go anywhere near it."

His voice is so concerned and raw.

He reaches over and opens the water, trying to set it to a warm temperature.

When he starts pouring some liquid from every bottle he can reach, I know for a fact he has no idea what he's doing, because who in their right mind would add this much?

"How many baths have you made?"

"One."

"This one?"

"This one."

His voice is so small—it's adorable.

I just burst out laughing.

The big bad wolf has made me a bath.

His pants are getting soaked, but he doesn't seem to care.

He's holding me like I'm the only thing keeping him upright—one arm locked under my arse, the other blindly reaching for whatever bottles are in his line of sight.

He's still pouring liquid after liquid into the bath, holding me to himself with a desperation like the world might end if he stops touching me.

When he grabs the salts, I decide he's officially lost the plot.

"Take your clothes off," I murmur. "Let's enjoy the water together."

He hesitates. He does not seem unsure. It's more this panicked look at what it would mean to let me go.

He reluctantly lowers me to my feet in front of him, his arm still crushing me to his body.

When he finally shifts to undress, it's a clumsy, half-desperate process.

He growls when his shirt catches, cursing low—but even then, he refuses to let go of me completely.

His leg wraps around mine, holding me there, as if his body is staking a claim he doesn't trust words to hold.

I glance down at the soaked fabric clinging to him.

At the thigh hooked around my own.

At the absolute refusal to give me even a second of space.

And something flickers inside me—sharp, hot, addictive.

I love it.

This isn't some soft, delicate affection.

It's messy. Overwhelming. Obsessive.

This constant, unspoken demand to keep me close. To keep me his.

It's not just in his touch.

It's in his restraint.

In how he holds on while giving just enough.

In how every movement says: *Mine. Don't go. Stay right here.*

It's extreme.

But so am I.

And maybe the most honest part of me, the part no one ever got even a glimpse of...

Wants this kind of possessiveness.

Wants him.

Unhinged and all.

The moment he's done and lies down, his back resting against the bathtub wall, his hand finds mine.

And once he's comfortable, he gently tugs at my hand.

I'm sore.

I know it physically.

My mind knows it too.

But let's be honest... it's Elijah—naked, wet, in a tub.

Who in their right mind wouldn't straddle him?

I place my legs on either side of him, lowering my pussy directly onto his cock.

The moment they make contact, he freezes in place—as if I've unleashed something feral inside him.

I circle my arms around his shoulders and settle my head on his chest.

He's so tense.

Completely frozen, breath panting, heartbeat out of control.

"It's okay, iubire scumpă. Breathe."

"Easy for you to say, Lisichka. I'm trying—with everything in me—not to get inside you."

His voice is so strangled, as if he's in real, physical pain.

I lift my gaze to his, and sure enough, he is.

He's in pain.

I reach between us, and the moment I touch his cock, he sucks in a huge breath and holds it.

I freeze for a second.

When he says nothing...

I guide him to my entrance, and slowly slide down his length.

"Fuuuuuuuck," he lets out, a guttural moan ripping from his chest.

I start rocking my hips gently, rubbing against him in delicious, circular motions.

This isn't about brutal fucking like before.

This is about relieving the fucking need to having him inside me since the moment he came back to the room.

The aching, maddening need to have him inside me.

To feel all of him.

Again.

"Nice and easy," I whisper, guiding his hands to my arse.

His grip tightens instantly—possessive and demanding.

I place my palms on his shoulders, not just for balance, but to feel him. To ground myself in the trembling tension beneath his skin.

The moment I straddle him and he fills me completely, I feel him in the very centre of my soul.

I don't move.

I let all the delicious sensation overtake my mind and body, as if we are one entity now—consumed and fulfilled in each other in the most intimate way possible.

Then I begin to settle with deliberate, gliding thrusts, each one letting me feel him fully—every ridge, every curve of his cock—deeply, maddeningly, consuming me.

Our bodies align—united, one—and I feel it again.

That need.

That deep, low ache that didn't exist before him.

A hunger I never recognised until he awakened it, carved it out of my very soul.

And now... I'm relieving it.

I shift my hips in slow, circular movements, sliding my pussy along his cock—coaxing friction, heightening the tension coiled between us.

His breath stutters.

A quiet groan curls out of his throat, strangled and raw.

He tilts his head back, eyes squeezed shut, the vein in his neck bulging as he fights to control himself.

"Lisichka..."

His voice is a broken plea, trembling with restraint.

The water laps around us—warm and fragrant—steaming with rich perfume and something else... us.

The scent wraps around us like silk, sinking into skin, into hair, into memory.

I roll my hips again—slower—and his whole body jerks.

One hand fists the edge of the tub while the other claws me closer, fingers digging in as if he's trying to pull me under his skin.

"Fuck..." he breathes, and it's barely a sound.

"I can't... Goddamn it!"

I smile against his mouth as I kiss him, and in that moment, I know.

I have him.

Not just his cock. Not just his body.

All of him.

Every inch. Every breath. Every broken piece.

All mine.

All of him is mine.

My movements quicken—grinding, bouncing, rubbing against him with more pressure, more intent, more possession.

His hands are everywhere—rough, desperate, shaking with the need for more.

He's whispering my name now, over and over, like a man possessed—ruined, undone, worshipping.

And I let go.

Let go into him.

Let him hold me.

Take control.

Submit.

Let him fuck me from beneath—his rhythm chaotic and perfect and filled with something more...

The complete knowing that we are one and the same, in every small or monumental way that matters.

And this treasure we've found in each other?

Absolute.

I arch back—one hand on his shoulder, the other braced behind me.

And he meets me, thrust for thrust.

His cock hitting that deep place inside me I didn't even know had nerve endings, but he's breaking it open, breaking me open—delirious in ecstasy.

When his mouth closes over my breast, teeth grazing, tongue circling.

When he gasps and pulls me harder.

When his voice cracks as he says, "Please, don't stop."

I feel it.

That breaking point.

That sharp, blinding moment where pleasure becomes everything—and it cannot be stopped.

And I know, when I fall over that edge, exploding into a million blissful pieces...

I'll fall into him.

"Fuck, Elijah. I'm so close..."

My moans are out of control, and now all I can think about is that blissful point where every sense explodes—where I see white, stars—where that sweet taste blooms on my tongue.

"Baby... baby... please..."

I don't know what he's begging for, but whatever it is—it's his.

All of me is his.

I want to explode in his arms again.

His thrusts are unhinged now, and water is splashing everywhere around us—our breaths and moans mingling in a symphony of filthy, depraved sounds.

He starts sucking on my shoulder, and the moment he bites down, thrusting hard at the same time, opening me up even more, I cry out so loud it tears from somewhere deeper than my lungs.

And then I detonate.

Like a thousand volts.

Shockwaves of pleasure rip through me, exploding across every nerve in my body.

All I can do is cry out, my pleasure echoing, vision gone, mind blank, and my anchor is Elijah—his moans, his voice, his filthy swearing tangled with the ocean outside and the sound of water splashing from his brutal thrusts.

It's my own personal corner of heaven.

"Lisichka, I'm coming, baby..."

It's all he manages before he pulls me down hard onto him and hot cum explodes inside me, my core going delirious with pleasure.

I roll my hips again—slow, grinding, desperate—rubbing him like a thief, stealing every last drop of his cum, claiming it as mine.

He stops breathing altogether, completely lost in his ecstasy.

I shift my position and wrap my legs around him, all while keeping him inside me.

I curl my arms around his shoulders, pulling him closer, cocooning him in me like a clinging little animal wrapped around her protector.

"Fuck, baby. That was insane."

His voice is raw, hoarse, and so damn sincere.

"Fuck, I love this position. It's like you're clinging to me."

I laugh—hard—because that's exactly what I'm doing.

Clinging. Needing. Keeping him mine.

Chapter Twenty-One

Elijah

I was privileged to a life of opulence and luxury from the day I was born. Luxury, power, and refinement were always part of my day-to-day life. My parents provided a life of comfort for me and my sister, giving us everything we could ever want.

What I have achieved since losing them is immeasurably superior to anything my father and his Pakhan could have even dreamed of. Yet all that power, luxury, unmistakable opulence—it all pales, dissolving into nothingness compared to having Lisichka in my arms, taking control and demanding her pleasure out of me like she just did.

It was undoubtedly the most beautiful moment of my life—when she took control and demanded her satisfaction. The way she conquered my entire being with nothing more than simple movements, touches, and whispers shattered my connection to reality completely.

By the time she submitted and I took over, fucking her desperately, there was no universe anymore—because she had swallowed it entirely into her existence.

All my insides are completely and utterly full of my Queen. I don't want—and I most definitely do not need—anything else except her.

The realisation slips in as the warm water caresses both our bodies and the perfume of luxury oils invades our nostrils. But to me... to me, all I can truly sense is our scent, mingling together once more. It's intoxicating and addictive—like our own personal brand of opiates.

"That smells really nice." Her breath tickles against my chest as she whispers the words.

"I know. You always smell mouthwatering."

She lifts her gaze to mine, and the way she clings to me like this—while I look down on her for once—shatters my mind into a thousand pieces. She is consuming me... everything about her is complete overload to my very being.

"Do you ever get your head out of the gutter?" she says in that unmistakable challenging tone of hers. Her point might stand stronger if my cock weren't still buried inside her—and at even the slightest hint of dirty talk, he twitches inside her.

"Apparently not, by the looks of it." She continues, rewarding me with one of those breathtaking smiles of hers.

I know now, without a doubt—the day I die, I'll die a happy man. Because the last thing flashing through my mind will be my Lisichka's smile. Whatever comes after this doesn't matter, because I have her.

"I was talking about the lilac," she continues, tugging at the hair on my chest. I wince slightly, though I kind of like it. "One of the bottles you used has lilac."

"Do you like it?" My tone is neutral, but studying my Queen is my life's greatest mission. I've researched and analysed every scrap of data I could ever find on her. I know everything out there is to know about her—yet the thirst for more knowledge eats me alive. I know there are still so many things I'm completely clueless about when it comes to her, and that doubt devours me.

"Yes. It's delicate and elegant. It's one of my favourites."

Jackpot. Yes. Give me more. I want more. I want it all.

Information: stored. Catalogued. Ready for future use.

"Plus, it's purple," she adds as an afterthought whisper.

Catalogued.

"What other flowers do you like?" Give me more. I beg you—give me more.

"I love lisianthus and white imperial lilies. Lisianthus have this almost unrealistic elegance to them, while imperial lilies are magnificently beautiful and have an extraordinary perfume as well."

I don't listen with my ears to the new information she shares with me. I absorb it. I drink it in—straight from her lips to my core, to the very centre of my mind and subconscious, where only she and knowledge of her live.

She's just shared something so deep, so personal. What she doesn't know yet is that every piece of information I gather about her is stored—weaponised to reshape my world so she'll love it more when she discovers more and more about me.

The next time I touch my phone, this information will be put to use. And she'll fall a little more for me.

"Enough about me." She pinches me again, but this time I don't flinch. Only the pleasure of her touch registers in my mind. "I already know you did your homework on me, and you know far too much about me as it is. How about you tell me more about yourself?"

"Ask me anything." I surrender completely to her will as I pull her closer to my chest.

She takes a moment, then asks, "Do you have any family?"

"No."

A few moments pass. She tries to pull back—and involuntarily, I tighten my grip around her so hard she can't move at all.

"Well, you're squashing me now, and I don't like it. Please let go." Her voice is calm and collected, but there's a definite tone of authority that tells me to obey.

So I shift my hands to either side of her hips, pinning her in place, and allow her to straddle me once more. I might have been semi-hard this entire time, buried inside her, but this new angle is quickly bringing me back to full, hardcore steel—ready to break her open again.

"Don't even think about it. The water helped, but I need a break." She holds my gaze, sealing the words of my despair.

If it were up to me, I'd be inside her for the rest of my life. But I know she has a say in this, so I reluctantly move my hands to her breasts and let her decide whether she wants to move off me for a while.

The moment she lifts from my cock, the loss of her warmth is so visceral, so palpably intrusive in my subconscious, that for a split second I want to lunge at her and force her back onto me. But the instant she winces in pain, I pull back immediately—knowing I need to give her time.

She moves across from me, and this fucking bath is so big I feel like demolishing it right now. What the fuck was I thinking when I decided on such a massive tub?

Actually—it was installed for decoration, not functionality. At no point in my life did I ever make estate decisions with a partner in mind. A point I'm rectifying as we speak.

But I digress.

She leans against the back of the tub, and only her ankles still touch me. An all-consuming panic overtakes me.

I'm on her so fast the water splashes out of the bath again. I take her leg, place her foot against my chest, and begin rubbing her thigh and calf in a soothing massage. Her head falls back, and I see how much she's enjoying it. So I take her other leg and give it the same attention.

When my mind—and my cock—are screaming at me to tease her, I lift one of her feet, gently, deliberately, and begin to lick and suck at her toes.

When she lets out that delicious moan, I know I'm going to devour all ten little piggies if it's the last thing I do in this life. I circle my tongue around each toe—nipping, sucking, pulling—while she moans and shatters under my touch.

"That feels amazing, iubire scumpă, and I cannot wait to incorporate it into some sex play. But I really need your mouth free to tell me more about yourself. I didn't have all your resources to study you, and it makes me feel uneasy. One-word answers are not acceptable, by the way."

I let the last toe slip from my mouth with a pop and place her foot against my temple. Goddamn, this woman is consuming me. There is no length I wouldn't go for her. If she wanted my life, I would gladly give it to her.

"I don't have a family anymore. Except the one I created for myself. But no—I don't have blood-related family."

She studies me for a second, then asks, "Did I not hear someone at the wedding speaking about your daughter?"

I smile and rub her foot, taking my time, savouring the feel of her skin against mine.

"Yes. I have a daughter. But she isn't my biological daughter. I took her."

"You took her?!" She tries to pull back, to sit up straighter—but fuck that. That's not happening.

"What do you mean?"

"I was in Africa on a business trip, bored to death by this business tycoon, in a deal I was being dragged into, when I heard this cry. This animalistic, primal cry of a little girl. There was only one other time I'd heard something like that, and I knew I had to act."

She pulls hard at her foot, and this time she succeeds in cutting all contact.

The moment her touch is gone, something in me fractures at the loss. She stands taller, and once again she looks down on me.

Her height, I notice, is actually much smaller than mine—contrary to what I first thought. But her presence, her authority—even over me—makes her feel as tall as I am.

Her features tighten at my words. She's not pleased—that much is certain—and when she stands to get out of the bath, I feel like I'll be the one screaming in pain.

"Lisichka, no..." My voice trails off as I reach for her hand to pull her back to me.

"Listen, fucker! I am not some small, little woman you can feed half-truths to and expect me to walk away happy." She lifts her leg and kicks me hard in the ribs.

"You fucking know your place with me, Elijah—or this is not going to work!"

She's right. I'm so used to keeping everything to myself. Everyone and everything is so detrimentally inferior to me that even speaking to them has always been a painful daily chore. And in that, I'm completely missing the truth—that she needs to know me, and I need to learn how to speak to her.

If my need to know her is like a living, breathing organism, then surely she must feel the same about me.

As she lowers her leg, I take it, kiss her foot, and place it against my chest.

"You're right. My sincere apologies, Lisichka." I study her gaze, and she reads my sincerity. Her features soften, just a little.

"Let's dry off, and then we can talk more."

I stand and gently guide her out of the bath, drying her carefully. The fact that she lets me take care of her—lets me touch her as much as I want, feel her skin against mine—is the most generous, electrifying gift she could ever give me.

When it's my turn to dry off and I realise I'll lose my connection with her, I don't think twice—I place my foot gently on top of hers, just so I don't lose contact completely.

"Oh shit," she squeaks quickly. "Is your toe supposed to look like that?"

I look down, and sure enough, I've put the foot with the pulled nail on her. It's red, swollen, angry—probably from the bath we just had. But for the life of me, no pain registers, because I'm completely lost in her.

"No. Sorry about that." I pull my foot back, forget about finishing drying myself, and take her hand in mine to lead us to the bedroom.

"Wait. What happened?"

"I accidentally snipped it off when I was fucking you in the office." Her face drops—and it looks adorably comical. "I was really engaged, busy, and lost my damn mind in you. What did you expect?"

"Well, no wonder my pussy is so sore. You pounded into me like a savage, barbaric man!" Her words are a faint insult, but the corner of her mouth betrays her.

"Come." She takes over and guides me onto one of the bath loungers, where I sit while she starts opening cupboards and drawers in search of the first aid kit.

When she finds it, she kneels before me—and no sane man would stay soft if the woman made for him kneels at his feet. Sure enough, my cock jolts to attention at lightning speed. But she ignores it—or at least tries to—as she gently cleans my toe.

"Does it hurt?"

"I'm not sure."

She lifts her gaze to mine and arches a brow. "Are you one of those who doesn't feel pain like the rest of us?"

"No. I most definitely understand physical pain. My brain registers it. I'm just consumed by you, and I can't feel everything the same right now. All my body, mind, and soul are singing your tune, my Queen."

She stops applying betadine where my nail should be, and our eyes meet again. It's written all over her features too—she knows exactly what I mean.

We're both trying our best to navigate what's happening between us, our bodies and minds struggling to keep up with the new information, the flood of feelings and sensations that shouldn't exist in the first place. It's overwhelming for both of us—overwhelming in the most delicious, delirious way.

She finishes dressing my toe, then stands. In the process, she flicks my cock with the tip of her fingers, and a full-body shiver rips through me.

"Good boy," she says, winking before walking toward the bedroom.

I'm completely lost in what just happened. Transfixed. Trapped in a world made only for the two of us.

She settles on the bed, her back resting against the headboard, then beckons me to take a seat beside her.

She is so beautiful—naked, radiant, standing tall in the middle of our bed. I only hope she understands that she's here with me from now on.

And I hope she doesn't notice when I place the second tracker—because that fine arse needs one. More importantly, the part of my brain poisoning me with doubt, whispering that she might run, needs to be silenced. At the moment, it torments me with fear that the first tracker will fail.

I rush to the door and grab the tray of food. She's sore, but she must be hungry too.

One look down and I know—it's chaotic. Complete madness, like a child or a very, very drunk man lost his mind in a pantry. There's no way we can eat this abomination of a meal. But on the other hand, I won't allow anything else near her.

Shit. I fucked up.

I place the tray on the bedside table and sit across from her, one of my legs encircling her body again. The moment our skin touches, it's like I can breathe again. My lifeline reconnects, and I just take her in.

She is magnificent. By far superior to anything I've ever seen. She truly is my equal.

"Very well," she says in a calm tone. "Now spill it."

Chapter Twenty-Two

Elijah

Perfect. She is perfect in every single way. Demanding, efficient, clear, ruthless. She knows what she wants, and she doesn't hesitate to demand it—even from me.

"Yes, I took her," I say in that warm voice that never ceases to amaze me simply by existing in me. I take her hand and trace lines across it with the tip of my fingers. I know I need to tell her everything about me. And I will.

I'm just afraid she'll be afraid when she learns all the horrendous things I've done. I've achieved extraordinary things, yes. But I've also done despicable things—at least by some people's standards. She is like me, and she will understand the logic behind my actions. But the delivery of that judgement might be more than she's ready for. And that is what I fear.

I draw in a deep breath and steady myself. This is it. The moment of no return.

"Yes, I took her. As I said, this man was trying to convince me to do business with his organisation. I wasn't even remotely interested, but another client insisted on the meeting. I was bored out of my mind that day, so I agreed.

Five minutes in, I knew it was a mistake. I was already planning my escape route when I heard the first scream—and everything in me stopped.

It was the same scream my sister made when she watched our parents being killed."

The moment the words leave my mouth, her hand tightens around mine, and I could not adore her more for it.

This is compassion.

Compassion... from a psychopath?

Yes.

We're not supposed to be capable of such a thing. And yet, she understands. She reaches through the memory, touches the wound, and makes a connection with me.

"So I made my way to where the screaming came from, and I saw a little girl being hurt. I wanted to kill them all for what they were doing. But as I was about to give the order, I realised—that wasn't my kill to make. It was hers.

So I took her with me. I gave her a chance to become everything she could be—and maybe, one day, to return and make that kill."

She cups my cheek and runs her thumb over my bottom lip, then leans in and kisses me. The kiss is so soft, barely there—completely at odds with the way we're both built.

"You gave her a choice," she whispers against my lips. "That's the greatest gift you could have given her."

"It's quite funny, actually. Her suitcases have been packed for years now, waiting for the day she goes back to make that kill. But they just sit there, untouched, in her apartment. I suppose she still needs more time."

"Now tell me about your family. We can come back to your daughter."

I sigh again, then shift beside her, my back pressing into the headboard, and pull her onto my lap. My intent was to feed her while I told her more about myself. But the moment she settles against me and notices the food, she bursts out laughing. Hard.

"Who prepared that?"

I say nothing.

She turns to me and arches a brow. "Were you drunk? Or perhaps high as a kite?"

She bursts out laughing again at her own joke, and I can't help but join her. The way she teases me—constantly pushing, constantly challenging me, it's such a fucking turn-on.

No one in my entire life has ever had the courage to talk back to me. Well... except Dominic, at his wedding, when he was freaking out. But that's in the past—overlooked, because he somehow made it work with me and Lisichka. Therefore, he gets to keep his life—and now even the estate I'd been planning to give them.

"Let's see," she goes on in a mocking tone. "Crackers but no cheese, pickles but no meat, cold cuts but no bread or butter, lollies, gummy bears..." She turns and gives me a once-over. "Gummy bears, Elijah? Seriously?" She shakes her head in disbelief, clearly assuming they're mine.

"Lisichka, those weren't mine. We have plenty of people living on the estate. At a minimum, over twenty guards stay here full-time, plus the rest of the staff."

"Yeah, yeah." She dismisses me with a flick of her wrist, then starts unloading the tray, setting things between us on my lap. I know she's doing it on purpose, to provoke me some more.

But the moment the jar of pickles lands on my lap, the cold shock makes me yelp instinctively—and she bursts out laughing.

I know that laughter now. It's the sound she makes when she gets exactly the result she wanted. The satisfaction of her challenge, her tease.

And I love it.

"Chocolate glaze but no ice cream. Well, for that alone you should be kicked in the balls—because there is nothing better in this world than ice cream. And for you to bring the tease but not the product? Beneath you."

She glares at me... then smiles and winks.

Ice cream. Check.

She finally gives up and leans back, then pushes everything aside, except the pickles. She studies the jar and nods in approval, not sure if it's to me or to herself. Then she opens it and takes a drink straight from the liquid.

I've never seen anyone do that before, and it surprises me. I didn't know people drank the liquid. But if my Queen does it... then it must be good.

"What? Why are you looking at me like that?"

All this information is stored so carefully in my mind that I'm already trying to figure out which country I could take her to that has plenty of pickles and ice cream. Maybe Turkey?

"Nothing, Lisichka. I'm just glad you found something you like."

"These gherkins are really nice. They've got dill and other spices in them, so the brine is delicious too."

Her eyes shift for a moment, and it's like a glimpse into a part of herself that's truly hidden from everyone. And she just opened it for me, let out a tiny treasure.

She takes a gherkin out, and the moment she bites into it there's a crisp crunch—followed by a little moan of pleasure slipping from her lips. She's really enjoying this pickle. Who would have known?

I can't even remember the last time I had a pickle, but whoever brought this into my house is going to be rewarded for it.

"Continue." She gestures at me with the pickle.

I don't even remember what I was thinking, let alone what I was about to share with her. Somehow—without even trying—she disarms me. Everything about her pulls me deeper into her orbit.

The moment she finishes her gherkin, she takes another sip of the brine, then replaces the cap and sets the jar back on the tray.

"I'm distracting you with my eating. That's okay." She smiles at me. "All of that can wait."

She pushes everything off the bed, then turns and straddles me. The moment her legs circle around me, I instinctively wrap my arms around her and pull her against my chest.

She rests her head over my heart, and the feel of her like this—both of us naked, completely engulfing each other—this sense of fullness overtakes me so completely that I shiver in her arms.

"You feel it?" she whispers against my chest.

"Yes." My voice is so small, so raw. "I didn't know this even existed."

"Same," she breathes, then presses a kiss to my chest. "Now tell me, iubire scumpă. I want to know it all."

I kiss the top of her head and pull her tighter into me. Every time she calls me by my pet name—her sweet love—I unravel a little more.

"I was born into the Bratva in Moscow. My father was one of the *Sovetnik*, sworn into the brotherhood since birth. He was the Pakhan's advisor. My father was a strategist, and no decisions in the brotherhood were made without first consulting him.

We weren't raised like children. We were raised as Bratva. We had a life of comfort and luxury, and we were exposed early to the true life of darkness and power.

When I was twelve, my father had a disagreement with the Pakhan over expanding the brotherhood's business into human trafficking."

I take a deep breath, because the thirst for blood that was born in me that day is starting to rise again.

"I always found that ironic—because of how my father took my mother."

"Wait." She quickly shifts in my arms. "Who did your dad take? Your mum? Why did he take your mum?"

"There's a bit of backstory there, but the short version is this: my father was on a business trip to Morocco, settling some shipment issues in the region. He was in the car, driving back to the hotel, and it was raining like hell.

Then he spotted her—on the side of the road. A woman dancing in the rain, arms wide open, her covering fallen from her head. She walked and spun, glancing up at the sky from time to time.

The moment the car reached her, he opened the door... and took her."

Lisichka jolts upright, and if glaring could kill, I'd be dead already.

"He did what?!" she yells in my face.

"It's okay, Lisichka. My mum was no soft woman. She once knocked him out with a frying pan for speaking back to her."

That seems to please her, because the murderous look eases a little.

"I'm not sure how they made it work in the beginning. I heard stories... but I know he never forced himself on her. She told me once the only reason he's still alive is because she allowed it. The fact that he never forced her in any way, that's the reason she loved him."

That makes my Lisichka relax further, and she settles back into my arms.

"Wait! Where were you planning to take me?!" she yells again, trying to pull back—but this time, I don't let go. I tighten my arms around her, imprisoning her against my chest.

"Yes. But there's no need to be mad about it—you came to your senses and gave in to us."

She pushes at my chest like a feral animal.

"Look at where we are, my Queen. Look at what's happened between us. Tell me I was wrong to want to be with you."

That makes her calm down, because she knows this was inevitable.

"Continue," she commands, biting my nipple.

Fuck, that hurt.

"My father did not want to get involved in human trafficking. He despised it, actually. I'm not sure where that hatred was rooted, but he couldn't accept expanding into that market.

I heard him arguing with the Pakhan at our house, days before the massacre—that people should never be broken down to such a degree that they're no longer human, just mere objects of transaction.

The Pakhan laughed in his face. Called him soft. Weak.

Two days later, the entire Bratva was ordered to execute us."

The pain of that day is as fierce in my memory now as it was when it happened. No amount of time, space, blood, or wealth could ever compensate or erase it.

She tightens her arms around me, and her comfort does exactly that—comforts me. For the first time since that day, I'm sharing this with someone. I'm sharing my pain.

"How did you escape?"

"I didn't. I was there the entire time." My voice is so raw.

"My father was overprotective about security—to the point of paranoia. Maybe that's why the Pakhan sent the entire Bratva to execute us. Every one of our homes had panic rooms and hidden spaces in the walls, places we could retreat to in case of attack.

When the first shots rang out, I was with my mother and sister. My mother shoved us into one of the wall spaces, but she heard movement near the door and slammed it shut before she could slip in herself. Through the crack, I saw it was one of our men with my father. My sister started screaming and pounding on the wall, begging my mother to open it. When she finally did, my sister leapt into their arms—but before anything else could happen, the attack hit full force. Screaming. Gunshots. Closing in at terrifying speed.

My father kicked the wall shut again, trapping me inside. I was left alone... forced to watch.

The Vor who had convinced the Pakhan to expand into human trafficking strolled into the room like he owned it. He laughed in my father's face, called him weak and pathetic, then turned to my mother and sister. He said it would be more fun to kill my parents first—so my sister would see it all.

And so he did.

He gave the order to execute our men. Then my parents. Then my sister.

The scream she let out when my mother collapsed beside her will haunt me forever. My father—who had always seemed the largest, strongest man in the world—fell like nothing. His body gave in, and the bullet cut him down as if he wasn't a giant, but just a mortal man pretending to be one."

We sit there in silence, my words still pulsing between us. Heavy. Irrevocable.

I know she'll ask more. I know that by the time the sun rises, she'll know me as well as I know her. Every secret laid bare. Nothing left in the shadows.

"Did your family know what you are?" she finally asks, pulling me back to the present.

"Yes. They figured it out quickly. My sister was four years younger than me, and once, when she was maybe three or four, she wandered too close to the guard dogs on one of our estates. They barked, and she came running to me in tears, clinging to me for protection.

I remember the rage. That day, something inside me snapped. My father arrived in the middle of the chaos, he saw me, and by the end, he knew. He could see it in my eyes, in the way I didn't hesitate when violence was needed of me and I had to protect what was mine. He was afraid. I saw it in him. He understood I was different.

But to his credit, Lisichka, he never made me feel ashamed of that hunger. From then on, he brought me into his meetings, into his interrogations, despite my mother's protests. Eventually, even she understood that I needed it—that release.

They were good parents, Lisichka. And then someone thought they could take what was mine."

"So, back to that day you lost your family. How did you make it out?" She lifts her gaze to me, studies my features, then, seeing only herself in them, kisses my chest and settles once more against me.

"I didn't. They looked for me for a while, then assumed I ran. I was trapped in the wall for two days until I finally picked the door mechanism to let myself out. The rotting corpses everywhere, the smell and the sight were a lot to take in. Without a doubt, for someone not like us, Lisichka, they would have lost their mind in that wall. The only mercy they did for me was taking my family's corpses away with them. Only the guards' dead bodies were everywhere. I went to one of the safes and took all the money with me. I ran and hid in one of the most run-down suburbs of Moscow for two months, listening to all the whispers on the street. I hid until they stopped looking for me. There, I was not myself. There I was just another orphan on the streets, begging for money and food. I dressed as a homeless kid, and eventually, when they stopped checking every exit out of Moscow, I took a train and made a run for it. Then I slowly made my way to the only place I knew would take me in. My mum's family."

"Right. Were you close to them?"

"No. Never met them before that day. My dad never returned to Morocco after he took my mum. He was desperate to keep her, and her family wanted her back, but they knew they couldn't stop in Russia to claim her."

She laughs softly in my arms, shaking her head. "Your dad was hilarious."

"He was. I enjoyed speaking with him. It was always pleasant, nothing like the suffocating feeling of speaking to others."

"Yep. I know what you mean. Anyway. Continue."

"My mum wrote to them from time to time, so I knew the address—I just never knew they were rich as well." I lift her chin with my fingers and smile. "You'll like this part, Lisichka. By the time I reached their gate, I had changed into normal clothes, but I had to catch a fishing boat from Spain to Morocco because I'd run out of money. So, the moment the guard saw me at their gate, I was dirty again—and smelly as well." She rewards me with that amazing laughter, and the memory of me all alone at the gate of strangers suddenly feels a lot easier to carry.

"They didn't believe me, of course, but at least they took me in until the DNA test came back. My grandma kept studying me the whole time, and when the results came in, she broke into tears, saying I looked just like my mum."

"When did you go back to Russia?"

"I was eighteen when I got everything ready to spill the blood of those who had taken from me. For me, the attack was inevitable. My grandfather organised a new, better deal with the port of Morocco for the Pakhan, and in return he invited him to Russia. He told the Pakhan he would bring containers of fabric, gold, and goods for him and his family to enjoy the riches of Morocco. What he actually brought were five containers full of our men, over one hundred and fifty with us.

By then, I was already doing well for myself hacking in all sorts of places, and I discovered that the Lieutenant General of Police in Moscow, equivalent to the Commissioner here in England, was dirty as hell. Unfortunately for him, he was also having an affair with the wife of the Minister of Defence. I very kindly sent him the pictures and videos of them fucking, and he agreed, very eagerly, to assist us in moving the containers into place for the takeover.

After we took over and I captured the Pakhan, he was less than thrilled when I tied the former Pakhan to my car and dragged him through central Moscow for everyone to see him bleed to death."

Lisichka lifts her gaze to mine, and there is no emotion there. Nothing. She is her true self in her truest form.

"He was naked," I say, matter-of-fact.

She bursts out laughing at the remark, her eyes shifting into those funny little semicrescents again. It's overwhelming for me.

"How did it feel?" she asks once her laughter settles. "To kill the man who took from you?"

I take a moment to weigh my words and settle my thoughts. "Empty." One word, spoken with truth. She studies me for a moment, and I realise she needs more.

"In that very moment, seeing him hurt, seeing inside of him, watching him in complete agony was delicious, of course. My body was humming with pleasure. But after I took complete control and became the Pakhan, I realised that the Vor's son, the one who started it all, had actually helped us kill his father. So I did not kill him. I kept him locked up for a while as I was setting up my operation in Moscow.

Once everything was in place, I realised I felt empty.

My father was not my Sovetnik. In my mind growing up, I always knew I would take over, but always with my father by my side. Now that I was Pakhan, and everyone was swearing loyalty to me, I knew I wanted nothing to do with any of it. Killing that fucker and dismantling his entire empire did not bring my father back, or my mum, or my sister. I was still alone."

I have never admitted that to anyone before. Sharing such a deep memory with my Queen makes me feel vulnerable—yet strong at the same time—because I know she will guard it with care. The moment she tightens her arms around me, I know I'm right. My past is safe with her.

"Oh, that's when I found Buddy as well," I add quickly, remembering that bit of information.

"Who's Buddy?" She tilts her head up to look at me.

"Buddy is my second-in-command."

"Is he the African guy at the wedding with the line scars?"

"Yes, that's him." I nod, then trace her jawline with my thumb. "I found him in the middle of the attack. The Pakhan was eating at one of the restaurants he frequented, and then he'd force himself on any of the women there. That is how vulnerability starts in an organisation—repetition, patterns your enemies can learn and exploit. I studied him for years to know everything about him. I knew that was the best place to strike. So I did. We killed everyone inside the restaurant and took the Pakhan.

As I made my way through the rooms, I came across one packed with people. They panicked at the sight of me—covered in blood, with a knife and a gun in my hands. They squealed in shock, crying, all of them except one. Naturally, I thought he was some kind of leader or one of the Pakhan's men. He was kneeling before me, my gun to his temple, ready to execute him. But when I looked into his eyes, there was nothing. Life or death meant nothing to him—me taking his life would mean nothing. That's when I knew he'd been trafficked too. His life wasn't his anymore, and he knew it.

I spared him and tried to shake him off, but he wouldn't have it. He swore his loyalty at my feet a few days later and refused to stop being my shadow, even after we beat him. He insisted his life was now mine, and he would not leave my side."

I look over at the time—it's almost 4 a.m. Fucking hell. I hadn't even realised how fast it passed. I pull the duvet over us. "Let's sleep, Lisichka."

She lets out a loud yawn, and I start laughing.

"I'm not bored, I swear. I'm just really tired. Someone fucked me real good, and I'm still trying to take it all in," she says, her voice adorably sleepy.

"You'll most definitely take all of me," I murmur, sliding my hands to cup her arse. "Let's sleep for now, my Queen. There's a lifetime for me to share myself with you."

Chapter Twenty-Three

Monica

My entire life, I dreaded going to sleep—because in sleep, I wasn't in control of my surroundings anymore. But falling asleep next to Elijah? It's the easiest thing I've ever done. I simply closed my eyes, and I don't remember a thing until now... when I feel something wet lapping at my core.

For a moment, I wonder, Why am I so wet? What happened to me? But then his tongue drags a long lick from my arse to the top of my clit, and a jolt of pleasure rips through me. That's when my brain finally clicks in—he's eating me out again.

I lift myself on my elbows and look down at this mountain of a man with his face buried between my legs, and I smile.

"Well, good morning to you too. Ohhhh..." My words trail off, and his reply comes in the form of rolling my clit between his lips—and it's pure magic. He pulls back just as he slides two wicked fingers inside me, dragging them straight to my most sensitive spot. Then he meets my gaze and winks.

"Don't mind me, Lisichka. Please continue sleeping if you like. I'm just eating my breakfast." Then he dives back in, lapping at my pussy like a man starved, all the while his fingers dancing inside me. I collapse back onto the bed—because fuck me, this is the kind of waking up a woman could get used to.

I stretch, and as I move my pelvis, he shifts with me, fucking me with his tongue while his fingers work my clit. That mix of sharp pain and extreme pleasure rips a guttural moan from me, and I feel my whole pelvis heat as blood rushes to the area.

"Yes, baby, give me more! Give me all!" Elijah's words are muffled against my pussy, and I feel myself getting wetter with every lick. He drags me to the edge of the bed and kneels before me, then lifts my arse and quickly shoves a pillow beneath my lower spine. My pelvis hangs over now, stretched almost straight.

He moves to my entry and starts savagely lapping again. I hear him cursing into my pussy before he latches his mouth over my pussy and sucks hard. I scream at the sensation tearing through me—it's delicious and maddening, filthy, dirty, depraved—and yet I want to give him everything he craves. I roll my hips against his face, and the sound of his approving moan is all the reward I need.

I start grinding harder, and then he begins working my clit in deep, painful circles. All my blood is dancing in my veins with pleasure and ecstasy, making me a wreck in his hands. He curses again, then completely lifts my arse off the bed and onto his face, tongue-fucking me with savage hunger.

His strokes inside me are precise, deliberate, and when he starts rolling his tongue over my most sensitive spot, I detonate. I roll my hips harder against his face, demanding my release, and he lets me. He licks my g-spot with the expertise of a man born to eat pussy, all the while rubbing my clit to madness.

I ride the wave of bliss, screaming my pleasure for his ears to devour, as white stars explode across my vision.

The moment I feel his fingers at my arse, I'm already coming down from my high. Then I hear him sucking on his fingers before placing them back on me. He traces circles around my back hole, all the while drinking me in and moaning his despair for more. It's filthy, depraved—his hunger for my cum—and yet it turns me on so much I can feel myself winding up again.

The moment his finger slips into my back hole, the edge of ecstasy comes rushing at me with lightning speed. He curses into my pussy again, then spits on my arse while gently fucking me with one finger. The extra wetness is exactly what I needed, and when he adds a second finger, I feel a sharp pinch on my arse cheek. The pain is perfect—exactly what I needed to detonate again. As he sucks my pussy, he finger-fucks my arse into oblivion, and I scream my orgasm with a force I've never felt before.

He rolls his fingers inside me, massaging in a way I can't even describe. There's resistance, yes, but no pain—only sensation. More than delicious. And I know I want more. I want it all from him.

"Baby, will you let me take your arse?" he breathes against my pussy, his lips trembling with restraint.

"Please..." His voice cracks—low, broken, desperate. Like he's ashamed of how much he wants it, and terrified I might say no.

This aching need inside me is relentless. A living thing. It coils through my belly, my thighs, my chest—demanding his cock, his mouth, his weight, his everything. I want it all. I want him to take everything. I want it all with him.

"Give me your cock, iubire scumpă," I whisper, my voice soaked in hunger, in surrender.

He moans—moans—like my words cracked him open. Then he presses his mouth to my pussy in one deep kiss before rising.

He's huge. Not just his cock—him. His voice. His words. His presence is overwhelmingly big. Everything about him is big. Monumental. His body is all muscle, tattoos, ridges, and valleys. He's so big he eclipses everything else. But right now, in this moment, he's just a man before his woman—on the verge of losing himself.

He locks eyes with me as he spits into his hand, rubbing it over my pussy and letting it drip between my cheeks. His gaze never leaves mine—not for a second—as he circles my tightest place with the flushed head of his cock.

"This might hurt, my Queen," he whispers, almost broken. "But I'll make it better. I swear." His eyes are full of concern and arousal, and I just want to bathe in them.

"You sure?" he asks, voice hoarse. "I'll be careful. I'll make it feel good. Just... say yes again."

"I want it." I hold his gaze. "I want all of you."

He groans, then pushes.

The stretch is instant and searing. My body clenches around him, resisting his size, and I gasp—eyes wide, fingers gripping the sheets as he presses deeper. The burn licks at my nerves, sharp and raw... but beneath it, something blooms. Fullness. Pressure. A filthy, addictive pleasure that makes my stomach drop and my nipples harden instantly.

He's slow at first. Unforgivingly slow.

My body strains to take him, stretched so tight it feels like I might tear.

I burn. I shudder. I *feel.*

He's inside me—really inside me. Not just my body, but everywhere. There's no part of me he hasn't claimed. And I let him. No—I want him there.

"Fucking hell," he breathes, sweat beading on his brow. "Baby, you're breaking me into pieces."

He pushes deeper, watching every flicker of expression cross my face—the pain, the awe, the desperate pleasure stirring in my belly. I whimper, overwhelmed. And when he bottoms out, I feel him everywhere. Stretching me. Holding me open. Owning me.

And then—his hand slips between us. His fingers sink deep into my pussy, gliding easily through how wet I am for him. They sink deep and slow, every movement magnified by the stretch. His cock in my arse. His fingers in my cunt. The pressure between them makes my entire body tremble.

"Iubire," I pant, barely able to speak.

"That's it," he growls, voice low and broken with restraint. "Feel how deep I'm inside you."

And fuck, I do. I feel everything—his cock dragging against my insides, pressing into the back of my cunt through that thin wall. His fingers plunging in, curling just right.

It's obscene. It's overwhelming. It's perfect.

My body clenches tight—one place squeezing him, the other sucking him in deeper, wetter, more desperate.

"Look at your arse taking my cock so well," he growls, thrusting harder into me now. "You'll take anything and everything I give you. Isn't that right, my Queen?"

I can't speak. Can't breathe. My body is nothing but heat and tension, a climax building so strong it feels like it could break me.

He groans like it hurts, like my voice alone drags him closer to the edge. "You feel that, my Queen? That's me everywhere. No part of you untouched." He leans over me, his mouth on my breasts now, lapping and nipping at them.

I nod, shaking, lips parted. "I feel... so much. I can't..."

"Yes, you can," he growls. "You'll take it. You'll take me. You'll take all of me!" His words are not kind—they're commanding, authoritative, demanding my submission.

He curls his fingers inside me as he thrusts into my arse, slow but deep, dragging a moan from the pit of my soul. My head falls back. My legs lock around his hips. I can't stop it anymore. It's building. Rising. Crushing me.

He starts rubbing my clit, slow, devastating circles—while his cock drives into me harder, deeper, his fingers matching the rhythm—and I break. Completely. Fully. Irrevocably. Lost in a sea of pleasure.

I scream my pleasure for the world to hear, sharp and exhilarating.

My whole body spasms violently, wave after wave of climax tearing through me. My vision blanks, and all I can see are white stars. That now-familiar sweetness spreads across my tongue like sugar melting, and my mouth falls open, trembling with the aftershocks.

I don't even register the power of his thrusts until his swearing drags me back to reality—a reality where he's still worshipping my body with barbaric force and a constant, unrelenting need for more.

"Fucking hell!" he grits through clenched teeth. "You're strangling me, baby—demanding what's yours out of me—I'm going to—fuuuuuuck!"

He drives into me with one last brutal thrust and groans, guttural and broken, as he spills inside me—hot and thick and endless. His arms shake. His jaw clenches. And then he collapses onto me, still pulsing, still deep, holding me with desperation.

I hold him back. Breathless. Satisfied. His heart hammers against mine, and I swear... it beats in rhythm with my own.

His weight on me is crushing, but in the best way possible. Because if I die today, if I die like this with the true weight of love pressing me down, I'll die a happy woman, with the image of Elijah burned into my mind.

He pushes up on his arms, his body still heavy over mine, and locks his gaze with me. I swear he's holding back tears—but that's insane, because we don't do feelings, let alone cry. Yet I see it. Something in his eyes is breaking. This was a lot for him too.

I say nothing once more. I don't know what to say. There's nothing that could possibly seal what just happened between us, so I just cup his cheek. He leans into my hand and closes his eyes.

"Is this love?" His voice is so small at first I think I imagined it. But when he sighs, I know he really asked.

"You know I don't know." I trace his lip with my thumb. "It's my turn to tell you I'm feeling everything you are—and I'm scared too."

That makes him open his eyes, and he is so incredibly handsome. The only man I've ever felt physical attraction to is buried deep in my arse, completely crushing me with his weight. He just gave me multiple orgasms, and now he's shivering in my arms.

"This is the first time you've admitted any feelings."

"Honestly, I don't know what to say. If I need to tease you or put you in your place, that's no problem. But this... this is so big I'm speechless. I just don't know."

He rests his forehead against mine and breathes me in deeply.

"You smell mouthwatering, Lisichka," he whispers against my lips.

"It's the lilac thingy in the bathroom." That pulls a laugh out of him, then he presses a gentle kiss to my lips before standing.

"You are so magnificent, Lisichka. Everything about you is designed to break me into pieces. It's very hard for me, baby." His words are so raw and sincere that something in me breaks. I can feel his pain at dealing with all these feelings and sensations.

"Iubire, listen." I lift myself on my elbows. "I'm not sure what this is called. I'm not even sure this is love. If other people even have this, I really doubt it." I pull a face at him, and he laughs again. "Where I'm getting at is, it doesn't matter what it's called. You—your feelings, your pain, your entire self, Elijah—are safe with me. I'm not going to hurt you."

As the words leave my mouth, a tear slips from the corner of my eye. I hadn't even realised I was fighting back tears, just like he was. He brushes it away, then places his thumb on my lips.

"I adore you, Lisichka. More than adore you. I live for you." He leans in again and brushes away another treacherous tear that escaped. "You are forever safe with me. I'm not going to hurt you, my Queen."

We hold each other's gaze, drinking in the other and the monumental moment that just took place. We've completely surrendered to each other.

He pulls out of me, and that delicious burn hits me once more.

"Two seconds, my Queen. I'll quickly wash my cock. I need to be inside you again. I need to fuck my pussy now or my mind might break in two." He bolts to the bathroom; I hear the water running, and the next second he's back with a towel, between my legs, wiping me clean.

"I need to fuck you again, baby. I need to come inside you, and I need to finish off the back of your thighs with my cum as well. I need it, baby. I really need to finish marking you as mine." His voice creaks with need as he wipes at my arse. Then I feel a prick on one cheek, then his teeth sink into my thigh, then the other cheek.

"What..."

"I'm going to mark you as mine forever," he cuts me off before I can ask what that was. "You are my reality now."

Then he stands and sinks his cock into my pussy, fucking me exactly the way his mind demands—raw, dirty, unhinged, and all mine.

Chapter Twenty-Four

Monica

This man is out to get me. I know it now—without a doubt—he's out to destroy me. Well, maybe not destroy exactly, but he is definitely out to ruin my pussy. I'm deliciously sore, content, and satisfied, and if I'm being completely transparent, I'm already planning some new positions that might play perfectly into his kinks. But that's for later. LATER. Right now, me and my pussy desperately need a break because damn—this man and his stamina. What the actual hell?! He releases in me or on me, and then, fifteen minutes later, he's back, asking for more.

When I woke up this time, after passing out. Yes, I did pass out. What else could I have done? He took my cunt, then started kissing and biting my body again. After that, I sucked him off for a bit, and he released on the back of my legs, completely marking me now. You should have heard the animalistic growl he made. One might swear it sounded like a lion marking his territory.

He massaged that cum into my skin until it dried, making sure none of it was wasted. His words, not mine. Then the sight of me, completely marked by his cum, made him hard again. He started fucking me once more, and when I winced in pain, he moved to my back hole, fucking it raw.

Am I complaining? Far from it. I didn't know sex could be like this, and quite frankly, I want more. Right after I get some liquid and food into my body, though, because we've been at this marathon fucking for almost twenty-four hours. And if I'm not fed soon, I swear I'll bite his cock the next time it's in my mouth.

"Iubire..." I nudge at his arm around my waist. "Feed me," I say, fighting back a laugh.

It's like magic to his cock—the damn prick twitches to attention against my arse cheeks again.

"Don't even think about it. You and your cock can take a much-needed rest."

"I don't need to rest," he whispers in my ear before biting down on my shoulder and sucking at the skin. "I can feed you more of my cum whenever you want." His torment continues with kisses trailing along my shoulder and back.

I can already feel myself getting wet—at his words, at his touch, at his lips on me. But then my stomach growls loudly, and he freezes, rigid, as if someone has actually dared to attack us.

"Lisichka, I'm so sorry." His voice breaks behind me, as if he's committed a terrible injustice. "Fucking hell... I'm really bad at this."

His entire body shivers as he tightens his arms around me. "I will learn, my Queen. I swear to you, I'll learn fast how to take better care of you."

I don't even get a chance to reply before he leaps to his feet and offers me his hand. He's most definitely displeased—and as endearing as I find it, there's no need for this. I'm not some delicate flower in the wind waiting to be rescued by the big bad wolf. I can demand what I want.

So I do what I do best, I pinch him back.

"And you better remember it, boy." My voice is all serious and authoritative as I look down at him.

He bursts out laughing and pulls me against his chest. That calms him down—for now, I hope.

"Come, my Queen." His words are spoken so softly, nothing like the fearless man I first met. This side of him—tamed, gentle, almost tender—throws me off balance. I let him lace his fingers with mine and guide me forward.

We leave the bedroom, and he leads me through another door. On the other side is a space that makes me pause. It's not just a wardrobe—it's an entire room, easily the size of my apartment.

Rows of perfectly tailored suits stretch out in front of me. Glass islands float in the centre, displaying watches like they're museum pieces. My gaze drifts across the opulence until it lands on something that makes me freeze: a section gleaming with women's jewellery.

I lift my eyes to him slowly, my hands curling into fists. And in that moment, I really, really want to punch him.

His features are still soft and broken, so I put my fury on pause — he's clearly beating himself up for apparently not being good at taking care of me. I say nothing and keep taking in the room. Opposite us, rows and rows of women's clothes, shoes, bags and every kind of accessory line the walls. An entire wall of perfumes. A. Fucking. Entire. Wall. Of. Perfumes.

I really want to kill him. Well, maybe within an inch of his life. But I will definitely do some damage.

I look up at him again, ready to at least bash him a bit. I try to pull my hand away and that's when I realise he's trembling. FUCK. MY. LIFE. Half of me wants to scream, *I don't want any of this!* — to beat it into him until the moron understands I don't want things. The other half just wants to reassure him that I'm fine. He's fine. We're fine. There's no need to be sad over something so small.

But that's the thing. To me it's small. To him... the idea of not taking proper care of me is breaking him.

I move in front of him, guide his hand to my hip and look up at him. He quickly circles his other arm around my waist and pulls me in. I hold his gaze until he's fully with me, not lost in his own prison.

"Thank you," I say, then lift onto the tips of my toes and kiss his chin.

He lowers his forehead to mine and breathes in. "You like it?" he whispers against my lips.

"Nope. But we can talk about it another time." Brutal honesty to the rescue. My remark makes him laugh, and that's all I need deep in my core — I got it.

"Well, if there's a lilac perfume in that floor-to-ceiling wall of perfumes you made for me, then it's a different story," I tease.

"It's already on its way, Lisichka. I want you to have anything and everything you ever imagined. Nothing is out of reach now, my Queen. The world will kneel before you — I will fucking bring it to its knees for you."

I don't even know what to say. I don't understand this feeling rising in me at his words, so I say nothing. I want to be with him because he is part of me, as much as I am part of him, but I'm quickly realising that, while gifts aren't my love language at all, they're definitely his.

Throwing away all his presents up until now didn't make him understand that I simply don't want things. Never did. I'm not sure whether it comes from how I grew up — having almost nothing, often going without food — or from the fact that I'm autistic, or even that I'm like Elijah in some ways, a psychopath. I just don't have love for things.

Clearly Elijah does, because he went above and beyond to fill this room with things for me.

"When did you do this?" I ask.

"Since that day in the shop, when you placed your hand around my neck."

"Oh! You mean the day I had my pliers around your balls?" I say, fighting back a laugh at his reaction.

"I knew it then, without a doubt," he continues, not missing a beat. "I knew you were like me. I knew somehow this world had made two of us. And I fucking found you." The words are barely out of his mouth when he crushes his lips to mine in a desperate kiss. His lips and tongue aren't sparring with mine. They're conquering me, stealing my breath, my sanity, my power. It's all-consuming, powerful and demanding. I need this as much as he does, and I surrender to him to take from me all that he needs, and to give me all of himself in return.

By the time he pulls back, only his arm around me holds me up — and we both know it. His lips hover over mine, his breaths coming in ragged pants, his cock nudging at my thigh.

"Feed me." I smile against his mouth, then dart my tongue out and lick his bottom lip.

"Lisichka, please," he says. "Every time you say it like that, my mind imagines you on your knees, stuffed full of my cock until I'm feeding you all my cum. Please, my love — I really am trying to do the right thing by you." His voice is raw and desperate, clinging to any scrap of self-control.

"That's because your mind lives permanently in the gutter." I feign innocence.

"That's because you put it permanently in the gutter, woman!" he fires back, then nudges his cock between my thighs and starts thrusting, dry-humping me.

It's not direct contact with my clit, not even penetration, but it's seriously hot as hell. I can feel myself getting wetter by the second, and the more ruthless his thrusts become, the more I want to give in and take another round of his cock inside me.

By the last thread of my sanity, I whisper against his lips, "Feed me, Elijah, or I might faint. I'm so light-headed."

That snaps him back to reality so fast he stops mid-thrust.

"Sorry, Lisichka. I'm really trying, baby, but everything about you screams at my senses to devour you somehow."

"I know! I think some clothes will calm that libido of yours." I feign innocence again, biting back a laugh at his expression. "Admit it, not seeing all of this goodness," I tease, wiggling in his arms and running my hands all over my body, "will calm that libido of yours. At this point, iubire, I'm starting to think you're pumping Viagra by the bucket."

He bursts out laughing so hard his head falls back; his laughter engulfs me in its warmth and serenity, and I'm transfixed watching this mountain of a man melt in my arms like this.

"Viagra or not," he says between fits of laughter, "you are all mine." He wipes at his eyes. "And for what you just said, prepare your arse, my Queen. It will be spanked raw."

The words barely register in my head before he scoops me up and throws me over his shoulder, no say in it whatsoever.

"Excuse me," I say, dangling off his shoulder. "Sane person to caveman."

That earns me a sharp slap on the arse, and I want to tell him what the fuck is wrong with him — maybe even kick him — but the moment I prepare my bite-back, I realise... I liked it. The sting, the burn, the rush of blood to the spot, the sudden wetness between my legs. I liked it.

Let me do it again...

"Excuse me, Mr Savage."

He says nothing.

Oh, it's on!

"Beg your pardon. You don't need to carry me over your shoulder while you search your mansion for more Viagra," I say in my most aristocratic voice. "That should be your tiny little secret," I whisper.

I register the sound and count to three in my head. Surely he didn't spank me three times — that would be absurd. Then my arse explodes in agonising fire; the deep sting of the slaps registers, my blood racing in the area, and I realise... *holy moly, I fucking like being spanked.*

WHAT! THE! ACTUAL! FUCK?!

It's one thing to be submissive. But *liking* being spanked? What the fuck is wrong with me?!

Before I can spiral further in my own head, I hear it...

Slap!

Slap!

Slap!

Slap!

Some land on my arse, others on my thigh, and one square on my pussy. The impact hurls me toward a climax at an alarming rate.

"Stop overthinking this, my Queen. Just give in." He traces a finger along my pussy, then brings it to his mouth and sucks it clean. "Don't think about what you should feel — think about what you are feeling." His voice grows more and more aroused, and I know the cliff of another orgasm is approaching at lightning speed. "Did you enjoy it? Because sure as fuck I did."

He places me on one of the islands of jewellery and settles between my legs. He's so imposing and beautiful — all dominance, demand, and control. I'm trying to process what I feel, what I like, what I don't like. Was there even anything I didn't like about it?

He holds my gaze as he slides his fingers across my pussy, then lifts them for me to see my own arousal. His fingers glisten with my wetness, and it's clear as day — my body enjoyed it faster than my mind could process.

Right. So not only am I submissive to him, but now I like him giving me pain in the form of spanking. My analytical mind offers me two options. One — fight it and tell him to fuck off. Or two — give in. FUCKING. GIVE. IN.

He traces his finger across my lips, and it takes me a moment to realise he's smearing my own arousal. I open my mouth to ask him what the fuck he's doing, but instead he shoves his fingers inside and starts fucking my mouth with them.

"Shhh," he murmurs in a soothing voice. "Just give in, my Queen." He starts peppering kisses on my breasts and along my abdomen. "We'll stop the moment you're not comfortable. We'll stop immediately if you don't like something, my Queen."

He straightens to his full height and looks down at me. "I'm begging you, please. If I mean anything to you, I'll fucking drop to my knees if you want me to. Please, don't shackle yourself to what's expected of you. Let yourself feel whatever you want to feel. Let yourself be free, my Queen."

Fucking hell — his words, his processing of this situation, his processing of his feelings... FUCK!!!

Why does he have to be better at this than me?!

Why can't I process this easier?!

"Lisichka... please," he says as he withdraws his finger from my mouth and sucks on it, all the while holding my gaze. "It's not easy for me either. The only difference is how we grew up. I know how to accept what's in me. I just want you to be free. Completely free. Completely out in the open. Completely happy with who you truly are. Because there is no one like you, my Queen. Truly, there is no one like you."

We stand there for a moment, just taking everything in. The truth is written all over his face. He really means it. He truly believes there is no one like me. And it's true — I don't think there's anyone like him either.

I don't know what to say... so I say nothing. Until it feels too strange, and I crack a joke to deflect.

"You taste better," I say, fighting back a smile.

He bursts out laughing, that deep, rich laughter with his head thrown back. It's beautiful, seeing him laugh so freely at my antics.

"We'll agree to disagree, Lisichka. I'll drink you again once I put some food in your belly."

"Feed me!"

"Oh, you whining baby," he says through fits of laughter. "Hang on." He keeps one arm on my leg while stretching the other toward a robe. He can't quite reach it, but he still doesn't move his hand from my leg.

I slide off the island and take his hand in mine. When he turns to look at me, his gaze is full of concern, as if he's done something wrong.

"This might be easier. Let's get dressed together."

"No, Lisichka. Please..." He trails off and gathers me in his arms. His body is shaking and I have no idea what's going on or how I triggered this. "I need you naked for a bit longer. Just a little longer — a few more days," he whispers into my neck. "We can put the robe on and I'll wrap it tight around you. Nothing will be seen. Even your neck will be covered to some extent. I just... I just need a bit more of you for myself."

Right.

I might not understand it, but I do accept it. Clearly this is another place where I don't fully get his version of things, but I can see it's important to him — so I will allow it.

I pull back until our eyes meet and smile. The relief on his face is palpable, more than I expected.

"What should I say to you? If I say I love you it feels small and ordinary. If I say I adore you it feels common. Tell me, my Queen — what should I say to you?"

I say nothing, because there's nothing I can say. He's the one figuring this out faster than me. I cup his cheek and run my thumb along his jawline.

"I live for you, my Queen."

Chapter Twenty-Five

Monica

I didn't expect the hallway to feel like this. Like a shrine.

The bedroom door closes behind us, and suddenly it's as if I've stepped into a world I'm not meant to touch. The corridor stretches longer than I remembered, polished black-and-white marble cooling my bare feet. Smooth, cold, almost too flawless to walk on.

A gold-lined runner floats down the centre, thick enough to swallow every step. Even it obeys the rules of this house — black, white, and gold. No room for colour. No room for chaos. Power restrained, indulgence in control.

The air smells faintly of something expensive — not perfume, but atmosphere. Like clean fire and polished stone. A scent so distinct I've never encountered anything like it until I stepped into this house.

Along the walls, sleek console tables stand like guards, carved from black lacquered wood with gold inlay so fine it looks like thread. Fresh white orchids bloom from crystal vases — not a petal out of place. Beside each one, a gold tray holds obsidian stones and black candles, their flames flickering as if bowing in prayer. Useless objects... yet perfectly, purposefully placed.

Above them, the mirrors. Large. Gilded. Heavy. Silent judges reflecting a version of me I don't quite recognise. My eyes catch on the centre of each frame — his initials, E.D. So discreet, etched into the gold, I almost miss them.

But once I see them, I see them everywhere.

The hallway isn't a hallway. It's a stage. Every inch whispers that someone crafted it to be admired, to be remembered.

He walks beside me as if it's nothing, as if this is normal. Maybe, for him, it is.

We reach the staircase, and the breath I didn't realise I was holding escapes in a slow exhale.

It's art. That's all it can be. Wide and sweeping, carved in polished black-and-white marble that catches the soft light above. The golden rail curves like a ribbon, warm and solid beneath my hand, lined with tiny engraved flourishes — swirling patterns that shimmer without ever demanding attention.

Each step isn't shallow but smooth, designed not for haste but to be admired, descended with purpose.

And then I see it... the painting.

At the top of the stairs, above us and angled ever so slightly forward, a single spotlight illuminates a painting. It doesn't belong. It's not elegant. It's not composed. It's heartbreak.

A man, gaunt and bare, pulls something massive — a stone carved in the shape of a broken heart. It drags behind him, cracked and bleeding gold. His knees buckle under the weight. His face is twisted in agony.

I can't move.

"Elijah..." I whisper.

He stops beside me, his eyes never leaving mine as I stand, completely mesmerised by the painting.

"That one's called The Weight of Love," he says, voice low. "It's by a contemporary Russian artist. When I saw it... it reminded me of you."

I look at him, breath caught in my chest.

"What it would be like," he says, "if I ever lost you."

The power of his words, the weight of the painting, overwhelms every sense. My vision blurs before I even realise it. I feel too much — out of place, broken yet full, confused by everything surging through me, everything my body does of its own will.

His hands wrap around me, pulling me against his chest as if he can sense the storm inside me. He engulfs me completely.

"Lisichka, I feel it too. It's overwhelming me."

I take a moment in his arms to sort through my own feelings. Yes, I'm overwhelmed, but I'm not afraid. I know I'm safe with him.

I press a kiss to his chest through the robe, letting him know I'm okay.

We continue our path to the kitchen, descending the stairs, and everywhere I look there's more opulence, more than I ever thought possible. To live in his world is... something else entirely.

As we make our way down the hallway, voices grow clearer, and the moment we reach the kitchen threshold I reach over and place my hand on Elijah's chest, signalling him to stop. I want to listen. I think they're talking about us. About me.

"I cannot believe this!" a woman's voice comes through. *"You're telling me that the lady of the house is a commoner? A florist?"* Her voice is agitated, arrogant.

I feel Elijah's body stiffen instantly, ready to spring into action, but I shake my head and smile. I want to hear what she has to say.

"I'm not sure what you want me to say. We were stationed next to a flower shop for a while, and then we moved to this apartment building," a man's voice answers.

"A florist? A nobody? It has to be some sort of sorcery! How can a filthy nobody entrap a man like our master? All of his wealth and power shared with a vermin like her?"

At that I bite back a laugh, as much as I can. When I glance at Elijah, he's gone—already gone. The moment I lift my hand off his chest, there will be only the psychopath left.

"She's clearly on the make, latching onto anyone with a decent salary, and now she's hit the jackpot. Who knows what sort of disgusting things she's been doing to him for the past day. An entire day?! I've never even heard of such a thing." The old woman keeps going, relentless.

"I think it's romantic. Especially how he ordered that no one even come close to their wing of the estate," a younger voice counters.

"Hush, you!" the old woman rebukes her. "What would you know? The lady of the house needs to be sophisticated. Refined." Her voice shifts into a posh, elevated accent — and that's when it clicks. She's talking about herself in her mind.

"Educated, and knowing her place around the master."

She pauses, letting the words hang. I keep waiting, eager for her to continue. I'm enjoying this, and in a few minutes, I'll be enjoying it even more.

"I'm not sure. But the boss was really clear about never even looking at her directly. Even when we were surveilling her, we were never allowed to meet her eyes. That made it a bit complicated when we were her shadows."

At that, I glare at Elijah and his antics. Seriously? Don't look at my face? WHAT! THE! FUCK?!

"See! What did I tell you? Sorcery! Why else would he not let anyone look at her? What is she? Some kind of witch who knows how to entrap men and make them do all sorts of crazy things?" the older lady insists.

"I don't think we should talk about things like this," a different younger woman cuts in. *"We all know how the master appreciates loyalty and respect. If any of this reaches his ears, we might lose our jobs."* Her accent is thick, and it's clear she's not British.

"Hush, you too!" the older lady snaps at her. *"I'm protecting our master from a witch. He cannot see it. She's working all sorts of sorcery on him and probably demanding he do despicable things to her. In... sex things."* She whisper-yells the last words. "You know some of these women take it in their arse? Or put it in their mouth? How degenerate is that?"

I'm about to pee myself with laughter, while Elijah is a living, breathing organism of fury. It's not annoyance. It's not simple anger. It's our primal call for blood — and as much as I hold him back, I know this is going to end in blood within seconds.

"Yes, she's surely doing all sorts of degenerate things to entice him. A woman like this would marry a coat rack as long as it had money and a title. Soon she'll announce she's with child — and it will probably be from some other man she's bedding on the side."

Oh, that sobers me up in an instant. As if I've summoned my own personal demon into action, I lift my hand from Elijah's chest and he turns the corner. His movements are sharp, mechanical, yet purposeful, so powerful he eats up the distance in a few steps.

I follow in silence as we enter the kitchen, taking everyone in. A man is seated at the island, two younger women are busying themselves with tasks, and one older lady is pacing up and down in front of the man on our side of the island.

I glance at Elijah just as he touches something on the wall. A compartment opens. In the next breath, he pulls out a gun and shoots the man square in the middle of his forehead. The women don't even have time to scream before the body hits the ground with a final thud.

When the screaming starts, I casually move past the older woman and jump up onto the island, my legs dangling off the edge. I don't even bother to look at the man anymore — he's Elijah's. He's a corpse taking his last few breaths. I sit between the two younger women and watch as what's about to become a bloodbath unfolds.

I look over at Elijah just as he lunges at the old woman and starts stabbing her. She doesn't even have time to scream — the attack is so brutal she drops instantly to the floor, and he's on top of her.

Obscene, macabre sounds fill the room, the knife piercing flesh in relentless rhythm, broken only by the occasional gurgled gasp. The scene overtakes everything, dragging the room into a complete transformation, into our truest form.

I glance over at the younger women, they're as white as snow.

"Please don't throw up," I say in what I hope is a calm tone. "Or faint. We need to establish a few things, to make sure we're all on the same page."

They don't respond. They don't nod. They just sit there, hands gripping the edge of the counter, staring at me as if I am death itself before them.

"Your friend here had the misfortune to think her opinion was wanted or needed. It was most definitely not. And as much as I found it amusing, clearly your master did not."

I glance over my shoulder at Elijah, and he's long gone. In his place there is only the blood thirsty psychopath. There's only a massacre on this side of the island: blood and body parts everywhere.

"You know as well as I do, Elijah appreciates loyalty and respect, and what was said in this kitchen was neither of those things. Therefore, her punishment was death."

As the words leave my mouth, something lands in my lap. I look down. It's an ear.

I look over again, he truly made a mess over there. I'll need to pull him back in a moment.

"Iubire scumpa, you're making a mess," I say, ever so calmly, pick up the ear and drop it next to him.

I turn to the women and can see it in their eyes. They're seconds from losing their minds.

"The old lady was right about some things. Your master and I care for each other fully, and we truly enjoy each other's bodies. So we'll come up with a schedule for when you're allowed in that part of the estate moving forward. We do not want or need your company in any shape or form outside of those times. Is that clear?"

They both nod so fast it's comical, like bobbleheads, and I smile.

Apparently my smile doesn't sit well with them, because they both flinch at it. Right. Noted. Don't smile at the help — they'll only be more afraid of me unless I put my mask back on.

"Do you have any questions for me?" I ask, trying to extend an olive branch.

They both shake their heads so fast I have to fight back another smile.

Yep, we're done here. I hop off the island and reach for Elijah's shoulder. The corpse is completely disfigured, unrecognisable from the person it once was. At my touch, he lifts his arm and slowly rises. He's covered in blood, body matter and sweat. At his full height, he looks larger than life. Monumental.

He drives a strong kick into the corpse, the unmistakable crack of ribs echoing through the kitchen.

The entire time, he never looks away from the women. He spits on the body, then stomps down hard, another sickening crack of bone filling the room.

"How dare she?" His voice is so dark and authoritative that the women let out an involuntary squeak.

I glance at them, tilt my head, and smile. If I thought they were afraid of me before, now they're beyond petrified.

But now... now they understand. I am just as ruthless as their boss.

"Iubire scumpa," I say in a calm, warm voice. "Come back to me." I run my hands along his back, trying to soothe him. "This is not why we came here."

The words make him drop the knife and take a deep breath.

When he turns, and I take him in fully, there's very little of the man left, and far more of the unhinged animal that just tore that woman apart.

The fact that I'm not hiding from him, or from what happened to this woman, that I'm giving everyone my true form, makes him pause and study me. He takes me in more and more with every passing second, until his features finally soften.

"Lisichka..." His voice is warm again, fragile. "My Queen, I'm so sorry."

His hands tremble in mine so violently it unsettles me to my core.

"My people are an extension of me. What happened here is unforgivable."

I understand his logic. I understand his point of view. I don't fully agree, and this will be a discussion for later. Not now. Not in front of the staff who just witnessed all of this.

I cup his cheek, and he leans into my touch.

We'll fix this later. For now, we need to deal with all the blood and the corpse.

"Go get cleaned up, and I'll make us some sandwiches. What do you say?"

His face twists into complete panic, and that's when I remember. His need, his kink, to always touch me. That's fine. But right now, he needs to wash this blood off, and I'm starving. His kink will have to wait.

"Iubire," I whisper against his lips, rising onto my tiptoes. "I'm hungry, and you're covered in blood. It'll take you minutes to wash, then I want to eat, and then we can talk some more."

When he just sits there, unmoving, I bring out my last weapon.

"Please, iubire scumpa." I whisper against his lips and kiss him softly. The touch is barely there, but a full-body shiver runs through him.

"Alex. Lockdown. LA LA protocol," Elijah commands sharply.

"Understood. Lockdown initiated," Alex replies.

"Alex, undo command," I say, holding Elijah's stare. "What are you doing, Elijah?" I measure him closely, ready to rip into him if he plans to force me in any way.

"I am not going to step away from you and leave you unprotected," he says, not backing down an inch. "Never, Lisichka. Do you hear me?"

"Alex. Lockdown," I command confidently to the security system.

"Understood. Lockdown initiated," Alex confirms.

"Iubire, let's break this down," I try to reason with him. "I'm in your home. It has to be the safest place for me, right?" He says nothing, so I soldier on. "The bathroom is one minute away. Undressing takes seconds, the shower two minutes, one minute to find something to put on, then one minute back. Total five minutes. I think I can manage for five minutes without you."

"No. You're coming with me." His voice is so agitated, like he's on the brink of losing it again.

"No," I say gently and place my hand on his chest again, and I realise his heart is racing as if we're under attack. "Iubire scumpa, please. I'm going to stay here with the girls and make food until you come back. Now go." I push at his chest gently. He doesn't move an inch. I smile, soften my features, and repeat my words.

"Alex. Eyes on our Queen at all times. Any threat—neutralised."

"Confirmed," Alex confirms.

"Alex, send a text to Buddy. Kitchen, seven minutes." With that, he leans down and presses a quick kiss to my lips, then runs out of the room.

I turn to the women — still white as snow, now even more terrified because Elijah isn't here.

"Right, ladies. Let's make some sandwiches. We have six minutes, apparently." I can't help laughing as I move toward the sink to wash the blood from my hands.

What the hell happened to my life that I'm now timing how long it takes to make a sandwich?

Chapter Twenty-Six

Elijah

Goddamn it!

What the hell is wrong with people?!

I'm screaming at the top of my lungs in my mind as I run full speed to wash up. What happened cannot—will not—happen again.

What the fuck? How could the help even think they could speak like this behind my back? Is this something everyone does?

I need to work with Alex and analyse their communication, cross-reference it with recordings from the past three—no, make that six—months, and execute anyone who might have said anything even remotely similar about my Queen.

What the actual fuck?!

I'm out of the shower with thirty seconds to spare and out the door in another ten. I bolt down the corridor — I've never hated my house for being large until this very moment. Everything I've designed and placed is arranged to intimidate and demand submission from the moment someone enters.

Now... now everything is pointless, because I do not care in the slightest if anyone knows who I am. All that matters is her. And right now... getting back to her.

I'm back in the kitchen in just over four minutes, and the moment I see her busying herself with food, I finally draw a deep breath.

Fucking hell... she's so beautiful in our kitchen.

I just stand there, taking her in. Her movements are clean, purposeful. She looks completely at ease in her element, as if she's been here my entire life.

She truly is... breathtaking.

"Good evening."

Buddy's voice snaps my attention back to the present. I have to give him credit, he didn't even stop beside me, as he usually would. Instead, he halted two steps behind the moment he realised Lisichka was in the room.

Clever man. He probably calculated that getting too close might trigger me. And he's right, it would have.

"You're not keeping to the schedule, iubire." She chastises me, then smiles.

She comes to stand beside me, takes my hand, then extends her right hand to Buddy, and everything in me screams to kill him again.

He's not allowed to touch what's mine! No one is!

"Breathe, iubire." Lisichka smiles at me again.

I don't want to breath I want to take his last breath from him for even breathing around you!

"Don't mind him," she continues as she shakes his hand. "You must be Buddy. I'm Monica."

"Don't you dare call her Monica." I say in my unhinged voice, trying with all in me to not pull another gun or knife and finish him off as well.

"Don't listen to him. You can call me Monica." She lets go of Buddy's hand and places hers on my chest. I try to anchor myself to the touch. The warmth, her scent, her voice. Anything to pull me back from the avalanche of feeling.

I'd been looking only at her face, and when I turn I see Buddy's eyes drop to her neck. I'm already reaching for a secret compartment to execute Buddy, when Lisichka stops me dead in my tracks.

"Oh, don't mind those bites either. His are on his cock." She starts laughing in that signature way she does when she's done something wicked.

I look at Buddy and his jaw is on the floor. I'm very confused about what I feel. Part of me wants to join in the laugh because this is Lisichka. That was a brilliant, smart-arse remark. But the other part of me remembers he looked at what's mine. Decision. Decisions.

I start laughing, savouring my woman, and pull her to my chest to feel her warmth and move her out of the way. With my other hand I reach for a gun. I don't even get time to aim before she steps in front of me, shielding Buddy with her body and glaring at me.

"Hand it over." Her voice is cold as ice.

"One." I shake my head. I truly need only one bullet.

"Hand it over before I get mad." I can tell by the tone she's already getting angry.

We hold each other's gaze for a moment longer, then I hand her the gun and look away. Fucking hell! I submitted!

She rises on her tiptoes and kisses me softly, then whispers, "Good boy."

"Come, let's eat." She glances around, uncertain where to sit. I can sense she wants to eat at the island, but the two bodies are still in the way.

Buddy looks over at both corpses and says nothing. He already knows what to do — this is part of why he was called here. A text would've been enough to tell him about the clean-up. If he's here in person, it means there's something else he needs to sort out.

"Come," I say, tugging at her hand, my voice warm again. I kiss the back of her hand and press it against my heart. It's been a few hours since I touched or tasted her, and I can feel withdrawal kicking in. This is going to be a fast meal and a faster conversation — that's for sure.

We make our way through the small hallway to the dining area, and I can feel her taking everything in, cataloguing it herself, noticing the details most people would miss. I'm not sure whether she likes or dislikes my tastes, but at the end of the day it's just a house. I could burn it down and rebuild it to her taste. My own is only hers now.

The moment the three-metre-tall doors swing open and the dining room is revealed, I hear her take a breath.

I designed the dining room to unsettle, not with grotesque décor or blatant intimidation, but subtly. True power hides in reverence, in awe. I wanted the room to feel like a cathedral. Byzantine, Eastern Orthodox, sacred. The kind of place where people forget to breathe and don't know why.

The ceiling is modelled after a barrel vault, like those in centuries-old Eastern Orthodox churches, where every stone carries the weight of prayer, sin and war. I chose limestone threaded with veins of gold, just enough to catch the light and feel divine. I commissioned frescoes, intentionally faded: angels with haunted faces, demons captured mid-sin, broken halos scattered across the span. Not a single brushstroke was random. I oversaw all of it.

The columns are carved from dark marble — almost black, yet translucent enough to glow faintly in candlelight. Each one tells a different story: angelic battles, demonic triumphs, salvation twisted into despair. They aren't there for beauty. They're there to remind anyone who sits at my table that heaven and hell aren't opposites — they're choices. And both are mine to offer.

The five chandeliers are crafted from Bohemian crystal — enormous, precise. I had them retrofitted to mimic the soft, flickering glow of flame. No harsh light. I wanted warmth, but not comfort. Illumination, but never exposure. Candlelight makes people feel watched in all the right ways.

It's a room built for dominance. For presence. For control.

She pauses and sweeps her gaze around, taking everything in. I'm sure she'll mention anything that doesn't please her. I look back and Buddy has taken the tray from the kitchen, giving us some privacy from the staff.

We make our way to the head of the table. I pull out the chair beside mine at the head and hold it for Lisichka to sit. This is not a marriage. This is not a partnership where one person has a little more than the other. This is equality. She is like me and I am like her — together we will rule the world.

Buddy doesn't say a word. He sets the tray in front of us and takes his usual seat.

I notice there's no cutlery, no plates, no cups, no wine glasses, nothing. But when Lisichka lays her hand on my leg and the connection to her snaps back into place, nothing else matters.

She reaches over, takes one of the sandwiches, and offers it to me. I accept without hesitation. I would eat live scorpions from her hand if she asked me. Then again, I can't even remember the last time I had a sandwich.

"Please, Buddy, help yourself." She gestures to the tray and smiles at him.

Oh, for fuck's sake. Rage explodes in me all over again.

"Cut it out, Elijah." She rebukes me and tries to pull her hand from my thigh, but I grab it quickly and hold it there.

I lean in and kiss her cheek, then nip at the bottom of her ear. At least that. Just a bit of her for me.

I turn and glare at my friend. He says nothing, doesn't move, barely breathes, waiting for my command.

"I want everyone from the UBT here in two days. Leave." Short, sweet, commanding. Done.

"Hang on." Lisichka cuts in. "First — what's UBT? And second, what do you mean leave?"

"He has his command. Why would he stay?" I'm confused by her words.

"Because we invited him to eat with us," she replies.

I pull a face. "Alright — I invited him to eat with us," she continues without missing a beat.

"He'll leave if he knows how to value his life," I counter.

"Grumpy. Haven't had any lately?" she bites back in that mischievous tone of hers.

"No, actually. I'm about to eat my dinner, then this sandwich. If you don't want him dead, I'd advise you to let him go."

She pulls a face at me, and I notice she's biting back a laugh.

Buddy, the very wise man he is, stands, says nothing, and leaves.

"Get your sweet arse on the table and let me eat," I command in that warm voice meant only for her. When she doesn't move and just stands there laughing, I push my chair back, reach for her, and place her on the table in front of me.

She instinctively drapes her legs over my thighs and her robe parts, giving me a glimpse of her pussy. And just like that, the only thing left in the universe is me and that cunt, finally coming together.

I lean in to devour my dinner.

Chapter Twenty-Seven

Monica

He's up to something. I can feel it in my gut. I can't see what it is yet, but I can feel it in the air. The fact he thinks he can hold it back tells me I won't like it. Not one bit.

I'm seated on the table in front of him, my legs resting on his thighs, my robe parted slightly. The air changes around me when he shifts — he becomes the beast that wants, no, needs to drink from me. He leans down for my pussy, and I clamp my legs shut at the last second; his face lands on my thighs.

He slowly lifts his gaze. Part glare, part confusion, part... fear?

I smile and play the innocent. Oh, two can play dirty. As he said, I am a Queen. And Queens get what they want. By the end of this meal, he'll tell me everything I want to know.

I hand him another sandwich, nonchalantly, then cross my legs, not the least bit bothered that he now has a front-row seat to my arse.

"This is so yum!" I say in a playful tone. "The girls really helped me make some yummy sandwiches."

He looks down at my pussy, then at the sandwich in his hand. The corner of his mouth twitches before he takes a big bite. He's fighting back a laugh — I can see it as clear as day. I also know he's onto me, but I'll get my way. Sooner or later, it's just a matter of time.

We sit there in silence, eating. I reach for another sandwich just as I shift position, crossing my other leg over and deliberately flashing my pussy at him.

He bursts out laughing and leans back in his chair, finishing the last bite of his sandwich.

"I'm not sure what you're playing at, Lisichka. But just know this... " He pauses and holds my gaze. "Your arse will wear my hand-marks by the time the sun rises, as proof of this forced obstinacy."

"Whatever do you mean?" I play the innocent in my best British accent. "I am innocent, master."

When I drop "master," his face falls. It's like I've pushed him into a reality where he sees nothing but me. His entire posture changes; the look in his eyes, the burning need to devour me now, is as palpable as the blood he spilled for me just minutes ago in the kitchen.

"Name it." His voice isn't his own — deep, animalistic, predatory, ready to hunt.

"What do you mean... master?"

He lets out such a deep grunt I flinch back involuntarily. He has never made that sound before. It doesn't scare me — it excites me. I can feel my core getting wet, my whole body humming with anticipation. All I want is to push and push and push until he fucking snaps.

One way or another I will get what I want — and before he snaps, I need to find out what he's up to.

He lifts my foot to his mouth and starts that nipping, sucking thing at my toes. It's tingling, arousing, dirty — and I like it. I love it, actually. I want more. More!

I lift the sandwich to my lips, take a bite, and play the innocent game a little longer. Thanks to this sandwich, none of the moans fighting to escape make it out. When he reaches the last toe and I'm still eating as if nothing is happening, I glance over at him — his forehead is shining with beads of sweat. He's barely holding back.

I say nothing. I don't look at him. I don't acknowledge. I don't engage.

"Lisichka..." His voice is deeper now, ferocious — any other person would have cowered before him.

"Name it."

I turn my gaze to him slowly and smile, but say nothing. I just hold his gaze in a silent challenge.

"Whatever you want, it's yours... just name it." He kisses my foot again and then places it on his chest.

We linger there for a moment, lost in a world of our own making — a weight and a gift all wrapped in one.

"I want to be your equal..."

"You..." he cuts me short, but I silence him by pressing my toes to his lips.

"No, Elijah. I want to be your equal. That means actual equality — not that you tell me things; it means you talk things over with me. You need to make room in your life for me. If this is something you cannot do, I can simply walk out that door."

He grabs my foot so fast I don't even see it until the pain registers — it's too late.

"That is never going to happen." His voice is pure ice — full of pain. "That option does not exist between us. Listen carefully, Lisichka, because we are never going to have this discussion again. There is nothing else except us. This is not a marriage, a partnership, a love, or whatever else you want to call it. This is the most core, fundamental connection between two people. I feel you, I know you, and I want you as much as I want to be alive. The moment something happens to you, Lisichka, know this: it is the moment I will die too and follow you into the afterlife to be with you. Never — and I mean never — will there exist a day when I am not with you."

He lifts my foot to his lips, kisses it, then presses it to his forehead. "Now stop torturing me and name it."

"What is UBT, and what did you ask to happen in two days? Also — the day you make a decision without me is the day you see the other side of me, boy."

He shakes his head in disbelief. In one smooth move he pulls me onto his lap and I straddle him, my core flushed against his hardening cock. His robe is in the way, but it'll be only seconds until he realises how much I enjoyed tormenting him just now.

"UBT stands for Unity Bridge Team. It's my inner circle." He wraps his arms around my middle and pulls me flush against him. "Woman, you don't need to drive me to the edge of insanity. If you want or need something, just ask. It will be yours." He kisses my forehead and breathes me in, lingering for a moment.

"Let me tell you everything you might need to know now, because you'll complain again about one-word answers and set off on a mission to kill me from the inside out." He kisses the tip of my nose, then leans back.

"The UBT is made up of Sofia, Buddy, Hunter, Vasile, Alec, Kirill, Stefan, Alexandra, Liam and Dominic. Dominic you already know, of course. In my organisation he's the man I send out to fix things for us. He likes to give himself titles, but they don't mean anything to me. I mostly keep him around because he's funny, just never tell him that.

Sofia is head of cyber security and my daughter, as you know. Buddy, you already know, is my right-hand man. Hunter is head of security, fire expert and a few other things; at the moment he's being tortured in one of our warehouses. Vasile is my chauffeur and bodyguard, you know him as well.

Alec, this one will make you laugh. Alec is an ex-porn star. He's got a lot of brains and worked hard to get where he is; he made it into the UBT, and a lot of people underestimate him because of his past. He works in cyber security with me and runs a few of my other side businesses."

He stops and studies me for a second. I say nothing. I want to get as much out of him as possible.

"You know Alec as well. He's the man Dominic fought at City Hall the day of the explosion at the Barrow.

Then there's Kirill. Kirill is the son of the vor who caused my family's massacre. After I realised I wanted nothing to do with the Bratva, I made an agreement with Kirill. He could be Pakhan, as long as he swore loyalty to me. That was more than twenty years ago.

Then there's Stefan. He's German and does similar work to Alec.

Then there's Alexandra. She's of Greek descent and works in the same field as Alec and Stefan.

And the last one is Liam, who is Irish."

His features soften so much it's like there's no predator before me, just a simple man completely drowning in love for his woman.

"Lisichka, please understand once and for all." He sighs and searches my eyes, silent. "When I called you my Queen, it's not because you are under me. It's because you are above me. You're not my equal because you are over me, my Queen. I need to make room for you in my life, and that's not because you are less than me. It's because it's been only me in my life until now. But now I know there truly are two of us," his words trail off and crack at the end. "I am not planning to rule, my Queen. I am planning to surrender it all to you. You can choose to rule on your own and let me have my time worshipping you, or you might choose for us to rule it together. I don't really care. I thought when I told you before that you can rule the world as long as I rule you, dominate you, and fuck the living hell out of you to my heart's content. All I care about is being with you. The rest of it does not matter to me anymore. I had decades of ruling without you. I have no interest in continuing to do it. All my focus now is on you and our future together."

His words are soft, sincere and clear. His vision for our future is defined and concrete. In none of it does he rule over me. Smart man, he knows I would never stand for that.

"What are you planning, Elijah?" I dare him head-on, wiggling gently in his arms, my voice sliding into my signature mischief.

"For now, I'm planning how to punish you for calling me by my name. The rest? Not much, I've got you in my life."

"Cut the crap. What will happen in two days? What have you ordered Buddy?" I press, teasing him, sizing him up.

He bursts out laughing so hard he shakes me with him. My response? I pinch his nipple — hard.

"Oh, you're going to be unable to sit on your arse for days by the end of this." He starts peppering kisses along my neck and shoulder. His lips on me do terrible things — lowering my guard and setting me ablaze. I involuntarily let out a moan, and he starts laughing again.

I need to take control of the situation! I need to redirect the attention from me back to the discussion. So I grab one of the sandwiches and shove it in his face.

"How much do you want me to eat, woman?"

"Just enough to replenish your stamina and fuck me just right. Now — shh — tell me more. Why is Hunter being tortured?" I finally say as I pull back. "What did he do? Did he take something as well?"

"Amazing questions. It's true, I test my people periodically by leaving information for them to steal if they want. That's how I found out Bogdan was a traitor. Unfortunately, Hunter wants the one thing I will never give him. My daughter."

The way he says it is so possessive — as if he actually has a say in it. I burst out laughing when I realise he's serious, that he believes this shit.

"What's funny?"

"You, of course. Do you think you actually have a say in it?"

"What do you mean? Of course I do!" His voice is so firm, as though he's raising it, and I simply arch my brow and hold his gaze. "Apologise, Lisichka."

"Does she love him?"

He doesn't want to admit it, but I can see it all over his face. "Then we can't do anything about it. If anything, we need to push them to pull it together and sort their shit."

His arms engulf me once more — I think it's more for his comfort this time than mine. He's as protective of Sofia as if she were his real daughter, and in many ways she is. He raised her. She's his daughter as much as Angela is mine.

"Can I eat you now?" he whispers into my skin. "We can talk some more later, if you like."

I don't answer with words. Actions speak louder. I grind my core against his cock, and that's all the invitation he needs. In the next second I'm flipped over on the table with him at my back. When I feel him pinning me down as he kneels behind me, I'm already moments away from detonating. He lifts my robe to expose my arse and pussy, then inhales me deeply. It's depraved. But I've waited the entire meal for this, and I'm going to enjoy the fuck out of it.

The first lick he gives me is so maddening, as if he ran a current through my veins and brought me back to life. The sensation is so familiar now — so electrifying, so intense, so consuming. But just as I feel myself losing control in the flood of pleasure he's pulling from me, he lands two sharp slaps with both hands on my arse.

I yelp so loudly it sounds strange even to my own ears, the cry bouncing around this ridiculously large room. Before I can catch my breath from the rush of hot blood to the area, he lands two more slaps, then two more. Then he grabs my hips, lifting and opening me up in that way only he can, completely opening my pussy for his taking.

The sensations are too much, too demanding, too devouring.

The moment he latches onto my clit, I detonate instantly. Hot ripples of pleasure pulse through me, setting my whole body on fire. I couldn't stop the spasms even if I tried. My vision blurs, my skin sings at his touch, and that maddeningly sweet taste overtakes my mouth once more.

"I told you, you're going to sit on my lap for a week after today, because your arse will be dark red by the end of it." The words are barely out of his mouth before he lands three more pairs of slaps on my arse, cutting off the end of my orgasm and promising filthy, depraved things for the rest of the night.

And I just want more...

Chapter Twenty-Eight

Monica

I am drifting in and out of sleep, wrapped in that beautiful perfume that hangs in the air, that scent specific to Elijah's home. When I eventually open one eye and look at the clock, it's 2am. These past few days have been extraordinary, far greater than I thought they would be, but in the midst of it all there is a familiarity in every gesture, every word, every touch that confirms to me that I truly am where I'm supposed to be.

For so long I felt I didn't belong. Certainly not beside my parents. There was a time when I felt beyond that point, as if I were floating in air, my daughter the only thing anchoring me to reality. Now... now I feel I do belong. I am exactly where I'm supposed to be.

My mind is reaching, caught between realisation, excitement, the weight of everything my body has been through, and the familiar, beautiful heaviness of Elijah's arm around my middle. After all that has unfolded since I arrived — the words, the acts, the sensations my body has discovered — I don't know which way is up or down, when I should sleep, or when I should demand more from him.

My back gently shifts against him and, as if on command, he starts kissing my shoulder and neck. The softness and possessive way his lips claim me is something I will never have my fill of. With a single kiss, he can ignite the fire within me until it consumes us both.

"Why are you awake?" My voice is drowsy, and I try to calculate how many hours I actually slept.

"How can I sleep when you're next to me? That would be a waste of time." He whispers the words onto my skin as he trails across my back with kisses before beginning to nibble.

Holy hell, I love that kiss-and-nibble thing he does on my skin. It's the perfect balance of exciting, tingling, arousing, drizzled with just the right pain. There's a reason I let him do whatever he wants to my body. He's fucking insane when it comes to fucking. Holy hell. My pussy hurts, and I've barely moved. My arse hurts because he made good on his threat and spanked me raw, but even so, toward the end

I found myself provoking him more. My arse and thighs are definitely red and pulsing now. Doesn't matter. It was worth it. Even the memory is turning me on.

"Hang on. How much sleep have you had since I arrived?"

Silence.

He moves lower on my back, and the only sound is the beautiful press of his lips and tongue on my skin. I start to turn, and in a flash he tightens his arm around me — as if I were about to pull away or make a run for it.

"Let me turn. We need to talk."

He lingers, lips pressed to the same spot. He takes a deep breath, pushes harder against my skin, then finally releases me so I can turn and face him.

"Iubirea mea," I say the moment we're face to face, cupping his cheek. "Tell me how much you've slept since I arrived."

I can see it written all over his face, this thing between us is consuming him. It's genuinely eating him alive. It's bigger than us, conquering him as if he were a mere mortal. He doesn't know how to process any of it. Not that I do, but for me... I deflect into selective mutism. I simply don't speak, don't think, the moment something feels completely out of reach of my understanding. I let it be and focus on what's in front of me. What I see. What I can understand. And what I understand is that this is real. As real as the need for the sun shining on us is my need for Elijah's presence and touch in my life.

It seems different for Elijah. He's consumed by it. For me it feels certain, permanent, absolute. I might be wrong, but it feels to me as if he's still scared he might lose me. I think that's what's breaking him.

"Who needs to sleep when I can enjoy you all the time?" The conviction in his voice is as absolute as if he were speaking of the most important thing in his life. Perhaps, to some extent, that is the case.

"Nope," I say cheerfully, swinging a leg over him. "From now on, when I sleep, you sleep. Understood?"

He leans into my touch, looks down between us, then up at me and smiles. He's a sight to behold when he smiles — the corners of his eyes thin into a beautiful line, revealing something I haven't seen before. He isn't the sort to smile to pretend or to please others, yet with me he does it so naturally, so effortlessly, like breathing.

"Lisichka, you ready for another round?"

Fuck no!

I'm wet, but I'm also very sore, and I'm not planning on any internal organ or vaginal damage any time soon — so, fuck no.

"Thank you, but no thank you," I say, trying to pull my leg back.

He grabs it so fast his fingers dig into my skin.

"Not so fast. You can't turn, look at me, or — worse — put your leg on me and think I won't want to get inside you."

Fuck — it's not going to end well for me. Distract. Distract.

"Did you find your guy?"

"What guy?"

"The Romanian one. The one who bombed you."

"Yes, we did. A few days later, like I told you we would."

"Did you kill him? Or are you still using him to bring your team together?" A smile betrays me. I still can't believe how he manipulates his own people like this.

"Lisichka, please. I am not manipulating anyone. Stop thinking that about me."

"You stop getting in my head!" I hate how he anticipates my moves. I guess it's part of thinking the same way, but I'm still getting used to that.

"I gave them a single point of focus. This does not constitute manipulation. And yes, I do manipulate everyone around me, but that is in our nature, so it does not count." He smiles, playing the innocent with me this time. "No — I did not kill him. I'm waiting."

It's like someone plunged me into an ice-cold bath. I freeze completely. I know what that means...

The moment our gazes meet, it's there — the confirmation that I really do know what this means.

I pull my leg away from him — there's no resistance this time. I push myself up, my back resting against the headboard. My blood is boiling to dangerous levels, my skin itches with fury.

"Don't you fucking say it," I warn him in my deadliest, calmest voice.

He raises his hands in a sign of surrender. "I wasn't about to."

He rises into a sitting position too, his back against the headboard. We stay there in silence. I curl tighter into myself, arms wrapped around my bent knees, and he sits beside me, not saying a word. It's the first time we're truly next to each other but not connected in any way, shape or form. What he's implying is something I never thought truly possible. I've dreamed it. Desired it. Desired it in such detail it consumed me. But I knew it would never happen. I knew it was out of my reach, so I buried it deep in my mind until it might as well never have existed.

Now Elijah is poking at the most sensitive place inside me, shaking me, demanding action with his silence. It's not that I fear him. It's not that I want to hide this part of myself from him — he already knows it. He may not know the details because I've never told a living soul, but he knows, obviously. I don't know where all of this inside me is coming from or what this feeling is truly called. So I do what I do best when I have no clue what to say: I stay quiet, pull my knees to my chest, and hide in plain sight.

There are no words, no touch, no prompt for me to say anything. There is just the silence in the room, that unmistakable perfume that hangs through the mansion, and the undeniable presence of the man next to me. Time stretches and becomes relative as it passes while I try to process this.

"Does she know?"

His words land like a vicious slap. I lift my gaze and glare at him with all my might, but the look that meets me isn't mean or cold. His eyes are soft, as if he's carrying this with me — a psychopath who cares. Given that we're the same, he cares for himself as much as he cares for me. I'm so confused by my feelings, by having choices. I want to hurt him for touching the one spot inside me that still aches. But on the other hand I want to hold him and love him that bit more for wanting to share my pain.

He doesn't push, repeat or insist with his questions. He just sits there, looking at me, giving me the space and time to process whatever's happening inside me.

"That she is a rape baby?" I finally say in a cracked voice. "She does not."

He takes my hand and places it on his chest, his heartbeat is out of control. I was right... he's sharing my pain with me.

I know what he wants. I know why he didn't kill the guy who bombed us. He wants me to go back and take my power. He wants me to face the man who hurt me and deliver his justice.

I feel numb. In shock. Maybe even weak... and I don't like it.

"You don't have to do anything you don't want, my Queen," he says in that warm voice of his. "But know this... whatever is in your past, or whatever's in our future, no one and nothing can hurt you again. I want to hurt that man more than I want to take my next breath. That being said, it's not my kill to make. So whenever you're ready, we'll go and face your past together."

I'm fighting the tears. My chest feels full and empty at the same time. I'm screaming and silent in my head all at once — a confusing, overwhelming flood of emotion running through me. Tears run down my cheeks of their own accord as I try and fail to hold Elijah's gaze.

"I'm not weak!" I yell into his face.

He pulls me onto his lap so fast I don't even see it coming. He wraps his arms around me and tightens his hold until it hurts again. "I would never think for one moment that you're weak. What happened does not make you weak, Lisichka. You survived it. All of it. And look where you are. Look what you are. Without even one touch of my help. You are truly magnificent, Lisichka."

His embrace feels calm, sweet and comforting. And I let it overtake me. I take complete refuge in his arms, and for the first time in my life I let myself cry — truly, fully cry for what happened. What happened to me was fucked up. It broke me to an elemental level. It cannot be undone. Kill or no kill, I will forever remain a rape survivor.

"I never said those words to anyone before," I muffle into his chest.

It's true. My parents never once spoke to me about what happened, and when they realised I was pregnant they kept beating me, trying to make me lose the baby. I wouldn't let them win. Every time they came at me I curled into a ball, wrapped my arms tight around my legs, and shielded my child the only way I could, with my own body. I took every blow, but I never loosened my grip. That's when they decided to get rid of me, to marry me off.

Slowly, I pull back and lift my gaze to Elijah... actually look at him.

"She is mine, Elijah. And she will never learn the truth. Do you hear me?" I give him my signature sizing look, eyes dropping over him. "This is not something that will be forgiven. She is mine alone. I made her, she is mine. Understood?"

"Crystal clear." His voice is comforting and at peace. I know without a doubt he will never let this secret out.

I let him hold me, taking comfort in his arms until all of these emotions and weird sensations in my body calmed down.

Chapter Twenty-Nine

Elijah

Everything for tomorrow is already in motion. All the details are in place, everything that needed doing was handled while Lisichka napped. Kirill is on his way to England already. My gift for my Queen will arrive this afternoon. I also checked the trackers I planted in her body — all three are working perfectly.

When that nagging voice at the back of my head said that it still wasn't enough, even I realised that putting another tracker in her would be too much. She might be furious — if she ever finds out.

The fact that I started the discussion about what happened to her, it wasn't really a discussion, more an acknowledgement that I knew. Then she didn't kill me as a result. That's a win. One thing I know now: it actually brought us closer, if that's even possible. It was tough on both of us, but it needed to be out in the open. Just as she should be out in the open for everyone to see.

This burning thing inside her needs to be extinguished, this hesitation. She wants to kill, it's within her nature. Yet she couldn't kill even the one person who deserved it most. Now that I've given her that choice, I could see so much running through her, but she deflated into her silent world to process it. She'll get there. And I'll be here forever, helping her through it.

There's no room to push things. Healing comes through pain, and I can vouch for that any day of the week — especially with her. I would never push her, or pretend I know what she went through, because I don't. No one does. It's her pain, her memories, she had to live with them. Even if she never tells me what happened, I have no problem with that — frankly, it's none of my business, and I'm not sure how I'd handle it. I might kill the fucker myself, but I know it's her kill to make, not mine.

We stay like this for a while, her in my arms as she dozes off again, and I can't take my eyes off her. She is the most valuable thing I have ever seen in my life — the ultimate, rare gem.

"Elijah?" Alex's voice alerts me just as Lisichka shifts in my arms.

"Not now." I try to whisper, not to wake her, but it's too late. Those big black eyes are on me again. It's like they pull me into their orbit, I'm completely devoured by her gaze and presence. Nothing could be important enough for me to look away.

"What happened?" Her voice is adorably sleepy — if I could lick and suck it all into me, I would.

"It's nothing, Lisichka. Go back to sleep."

"Elijah. It's under the P1 protocol," Alex insists.

Fuck — it had to be a P1. What the hell did these idiots do? I couldn't even have a few days to myself.

"Continue," I say, sharp.

"Sofia has activated the drones. She configured the coordinates for Romania. She requested six bombs to be loaded onboard."

"Fuck's sake!" my voice snaps, frustrated. This means I have to deal with her tantrum. When Lisichka rises, the duvet slipping from her shoulders and I can see her gorgeous breasts, I know this is absolute rubbish: instead of enjoying them and adding to the bruises on her chest and abdomen, I'll have to find the willpower to pull away, put my pants on and go talk some sense into Sofia. It's fucked. I want my space. I want my time with Lisichka.

"Calm down, iubire scumpa," she says, placing a hand on my chest and smiling. "The real world was going to come crashing in sooner or later."

"I prefer later. Much, much later." I reach for my phone. One of the guards watching Hunter has just texted me. The moment I read it, I want to tear him apart with my bare hands. I fire back a single reply.

Elijah

I should have killed you a long time ago.

The moment I look up from my phone and those eyes meet me again, there's no room for negotiations. We're going to deal with our first P1 together. My Queen has made up her mind, and we're going to sort this mess now.

"Come," I prompt, offering my hand. "Let's get ready. We'll go to the Barrow. Let me show you your empire, my Queen."

"You are hilarious," she says, dismissive.

"I truly did create an empire, my Queen."

"I don't doubt that," she says, walking ahead of me, her naked body on full display, her arse cheeks wobbling slightly. There's no stopping it. She drives me crazy by simply existing. To see her like this and not get hard would be a sinister joke, or something definitely wrong with my cock.

"It's hilarious how you call it 'my empire', yet I haven't decided what I'm going to do."

She reaches for one of the dresses I bought her and lays it on the side of the wardrobe where my most expensive day-to-day suits used to live. She doesn't know. I would never tell her. I moved them without thinking, like a sacrament. Something inside me screamed so loud the moment she walked into my life that every small, ridiculous corner of my world rearranged itself for her. I give up the things that once comforted me without a second thought, folding them into the edges of her world. I want nothing in return. Not praise. Not recognition. Just her — the way she is, the quiet of her breath, the natural presence and fulfilment she brings into me. Those are my treasures.

I redesigned the wardrobe down to the smallest detail, so that when she turns every accessory, piece of jewellery, and each perfume is within a step's reach. All her clothes, every item inside, was carefully bought, planned, and placed based on what I know and have observed of her. Everything, except the jewellery. She doesn't have much of her own, and I hate that. I want her covered in gold, platinum, diamonds, and the rarest stones. Perhaps the gift on its way will please her, perhaps it will open the door for me to finally shower her in jewels.

"Stop looking at me like that and get dressed," she says over her shoulder.

If I can't touch her while she's getting dressed, then at least I can devour her with my gaze and not lose the connection. I step back, careful not to sever it. That would hurt like hell, and then smash my foot against the corner of one of the floating islands of accessories. Fucking hell, it hurts. Doesn't matter, though. I might not be physically touching her, but I'm still on her.

I start getting dressed, dragging my underwear on, but the moment I do, I realise I'm still covered in her cum from our last fucking. I glance at her, she didn't mind wearing me on her skin and walking out like that. And I sure as fuck don't mind being covered in us, in her, as I step into the world. Her scent clings to me, intoxicating. What sane man would ever want to wash that away?

I get on with it, forcing myself to speed up, pulling my clothes on at what has to be the fastest record in the world.

Twenty minutes later, Barrow comes into view. I squeeze her hand, resting on my thigh.

"That is our main building in London, my Queen."

Her curious eyes sweep over the skyline until they land on the empire I've built in this country. I study her as intently as she studies everything else. That gaze, the spark of curiosity, will forever live in my memory as the moment she first saw my accomplishments.

"Drop us off at the entrance, Vasile."

She's the one who entwines our fingers the moment the building comes fully into view, and my heart dances in my chest. She cares for me as much as I care for her. Not only did the world create two of us—and I found her—but she feels the same way about me as I do about her.

All these feelings she's stirred inside me are no longer unfamiliar, no longer unusual or oppressive. They're mine. They're hers. They're ours. Born from her, because of her. So how could they be anything but wonderful?

Me. Feelings. And wonderful—all in the same sentence. Who would've thought?

I truly feel like I'm losing my mind around her. There is nothing in my life, nothing in my future, except her.

Vasile opens my door, and I gently tug her out of the car with me. The first thing she does is look up, taking in the entire building.

"Did anyone ever make fun of you saying you built something this big to compensate?" Her expression is straight, serious, but the tone of her voice betrays her. "Because I can set them straight and tell them your cock is bigger than the building."

She turns and winks at me.

I can't resist her. I pull her to my chest and start laughing. Holy hell, she drives me crazy! I love how she teases me constantly—always keeping me on my toes. Always a sassy remark. A cheeky bite. I love it.

"Unfortunately, they did not. Thank you for the offer. It really means the world to me," I say, pressing a kiss to her forehead.

I can't kiss her on the lips now. Not because I don't want to—my entire being hums with the need to kiss her. But if I do, I'll need to fuck her straight away. My cock twitched the moment she made that joke about him, and I'm not sure she'd let me take her here. So I hold it in. For now.

We make our way into the building, and everything about it screams power and wealth. I've never been prouder of not sparing a cent when we built it. This place represents my strength, my success—and now, it's hers. She deserves nothing less.

"That is a strange thing," she says, pointing at the very large, very expensive sculpture inspired by the famous floating skirt of Marilyn Monroe. Every single man who's ever walked through those doors has commented on how stunning it is. And here comes my Lisichka, calling it the opposite.

It will go. It has to. She called it strange, and I might not have an eye for art, but I do have an eye for my Queen. If she doesn't want it, the sculpture will be gone.

The moment we step into the elevator, I pull out my phone and text the building manager: have it removed this week, and send me a catalogue of contemporary artists so Lisichka can pick whatever she wants.

We're not even out of the elevator when we hear a commotion from the security room, one by one the staff pour out and scatter in different directions.

"FUCKER!"

"MOTHERFUCKER! ASSHOLE! DIPSHIT! FUCKER!" Sofia's voice rages from within.

I glance at Lisichka and feel embarrassed. It's the first time she'll meet my daughter, and she's fucking embarrassing me. I'm not sure whether Lisichka is taking in the space for my sake or simply because she's curious, but I'm grateful either way.

We walk toward the security room, and I make a point of staying beside Lisichka — not ahead of her for even a step — my hand holding hers the whole time. Soft whispers follow us as people pass, but I don't bother to acknowledge them. All the while I am claiming her for everyone to see. They'll know soon enough that she is their Queen, and they will bow down to her.

It takes only one look—one moment—for our gazes to meet, and we're in agreement. This is on me to fix. Lisichka will not intervene. I need to clean up this mess.

"Fucking pussies!" comes from inside the room just as we're about to enter.

I stop in the threshold, shoulder resting on the door frame, still holding Lisichka's hand even as she hangs back. I know this is my mess and I will clean it, but there's no way I'll let go of her. Not for a second.

I'll fix this, then introduce them, and make it perfectly clear to Sofia where she stands with Lisichka.

All of that must wait, because Sofia has clearly lost the plot — one look at the state of the room says it all. Her breathing is out of control, her whole presence unravelled. No wonder she did something this foolish.

"I like what you've done with the place," I say the moment she notices me. My presence snaps her back to reality, then her features twist into pure panic as she realises the drone is already on its way.

"I cancelled the drone, little one." We weren't even out of the mansion when Alex confirmed it was already on its return flight.

"I needed that." Her voice is so small, completely at odds with the woman she usually is. It throws me off for a second, and if I didn't feel Lisichka's warm hand in mine, grounding me, comforting me, this conversation with Sofia would have gone very differently. Because this truly is her worst fuck-up.

"Sure. For what?" I continue in my calm, collected tone. She's hurting, it's written all over her face, so perfectly mirrored in the chaos of the room she's created.

"To send a bomb to Bogdan's associates, of course," she replies in an exasperated tone, as if I'm wasting her time.

Her tone is unnecessary and unacceptable — if it were any other person, they'd have a bullet in their brain by now. Given it's her, and given the small caress of Lisichka's thumb on the back of my hand, I know I need to fix this, not dominate it into submission.

"I see," I reply, straightening my stance. "Have you considered the casualties?"

Boom — it's written all over her face. There's no logic, no rationality in the decisions she's made for some time now. More accurately: since that man left the organisation.

"Have you at least considered the percentage of casualties?" I continue, driving the point home.

"Dad..."

"No, little one. We are better than that." My voice is short, commanding and final. "Just because we can hurt someone doesn't mean we should."

I let the words settle, letting her feel the true weight of them. She really fucked up, and now she knows it.

"I'm sorry." Her voice is so small and weak.

"Little one..." I say gently, as her eyes plead for a way to make it all disappear. "You need to make a choice, little one." I know I have to put an end to this. My heart physically breaks as I release Lisichka's hand and move to comfort my daughter.

I approach Sofia and repeat myself, driving the finality of my words home. "You need to make a choice, because this ends now."

I place my hand on her shoulder and squeeze gently. Her entire body trembles beneath my touch. I don't know if it's my words, my touch, or my presence that offers her any comfort — but I do know my actions will. This ends today, by her hand or by mine.

"You need to go kill him, little one. I am not going to do it for you."

Her reaction is a pain I've never seen on her face before. Regardless of the agony now, in the long term it will be far more devastating if I don't intervene. I can see her features morphing into different shades of gruesome pain. She does not understand what I am doing for her. Perhaps she never will.

"Dad... I, I..." Her voice breaks so badly she can't finish the sentence.

"You can, and you will, little one." My tone is final, cold.

"Dad..." she insists in a weak, pleading tone.

"It was your decision, and you need to live with the consequences of your choice. I let things go on long enough, and now it's time for you to clean up after yourself," I say, my voice unyielding. I squeeze her shoulder again, and for a fleeting moment I feel Lisichka's fury radiate toward me.

I deliver my decision.

"Tomorrow, Sofia."

I let go of Sofia and move quickly out of the security room. I'm losing control. It feels like the air is drowning me, gravity ripping me apart because I'm not beside Lisichka and my brain goes completely paranoid that something has happened to her. The moment my eyes land on her, my body relaxes. In two strides I reach to engulf her, but she pulls away and I feel my legs give in beneath me. I study her gaze and know I've upset her.

"Lisichka?" I don't even dare prompt her to tell me what's wrong. I'm already calculating every way to chain her to me. There is no escaping me, if that's what she's thinking.

"It was not your finest hour in there. You're not very good at this. Are you?" Her tone is dismissive and she looks down at me again.

I say nothing. I have no reply. I thought I'd done well.

She passes me, dismisses me with a wave of her hand, and walks into the room like she owns it. She pulls a chair next to Sofia and sits.

"Hi. I'm Monica," she says, extending her hand to Sofia. "I'd like to apologise on behalf of your dad. He can be an insensitive prick, by the looks of it."

She glances over Sofia's shoulder at me, shooting daggers with her gaze. "I assume she knows about you, iubire scumpă?"

I nod, and that's when her features soften again. She turns back to Sofia and takes her hand once more into her own.

"Listen — your dad truly isn't capable of processing situations like this. What's happening to you is purely emotional, and as you know, he doesn't do feelings." She pats Sofia's hand as she speaks.

"Iubire, what would you have done in Sofia's place?" she asks me, not bothering to face me.

"I would have kidnapped you and locked you up for the rest of your days."

“There you go,” Lisichka says, final. “Please forgive his ignorance when it comes to feelings, and the way he has to pretend around others while someone is breaking down.”

"Pretend?" Sofia says in a small voice. She is so aware of Lisichka and the fact that she is touching her.

"Yes. The thing is, I am like your dad. The only difference is that I was born and raised in the world of neurotypical . Therefore I had to adapt and learn how I should react to situations like this."

Sofia, pulls her hand so fast, Lisichkas hand plops on her lap.

"I don't need your pretend pity. Please leave."

Lisichka straightens just as I move to stand beside her, and I glare at Sofia. She will not disrespect my Queen. She might be my daughter, but this is not something I will allow.

Lisichka reaches for my hand and prompts me to look at her, the moment our eyes meet, she lets me know she’s got this. I need to let her act as my equal.

“It’s not pity. It’s understanding. I don’t have feelings, just like your dad. But I studied human behaviour to the point of obsession so I could blend in anywhere. I know you’re hurting beyond anything you ever thought possible. We don’t want that for you.”

Sofia’s features relax a little. Her entire body is trembling, probably from the shock of my decision.

“I agree with your dad. However, as far as I’m concerned, I want you to go and talk to him. Not kill, not hurt. Just talk. Today.”

Sofia’s gaze snaps to me in complete bewilderment. Someone has contradicted me openly. Someone has given a different order than me, and that has never happened before. I understand her surprise, but I also know this is the new normal they will all have to live by.

When I nod my approval, Sofia falls to her knees and begins crying hysterically. Lisichka rises, our hands still intertwined, and looks up at me with a smile. My heart is full. Full of her. Full of awe for her. Full of her wisdom.

What happened here was beautiful. A psychopath showing compassion to the point of sparing a life — all because she knew exactly what she should do in a moment like this. It was such a deeply learned behaviour that it came as second nature to comfort my daughter.

"I know you need a hug right now, Sofia, but I'm not much of a hugger. So I'm going to give you another pat." She reaches over and pats Sofia on the head twice. "Go make your final decision. It's your life and you need to live it as you like. Do bring a gun with you just in case you need to shoot him dead. Better prepared than unprepared."

We walk out of the room and make our way to my office. Once we're alone she turns, and I know it's coming. She is not impressed.

"You will never speak to a woman about feelings in that way again. Understood?" Her voice is so sharp and dominating that I only manage a small nod. Words are redundant now — she clearly understands these things far better than I do.

"If that woman in there loved and cared for that man even a tenth of what I feel for you, she'd be on the brink of losing her mind from the pain right now. I'm not going to have someone who hasn't studied this behaviour going around blabbing, ordering people about and demanding she shoot the man she's breaking apart for."

I nod again and say nothing. She holds my gaze for a beat, daring me to contradict her — but I don't. I know I'm not the best at this, she is.

I am utterly mad for her — it hurts in a way that unthreads me. My mind, my body, my sense of reality all ache. I am consumed by my Queen. This is no ordinary love, it is obsession, a desperate, possessive hunger. She is everything... more important than air.

"You're doing it again," she says as she walks to the floor-to-ceiling windows. She lets go of my hand and I feel like I might scream at any second. Until tomorrow — until tomorrow, blasphemies like this could take place. After that, she will not take a single step away from me. If I am consumed by her to the point of madness, she must be as well, and we will carry the weight of it together.

I sink into one of the couches and let myself take her in, observing and memorising every detail of her body in that dress. It's like pouring gasoline on fire — instant and consuming — my cock springs to attention in a heartbeat.

"Come," I say, prompting her to turn and walk toward me. She can read my mind as easily as I can read hers, because she lifts her dress and straddles me.

The moment the heat of her pussy presses against my cock — even through the clothes — I feel like I'm on fire. The need to be inside her consumes me, alive and breathing, demanding, relentless.

"How do you feel about me fucking you right here?" I murmur as I press my mouth to her breasts.

"Thank you... but no, thank you," she replies, and then she starts grinding on me.

"How about I slide your knickers to the side and fuck you with just the tip of my cock until you explode?" I counter, my tone playful, hungry.

"Thank you... but no, thank you."

I change tactics and meet her thrust for thrust as she grinds on my lap. The friction, the feel of her in my hand, is enough to make me come if she keeps this up. We stay locked in the rhythm until her stomach growls so loudly it freezes us both in place.

She pulls back, and the smile on her face tells me she's about to pinch me the way she loves to.

"You suck as a boyfriend. You need to take better care of me. You really aren't having a good day today, are you?"

I grab her hips at that, grinding her against me, pressing my cock against her until she lets out a moan of pleasure.

"You're right, Lisichka." As much as it pains me, I know fucking her now isn't the right time. I kiss her breast one last time, then look up at her.

"Let me take you out for a meal."

This pleases her — and I know the perfect place to take a Queen.

Chapter Thirty

Monica

We drive to a restaurant so posh that even the butler, if that's what they're called, oozes arrogance the moment he opens his mouth to greet us. I wouldn't dine in a place like this even if the food were free and they kissed my arse on the way out.

Why does Elijah enjoy places like this? Seriously, what's wrong with KFC, Morley's, or Greggs?

The restaurant sits discreetly tucked between heritage stone façades in Mayfair, the cobbled street outside gleaming under golden streetlamps. Inside, it's all velvet hush and quiet grandeur: mahogany panelling, towering wine walls lit from within, and a ceiling so high it echoes the delicate clink of cutlery like a sacred ritual.

Waiters move with military precision, dressed in tailored suits and white gloves, their expressions hovering between polished indifference and silent judgment. The air carries a trace of truffle oil and aged Burgundy. The clientele, draped in couture and old money, barely glance up from their crystal flutes. Even the lighting is dramatic: low, moody, deliberate.

It's the kind of place where you don't ask for a menu, you're presented with an experience, or they already know your preferences.

We're guided to a secluded section, out of earshot. The staff clearly know Elijah, each of them offers a small bow as we pass. He doesn't need to ask for the table or say a single word the entire time.

Another noticeable detail: our bodyguards enter with us and position themselves in various locations, as if it's a rehearsed dance they've practised a hundred times before.

I understand that the intent of the restaurant, its taste and grandeur, speaks, like Elijah's house, to his wealth, style, and ambition. But it doesn't speak to mine. We may be the same, but I am simple and quiet in things like this, where he wields his wealth to intimidate and manipulate. To me, it feels almost obvious. Painfully so.

We're guided to the table, and when the waiter moves to pull out my chair, Elijah growls. An actual growl that makes the poor man flinch in fear.

"That won't be necessary. Move."

If tone and glare could kill, this poor boy would already be bleeding on the floor.

Elijah moves behind me and holds my chair as I sit, then drags the chair across from me to place it beside mine, putting his back to the room. I don't like it. Something about it sets me on edge. If I've learned anything about him in the past few days, it's that his desperate need to touch me, fuck me, or drink me in overrides everything else. But he shouldn't be this careless, turning his back on a room full of people and entrance points.

I don't say a word. I place my hand on the opposite side of the table, to my left. That would shift his back to the window and wall. That's all I do. Then I lift the glass of water and take a sip. The beauty of being with someone at my level is that I don't need meaningless conversation, no empty back-and-forth that drags on and sucks the life out of me.

He immediately stands and moves his chair once more to my other side. When he sits, I take his hand in mine and smile. He did well. He deserves this smile.

Multiple waiters arrive like a small army, making a fuss around us, pulling curtains to cover the window so we sit in more privacy. Others start pouring champagne, wine, and other beverages into an array of glassware before us.

"The usual, sir?" one clearly British man asks, trying to speak with a French accent. His attitude, like everyone else's here, is arrogant and exhausting. I can't help but let out a small laugh.

In a split second, I feel Elijah shift into predator mode. The air in the room changes. Heavy, dangerous, and I know he's seconds away from spilling blood.

"Leave." His voice is so calm, cold and deep. It confirms my senses. Something triggered him and he is about to snap.

I turn to assess him and see what triggered him, but the moment my eyes land on him it's obvious. He's jealous. I tilt my head, trying to make sense of it, and then it clicks: someone else heard my laugh, and he's losing his mind over it. I can't help myself, I burst out laughing.

"I would not do that if I were you," he growls at me. "Not if you don't want everyone in this room executed in the next few minutes."

This is one of those moments when I know what's expected of me. Something like, "Oh no. Please, I beg you, spare them," or, "Please don't. Oh no, you're a monster." In reality, I couldn't care either way.

What I actually like — and this is truly what I think, not what's expected of me — is that I like it. I like that something as simple as my laughter he wants all to himself. I love that he's so consumed by me that he can't share even the smallest piece of me with others. It gives me a sense of assurance and certainty that I'm not alone in this. That whatever is taking over me is consuming him in equal measure.

So if nothing else... bring it on.

I smile at him, letting him see exactly what I think, then move my hand to his thigh and pat it once. I look away and pick up the flute of champagne, letting my hand travel upward along his thigh until I reach his cock. I give it a tight squeeze, and it hardens instantly at my touch. I smile into my flute and take a sip.

My gaze stays firm on what I'm doing, completely nonchalant as if nothing at all is happening under the table. Elijah's arms rest on the table on either side of his plate, his gaze burning into me. I continue my mission, alternating between stroking him, groping him, and flicking him. Each time I change my tactics, he lets out a small breath, and I absolutely adore the effect I have on him.

Everything I'm doing is turning me on as much as it's consuming him, and I'm seconds away from taking his cock out and jerking him off just for the pleasure of it — when the unthinkable happens.

I don't see it until it's already happening, because I'm too busy imagining all the filthy things I want to do to Elijah. When this red-haired woman walks over and places her hand on his arm. My hand stills on his cock when it happens, and instantly I feel him soften.

I turn my gaze — and that's when I see her, and what she's done.

Elijah told me about his red-hot fury. I understood it on an intellectual level — of course such things happen, when all rationality flies out the window and what remains is the most unhinged version of ourselves. But until this very moment, I truly believed I was above it.

Turns out... I'm not.

"Elijah, darling, it has been some time." She trails her fingers up and down his arm.

I say nothing. I take her in — from her refined clothing to her perfect manicure, her velvet, wavy red hair, to her stunning face with big blue eyes, full lips and a tiny nose. She is most definitely every man's dream of a woman.

"Remove your hand if you don't want me to chop it off and choke you with it," Elijah says, his voice so calm it would terrify any grown man.

"Oh, my darling, you say the funniest things," the redhead laughs, running her fingers up and down his arm again. "Although I wouldn't be opposed to a little choking, darling," she says, and bats her eyelashes at me.

It's futile, all this display of belonging she's putting on. She's already dead, she just doesn't know it yet.

"Call me." She turns and starts walking. I watch her swing her hips in what she thinks is a seductive saunter, then I turn to Elijah. There is no mask on my face. It's the pure version of me he so desperately wanted out in the open. The corner of my lips tilts up and I stand. In one motion he flicks his wrist and a knife appears in his hand, he turns the hilt toward me in offering.

I study his gaze for a second, completely surrendering to my decision. If I kill him or her, he will not stop me. Smart man.

"Good boy," I say, take the knife, and stride after her. She's almost at one of the exits Vasile is guarding. When she steps in front of the door, I reach her and, in one motion, grab a fistful of hair, pull, and slice it off. With it in my hand, before she can scream, I kick her squarely in the middle of the back. She lunges forward and collapses outside, and our guards are on her in seconds.

"Cut out her tongue. Sever her hands and hips. Let her bleed to death." My instruction is direct—cold, sharp, final.

I hold Vasile's gaze the entire time. When I finish speaking, he dares to glance over my shoulder at Elijah, as if silently asking for permission.

Big mistake.

The tip of my knife is at his neck in seconds, drawing a clean drop of blood.

"Don't you dare look past me like what I said isn't an order." My voice is steel. "You'll go and do as you're told."

He nods, and more blood spills from the motion.

I want to hurt him now. Almost as much as I want to hurt her. But I pull back, lower my blade, and walk to the table.

It's really interesting how, even though some of the staff have clearly seen the commotion, perhaps even some of the guests, not a single person comes to help that woman. I guess when you're this rich and influential, if it's not something you can gain from, there's no reason to lift a finger.

When I'm seated, everything in me is screaming for blood: to hurt, to dominate, to demolish. I know this isn't the time or place to lose complete control, so I rein my fury in. Then I look at Elijah and he looks... happy.

What the fuck?!

"Are you having a stroke, Santa?" My words only amuse him further.

"Jealous, Lisichka?" he wiggles his eyebrows at me.

"Stop that right now!" I snap. "What are you, eleven?"

I grab the knife again — I'm not sure why, purely for self-defence.

His face does that funny thing again, he absorbs me into himself and I feel my fury drain away. I truly didn't think this day would come in any way, shape, or form, and I thought I was above such feelings, but I'm clearly not. More than that, now he knows I would kill anyone who touched him.

I let go of the knife, take a sip of wine, and admit my truth.

"Yes."

We stay in silence for a moment, our bodies not touching, but his presence all-consuming at my side.

"You better go take care of your mess next time."

"There will not be a next time, my Queen. I will order them all killed right now." His words are so clear and absolute, but the remnants of my fury are still lingering at the back of my mind.

"What the hell did you do with this woman for them to take such liberties with you?" My voice comes out demanding and hurt, and that just triggers me all over again. When I realise it, I turn and glare at him.

He moves so fast, taking my hand and pressing it to his chest, the roaring beat of his heart steadying the fury inside me.

"Lisichka, I told you all my sex partners were mechanical. There was nothing there. I used a few escort services, they were ordered to sit on the bed with their legs open. I didn't undress. I just unzipped, pulled my cock out, put two condoms on and..."

"SHUT THE FUCK UP!" I yell, startling even myself. Oh, this is new... wow. I actually care about this fool.

I look at him again and he's beaming with happiness. Joy flows out of him in rivers, his eyes do that thing again. I'm confused by all these reactions and feelings running through me. Sure enough, the cat's out of the bag: I'm as possessive of him as he is of me, and he knows it now.

"It was nothing there, my Queen. Ever. You know we're incapable of it." He lifts my hand to his lips and kisses the tips of my fingers, then places my palm against his forehead. "It's never been anyone else but you. There is nothing else but you in my existence."

I want to give him a hard time about it, but if I'm honest with myself, he's telling the truth. Just as I was never attracted to anyone before him, he would not have seen another woman as a woman.

When my palm relaxes against his forehead, he lowers it and presses another kiss to the back before placing it over his heart. It's still pounding out of control, as if he's the one on fire, not me.

"Have you..." He doesn't even finish the sentence. True to who he is, he can't bring himself to ask if I ever slept with Dan.

"Once," I say, and take a sip of my wine. Fuck the champagne and these pretentious rich shitheads. I'd take wine over this overpriced fizz-flavoured water any day.

I feel Elijah's heartbeat spike under my fingers, and I turn my head to look at him. Really look at him.

"I wanted to see if it would be different, if it would make sense to me what everyone kept going on about sex. It didn't. I felt nothing." His features relax at my words, but his heartbeat is still out of control.

"At least you got a release from your encounters. I didn't. It was nothing, and it sealed my deal with Dan that he could do whatever he wanted, and we would both live separate lives."

That makes Elijah relax a little. I knew this conversation would come up sooner or later, it was just a matter of time.

"Also, I want Kai as my bodyguard. I don't trust your man anymore."

That makes him freeze. He says nothing, just presses my hand tighter to his chest, his eyes calculating, measuring each word before he dares speak. Kai was another discussion waiting to happen, so if we're clearing the air, it has to be now.

"Why?"

He's lucky I'm not like other women, otherwise I'd go into full-on attack mode right now. Why does he call me his Queen and then question my decisions? Lucky for him, I'm not like other women.

"I don't trust your man after this little episode, and I've known Kai for years."

"He's ex-Mossad. He cannot be trusted."

"He can. And we will."

I can see how he's calculating every possibility to stop this, kill Kai, or change my mind without serious consequences. Only problem... I'm his equal. I'm doing exactly the same, as he weighs points and strategies, so do I. At the end of our silent battle we both know Kai is staying, and Elijah is not pleased.

"No, I never felt any attraction to him," I answer his silent question. "Yes, you can kill him if he ever crosses the line. But only after we've both assessed the evidence." I keep answering his internal interrogation. He nods, then stands, kisses me, and breathes me in.

"I will kill him. No questions asked if he crosses the line," he whispers against my lips, then sighs. "You're far too valuable for anyone else to come near you."

That might sound strange to someone else. But to me? I know exactly what he means.

It's not about jealousy, it's that he doesn't have the words, the language, the expression to match the level of worship he holds for me.

Which is honestly kind of adorable, considering he's a genius.

But I guess emotions make a fool out of even the smartest men.

The food arrives — small, pretty, pretentious... but delicious.

I'm still hungry, I think to myself, already planning what I'll order from Morley's later.

The next course comes, then the next. The portions are tiny, but by the time the fifth dish lands, I've had five different things. When the sixth arrives, I'm full.

I need a breather. No matter how good it tastes, there's no way I can eat much more.

"Tell me how it works," I say, and it only takes one glance for him to know exactly what I'm referring to.

"In various ways, but the most effective one is through online meetings. The virus infiltrates as an additional attendee, records and transcribes the entire meeting. At first, it was just a basic AI. But now, Alex runs the information, selects it, catalogues it, and stores it until we need it."

I nod my head, because that's pretty cool. How he's there, but not there. Knows how to steal the information, store it, and then release it. I'm impressed.

"How rich are you?"

"Five hundred."

To a different person, it would have seemed so strange to ask such a question or to answer it. To us, it's just a number. Our true power lies in our minds and character.

"In the bank. The entire portfolio, I'm not sure. I can get those numbers for you if you like."

"You have five hundred million in your bank and you sent two billion to my charity. You're an idiot." I side glare at him. That was not logical at all.

"My Queen." He tilts my head towards him, his fingers lingering on my chin.

"WE have five hundred billion in the bank. It's not mine, I added you to everything that I have a while ago."

I have only what I can call a very human reaction and stare at him. He bursts out laughing and makes a remark about my eyes being big as a sorcerer, but I cannot quite hear it because the number he said, it's not something normal.

People should not be this rich.

What the actual hell?!

"Why?"

"You already know who I am. I invested my money well. But the most profitable part of my business was, and remains, the information market. Especially if you play both sides."

To that, apparently, I make a face again, because the prick just starts laughing.

"Don't be like that, Lisichka. I was bored. I had to entertain myself."

"Have you ever heard of a fucking book?" I snap at him. "That's entertaining as well. Go in that direction."

"Hilarious," he says, placing a kiss on my nose.

Then it hits me. He said there's nothing else but me, so that means all the time and energy he was putting into all those businesses would now be redirected to me.

Oh shit. Is that what he's planning for tomorrow? It has to be.

We finish our food and make our way through the busy streets of London. I'm still trying to figure out how to process the new information I've just deduced.

My gaze drifts out the window — and there it is, one of my favourite Asian shops coming into view.

He can offer me true luxury, truffle, and caviar. But I can teach him about lychee and pandan.

It sounds so stupid... I'm doing it.

“Have you ever tried a lychee drink, iubire?”

He looks at me, confused.

I turn to Vasile. “Pull over in front of that shop.”

We’re not supposed to stop here, and we both know it, but I don’t care. That means Vasile will have to stay in the car while Elijah and I head inside.

The other guards will surround the shop in no time, but at least we won’t have a hovering giant breathing down our necks.

When we enter the shop, that distinct scent unique to small Asian stores hits us instantly. I take a moment to savour it, there’s comfort in its familiarity. It was one of the hidden gems I discovered when I first moved to England: my love for Asian cuisine and culture. So much difference, yet so many beautiful similarities between the nations. I was fascinated for years, always eager to learn more.

I’m not sure how much Elijah is enjoying this, though. At first, he simply tightened his grip on my hand. Now, he’s stepped behind me completely, circling his arm around my waist — becoming a human shield, blocking anything from behind.

I'm part amused, part annoyed. This level of protection is completely unnecessary. But if I'm honest, having him behind me actually makes it easier to weave through the narrow aisles, crammed with shelves stacked high and boxes shoved into every spare inch of space.

Still, I can't help myself. I start moving a little more unpredictably, just to mess with him. When I feel his panic start to radiate — like a heatwave of overprotection — I finally steer us toward the aisle where I know the juice should be.

We try to squeeze between some boxes to reach the shelf, but it's useless, we'll need to go around. That's when I notice a small shoe peeking out from behind one of the stacks. Someone's back there.

"Hello? Can you please help me?" I call out, curious to see who it is.

A small young Asian woman rises from behind the boxes. She's actually shorter than the stack, which is about my height, and even now she's barely visible. Truth be told, I've never been in an Asian marketplace that wasn't filled with boxes in every direction, this is hardly surprising. But the girl catches my attention.

She has impossibly smooth skin, a small round nose, and lips shaped like a perfect strawberry. Her jet-black hair falls pin-straight down her back. Her features are simple, but she's beautiful in a clean, effortless way — untouched. The moment our eyes meet, her black eyes lock with mine, and even though she's smiling, they speak volumes.

Unimaginable pain.

Elijah is on high alert and I feel like smacking him, just to get him to back off and let me observe the girl more closely. There's something about her. Something that's stirred my curiosity in a way I can't quite explain.

"Do you know where the lychee juice is?" I ask, my voice warm.

"Yes. Right there behind those boxes—next to where my sanity has left me."

The way she delivers it, with total sincerity, makes her dry humour even more hilarious, and I burst out laughing, leaning back onto Elijah for support.

I glance up at him. He looks stunned, like he has no idea why I found that funny.

Never mind him. He's probably panicking about why I brought him here in the first place. I'll force-feed him lychee for a week to make up for it. Anyway, that's for later.

I like her... Let's see what else I can get out of her.

She tries to move the boxes but gives up, then squeezes her tiny body between them to reach for a six-pack of lychee juice.

"How many do you want? They come in packs of six!" she calls out.

Elijah does that signature flick of his arm, and the knife appears in his hand. I immediately step in front of him, covering him instinctively. We lock into a silent war.

I don't have to say a word—he can read it in my eyes: *Put that knife away now or I'll shove it straight into your cock.*

The corner of his lip twitches in amusement. Of course, that's all it takes for him to start getting hard.

"I'm not getting any younger. One or more?" the girl yells again, arms stretched out with a pack.

I like her. I want her.

"Give me all that you have, thank you."

I don't take my eyes off Elijah until he gives a subtle nod, silently agreeing to let the girl be.

"I need an assistant," I whisper to him, smiling before winking when he pulls a dramatic, exasperated face.

"I can get you an assistant," he whispers back.

"Do I look like someone who needs an assistant, or your help, boy?" Now he's getting on my nerves. He better settle down if he doesn't want a real fight on his hands.

"There you go," the girl says as she squeezes her way out of the tiny nook she was in. She lays all the packs directly on the floor.

"You don't have a basket. Let me get you one or would you prefer a box, perhaps? Pick any you like. They all carry my will to live by this point."

I burst out laughing again and glance over my shoulder at Elijah, who just rolls his eyes.

I want her, I tell him with my gaze.

"A box will be perfect, thank you," I say, smiling politely at her. "What's your name?"

She stands a little taller, sizing me up as if *she's* curious about *me* now.

Elijah just shakes his head in disbelief at the girl's audacity, and I can feel his fury radiating off *her* like heat.

"My name is An Hong Mai," she says, the words landing with quiet honour—spoken as if they mean something.

She's an interesting little thing.

"It was lovely meeting you, Hong Mai. Thank you for the help."

I take one of the empty boxes and make quick work of arranging the juice packs with the barcodes facing up, so the cashier can just scan them and we can be on our way.

All the while, Elijah paces and fusses behind me in the cramped little shop. Don't pack that, don't lift this, on and on.

Give me a break... or give me a gun so I can shoot him.

When we get in the car, I make a point of not sitting next to him or allowing him to touch me in any way.

The air inside is thick. You could probably cut it with one of Elijah's mysterious disappearing knives.

Mental note: remember this moment and make a joke at his expense later.

After a few silent minutes, I place the box between us like a barrier. He lets out a sigh.

Out of the corner of my eye, I try to gauge his posture as I reach for one of the juice boxes.

I open it casually, as if it's nothing special, and take a sip.

It's just as I remembered—sweet, full of flavour, and delicious.

One of Asia's little hidden gems.

"Can I have some?" The mighty Elijah, asking for juice like a little boy.

"It depends. Can I have her?"

"You can have anything you like. We just need to run a check on her."

"Why would I do that," I say, my voice low and cool, "when I can ask her... or get it out of her?"

"Lisichka, please. I can't have anyone around you who hasn't been thoroughly vetted." His voice is laced with frustration, again. I didn't appreciate it the first time, and I don't appreciate it now.

I say nothing. Just keep drinking my juice. I roll the window down and let the fresh air in, letting the sounds of the city wash over me. I already know, I'll get Hong Mai one way or another. I just wonder what she's hiding, because every instinct in me screamed to take her.

Elijah reaches for my hand, takes it gently into his, and presses a kiss to the back of it. "What my Queen wants is what my Queen will get. She's yours to do as you please."

I turn the straw of the juice box toward his lips, watching with amusement as he takes a long sip.

"Delicious," he murmurs, eyes locking with mine. "But you taste better."

He smiles, and it's *that* smile. The one that turns my insides to molten heat and sets my core ablaze.

I've been thinking about this for a while now.

Maybe... maybe it's time I tried it.

How would he react if I were the one to drop to my knees this time? How would he react if I initiate to suck him off?

Chapter Thirty-One

Elijah

Her present has arrived.

It took them months to create what I envisioned only days after we met, but it's finally here.

Today is the day the entire world will either bow to their Queen... or be put down without a second thought.

Everything has been organised down to the most meticulous detail, with updates reported to me by the hour.

I managed only a few hours of sleep last night, my body finally giving out. I slept with my arms and legs wrapped around Lisichka, dozing in and out, terrified something might happen, or worse, that she might choose to leave while I was unconscious. At this point, I don't know if I actually rested or if I'm even more exhausted.

One thing is certain. I have never wanted anything more.

I need her to be recognised as what she truly is. To take her rightful place in this world.

This need... this all-consuming obsession to possess her, to force her to be mine, is devouring me.

There is nothing left of me.

Only her.

I understand my father now. If he felt even half of what I feel for Lisichka, I understand why he never allowed my mother to take even the smallest step away from him. Lucky him — she felt the same.

I can't even imagine what would've happened to me if my Queen hadn't wanted me back.

What truly matters is that she's here now. In my arms. I can touch her, feel her skin against mine, breathe the air she exhales, bathe in her presence, and let myself be consumed by her.

"Seriously, put that thing away or let me borrow your knife again," she says over her shoulder in a sleepy voice.

"I'm not doing anything." I laugh at her antics.

Oh, I love how she plays with me, makes my entire body sing in anticipation.

"Right. So that steel cock making its way between my legs, poking around, does indeed have a brain of its own, and it's not you?"

I burst out laughing and tighten my arms around her.

"Yes. It's scientifically proven that cocks have a brain of their own."

With that, I start kissing her shoulder and nibbling on it the way she likes. Then—this time consciously—I press my cock closer to her entrance.

It doesn't matter how many times I've had her.

It doesn't matter how many times I've drunk her dry.

The need for more only grows—stronger, deeper, more demanding.

If I didn't know any better, I'd truly think she did something to me—reduced me to this primal, unhinged version of myself.

"Don't even think about it!" she yells over her shoulder, clamping her thighs together.

"I'm sore, and we were at it for hours last night. I'm dehydrated, I'm starving, and I need to pee. So let. Go. Of me."

Let go of me...

More horrifying words have never been spoken in my presence.

Let go of me...

NEVER!!!

Instinctively, I tighten my arms around her even further, until I physically can't squeeze any more. My entire body shivering around her, desperate to draw more from her, to pull her into me, to never let her go.

"Let go, Elijah. You're hurting me."

That was the kick I apparently needed. I release her immediately.

I don't want to hurt her. Not in any way.

"...Apologise, Lisichka."

"Stop apologising and take better care of me." She quickly gets up and runs toward the toilet. "Or I might have enough of you one day and leave."

The moment the words penetrate my ears, my brain registers the sarcastic tone, it's a joke. But that doesn't matter. It flicks a switch in me, igniting something primal and uncontrollable.

If I wanted to trap her to me before, now... now there is nothing—and I mean *nothing*—that will ever allow her to leave my side.

She doesn't have free will when it comes to being with me anymore. I'd rather have her hate me and still be next to me than love me from afar.

Fuck that. All the way to Sunday.

Absolutely, categorically NO! NEVER!

If I had any reservations about my present before, she just obliterated them with that one line. Joke or not, it's happening. And to hell with the consequences. Whatever storm she brings has to be better than this rotten feeling of not having her.

The rest of the day flashes by in a blur of preparations, emails, and my constant monitoring of her every move.

It's intoxicating—seeing her not only in my personal space, but in the mansion, among my people. The way they fear her. The way they bow.

I love it.

They should worship the ground she walks on.

Or I will force them to.

"Should I wear something specific?" she calls out, eyeing the endless rows of clothes I arranged for this occasion.

She spent months tormenting me from her daughter's apartment. I spent those same months planning, designing, and executing every monumental detail—down to the last delectable thing I wanted for her.

From the clothes in this wardrobe to the accessories, perfumes, and jewellery, every inch has been touched by my love for my Queen. All of my estates bear her mark now.

The first property to undergo such a transformation is the one in Italy.

I can't wait to see her face when we arrive at the villa in Portofino.

The villa in Portofino had always been a statement.

Perched above the sea like a crown—sharp edges and indulgent restraint.

Every inch of it bore my taste: white marble, gilded veins, the cold satisfaction of symmetry.

But now... now it's hers.

It's all hers.

The gardeners planted over a hundred lilac trees across the upper terraces, because she once indulged me with a passing comment that she liked the scent.

Everything is in love for her.

Even the mosaic tiles throughout the mansion—torn out and re-laid—white and lilac, swirled in perfect harmony, like her laughter wrapped around my throat.

The drapes, the walls, the goddamn plates—everything redesigned, reupholstered, redone.

And I don't give a fuck what anyone thinks.

If the world knew I redesigned a ten-bedroom estate to match her favourite colour, they'd call me insane.

But they don't know what it means to be consumed like this.

To build cathedrals out of worship.

To bleed luxury into devotion.

Anyone close to me would expect to see my signature gold initials—E.D.—discreetly tucked throughout the estate.

But this is the first property where I updated the initials to **M.E.**

The world will see hers before mine.

Deliberate. Intentional. Good.

Let them know whose crown I kneel before.

It's for her.

It's always been for her.

Everything in this world is for her now.

"Iubire?" She turns to me, concern in her gaze.

She doesn't realise I just had an idea, for the estate in Japan. A way to include her in that, as my next project.

"Are you all right? Do you want to reschedule?"

She places both palms on my chest as she steps in front of me, and instinctively, I wrap my arms around her.

She fits so well in my arms.

All of this. All of her.

Fits perfectly with me.

Nothing is forced.

Nothing is pushed.

Nothing is out of place.

It's perfect harmony.

Perfect symmetry between us.

"No," I smile and kiss her forehead.

"I was planning a trip to Japan just now... and studying you at the same time."

"I think you've studied me enough, thank you," she says, her tone playful and dismissive.

"No. There will never be *enough* studying of you."

That's all it takes, my cock starts to harden. At this stage, it doesn't even surprise me anymore.

The things we've done, the memories we've made... They play and replay in my mind like a fever dream I never want to wake from.

I could be inside her every second of every day and die a happy man.

If anything, I need to control it. Force my body to stay calm around her. Tame the obsession, if only for her sake.

"Don't even think about it," she says, alarmed.

I smile and drink her in again.

Oh, for fuck's sake. Her being this adorable does not help the situation, now my cock is twitching, demanding satisfaction.

"I'm sore. And we said we wouldn't do it again until tonight. Promises are promises," she says in a playful tone. "Keep your word, Elijah."

She delivers those last words in what she thinks is a cold, daring voice, but to me, it's just that much more endearing.

The way she lowers her tone for effect... it kills me. It's so her, and I want her even more for it.

"Yes, yes. How about I lick you until I get a drink of you?" I wiggle my eyebrows at her. "I haven't had any since last night, so really, I'm being more than considerate. You should cooperate, take a seat on one of the floating islands, and let me enjoy you."

"Absolutely not!" she snaps. "People are already arriving. We're not doing anything."

"My Queen, please..." I grin. "Everyone else is early, regardless of the time. The Queen is always right on time."

She smiles at that and leans her head against my chest. Her heartbeat is agitated, and her body trembles with a soft shiver.

"Are you okay, Lisichka?" I was so consumed with my own feelings, I barely noticed something was bothering her.

"I'm not wearing make-up. Or putting on some stupid, complicated dress," she mutters into my chest.

That caught me off guard.

It had never even occurred to me as something we needed to discuss.

"You can do whatever you want." I'm honestly surprised we're even having this discussion.

"You're the most beautiful thing I've ever seen in my entire life, Lisichka."

At that, she lifts her gaze to mine, studying me. She stays there, eyes scanning, assessing—calculating and recalculating outcomes. I can read it all over her features.

"Fine. Maybe a lipstick," she says at last, and smiles at me.

"Whatever you want. Everything's there for you, and if you need anything else, we'll send someone to get it." I kiss the top of her head and linger there, just breathing her in.

"I do have one request about the dress... if that's okay with you."

As we make our way to the grand hall, I take my time absorbing my Queen into memory once more, etched in the dress I chose for her.

I wanted it all for myself, and this dress is the embodiment of her—of how I feel about keeping her mine.

The gown is high-collared, long-sleeved, severe in silhouette. Yet it clung to her with the quiet authority of a queen who needed no bare skin to command the room.

The ivory fabric moved like liquid obedience, heavy with intention, stitched with the kind of restraint that whispered power, not submission.

No embellishments. No distractions.

Just sculpted simplicity in the purest tone of devotion.

Every line of it mirrored her control, her defiance, her elegance.

The moment we reach the doors, I prompt her to stop and wait. My guards step forward to open them.

A hush falls from the other side, that silent chatter of anticipation, a tension so thick it hums in the air.

Everyone is waiting.

Twelve-foot slabs of blackwood parted like a book written in blood and sealed in tragedy. I designed them myself when we constructed the mansion, carvings from Slavic folklore, only wrong on purpose. Bent. Broken. Reimagined through my lens. The wolves bore too many teeth. The saints had their eyes stitched shut. And the silver inlays bled into the grain like veins beneath skin. Every inch a warning disguised as art. Intimidation in the most intimate, indirect way.

We walk into the hall, slow, measured. As always, I give people time to feel the weight of my approach. Our steps echoed on the marble like they belonged to someone who should be feared... but never fled from. A sense of self-awareness that tricks the mind—even when it senses danger, it deceives itself with assurance. *"Stay." "You're safe."* Until it's too late... and you're already in my web.

The hall exhaled silence the moment I came into view.

Vaulted ceilings, high enough to swallow hope.

Walls draped in velvet so dark it could have been mourning something. Or someone.

The chandeliers didn't sparkle—they hummed. Soft glass orbs glowing like distant planets, suspended above a table too long to ever forget who sits at the head.

Me.

Always me.

Until now.

It's not ostentation.

It's declaration.

Every detail exists because I willed it into form. Every shadow, every note in the air. The violins whisper through hidden speakers, a melody deliberately imperfect—dissonant threads woven through harmony, just enough to unsettle. Every slip, every fracture in the sound is purposeful, a manipulation of the senses.

It doesn't matter if they recognise the music.

It matters that they feel it.

I glance at my Queen and the corner of her mouth twitches, she's fighting back a laugh.

She gets what I'm doing before anyone else does: every detail is controlled, from the music playing like a haunted whisper through hidden speakers, to the perfume in the air now twisted by Lisichka's scent, to the light, to the very weight of it all.

I control it. I hold it all in the palm of my hand.

She walks beside me. My Lisichka. My Queen. Not behind me, as others do, as anyone should. She walks beside me because she is an extension of me. The only extension of me.

Heads nod, not in obedience, but in something more intimate: *reverence.*

Everyone here understands exactly where they stand in my world. And they feel it. The gravity of this gathering is beyond any of their control. Beyond their power.

Her present in my pocket feels heavier than before.

Not physically, emotionally.

I crafted it to outlast both heaven and hell.

Two cuffs—one for her, one for me. No key. One lock. A promise cast in precious metal. The weight of them is deliberate. She'll feel it, just like I do. Every diamond cut, set, and forged with the kind of devotion most men spend lifetimes avoiding.

The chain between the cuffs is not an afterthought. It's thick. Unapologetic. Loud in its silence. Laced with diamonds so vicious in their brilliance, they catch the fire of every light and spit it back like shattered rainbows.

You can't look at it without seeing everything we are..

Beautiful. Brutal. Bound.

And then there's **the cross.**

My home.

Not a delicate crucifix, not a religious icon.

This is the Bratva cross.

Squared edges. Blackened steel. Etched with our lineage, our code. Each arm tipped in sharpened angles—four blades of loyalty, honour, obedience, and blood. A single crimson gem in its centre, buried deep, like the heart we offer in silence.

It doesn't hang. It anchors.

Heavy, unyielding, carved for those who understand that power is pain worn with pride.

A symbol of my dominance.

Unity.

Protection.

Sacrifice.

Because that's what I'm doing right now.

It's not the dominance I'm publicly claiming—it's the sacrifice no one, not even I, thought possible.

It's not a chain with a cross around her neck to mark that she belongs to me.

It's a chain I will place around us both.

Long enough to move.

Short enough to bind.

Ensuring there is no moment in my life where I'm not with her.

This isn't just "You belong to my Bratva" or "You belong to my empire."

It's ***You belong to me.***

You are mine.

And from this moment onward, we are one.

This isn't just a ritual. Or a claim.

She'll be bound to me—physically, emotionally, spiritually, and through power.

I really just hope she takes it well.

If not, well... that's why I designed the diamonds to be so damn magnificent. Hopefully, that tips it over the edge and I don't get myself killed tonight. Worst case, I still have all three trackers in her body active.

There's no escaping this.

There's no escaping us.

Everything is intentional, down to the very last detail.

It might even be heavier than I'd originally planned, but even that has its place.

The weight of it was made for the world to bear.

The weight of us.

I stop near the head of the table.

The others remain silent, as they should, as we make our way.

Good.

They understand the gravity of this.

Not the ceremony.

Her.

My fingers brush the chain in my pocket again.

Not to bind her.

To bind *myself.*

I'm an intelligent man. I know exactly what this is. I am willingly giving my power to the one variable I can't control. But there is no other outcome that can keep my sanity and my life intact.

You don't understand, I think to myself, releasing that thought into the universe for the first time in my life.

This isn't about love. It's about the one thing I never meant to have—a reason to lose.

I kept my roots in place, and everyone at this table wears a chain, showcasing my legacy within the Bratva. A mark of their place in my world, in my empire. Some chose tattoos as well, but I never enforced that. The chain is enough.

It's a claim. Of my protection. A silent vow that I watch over them—that they belong to *me,* kneel only for *me,* and owe their loyalty and respect *only* to me.

We take our place at the head of the table. I gesture for the others to sit.

"She is your Queen from this point onwards."

I cut straight to the point — there's no time to waste. No softening the claim.

"In a P1 situation, there is no limit to get her to safety. Even before my own."

I pause.

Letting the words settle.

Letting the shock take shape — the understanding that Monica is no longer just mine. She's theirs. She's above them.

My gaze travels slowly down the table.

Sofia.

Buddy.

Hunter.

Vasile.

Alec.

Kirill.

Stefan.

Alexandra.

Liam.

Dominic.

I read each of their faces, one by one.

Assessing.

Weighing.

Making sure they *understand.*

"There is no world that will exist without her in it. And if she's gone..."

I pause again, my voice dropping like a blade.

"You have my permission to shoot me dead on the spot, because I will destroy the world and everyone in it."

A collective gasp ripples down the line.

Predictable.

Small.

As expected as the outrage about to come from what I say next.

"*Alex* has been programmed to deploy nuclear bombs — and multiple chemical weapons — across the globe."

I let that sink in.

Level. Steady. Final.

"As I said... in the event of a P1, your only task is to get your Queen to safety."

I pause.

Because I can't say it.

I *won't* say it.

The possibility of her being dead is a thought I can't allow to live in language — not even in theory.

I take a breath.

Press it down.

Force my voice into steel.

"Because if she is gone..."

Another pause, tighter this time.

"You better kill me on the spot."

A beat.

"Or I will destroy the entire world."

"Dad..." Sofia's voice is soft beside me.

"You no longer have Global Admin access to Alex," I say without looking at her. "He's been reconfigured with the necessary protocols for this event."

"Dad!"

Her voice sharpens, panicked now. She rises to her feet, and I finally turn to meet her gaze.

The look on her face says it all. It's not fear. It's hurt. The kind that only comes when the person you trust most draws a line — and places you on the other side of it. For the first time since she entered my life, I've shut her out.

"No, Sofia." I gesture for her to sit.

"You made your choice. And so did I. You chose Hunter, and I'm happy for you both."

I let that hang in the air for a beat.

“But just as I gave you all the freedom to build lives beyond me,” I scan the table, locking eyes with each one of them, daring anyone to challenge that truth, “I deserve the same.”

“And somehow, in some *unbelievable* universe, my Queen was created — and I found her.

There is *nothing* in this world, in this life, in this entire goddamn universe that holds a higher priority for me than her.”

"My King..."

Monica’s soft voice carries a trace of concern.

Her hand rests gently on my arm — to soothe me, perhaps. To stop me from escalating further.

"As I said, there is no limit for my Queen. You all have your orders."

In a single, fluid motion, I lock the cuff around her wrist, and then around mine.

The click echoes through the hall.

Sacred.

Tragic.

Final.

In the perfect silence of the hall, I hear it. Not the sound of metal. But the moment my universe became... **breakable.**

This isn’t a chain around her neck to mark possession. It isn’t meant to dominate or submit. It’s a chain forged for intimate allegiance. Not to lower her status — but to elevate her. To bind us in equal measure. To ensure our consequences are shared. Always.

Vasile rises from his seat. I don't hesitate. My wrist flicks, releasing the blade, and it flies. It slices past him with such speed, everyone sees it only when it’s too late. He jerks his head just in time, but not fast enough. The blade nicks his ear, clean and sharp. Blood trickles down.

He doesn’t say a word. Just sits back down and presses a napkin to the wound to stem the bleeding.

There’s no need for words. I gave an order. They will follow.

This isn't a democracy. I don't ask for opinions or advice. Why would I?

They are all drastically inferior.

To me.

To her.

Even before, I barely tolerated their feeble attempts at strategy, always five steps behind.

But this? This insolence from Vasile? It will be remembered. Not now. Not here. But a scratch from my blade is nothing compared to what's coming.

I feel a gentle squeeze on my arm.

When I glance down, I see her hand—her beautiful left hand—cuffed to mine.

Bound to me.

It's even more breathtaking than I imagined.

I chained my right hand. Gave it to her.

Even that detail isn't accidental.

It's a gesture.

A truth.

I've given her my right hand—because she is my right hand now.

If she chooses to, she can rule it all. Every piece of this empire.

Her left hand is the one cuffed. Because all I want from this moment forward... Is to worship her.

My finger traces the bracelet on her wrist, and the contrast between the cold metal and her warm skin sends a rush through my senses.

It's almost overwhelming—how perfect it feels.

All the emotions from before surge back, crashing over me like a tide.

I am one with her now.

There's only one thing left to do.

I raise two fingers—first to my temple, then to my heart.

In an instant, every person in the room mirrors the gesture.

Then, a single tap to their chests.

No words.

No applause.

Just silent acknowledgment.

Now they all know where they stand.

And so do I.

Our gazes meet, and I see it clearly in my Queen's eyes—surprise, fury, and unease.

It's enough to make my body tremble. She can rattle me with a single look.

I steady myself, clear my throat—for the first time in my life—and speak.

"I'm not above you. I'm bound with you. Your pain is mine. Your blood, mine. Your life... mine. As all of me is yours."

And in that moment, I realise something for the first time in my entire existence.

I'm not the most dangerous person in this room anymore.

She is.

Chapter Thirty-Two

Monica

I'm chained? What the actual fuck did he do?!

I'm going to kill him the moment we get to our room and spare the world another imbecile — because clearly, he's not the genius I thought he was! That man wouldn't have done something this stupid.

I knew it. I fucking knew that whatever he was planning today, I wasn't going to like it. The part about claiming me in front of his beloved UBT was clear as day — saw it coming a mile away. The indirect manipulation? Typical him. I saw that too, and I even found it hilarious how much effort he put into that shit.

But this?

The chain makes a small noise as we walk back to our room in silence.

This is unacceptable. He cannot do this.

He cannot have this!

Elijah isn't saying a word as we get closer to the room. We're in the last corridor now, and the air is thick with that inevitable doom — the moment the fight will begin.

He knows he's in deep shit.

But to my surprise, even knowing he's about to get it, he's as calm as ever. As if any outcome would suit him just fine.

I hate that.

I truly hate how easily he can force me to bend to his will.

The moment he pushes the door shut and the lock clicks, I leap at him — fast.

I wrap the chain around his neck in one swift motion and slam his back against the wall.

"What the fuck do you think you're doing, boy?"

My voice is calm. Low.

The perfect blend of terrifying.

He smiles.

The fucker actually smiles while being choked.

I tighten the chain, making damn sure it'll leave bruises around his neck for this.

"Be with you," he says in a choked voice. "In the only way I could survive it."

"Look, I know you have this need to possess me — it's clear as day. And I also understand you've got this proprioceptive need to constantly touch me. I get that as well.

But fuck me sideways, Elijah!

From that to chaining me to you is a long fucking way — and you crossed the line, boy!"

I yell the last words right in his face.

I'm actually choking him now — his face is turning red.

Part of me likes it. I want to do this. And part of me is choking with him, feeling the burn in my lungs alongside his.

Ugh.

This whole feelings nonsense is exhausting. Fine, I think to myself, and loosen my grip.

"The only way I could survive," he repeats through coughs.

"Not my problem," I spit back. "Take it off."

"It doesn't come off, my Queen."

I glare at him, at his unimaginable stupidity for doing such a thing.

"Take it off!" I yell at full volume.

"My Queen, it won't come off. I designed it so that the moment it clicks shut, it can't be opened again."

His tone is that warm, reassuring nonsense he always pulls.

I hate it.

I fucking hate it!

"I will chop off your hand, Elijah! Take. It. Off!"

His gaze softens.

His breath lingers on mine — his scent, his presence — breaking me from within.

I fucking hate it!

I fucking hate having feelings!

This crap shouldn't even exist, because clearly, even the most intelligent people are reduced to pure stupidity like Elijah... or pure confusion like me!

Why does this shit even exist?!

I want no part in this business of *feeling*.

I need rational, cold decisions — not this nonsense lurking around every fucking corner!

Fuck me!!!

"I will give you my life and my heart, if you want. Ask anything of me. But the chain will remain on us."

"MOTHERFUCKER!" I scream in his face.

He trapped me.

He actually managed to trap me.

This is far worse than what his dad did to his mum.

He trapped me.

"Very well, Elijah.

I would like your heart in my hands," I say, locking eyes with him as I deliver my request.

"I will peel these handcuffs off your corpse... and free myself."

His gaze softens again, and the look in his eyes isn't just resignation. It's... triumph. As if he's finally figured out what I want, and he's ready to give it to me.

He reaches to his left until there's a soft click... then pulls out a knife.

"Seriously?! What is it with you and secret compartments?" I say, exasperated.

"Don't judge me. I had a spy era of interest, and I designed the mansions myself because I didn't trust the architects — or anyone else — to know the full blueprint of my homes. That would be stupid. Or a complete security nightmare.

I was going to teach you..."

His words trail off.

"Well, I would have taught you the logic behind them. Where they are, how to access them in case of an emergency."

I glare at him again and pull back, putting some space between us. The stupid chain makes that sound again, scraping at my last nerve.

There are no words to exchange.

No pleas. No tears. Nothing else.

I gave him an order, and he needs to obey.

The look in his eyes is pure devotion, as if I'm truly the most precious thing he's ever had.

And for a man who lives in such luxury, opulence, and power... That look is more than I ever imagined he was capable of.

He truly sees me as above him.

It's clear as day.

I see myself as so simple.

So clear.

So clean.

There's nothing spectacular about me.

I just... *am.*

Yes, I'm intelligent — but I'm not extraordinary in any way.

Or at least... I can't see it.

But I see it in him.

And somehow... he's seeing it in me.

He thrusts the knife toward his chest, and I cover his heart with my palm. The blade cuts through my hand, the tip still reaching him.

"FUCK!" he yells at the top of his lungs.

"What have I done?!"

He pulls the knife out, and I watch the pool of blood spill from him, mingling with my own.

There's something almost absolute in the simple intimacy of our blood uniting.

He claimed me in his world.

Declared me his Queen.

Chained me to himself.

And now...

I've claimed him.

Sealed our bond in blood.

Accepted our fate.

It's done.

Our bond is bathing in blood, and there is no coming back from this.

The pain doesn't register.

His voice doesn't register.

The only thing I feel is the warm, sticky sensation of our blood mingling, pouring down my arm and his chest.

I could have been free.

But the moment the corner of my eye caught the glint of that blade... I knew.

Deep within me, I knew. I would rather die than let anything happen to him.

I chose him.

I chose *this.*

And I sealed it in blood.

"Lisichka, please. Baby... answer me." His voice is so scared as he presses down on my hand to stop the bleeding.

I lift my eyes to his, and I see it staring back at me.

We are one.

"I chose you."

A full-body shiver runs through me at the sound of my own words.

It's done.

We are one.

Chapter Thirty-Three

Elijah

She chose me back.

My Queen chose me back and spared my life.

If it weren't for the fucking blood pouring out of us, I swear I'd be floating in the air right now.

Goddamn it.

It actually worked.

My plan actually worked, and I survived it.

My body takes over. I wrap my arms around her, and it's my turn to take her breath away. My tongue dances across her entire existence, absorbing her into me.

"I live for you, my Queen," I vow onto her lips.

I take a deep breath in, breathing her in. I feel completely and utterly consumed by her. But then the sharp scent of copper registers, I pull back.

The top of her dress is now soaked in blood.

"Come, Lisichka. Let me call your doctor."

"My doctor?" she says, confused.

"Baby, please. You know me well enough by now."

She studies me for a second, and then I see it. The exact moment the pain in her hand starts to register.

"You got me a doctor, didn't you?" She watches my face, analysing my reaction.

I say nothing.

Play innocent.

Keep pressure on her hand while trying to dial with the other.

"What's next, Elijah? Did you already pick the names of our kids?" She provokes me, pushing for a reaction.

Fuck yes I did.

If it were up to me, I'd make twenty babies with her. I doubt she'd let me, or if it's even biologically possible anymore, but I'd pump her full of my cum any day, every day, until she gives me her babies, and I can look after them all like they're made of her.

"I'm getting Kai!" she yells at me again, realising she's just hit the jackpot.

I say nothing, still scrolling to find her doctor's number.

"And Hong Mai."

The corner of my mouth lifts, because this is a no-brainer. I already decided she can have both. She can have a thousand Kais and Hong Mais, as long as she's chained to me and I can protect her from everything that might ever come her way.

"Agreed," I say, and press dial.

I take her to the bathroom and press bandages to her hand and my chest until Dr. Sally arrives ten minutes later.

It pays to have money in situations like this. I can call in favours from anyone, just to get my Queen to safety.

Not to mention the discreet care that comes with situations like this. No paperwork, no unnecessary questions.

Just: *"What seems to be the problem?"*

"How can I assist?"

"Not to worry — you'll be back to full health in no time."

Didn't particularly like how she looked at my Queen, so I'll follow up, and make sure she likes men. Otherwise, Lisichka will be getting a new doctor. I know she's beyond beautiful, but if this doctor could do her job without looking directly at what's mine, it would be much better for her.

"Stop it," Lisichka whispers discreetly to me. "You're going to scare her."

I turn my gaze to her, and she is *not* impressed. Not sure what I did wrong. I just sat here and said nothing.

"You're looking at her like you're about to rip her eyes out."

"She was looking at you funny. I don't like it," I mutter, turning my gaze back to the doctor.

"You have issues, Elijah. Let's face it," she says, fighting back a laugh. "That *funny look* is called compassion."

"I don't like it. You're getting a new doctor."

She starts laughing hard, and the chain makes that sound again.

To me, it's the call of our bond. The one she *bathed* in blood.

This turned out even better than I imagined.

She chose me.

She didn't just choose me — she made a blood oath.

And now... there's no escaping me.

Not in this life.

Not in the next.

I'm so consumed replaying everything that's happened. Her words, her voice, the moment. I don't even register the doctor moving onto me, until I hear a growl come out of Lisichka.

I turn.

If looks could kill, the doctor would already be long gone.

Dr Sally is taping up my chest again, touching and probing, and I can see it all over Lisichka's face. She's probably murdering the doctor in her mind right now just for touching me.

This time, I'm the one laughing.

She can sing that song all she wants about me being possessive and having issues, but look at her, she's right fucking there with me.

"You have issues, my Queen," I say, challenging her back with a grin.

For the rest of the time we're being looked after, our eyes stay locked. I could stay like this, just looking at her until the moment I die, and still consider my life complete.

I found her.

I actually found my pair.

"Your services are no longer required," Lisichka says calmly. "Get out."

The corner of my mouth twitches, because this is honestly more hilarious than anything she's said or done so far. But if I laugh right now, I might get stabbed again. Or worse, she might do something stupid like pour bleach on me just to clean off the other woman's touch.

Imagine my surprise when I see my Queen kneeling before me looking up.

I swear, if I'd been standing, my legs would've given out.

Holy fuck!

My Queen is on her knees —willingly —before me!

I forget how to breathe, frozen in anticipation of what she'll do next. When I feel her hands on my belt, making quick work of it and my zipper, then touch my cock, my entire being comes alive, tingling with pleasure.

This is actually happening. It's fucking happening.

I look down, and my cock is fully hard in her hand as she jerks me slowly, studying it from every angle. The moment the tip of her tongue flicks the sensitive underside of my cock, a moan explodes out of me so loud it stops her in place.

"Fuck, baby! Are you sure? I mean, I really want this."

My entire body is trembling in anticipation. I really want her to suck my cock — to feel her lips on me, to feel her throat around me again.

She's never kneeled before me.

Has never initiated it.

She always submitted and took everything I gave her. And now... now we're at the point where she wants this as much as I want it. She wants to suck me as much as I want to suck her. She wants to drink me in as much as I'm desperate to drink her dry.

Her answer is simple — she gulps my cock down in one go. And when I feel her throat strangling my cock, I don't think. I just react — trapping her again on me, moving my chained hand to the back of her head. Part of me expects her to pull back or tap me to let go, but she actually relaxes on me, letting me enjoy the gag reflex and the way it tightens around my cock each time. She gags three times before I let her take a short breath. Then she lets go completely, lets me fuck her mouth to my pleasure.

The obscene sounds her throat makes as I thrust in and out of her are the most delicious, erotic thing I've ever heard in my entire life. The way she tries to roll her tongue around my cock every time I thrust in, or the way she sucks on my crown when I pull back, it's making my head spin with pleasure. If I don't pull out, I'll spill my cum down her throat.

As appealing as that is, I want to seal our bond with my cum in her cunt tonight, all night. Tomorrow? Tomorrow is free game for anything and everything filthy that comes to mind. And I've got an entire genius brain to work with to fuck her until the day I die.

"My Queen, I'm seconds away from coming, and I want to be inside you."

She doesn't miss a beat. She stands, pushes me back onto the bathroom couch, lifts her dress, and straddles me. She raises her hips, pulls her underwear to the side, positions me at her entrance, and then lowers herself onto me. The last of my restraint snaps the moment I'm engulfed in her heat.

Holy fuuuuuuuck!

There will never be a day I sink into her cunt where I won't feel like my entire mind is reduced to mush.

I really want to pound into her. To thrust like a madman and make her break in my arms. But I also understand she's on top of me. She picked this position. She's choosing me again... so I let her.

The look in her eyes tells me I'm right. And as she starts moving — fucking herself on me — I let her. I promised her full control. I promised her ownership of everything I have... of me. Now I have to deliver.

Her movements are small and grinding at first, but as I relax beneath her, handing her the keys to my empire and my life, she leans down and starts kissing me. All the while, her pussy thrusts and bounces on my cock in the most maddening dance of pleasure.

Her breasts grind against my chest. Her pussy is squeezing the life out of me. Her scent is driving me to the brink of madness. And the obscene sounds coming from her cunt — wet and filthy as she fucks herself on me, are devouring every last piece of my sanity.

I'm seconds away from coming — there's no stopping it, even if I wanted to.

I gave her full control, and we both know it. So I do the only thing left to do. I grip the chain, pull it between us, lift the cross to my lips, and *kiss it,* all while our eyes stay locked.

I feel the first spasm around my cock a second later, and there's no holding back. She's shattering around me, and my body lets go with hers.

The entire universe ceases to exist. There's only the feel of her wrapped around my cock, the unimaginable pleasure tearing through my mind with every release of cum, and the complete surrender of my body to her.

The moment my vision returns, she arches her back and tilts her head, and I know it's my call to take over. So I do. I thrust up with vicious intensity, rolling my hips on the pull-down to hit her sweet spot, and her moans grow louder and louder the more I fuck her like a man possessed.

It doesn't matter that I just came. It doesn't matter that I've probably torn my stitches. All that matters is getting as deep within my Queen as possible — and so I do. I grab her hips and pull her down on me until I feel the tip of my cock being strangled inside her.

The sensation slams into me as I feel myself buried so deep I momentarily black out, because every time I think I've reached the limit of worshipping her, she finds a way to pull me further into her orbit, obliterating whatever's left of me.

That's it! It's fucking *on* now!

I flip her over and start thrusting brutally into her, with a speed I didn't even know I possessed. Her cries — of pleasure, of pain, of more — are consuming me, urging me to take more.

I look down at her breasts, and the chain is resting on one of them. The rainbow light dancing off the diamonds makes my cock twitch inside her cunt with so much possession it blinds me.

She is mine.

Only mine.

She accepted this.

No — she didn't just accept it.

She *chose* me back.

Thrust!

She *chose* me.

Thrust!

She *wants* me as much as I want her.

Thrust!

I lift my gaze to hers — and this time, she's the one who traps it.

She lifts the chain between us, and this time it's not defiant. Not broken. Not uncertain.

It's just true.

"We are one," she breathes — and I forget how to breathe.

There's nothing else to say. Nothing left to do.

I let go in the same moment she does — our bodies connected, our senses exploding, our lives surrendered, our path one.

We are one.

It's real.

Chapter Thirty-Four

Monica

I wake up deliciously sore all over. He fucked me twice, then moved to my arse, then we showered, and then he came down my throat — twice. At this stage, I feel like he's popping Viagra like M&M's. How the hell does he have so much stamina?

As I try to fully wake up, the memories play again and again in my mind. Then I feel his cock, already probing between my arse cheeks in shallow thrusts.

"Don't even think about it," I try to warn him off. "You stuffed me full of your cum last night, that'll do for the next week."

At that, he freezes mid-thrust, and I let out a giggle, involuntarily.

"Lisichka, don't say that. That's not funny," he says, sounding genuinely hurt.

I look over my shoulder and smile. "Stop popping Viagra like they're vitamins and maybe you can control your libido."

He resumes the thrusts between my arse cheeks and bites my shoulder.

"I would, baby. I'd take a bottle of Viagra if I had to, as long as I get to stay buried inside you."

With the next thrust, he stops at the entrance of my arse, and I feel him guiding the tip of his cock in slow circles over it. That's his move — to relax the tight bundle of nerves before he gets in there and fucks me raw.

"Behave," I try to settle him. "I need to go to the toilet anyway."

That's when it hits me. How the fuck am I supposed to go to the toilet chained?

"Oh, Elijah — seriously, this was so stupid of you to chain me. How am I supposed to go to the toilet?"

"With me beside you."

"Nope."

In one move, he jumps on top of me, his chained arm trapping mine, his cock pressed between us, smearing precum all over my lower abdomen.

Hell. I didn't even realise how turned on he was until now.

"When are you going to understand?" he growls, eyes locked on mine. "There is nothing in my universe but you. I will wipe you clean every time you need to go to the toilet. I'll fucking lick you clean if you ask me to." He leans in, his breath lingering on my lips.

"There is nothing in this fucking world I wouldn't do for you, my Queen."

His words land on my mouth, as much as they land on my heart and mind — and as much as I want to fight him off, I can feel myself getting worked up.

"Lick me clean? That's gross," I say, trying to fight back a laugh. "Grossity gross gross," I add, and start laughing just as he starts thrusting between us.

I know I shouldn't be getting excited or aroused by this, but at this point, everything about him turns me on without him even doing much.

The way his cock rubs between us, pulling upward with every thrust, is making my clit twitch with each sensation. My breasts tighten under his chest, and I can feel it — if he keeps this up, I might actually come from a dry hump.

He moves his arms behind me and pulls me closer, removing any remaining space between us, then starts kissing, sucking, and nipping at my ear — all while increasing his thrusts.

The sensations are overwhelming.

His breath in my ear.

His scent in my mind.

His pull and friction on my clit.

His relentless rubbing of my nipples.

I can see the cliff of my climax approaching, and when he lifts me slightly, moves behind my neck, and starts to suck and nibble, I come so abruptly and violently that the scream and spasms tear through me without warning.

I've never experienced a dry orgasm before — but with Elijah, every single touch sends an electric shock through my system.

He starts thrusting more brutally into my orgasm, while his lips and teeth do real damage to my mind and neck.

As I start coming down from the high, I move my free hand to his arse and spank him once. He laughs into my neck, so I trail my fingers to the curve of his arse cheek and start teasing the tip in a slow, up-and-down motion.

He rewards me with a guttural grunt that makes me pause for a second.

"I like it. Keep going, Lisichka."

That's the thing with Elijah. It's always pure instinct. There's nothing planned, mechanical, or rehearsed between us. It all feels so organic — as natural as breathing.

I lift my fingers to my mouth, wet them, then place them on the tip again and start massaging the area. The moment I start kissing his chest, his shoulder, and any other part I can reach, his thrusts become so unhinged I know he's seconds away from covering me in cum again.

I know it now, by his breathing. Just before he starts shooting his cum, his breath pauses... and then comes that soft, almost broken cry of surrender, right before the heat of his release explodes on or inside me.

Same now. That shift in his breathing hits... and the moment I hear that cry, I start meeting him thrust for thrust, while relentlessly rubbing that sensitive spot between his arse cheeks.

Hot ripples of cum explode between us, and I push at his chest with my chained hand — I want to see it, to watch his release.

When I look down, thick white streaks of cum shoot up between us, landing on my abdomen, my chest, and finally my chin.

I open my mouth and stick my tongue out, but nothing reaches that far.

I glance up at him in disappointment, but he's in a world of his own, completely lost in his pleasure and the sight of me with my mouth open, waiting.

I say nothing.

I simply gather some of his cum from my chin and chest, suck my fingers clean... and smile at him.

"Now you do things like that and expect me not to want to fuck you every second of every day? Seriously, Lisichka. That right there earned you another fucking in the shower. Don't say I didn't warn you."

He lowers his lips to mine and starts to kiss me savagely, and I just laugh, because for the first time in my life, I feel happy.

I feel full.

I truly am not alone.

This feels complete.

When he stops kissing me, I can feel his body shivering above mine and I know, I know he's feeling it too.

I will find my peace and live my life with Elijah, I think to myself.

The thought isn't even fully formed in my mind when he pulls back to study me.

I say nothing at first. I just allow myself this moment — this moment of bliss.

"Let's go to Romania."

Four words.

A lifetime of pain in the shadows.

"Fuck yes!" he shouts, jumping off me in one go, completely forgetting we're chained. He pulls me up with him.

"Apologise, Lisichka," he says, then jumps back on me and starts kissing me everywhere.

"You make me so happy. More than a man like me—hell, more than any man—deserves. I'm beyond intoxicated by you. You consume me. I'm so happy we're going to get you peace. Let's go show the world who we truly are, my Queen."

I only laugh, because I feel the same way.

There's no need to say anything. We both know the truth: if I didn't feel this way, he wouldn't be allowed anywhere near me.

The fact that I *let* him do all these things to me...

The fact that I *accept* his nature in its rawest, truest form...

That *is* my declaration.

That's how he knows how completely consumed I am by him.

"Alex. Message Buddy — we're going to Romania. Message the pilot to get the plane ready in one hour."

"*Confirmed,*" Alex replies, without missing a beat.

I glance over at Elijah with a smirk. "Butler?" I tease.

"*I heard that, my Queen,*" Alex says. "*Butler — and more.*"

"You're offending my AI? My very capable AI?"

"I wouldn't dare challenge you both." I laugh and wiggle in Elijah's arms.

An hour later, we're in the car on our way to a private hangar for the flight to Romania.

At the bottom of the plains stairs, Buddy is waiting as the car rolls to a stop.

He smirks and gestures toward the chain between us. "I see you both survived... this."

"Yes," I reply dismissively. "He parted ways with one of his balls as payment for such insolence."

I say it in a dead-serious tone.

Elijah bursts out laughing — that signature, carefree laugh of his, head tilted back — catching Buddy completely off guard.

"What?" I frown, unimpressed with Buddy's reaction. "You've never seen Elijah laugh before? What's that face about?"

"No," Buddy admits, blinking. "No, I haven't. Before you, he barely looked at anyone, let alone engaged or laughed."

"For the record, both my testicles are exactly where they belong," Elijah cuts in. "Also, don't be so dramatic, Buddy. No one else ever existed for me before her. Everything — all of this — is because of her. For her."

Buddy nods. The humour fades, replaced by something else. Complete obedience. Absolute loyalty.

"I did cut off one of his balls," I say as I pass him, making a slicing gesture with my fingers. "Don't listen to him," I add, pointing at Elijah.

Buddy says nothing, but I catch the corner of his mouth twitching, fighting back a laugh.

Elijah guides me onto the plane, and everything — once again — is so obscenely luxurious it practically screams wealth and power. I roll my eyes in annoyance.

Then I notice it. Even the glassware has his initials — E.D. — discreetly engraved in gold.

I glance at him and make a gagging noise.

That does it.

Without a word, he changes direction and heads to the back of the plane. When I realise where he's going — a bedroom — I immediately drop into the nearest seat and smile up at him like butter that wouldn't melt.

He holds my gaze for a moment, a silent battle of wills. Then, finally, he smiles and shakes his head.

"You do realise I can fuck you right here too," he says, completely matter-of-fact.

"Not if I have a say in it," I shoot back with a smile, challenging him.

He chuckles, shakes his head again, and takes the seat next to me.

"This won't do," he murmurs, then pulls me onto his lap sideways.

I don't protest — because let's face it, I'm not an idiot. Elijah's lap or some overpriced seat? I'll take his lap any day.

I wiggle into a comfortable position and lean my head against his chest — his heartbeat the only drum, the only sound tethering me to reality. I feel so content in his arms. I stay there, listening to the steady rhythm of his heart. I don't register the conversation around me, the music, or even the sound of the plane. All that matters is Elijah's heartbeat.

Then it starts... the memories. My family. The way I grew up. Everything that was done to me.

I don't move. I don't speak. I don't give any sign.

But the moment the first image of pain flashes through my mind, I feel his heartbeat shift — picking up, pulsing harder beneath my cheek. Seconds later, he's glancing down, searching my face. Then I hear him quietly dismiss Buddy and the staff.

And just like that, we are alone.

I say nothing. Do nothing. Just sit there and listen to his heart.

He doesn't ask anything. Doesn't prompt. Doesn't push.

He just sits with me, puts on a movie, and gives me all the time and space I need.

"It's really stupid..." I finally whisper.

"I doubt that," he replies — in that quiet, signature tone he uses only with me. I notice it now. I feel it.

"I thought he was a safe person. And I was stupid."

Elijah doesn't say anything to that.

He doesn't move.

Doesn't even tighten his arms around me.

And I'm so grateful to him for that. That he can be still. That he can be cold.

He doesn't push. He doesn't probe.

He just lets me *be*.

"I'm supposed to be this genius of a woman," I murmur. "Capable of extraordinary things... but I couldn't see the predator right in front of me."

Silence wraps around us again, and I focus on his heartbeat — my anchor — but the itch won't go away.

This unbearable itch to tell him what happened to me.

It's eating me alive.

My insides are screaming to tell Elijah the truth.

I try to steady my voice, to sound like the woman I am now.

But the moment I speak... it's the voice of a teenager that comes out.

"I really thought he was a safe person. I really did."

I turn my face into Elijah's chest and breathe him in. His scent is so familiar now... so comforting. So whole.

"When I was little, we used to play on these steps, right on the path between my apartment building and his. He'd come home from work and always made a point to talk to all the kids playing there. Always so kind. So nice to us."

I pause, feeling the warmth of Elijah against my cheek.

"Not like the other neighbours who'd tell us off for making noise or tell us to go play somewhere else. He never did that. Sometimes he'd even bring us sweets. Smile at us. Ask about our day..."

My voice trails off.

"I just... I didn't see it coming."

My body is trembling, my palms are sweating, and I can't seem to breathe properly.

I might go into a panic attack at this rate.

But I'm going to do it.

I'm going to tell Elijah.

"When I was nineteen, I was coming home from school one day. I needed to visit a colleague who lived in the same apartment building as him, so I had to take the elevator.

I got in, it was empty, and just as the doors were about to close, he called out.

I stopped the elevator and let him in." I pause, trying to steady my breath.

"Let's just say... back then, there weren't a lot of people who liked me.

My mask wasn't fully formed yet.

I still believed that if I showed others pieces of my true self... they'd appreciate it.

That they'd respond with kindness, maybe even show me their true colours too.

That they'd accept me for who I am."

I look up at Elijah, searching his face, trying to see if he's judging me. If he thinks that was the most naïve, stupid idea possible.

But there's none of that.

Only concern. Only care.

He says nothing. Does nothing.

And if my ear weren't resting against his chest, I wouldn't even be sure he was still breathing.

"When I saw who it was, I smiled.

I fucking smiled, Elijah—because I thought he was a safe person.

He was always nice to everyone.

Even to *me*."

I sigh.

Everything from that day rushes to the surface all at once.

The smell of the elevator.

The sharp, crisp sounds it always made.

The flickering lights.

The familiar annoyance I always felt whenever I had to visit that colleague of mine.

I remember every single detail of that day.

"We made small talk, and then... he asked me if he could hug me.

I genuinely didn't think anything of it—he'd hugged me before. He'd hugged others, too. So I said... sure."

The moment his arms were around me, I felt it.

Something was different this time.

"He reached over and stopped the elevator—while still pressing his body into mine.

Then he hugged me again.

But it wasn't a hug."

My voice is breaking. Tears are running down my face. My whole body is shaking.

"His hands started moving over my body.

He told me his wife didn't care about him. That he needed me.

That he needed this."

I'm completely frozen. I've kept his secret for over twenty years. There are no words to describe what that's like. That kind of pain. What it means to finally say it out loud. To finally have someone you trust enough... to let them see the darkest part of you.

Elijah doesn't react, except for his heartbeat, which skyrockets under my ear.

He stays completely still, letting me take my time, letting me take anything and everything I need from him.

He lets me find my own pace in telling my truth.

"When it was all over, I made my way down the stairs and home.

I didn't see a single person on my way back.

Not one.

No one stopped me. No one asked what was going on.

Why I had blood on me. Nothing."

I shake my head in disbelief—at myself, at my own desperate hope.

"It's stupid, Elijah.

I just wanted one person... anyone... to stop me and ask if I was okay.

To ask what was going on before I had to go home to my parents.

Just one person to care. I just thought someone should care."

I sigh.

"I remember it so clearly, so vividly—my mum's reaction when she saw me.

I remember everything.

The unbearable smell of borscht, always lingering in the air.

The dim light in the hallway.

The moment she realised what had happened to me.

And the pleasure on her face... that she could beat the living hell out of me again."

That confirmation pulls a reaction from Elijah. He tightens his arms around me, and I notice he's trembling too. I was so consumed by my memories, by my pain, I didn't even realise he was breaking beside me. I look up—and sure enough, he's trying to hold himself back.

But it takes one to know one... and there will be a lot of people screaming in pain at his hands today.

I lift my hand and cup his cheek. He leans into my touch and closes his eyes.

I might be broken. I might be different than others.

But I'm not alone anymore.

There are two of us now.

When he opens his eyes, I see it—clear as day.

He wants to kill my parents.

He *really* wants to kill them.

"No," I say simply.

"Lisichka, after everything they've done, they have to be fair game." His voice is so pained, so pleading.

"No, iubire scumpa."

I move my hand to his chest and tap it gently.

"I didn't have a choice in who I came out from. And even if they were the worst parents imaginable, I'm still alive because they participated in procreation. That's about the full extent of their contribution."

"There you go. My point exactly."

"Even so.

It's a no."

"Ladies and gentlemen, we have commenced our descent. We will arrive at our destination in ten minutes. Please fasten your seatbelts once the sign comes on. We hope you had a pleasant flight."

The pilot's voice interrupts us.

Elijah doesn't say another word. He doesn't pressure me, even though I can feel it—every fibre of his being wants my parents' blood for what they did to me.

But he doesn't even know the full extent of it.

And, quite frankly, I'll never tell him.

There's no victory in revisiting that pain. He can't travel back in time and change it. So what's the point?

The moment the plane lands and comes to a complete stop, the stewardess opens the door, and that familiar smell of home hits me.

It's familiar... and it's not.

It's terrifying... and it's not.

All of my senses, all of my emotions are suspended—floating into nothingness and consuming me so completely that I feel overwhelmed.

I glance down at my hand, where Elijah has intertwined our fingers. The diamond bracelet dangles from my wrist just as his matching one does from his.

If it weren't for him guiding me to the car right now, I'm not sure I'd even remember how to walk.

This is the first time I've come back since the day I swore I'd never set foot in this country again.

There was only pain and sorrow for me here, and the only good thing that ever happened to me is back in England.

I would have never returned... if it weren't for Elijah.

The moment we're in the SUV, I think he's going to pull me onto his lap again. But he doesn't. He just moves my hand onto his thigh and places his own over mine, trapping me in.

I give him a small squeeze to let him know I'm okay, then turn to look out the window.

Everything has changed—buildings, cars, traffic, people, advertisements everywhere.

It's all so different... and yet, somehow, it feels exactly the same.

I didn't give Elijah the address. I didn't need to. I know he already knows everything about me. So I lean back in my seat and take it all in.

When the apartment buildings come into view, my hands start trembling, my palms slick with sweat.

He turns to me and studies me for a long moment.

"My Queen," he says, voice low, steady. "I will bring all of them to their knees in front of you. Just say the word."

The truth in his eyes is as clear as his feelings for me.

He would bring *everyone* to their knees for me.

But this shaking, it isn't fear.

"It's suppressed fury, iubire scumpa. Not fear."

He narrows his eyes at me, trying to understand what I mean.

"I understand now that I have the power to do with any of them whatever I please. All of that anger, all of that pain I had to live with and suppress every single day, it can finally be released. Avenged."

I turn to face him fully.

"I truly understand now, I can do *whatever* I want."

A smile spreads across Elijah's face at my words. He looks so pleased with himself, pleased that *he* was the one who brought me this power, that I finally understand my own strength.

"You said it to your daughter, iubire scumpa. Just because we have the power to hurt someone doesn't mean we should."

"Nope! Nope!" he raises his voice and shakes his head. "That was different, and you know it. Lisichka, please! They have to die. They have to suffer for what they've done."

The car comes to a stop in front of the apartment building I once called home. I look at it now—someone painted the exterior this grotesque pinkish colour that somehow warns people, without a single word, that horrible human beings live inside.

I don't say a word. I open the door and step out, Elijah right behind me, shielding me with his body like we've entered a war zone.

I look up and take in the four-level apartment block. The strange colour looks even more grotesque in daylight.

I tilt my head to the right, and there they are.

The steps I used to play beside when I was little.

As if on cue, Elijah steps into my line of sight and blocks the view, probably realising what they meant to me.

I start walking toward the front entrance of the apartment building. A few neighbours are at their windows, spying on everyone who comes and goes.

Some older women sit on the bench out front, and we exchange polite greetings as we pass.

They know me, or rather, they used to know me.

They knew the child who lived here... right up until the moment I left and swore never to return.

But this version of me?

The real version, dressed like this, with a man like Elijah at my side and guards surrounding us? That, they've never seen before.

Elijah quickly instructs the guards on how to position themselves, and then we start walking up the stairs to the first level.

I've never understood why in England they count the ground floor as the first storey—when it's clearly just the ground.

Anyway.

The men begin power-walking ahead of us while Elijah deliberately slows his pace.

"You might get attacked with some borsh or a broom, but that's about it, Elijah. Relax."

"I will eat all the goddamn borsh in this building if I must, but your safety is more important than air in my lungs right now. Let them do their job, Lisichka."

I turn to him, and he's freaking out.

I'm not sure if it's from fear of physical danger or emotional damage, but he's fully slipped into paranoid, possessive psychopath mode.

I let him be.

When I see the door to my parents' apartment, the only thing I can think is how grateful I am that Elijah is here. They couldn't beat me again, not because I know how to fight now, but because I would never let them.

And the fact that Elijah is here?

That feeling of gratitude... it's not about protection. It's because *I'm not alone anymore.*

Come hell or high water, I'm facing my past today—and I'm finding peace with it.

I knock on the door.

And even before it opens, I already know I won't like what's waiting on the other side.

"Bună, mama," I say, as my mother appears in the doorway.

Chapter Thirty-Five

Monica

„Ce înseamnă asta?" (What does this mean?)

Her voice drips with simple disgust at the mere sight of me. Twenty years apart haven't dulled it, her revulsion is just as sharp.

She doesn't even speak to me, not really. Her eyes dart over my shoulder to Elijah, taking in the man behind me, then shift to the guards lining the hallway... and the few smirking down from the stairs.

„De ce ai venit? Nu am nimic ce să-ți dau. Pleacă." (Why did you come? I have nothing to give you. Leave.)

She spits the words like poison and moves to slam the door in my face.

Truth be told, I have no idea why I even came here.

We're in Romania so I can kill that bastard, that's the mission. So for one absurd moment, my mother's reaction is almost comical. Both Elijah and I thought this confrontation might matter, but now? I can't even imagine why.

I don't know what I planned to say. Maybe nothing.

But one thing is certain... *she doesn't get to slam the door in my face.*

I lift my boot and plant it against the frame, halting it with the kind of ease that she most definitely did not expect.

„Nu-ți dau nimic! Pleacă!" (I won't give you anything! Leave!)

She screams now, a shrill, desperate kind of rage, and I can feel Elijah shift behind me, just a twitch, ready to strike for what she dares do in front of him.

„Nu am nevoie de nimic, mama." (I don't need anything, mum.)

I meant for it to sound strong. Sharp. Like the woman I've become.

But no. That fucking child buried deep inside me spoke instead. And I fucking hate her for it.

„De ce ai venit atunci?" she demands. „Nu-ți dau nimic. Să-ți fie clar!" (Then why did you come? I have nothing to give you. Let that be clear!)

I'm not even sure what she's going on about. They never had anything. Not back then, not now.

Even if I were in trouble, which I'm not, she wouldn't have a single thing to offer.

„Sincer?" (Honestly?)

I meet her gaze, steady, flat.

„Nu știu de ce am venit." (I don't know why I came.)

„Atunci du-te de aici. Nimeni nu are nevoie de tine." (Then leave. No one needs you.)

The words hit harder than I expect. Not because they hurt, but because she said them so easily.

As if I were nothing.

It clicks something back into place.

„Eu am avut nevoie de tine," (I needed you,) I say, low, almost a whisper.

„Eu am avut nevoie de o mamă toată viața mea. Și când n-am găsit una, am devenit eu mama pe care am vrut s-o văd în lumea asta."

(I needed a mother my whole life. And when I couldn't find one, I became the mother I wished existed in this world.)

The words might be small. Shaken, even.

But they cut.

Her face turns red. That trembling, violent edge of hers rises fast. I can see it, plain as day. She's about to strike.

And for once, I almost hope she does.

She glances over my shoulder, and whatever she reads on Elijah's face makes her pause.

She knows she can't fight us alone.

So she screams for my dad. Not words, just a raw, high-pitched panic, as if someone's physically hurting her.

„Da' ce s-o întâmplat? De ce răgnești așa?" (What happened? Why are you roaring like that?)

His voice cuts through the house before we even see him.

And of course, he's in his underwear, again. His stomach hangs over himself like it's trying to smother the very thing that made me dry heave every time I saw it.

I used to run. Every time at the sight of him in his underwear. Revolting!

„Ce înseamnă asta?" (What's the meaning of this?)

His tone is menacing now. He shoves my mother out of the way like she's nothing.

Then his eyes land on me.

Then Elijah.

Then the men behind us.

„Îmi pare rău, Domnule. Nu știu cine e femeia asta. Fă cu ea ce-i vrea." **(I'm sorry, Sir. I don't know who this woman is. Do with her what you will.)**

That's what my father says.

Cold. Final. Like I'm nothing.

He doesn't even see my boot in the doorway when he tries to slam it shut.

I hear the impact, but I don't feel it.

I'm still stuck on his words.

What the actual fuck?!

Both of them thought I might be in trouble.

And yet, without so much as looking at each other, they turned their backs on me. They completely abandoned me.

As if that's normal.

As if that's what you do to your own child.

But for my father... to say he doesn't know me?

And for someone like Elijah — someone terrifying in ways they couldn't even imagine — to be told he can do whatever he wants with me?

Well.

That is unforgivable.

I say nothing.

I do nothing... except step aside.

That's all the invitation Elijah needs.

In one breath, he's in my father's face. His left hand snaps up, fingers locking around his thick neck.

No warning. No words.

Just grip, hard and unrelenting, his fingers sinking deep into meat and panic.

„O să vorbesc încet, să înțeleagă și un dobitoc ca tine." **(I'll speak slowly, so even an idiot like you can understand.)**

My words came out lower than I wanted. But they landed.

Elijah's, though, just now — his are ice and ruin.

„Singurul lucru pe care l-ați realizat în viața voastră a fost să o creați pe Monica. Restul e gunoi. Voi sunteți gunoi. Și singurul motiv pentru care nu vă omor azi, în chinuri groaznice, e pentru că ea v-a lăsat să trăiți." **(The only thing you've ever accomplished in your miserable lives was creating Monica. The rest is trash. You are trash. And the only reason I'm not killing you today, in agonising pain, is because she allowed you to live.)**

He slams my father against the wall. The impact ripples through his gut, one wobble, two, before he staggers in silence.

Then they both look at me.

And for the first time, I let them see it.

All of me.

No mask. No charm. No filter.

Just *me.*

And their reaction?

Delicious... **They're afraid.**

There.

That's why I came.

Not for answers. Not for closure.

I needed them to live in fear. The same way they once made me live in it.

I place my palm on Elijah's shoulder. He knows. We're done here.

I fucking love my relationship with him. No meaningless conversation. No useless words, no commands, no promises. I can have a full-on conversation — or a full-on fight — with him through a single look or a small gesture.

This is how a relationship should be.

Fucking effortless.

I intertwine our chained hands, letting the metal shift with purpose. I make sure the chain dangles, the cross dangling, just enough for my parents, and our nosy neighbours, to catch a good look.

Let them talk.

Let them whisper.

It'll take me some time to process everything that happened today.

But if I'm being honest?

I liked it.

Coming here...

Yeah. It was definitely the right call to come.

The idea doesn't even have time to form, before a voice cuts through the air and the ground beneath me threatens to give way. Like I might fall into an abyss I sworn I'd sealed shut.

„Monica! Tu ești?" The voice I hopped I'd never hear again.

I take one step, just one, toward Elijah's back. And that's all he needs. He moves in front of me instantly, shielding me with his massive frame.

No words. No delay.

Just instinct — his and mine.

„Ai persoana greșită." **(You've got the wrong person.)**

His voice is cold enough to freeze blood, steady, dominating, absolute.

„Îndepărtează-te. Acum!" **(Step away. Now!)**

The last word isn't spoken. It's delivered, like a threat with teeth.

I can't see what's happening. But I hear it, the sudden shift, the sharp retreat, footsteps scattering fast.

I didn't know Elijah spoke Romanian. I'm not surprised, of course he does. He's a genius. But he's never mentioned it. Not once.

And right now? I could fall to my knees and thank him for shielding me.

I wasn't ready. Not after facing my parents. Not for *him.*

What the fuck is happening to me? Why am I so consumed by these fucking emotions? I hate them. I hate them *so much.*

"Easy, my Queen."

His voice is low, steady. A quiet tether as I cling to his back. He wraps his arms around me, shielding me even now.

Without missing a beat, he starts barking sharp, fast orders. He tells the guards to go after the man, to take him to some warehouse they've secured.

I hear footsteps pounding away.

And then...

Silence.

Just the sound of my own breathing, shallow, fast, and too loud in the stillness.

That's all that remains.

Elijah pulls me to his front and wraps his arms around me, firm and steady. He presses a kiss to my forehead, slow, deliberate.

There are no words.

No promises.

No judgment.

No pity-party.

Just silence.

And... I'm truly grateful for it.

When I can feel my legs again, I pull back. We walk in silence to the SUV. We drive off, other cars in front and behind, like I'm some kind of fucking royalty.

I'm not.

I'll never be.

Just look at where I came from. Look at *them.*

But today... Today carried immense weight and I'm too fucking exhausted to overanalyse any of it at the moment. So I stretch out in the backseat, my head resting on Elijah's thigh, and I let sleep take me.

I've had enough of this shit. That's the last thing I think, before everything goes black.

Chapter Thirty-Six

Monica

I open my eyes, and the first thing I register is Elijah's soft breath on my back.

He's asleep.

I've never seen him asleep before, but right now, he's out cold. I don't even dare move a muscle because—holy shit—Elijah is asleep. He must have been completely exhausted from everything that's happened over the past few days.

I glance around the room. We're in some sort of hotel—well, a pretentious hotel, that is. It's clean and elegant, but something about it feels... off. Too polished. Too sterile. Like it's trying too hard.

I try to scan the space without moving too much, hoping to spot a guard. But I can't see anyone. Still, I highly doubt Elijah dismissed them all.

They're here somewhere.

I let the time pass, relishing the feel of Elijah's skin against mine, the soft fan of his breath on my back, and the deep relief within me that he finally got some sleep.

I came back.

I actually came back to Romania.

And yet... it doesn't feel like anything I'd imagined it would.

It feels completely different—because I have Elijah now.

And with him, everything is easy.

Just easy...

I know that if I ever have a low moment — for whatever reason — he'll step in and finish what I couldn't. Just like I stepped in with Sofia.

Our relationship works. We complete each other.

We might be different from your average couple, but for us, everything makes perfect sense.

It's naturally easy. We support each other in the most elemental way possible.

"Have you been awake long?" he whispers in my ear, then kisses the tip of my shoulder.

"You slept," I murmur, tightening my hold on the arm he's wrapped around me. "Slacking on the job?" I tease.

He laughs, then nibbles that spot on the back of my neck that instantly makes me tingle.

"Iubire..."

"Hmm?"

"No."

"Why not?" he asks between kisses and nibbles.

"I'm not sure." It's the truth. I have no idea why. "Something feels wrong... off, somehow."

He turns me and rolls on top of me, holding his weight on his elbows. The look in his eyes is part amused, part concerned. He's clearly not sure if I'm joking or if something's actually wrong again.

So I smile.

For a second, he thinks I'm just playing around, then he sees it. He realises I'm trying to hide it.

"Fuck no, Lisichka. Don't you dare. You gave me your word," he genuinely sounds hurt.

So I tell him the truth.

"I'm not sure, iubire scumpa. Something feels off. I don't think I can do it here."

"Do you mean the hotel or Romania?"

I try to look away, but he grabs my chin and brings my gaze back to his.

"The second." My answer is short, clear — and it hits him like I just slapped him.

"You're telling me I'm not getting any pussy while we're in Romania?"

It's the first time I've ever seen genuine shock on Elijah's face. It's actually a little amusing. I would laugh... but something tells me he might not appreciate that right now, so I hold it in.

I nod.

He stands and straddles me, his weight pinning me in place with the sheer size of him.

The ever-problem-solver comes up with a plan in mere seconds.

“Very well. We can shower and get ready to leave in twenty minutes. The travel to the location will take another twenty. Kill them both in five. Then the drive to the plane. All up, under one hour. That gives the pilot enough time to prep, and we’ll be in the air in an hour... and I’ll be inside you in about an hour and three minutes, give or take.”

“No.”

He rolls his eyes and collapses beside me.

"I don't want to hurry you, Lisichka, but you need to understand. This hunger inside me for you can only be held back for so long."

His words are sincere. The look in his eyes is sincere. The shiver that runs through him is sincere.

I feel for him, I really do. I want him just as much.

But like I said... I can’t quite pinpoint what’s wrong, I just know something feels *off*.

He sighs and rolls onto his back.

"I truly don’t mean to hurry you, but please do hurry up. I might actually develop blue balls by the end of this."

His voice is serious, but I can’t hold it in any longer. I burst out laughing.

When he turns and looks at me, I stop laughing altogether.

Because damn... he’s *really* serious.

Quick! Quick! Distract!

"You slept, iubire scumpa," I say cheerfully, turning toward him. "That makes me very happy," I add, then kiss his bicep.

"Okay, okay! If I’m not getting any pussy, then you are not allowed to tease me in *any* way, woman! Goddamn it!"

He grabs my hand and places it on his hard cock, and I burst out laughing.

"Is that all it took? Come on, lay off the Viagra," I say between gasps of laughter. To which he whips it out and starts whacking me with it.

"What the hell are you doing?!" I cry out, laughing so hard I can barely breathe.

"Anything and everything I can, given the situation and your filthy mouth," he says, then starts kissing and nibbling at me.

"Hang on! Are you sucking me off on the table?"

The look on his face is so hopeful I almost say yes... but then I shake my head.

"Anal! You have to give me anal!"

This time I do laugh, because it's hilarious, but I shake my head again.

"Dry! Like last time—you were sore, you came! Lisichka, you came! I can make you come from dry fucking," he says with so much conviction my heart melts right in front of him.

I wrap my arms around him and sigh.

"That was a good laugh. I needed it," I say, then flick his cock.

I burst out laughing at his groan, then take pity on him and jerk him a few hard times. He lets out a moan just as I release him.

He looks at his angrily twitching cock, then at me.

"You're mean," he says, then moves to tuck it back into his jocks.

I take his hand and rest it on my breast, stopping him. If he took the time to undress me last night, he needs to sleep naked from now on too.

"Leave it out. I like looking at your cock," I say with a smile.

"He liked your gaze on him, but I really need a bit of you. Any of you." I can hear it in his voice, he truly needs this.

"If this feeling goes away, I promise you'll be the first to know."

As the words leave my mouth, I realise something important. Whatever this is — this feeling or heaviness inside me — it has nothing to do with Elijah. So why should he be the one who suffers because of it?

"Iubire," I say in a small voice. "I might not be in the best place to enjoy myself with you right now, but it could be kind of hot if you jerked yourself off." I flutter my eyelashes at him.

"And for me to watch you," I add in an amused voice, then bite my lip, only to completely lose it laughing at his reaction to my plan.

"Really?!" His voice is full of surprise, then he pauses to reconsider. "It could be hot, actually. Is this a fantasy of yours?"

"No, not really. I just thought, there's no reason for you to suffer while I sort my shit out."

"Lisichka," he says as he lifts my hand to his chest, where his heart is drumming out of control.

"I'm not suffering. Not even a little. And this isn't you sorting your shit out, it's *always us*, remember? We'll sort it together the moment we walk out that door."

"Yes, yes. Less talking, more jerking," I reply, then glance up at him again.

My gaze bounces between his cock and his eyes, clearly signalling him to get started.

He bursts out laughing at my sudden eagerness, especially after my firm no just moments ago.

"You sure this isn't a fantasy? Because you're definitely acting like you're in the mood now."

I shake my head again and, this time, just point at his throbbing cock.

"Do you have any preferences? Position? Anything else that could make you enjoy this more—with me?"

His voice is getting rougher, thicker with arousal, and I'm ridiculously happy that this is turning him on just as much as it is me.

"Nope. Right here on our side will do. Now get going."

He smiles and leans in to kiss me, but I pull back.

"How can I look at you if you're kissing me? Get going, boy. Let me see those balls bounce with every jerk."

He leans his head on my shoulder, then laughs so hard the bed starts shaking beneath us.

"Bouncing balls? The mouth on you is something else. Sometimes I think all that intelligence is going into finding new ways to make me lose myself in you."

He pulls back, and the moment our eyes meet, he's so aroused—so completely in the moment—that I know this is as hot as it could possibly get.

His strong hand wraps around his shaft, and he begins to jerk himself off, from base to tip. Once. Twice. Three times. Then he looks up at me.

Whatever he sees in my gaze makes him smile, and the sight of Elijah's smile, with his fingers wrapped around his cock, is a sight to behold.

Holy fucking shit. Seriously. Fucking hell.

My mouth is watering from the sheer beauty of him.

He's stunning—masculine in the most devastating way possible—but to watch him like this, touching himself while staring at me...

Taking in my body without laying a single finger on me...

All while his cock is weeping precum...

It makes my head spin.

I glance down at his hand again. He's loosened his index finger, and with every stroke, he rolls it gently over the crown.

His moans—raw, primal, guttural—hit something deep in me.

Without even realising, one of my hands moves up to play with my breast, teasing and pinching the nipple as the pleasure builds in waves.

He is so beautiful. So handsome. So all man.

From the inside out, everything about him is pure, raw power.

We're lying on our sides, face to face.

Our bodies might not be touching, but our minds—our most intimate inner beings—are completely connected.

And it's deliciously hot.

I lunge at him in an all-consuming kiss—teeth clashing, tongues swirling, moans tearing out of us.

I was right. He's jerking so hard now, the bed is trembling with every movement.

There's no way around it. I'm soaked.

I'm so turned on, my entire being is crying out for release.

Not just my pussy, all of me is pulsing with desperate need.

Because it's not just about lust anymore.

It's him.

It's us.

And I'm enjoying every second of this with Elijah.

I pull back and slide my left hand—the one still chained to him—down to my needy clit, all while holding his gaze.

The moment I make contact, whatever he sees in my eyes pulls a deep, guttural groan from his chest.

A big smile spreads across my face at his reaction.

It takes three rolls of my fingers and the sway of my hips for me to detonate into a million little pieces at the sight of my love before me.

When I hear that shift in his breathing, followed by the broken little cry that tells me he's seconds away from release.

I want it.

I want it all for myself.

In a split second, my mouth is on his cock, just as he lets out a guttural moan and lets go.

I take his crown deep into my mouth and start sucking him dry.

"Holy fuuuuuuck!" he yells at the top of his lungs.

"Fuuuuuck, baby! Goddamn it!"

A stream of swear words spills out of him as ripple after ripple of cum explodes into my mouth.

When his body finally relaxes and I know he's done, I jerk him three more times, sucking on him with each pull just to make sure he's completely emptied.

Then I look up and hold his gaze as I let go of his cock with a soft pop.

I smile.

Slowly, I open my mouth and show him his cum resting on my tongue—then smile again as he completely loses himself in another round of stunned, filthy curses.

"Fuuuuuck, Lisichka! You expect me to stay sane and then you pull shit like this? Fucking hell!"

His voice is a perfect mix of awe and complete bewilderment, like he has no idea what he's supposed to say or do next.

The moment his eyes drop back to my mouth again, I close it—and swallow.

Then I open it again and smile.

When he reacts the same way as before—swearing the filthiest, most unhinged things I've heard from him in a while—I burst out laughing and flop onto my back.

I didn't want anything. Not really.

But now that we've done what we've done, I feel better.

I turn my head toward him, and he's shaking his head, like he's trying to chase away a thought. He really does live for me now. Everything about him is for me.

"Thank you," I say, then shift my gaze back to the ceiling. "I feel better now."

He doesn't say anything. Doesn't move. He wants more, but he lets me be. Lets me exist in my truest form.

"I needed that. Thank you, truly."

A few moments pass in silence before I roll onto my side and face him.

"First of all, you never need to thank me for sex. I am 100% at your disposal, twenty-four seven," he says with so much conviction that I can't help but laugh—it's hilarious the way he says it.

"Second—holy shit, that was hot. I feel like I should be thanking you. No blue balls for me, for at least a few hours."

At that, I raise an eyebrow. He really should lay off the Viagra.

"Thirdly... did I do something wrong? Is that why you didn't want to fuck the usual way? Did I say something?"

I shake my head and try to look down, but he reaches over and lifts my chin, bringing my gaze back to him.

"Are you sure? We can talk about it, whatever it is."

I shake my head again.

"It's not because I shoved your dad into the wall, right?"

I make a confused face, then shake my head once more.

"Good. Because I'm not sorry about that. If anything, I think I showed remarkable restraint by stopping there."

"You did well, iubire scumpa. It's not you. Not in any way. If anything, I felt so much better because you were—because you are here with me. It makes a world of difference."

That was a bit much, and the sweet, beautiful taste still lingering in my mouth is starting to fade, so I try to distract him again.

"Did you rest well?"

"Yes, actually," he says, moving closer and kissing my forehead. "And now I feel good as well, after what happened. You were smoking hot when you were rubbing your clit. We're doing that again soon."

He sighs, then holds my gaze captive in his while trying to study me.

"It's the first real sleep I've had since you gave in to us. Don't get me wrong, I dozed off here and there, but every time, I'd wake up within minutes just to check on you. To make sure you didn't take off."

He lifts my left hand—the one chained to him—and kisses the back of it. Then he kisses the bracelet around my wrist... and finally the little cross dangling from it.

"Are you truly okay with this? Because this is the real reason I was able to fall asleep. I knew I'd bound myself to you in every way I possibly could. And you did the same for me. I knew I could let go... sleep... and when I woke up, *you'd still be there next to me.*"

His words are so powerful, so vulnerable and sincere, they melt my insides.

I had no idea he was plagued with so much pain at just the *thought* of me leaving.

He had to fucking chain me to him to be able to sleep.

That is possession on a whole new level... and **I love it**.

I cup his cheek, and he leans into my touch.

I smile at him. This man is the most dangerous creature anyone could ever cross paths with, and yet he's melting in front of me. He gave himself to me just as much as I gave myself to him. That's why this works.

It's complete surrender on both sides.

My smile grows wider, and he picks up on the change instantly.

I start laughing, then say, **"Let's go kill some bastards."**

Chapter Thirty-Seven

Elijah

It's a good day.

Life is good.

I had proper sleep. I had a proper fuck.

And yes, I still consider that a fuck—because holy hell, it was hot as sin and she swallowed my cum. That counts in my books.

Now, we're heading out to bring the last piece of my Queen into the open.

She's sitting on my lap in the car, looking out the opposite window.

She's not fidgeting.

She's not nervous.

She's not even breathing irregularly.

She's just like me. Calm and collected when it's time to deal with an inconvenience.

Though this isn't an inconvenience for her. This is her stepping fully into my world. And it's not an inconvenience for me either, because what she carries, is mine now. All of it.

That said, we did move Bogdan to this location as well, and he is an inconvenience. He'll be put down like the dog he is within minutes. Unless Lisichka wants to play with him first.

I'm completely confident in my decision to give it all to her. Whatever she wants, however she wants it.

I've ruled from the shadows for decades, and it brought me zero pleasure.

Sure, there were times I felt a flicker of excitement while playing with people, manipulating global outcomes like pieces on a board. But nothing, and I mean *nothing*, has ever come close to what I feel since Lisichka came into my life.

The fact that she willingly gave in to us—that she chose to start this relationship with me—I know that's what drove my mind completely haywire.

I couldn't think straight until I came up with the perfect trap to bind her to me, and for her to give in to us again.

Imagine my relief when she chose me back, and didn't let me die right there in front of her.

Her hand is still healing, and I've been checking on her progress every six hours, much to her displeasure. I forced her to take antibiotics just to be safe, and when she refused, I told her I'd smash it into her food if she didn't listen to reason.

She took the tablet, and *accidentally* stepped on my foot. Very hard.

I'd break my foot off and give it to her if she asked. But the way she toys with me and provokes me at every turn? It makes her so deliciously appetising to conquer. I truly can't get enough of her.

I glance at my watch, three minutes to destination.

It's been thirty-eight minutes since she swallowed my cum, and already I can feel the need for another taste of her.

I pull her blouse to the side, revealing her shoulder. The sight of her creamy, smooth skin makes my mouth water and my head spin instantly. I start kissing her at the tip of her shoulder, then trail my lips toward her back. She's incredibly sensitive there, especially where her shoulder meets her neck. She always lets out a very specific moan when I nibble that spot.

This time is no different. She rewards me with that sound, the one that makes my cock throb and her arse wiggle in my lap.

"I think you're well looked after at the hotel. At least until the plane ride home."

She called it *home.*

Her home.

My home.

Our home.

I kiss that spot again and linger, breathing her in.

What she doesn't know is, we're not going to England. From here, we're heading to Italy, until everything is prepared for the wedding.

I didn't ask her.

And I'm not planning to.

Because asking gives her the option to say no.

I've given her everything I have. And more importantly, everything *I am.*

This one thing...

This one thing, I'm stealing is her *no.*

Keeping it for myself.

She *will* be mine.

Whether she wants it or not.

She will be mine.

"What are you planning again?"

Her words are sharp, suspicious, as she studies my face.

She grabs my jaw and presses her forehead to mine.

"You're making that face again, the one that means you're planning something I won't like." She speaks against my lips, her breath tickling me with every word.

"Lucky for you, I'm your kind of crazy. But whatever it is you're planning, it better not be a chain around my ankle. Because I swear to God, I *will* cut off one of your balls. No questions asked. One ball. Plop. Right on the floor."

...And just like that, my erection dies a sudden, painful death.

"You happy now?" I say, feigning offence. "He ran away at your mean words."

She starts laughing, and every time I hear that sound, it's like she reaches into the darkest parts of me and pours her light into them.

The car comes to a halt.

I know what awaits on the other side of that door is not for the faint of heart.

She has all the time in the world to change her mind. I haven't mentioned it once. Didn't cross my mind to guide, suggest, prompt, or manipulate in any way. Not that manipulation would work on someone like her, but still. I gave her all the freedom in the world to choose what she wants.

In a split second, she plants such a passionate, deep kiss on me that I miss the beginning entirely, because she just starts devouring me.

The next moment, she's off my lap and reaching for the car door.

We're at the warehouse entrance in mere seconds, and I can feel the buzz radiating off her, electric and wild with what's about to happen.

She's excited.

She's looking forward to this.

And all traces of the girl who was in shock yesterday? Gone.

This is my Queen.

And she's about to cross over into my world completely.

Bring it on.

Chapter Thirty-Eight

Monica

I'm so excited. I'm fucking developing little wings and flapping all around like a rabid thing, high on the thrill of finally scratching this itch I've carried for far too long.

I've waited.

My entire life I waited for this moment.

My first kill...

And tonight, I get to alleviate the need from my own chest, and shove it right back down someone else's throat.

The rush makes me laugh, and jump up and down next to Elijah. He smiles at me, pleased with my reaction.

Then the doors open, and the cold hits me.

Both temperature... and atmosphere.

The warehouse breathes around us. Tall. Skeletal. Buzzing under flickering lights that seem to hesitate before revealing the scene.

The only natural light filters through narrow windows along the top edge of the walls, casting long shadows over the four guards standing in each corner, silent, waiting, watching, expecting their next orders.

In the centre of the space sit two men in metal chairs. One is the man who once thought he could break me. The other... I assume that's Bogdan.

To the right of my rapist stands a tall, wide table. From a distance, I can't quite make out what's on it. But as we approach, it becomes clear.

A collection.

A display.

Torture tools, arranged in neat rows, some familiar, most completely foreign.

At the edge of the table, several jars are lined up. Some filled with dark liquids. Some with powders I don't recognise. One holds... something alive. Maggots, I think.

I don't even realise I've stopped walking to take in everything on the table, until I feel Elijah's presence just behind me.

The table stands before me, lit by a single strip of flickering light above. I let my gaze sweep over it slowly, like I'm taking in a piece of art.

I look up at Elijah. He's already watching me.

I smile... wide, slow, deliberate.

And he knows.

He knows exactly what I've just found.

I turn back to the table and raise my right hand.

My fingertips trace over the cool surface of metal, grazing each piece as if saying hello.

Not to the tools — but *to myself.*

To that locked, caged part that has always been there.

Waiting.

Whispering.

Wanting.

I drag my fingers across the first object again and let myself feel it.

It looks like a bear claw. Curved and wicked, the steel spikes catch the light like tiny daggers. Each tip is sharpened into a fine point, the arcs shaped to tear flesh from bone in long, satisfying ribbons. It fits in my palm like it was made for me.

Heavy.

Personal.

Intimate.

I move to the next in line, some sort of bone saw. A compact, serrated blade attached to a smooth black handle, worn from use. Not mechanical, but manual.

Slow. Intentional.

This isn't for efficiency. This is for control. For pain. For feeling every movement vibrate through your wrist.

The next piece is some sort of nasty syringe, possibly made of glass. Thick, old-style, with a wide needle and cloudy residue crusted inside. The liquid next to it is yellow. Or green. I'm not sure.

But *I know* it burns.

I don't know how I know... but I do.

It's not the pain that matters. It's the helplessness it leaves behind.

I can feel it, the way it would ravage whoever receives it.

I pick up several others and analyse them as best I can, deducing their purpose and contents.

Then one more stops me.

Something delicate. Surgical.

A wire loop — thin, almost innocent. There are other surgical tools on the table, but this one... it's different.

A fine wire, threaded through a small handle, with a tightening mechanism. It's used for cutting, I assume. I take a closer look, test its movement, and yes — it's for cutting.

But slowly.

Quietly.

From the inside out.

How fascinating. That someone would put time, money, and effort into creating something like this, and using it.

I turn to Elijah and place both my palms on his chest, looking up at him. He pulls me into him immediately, arms tightening around me.

"You are a good man, iubire scumpă. You are good to me."

More sincere, more vulnerable words have never left my lips. And we both know it.

He buries his face in the crook of my neck, and I do the same.

We melt into each other — not just bodies, but minds, hearts, beings, histories.

Entwined.

To the outside world, it might seem wrong.

Dark.

Deranged.

Two people, completely and absolutely giving themselves to each other — in the middle of a warehouse, with two men bound and gagged beside us. Torture tools gleaming in anticipation just inches away.

To others, it might seem that way.

But to us...

This is perfect.

Absolutely perfect.

I pull back and look into his eyes and see myself in them and I smile again.

"Shall we, my Queen?" he says in that kind voice he has for me.

"We shall," I reply and turn to the men. I did not even notice that both of them were screaming this entire time. It did not register until now. Fascinating.

I look up at Elijah and smile again. "Which one should we start first?"

"Ladies choice. Given you're a Queen you can have them both if you like." That pulls another gagged scream out of both of them, but a single glare from Elijah temporarily silences them.

I look at them both, trying to decide what I want to do. Then I realise I don't want anything to do with this Bogdan. I want to take my time and enjoy tormenting my rapist.

"I have no need for your man. I want to play with him," I say and point to the bastard that tormented my mind for years.

"Not a problem at all, my Queen," Elijah says and kisses my forehead again. It did not pass my notice how he always calls me his Queen in front of all his staff, Buddy included, but in private he called me Lisichka, his Queen, his baby. The last one is when he is completely losing connection with reality, but still it counts to me.

"Do you want me to clean up after myself and then we can focus solely on your concern?" It's amusing to me the way he is formulating his sentences as we would be spending a nice evening out discussing mundane issues and not the way we're about to execute two of the most despicable people that live.

"By all means, My King," I make a point of smiling up to him when I call him that. "Let's practice on your guy and I can familiarise myself with all of my toys."

Elijah nods, pulls back and looks down on Bogdan.

I have never seen that look that Bogdan has right now, on anyone's face before. I'm not even sure there is a word for it. It's more than fear, panic or resignation that death is mere hours away. It's almost as if he is playing and replaying all the possibilities of torture Elijah might unleash on him.

"Long time no see, Bogdan." Elijah says as he takes his gag off. The bloody thing is not even fully off and the guy is on full auto mode trying to plead for mercy.

"Oh stop it." Elijah dismisses him. "You made it to the UBT. You already know how this works. You also know I don't like a lot of talk so stop it." His tone now is his usual cold and calculative self that dominates every room Elijah steps in.

He looks over his shoulder to where Buddy is waiting and, with a flick of his hand, Buddy moves into action and directs all the guards outside.

"I thought you might want the intimacy, my Queen."

"My Queen?" Bogdan spits out. He turns to me and sizes me up. He knows I'm Romanian like him, and I can see it in his eyes, the gears turning, calculating how he might plead with me for his life.

He truly believes I'm Elijah's weakness.

Not his strength.

"Tu știi cine e monstrul ăsta?" (Do you know who this monster is?) he asks me in a disgusted voice.

"Tu știi ce lucruri oribile a făcut? De ce e capabil?" (Do you know the horrible things he's done? What he's capable of?) His voice is trembling now, he's playing his part to perfection, and I'm fighting the urge to laugh in his face.

"Tu nu știi ce o să-mi facă dacă nu-l oprești." (You don't know what he'll do to me if you don't stop him.)

There. That's where he was going with this entire nonsense.

I burst out laughing, so hard that Elijah joins me, and it takes me a while to recover.

When I look up, both of the captured men look so confused and terrified by my reaction that I almost lose it again.

I look up at Elijah, and goodness, I melt for this man.

"He doesn't know you speak Romanian, I presume?"

"My Queen, please," he says, a smile tugging at his lips. "I started learning it when you came into my life. I wanted to know how to love you in your mother tongue. I would learn all the languages of the world if it would prove to you what you truly mean to me."

I lift up on my toes and place a soft kiss on his lips.

He's so sweet.

My big, bad wolf is so sweet.

"There, there, my King. They do not deserve to hear such beautiful words," I say and wrap my arm around him. A shiver runs through him, and every time I notice it, I find it so fascinating that someone as cold and calculated as him can have such a human, realistic reaction to me.

„Singurul motiv pentru care ai reușit să iei codul a fost pentru că ți l-am lăsat intenționat să-l furi." (The only reason you managed to take the code was because I left it there on purpose for you to steal.)

„În niciun moment nu te-am pierdut din vedere. Știam exact unde erai. Ce ai..." (Not for a single moment did I lose track of where you were. I knew exactly where you were. What...)

„Dar m-au căutat!" (But they were looking for me!) Bogdan interrupts Elijah and protests vehemently. "You killed so many of my friends!"

Elijah punches Bogdan hard in the stomach. A popping sound reverberates through the warehouse. He's completely out of breath, and when he finally manages to inhale, a violent coughing fit follows, ending with him coughing up blood.

"Listen carefully. You don't get to interrupt me. The code you thought would let you remotely access ordinary people's computers and drain their accounts without them even noticing? It won't work. It's still my code.

Did you really think I'd leave something like that lying around for someone like you to take?

I periodically test my people, see if they'd take money, code, information, anything from me. You were just stupid enough to fall for it and steal something that doesn't belong to you."

Now it makes sense why he sent the guards away. They didn't need to know that Elijah is playing them all. Buddy is still in the room, so I assume he already knows about all these side gigs Elijah runs.

Bogdan's face crumbles with the realisation that he's been played so thoroughly by Elijah — a possibility that never even occurred to him.

There is no bargaining chip.

No salvation.

Absolutely nothing he can do or say to fix this or to save himself.

I see it clearly, the moment his mind switches, deciding that maybe if he makes Elijah mad enough, he'll put a bullet in his head and not torture him to death.

"You think you're so smart? I already took some money from people using your code. How do you think I funded my escapes?"

"I already sent it back to them," Elijah says dismissively, turning to the table.

"My Queen, what would you like to try?" he asks me with enthusiasm, and I adore it!

"No! I stole over a million dollars! There is no way you could have sent it all back! The code words!"

Bogdan's words are now hysterical and babbling.

Elijah just turns his head and sighs.

"You're an imbecile. A sloppy imbecile. It took me seconds to send the money back to the people. They never even noticed your presence, because there was no presence to detect. I added my money to your account so I could keep chasing you. There was no real code for you to use. I funded you to run from me... and now that I have better interests, this has to come to an end."

I look past Elijah to study Bogdan's reaction, and it's absolutely delicious.

His reality is crumbling.

Everything he thought he knew, accomplished, even possessed... has disappeared in a split second.

His reality never truly existed. It was all at Elijah's pleasure — Elijah's creation.

And now, he's taken it all away.

"My Queen, are you interested in trying anything specific from the table?" he asks me in that kind tone.

"I don't even know what most of these things are," I admit, pointing to one of the jars lining the edge. "What's this white powder?"

"Oh! That's a good one. I hoped you might pick that one."

He looks at me with so much love and smiles.

"That powder, if ingested, damages the organs, melting them from the inside out. The organs dissolve in mere hours, and the death is excruciating because it heightens the nervous system and the brain's pain response.

I was told to inject adrenaline with it, because the possibility of a heart attack is around 80%."

I look at him.

I look at the jar.

Incredible! Who would spend time and effort developing such things?!

Then I realise... Elijah would.

Motherfucker.

He probably created a laboratory just for this — strictly for this.

He bursts out laughing the moment he realises I've figured it out.

I say nothing, because I'm completely fascinated by what is actually happening.

I can feel his arms pulling me into him before I can even try to pull back.

"Is that okay?"

All laughter has vanished, because I didn't join in, and now he's completely concerned that I might not be impressed.

I smile up at him and rest my head on his chest.

His heartbeat is so comforting to me. So peaceful.

Regardless of whether it's drumming out of control or simply singing my melody, I love just listening to him.

"I know now what part of your business I want to be involved in."

At that, he tightens his arms around me to the point of pain, lifts me into the air, and lets out a deep growl.

"Yeeees! Fuck yes! My Queen, ladies and gentlemen!"

He starts kissing me everywhere he can reach, and I start laughing at his antics.

"There, there, big bad wolf. I told you these people don't deserve to hear any of this."

He sets me down and places another kiss on my forehead.

"Right. Anything in particular I need to know about this powder?"

"Not really. In powder form, it's harmless. But if you combine it with liquid — that's when it gets deadly. Good thing he's bleeding."

I look up at him and glare.

Did I just get played?

Did Elijah just push me into picking the powder and create the perfect opportunity for me to use it?

"I swear to you. Never. I would not dare." He immediately tries to placate me. "It was a pleasant coincidence."

"Shut the fuck up! Pleasant coincidence my arse!" I cut him off because frankly, it doesn't matter, whether this idiot of a partner planned it or not. What matters is that I get to play with something new.

The next second, Elijah punches Bogdan in the throat so hard he's gasping for air, then signals me to add some into his mouth.

There was nowhere he could go. Nothing he could do. It was done and dusted, and the gag was back on within seconds.

One down. One to go.

I look at the bastard who hurt me.

The thing is, he didn't just hurt my body with what he's done.

He shattered my trust in humanity.

He crushed that small, pathetic hope that someone might like me.

He broke something in me on a molecular level, so deeply that until this very moment, I didn't think I'd ever truly get over it.

Cover it up? Yes.

Actually face it? Let it go? No.

And I know now... this will never fully go away.

I pull the gag off, and he's crying so hard, blubbering for mercy. It's infuriating. Annoying.

I sigh and glance at Bogdan. His skin's gone from ghostly white to a deep, burning red. Good. He's well on his way to complete agony.

I turn back to the snivelling wreck in front of me, shake my head, and look up at Elijah.

“Could we cut his tongue out?”

"Yes, absolutely," Elijah replies without hesitation. "However, if you still want to play with him after that, we'll need to manage the haemorrhaging that'll happen. The tongue's an organ that bleeds profusely when cut, so we'll have to act quickly."

I nod in understanding and smile.

Fuck, he knows a lot.

"What are my options?"

"We can burn it. We could apply a solution to stop the bleeding. We could use powder as well... and a few other methods."

Ha!

He thinks I didn't catch it, the way he's holding something back from me.

I bet it's the maggots.

"Right, so we could burn it?"

"Yes. The only downside is that it'll smell."

I nod my approval.

Within seconds, he reaches for the pliers, pulls the tongue out as far as it will go, then prompts me to make the cut.

He was right. We had to move fast to cauterise the wound and keep him from bleeding out.

He passes out from the shock, his head lolling to one side.

Looking at him like this...

He seems so mortal.

So breakable.

Nothing like the man who once laughed with us on the stairs — or the monster who demanded something from me that even his own wife wouldn't give.

Bogdan's screams register for the first time.

I was so lost in my own little world that I wasn't in the warehouse anymore. I was in the darkest places of my mind.

I'm not enjoying the screaming. Maybe it reminds me too much of all the yelling my parents used to hurl at me growing up.

In one motion, I take the wire and snap it around his neck.

He's gone in mere seconds.

"I didn't like his voice," I say to Elijah.

"It's your day, my Queen. You can do whatever you like."

I look at the table—and it's the bear claw I want to try next.

In one go, I lunge it into his thigh. It makes a squelching sound I wasn't expecting.

The handle fits perfectly in my hand, but when I try to pull it back out, the fucker won't budge.

"My King."

That's all I say once I realise this piece of equipment needs more strength than mine. Without a word, and never breaking eye contact, he intertwines his fingers with mine on the grip and pulls hard. The force of it sends a deep vibration through the handle, pulling me with it.

In one go, the bastard jolts awake and lets out an almost silent scream of agony—just like the one I had to scream all those years ago.

One after the other, he screams and thrashes from the excruciating pain of his thigh muscles being torn into ribbons. The bleeding is severe, and I listen as an excited Elijah starts explaining my options to stop it this time.

When he gets to the maggots, I nod—because I *knew* it.

I know how Elijah operates now.

Every version of him is clear to me.

I take the jar of maggots and sprinkle them onto his thigh.

Sure enough, the tiny little things get to work fast.

Not sure what type they are, but holy hell—they *work*.

Well... for the bleeding, of course. Not for his pain.

I take several hours playing—discovering tools, techniques, even resuscitation methods, because the bastard tries to die on me several times.

One discovery more fascinating than the next.

By the time I'm finished and finally let him die, both Elijah and I are covered in his blood.

There are countless cuts, wholes, broken bones on this rapist's body. Each one symbolising my pain, my brokenness, and everything he took from me.

And now... now he's gone.

And the only thing I feel is *relief*—relief that there is one less rapist out there who could break a woman.

I throw my last tool onto the table and exhale.

I can breathe.

For the first time in my life... I can *truly* breathe.

Elijah's warm hands land on my shoulders, his breath a soft caress against my neck.

"Are you okay, my Queen?"

When I don't respond—don't move, don't react—he wraps his arms around me, holding me so tightly to his chest it aches all over again.

"Did I push you too far? Did I do something wrong? Are you mad at me?"

My only answer is to lean my head back against him.

He loosens his hold instantly, recognising this for what it is—my silent mode.

The part of me that needs stillness to process.

To accept.

To *be.*

I whisper the only truth that matters right now.

"I can breathe."

Chapter Thirty-Nine

Elijah

I had planned to take her to Italy, to show her the first mansion I had restored from the ground up for her. But that plan is gone. I couldn't wait. I needed to act—now—to quiet the hunger clawing inside me.

After what we shared in that warehouse, the way she surrendered to her true form, the way she drew me in, let me complete her as much as she completes me, I could no longer hold back. Every part of me screamed to make her mine. To drag the entire world to its knees and force it to bow before its Queen.

She belongs to my world now. And the world will bow to its Queen.

It's September. More precisely, the 21st of September. I'm texting like a maniac on my phone, and out of the corner of my eye I can sense her studying me. Her curiosity comes in waves, though she says nothing.

I glance up to gauge her next move, but she only smiles, yawns, and settles into the seat, her head resting on my lap. I love the way she surrenders so completely, placing such blind trust in me, especially knowing exactly who I am.

There are no more masks between us. No more half-truths or half-desires. We are all in, both of us, and we both know it.

After everything was done in the warehouse, we changed into clean clothes and washed in the grimy little sink shoved in the corner. It was filthy in itself, but we had nothing else, so we made do.

I watched her as she changed, as she bent over the stained basin to wash. She kept glancing at me from the corner of her eye, and every time our eyes met, I saw it—the quiet settling over her beautiful features. A peace she had never worn before.

My Queen had found her peace. What more could a man ask for?

There were no words exchanged, no guidance of any kind. The moment we finished at the warehouse, we burned it all to the ground — the bodies, the memories, the pain — everything up in flame. It was as clear as day: she was healing. She embraced her true self and liked what she saw.

I didn't probe, didn't ask, didn't speak. I stood there as a spectator while a true Queen was born before me, and I knew my life was bound to a woman who would take care of me just as much as I would take care of her.

I run my hand over her beautiful hair, my fingers gliding through the silky strands. Her breathing has evened out for some time now, the weight of it all claiming her as its prisoner. Or perhaps this is the first time she's truly slept deeply, because her entire body is loose and unguarded, almost comically sprawled in the seat beside me.

She has completely let go, her body and her mind finally at ease—for the first time in... forever.

I'm so pleased with myself for giving her this peace. Terrible things have always been part of my life, and over time I did worse and worse. But if I have done one good thing in this world, it was bringing Lisichka the peace she needed. If I die today, I will die loved — and my life will have had meaning because of her.

When the car comes to a stop beside the plane, all my men get out of their cars. Some take up positions at the entry points; the rest circle our vehicle, shielding it with their bodies. I appreciate their loyalty. I respect what they do, and I see their respect for me and for what is mine.

I know we'd be sitting ducks in the car, but as her hair flows through my fingers once more I cannot bring myself to wake her. She needed this—more than anything—and I'll give it to her. This moment of complete surrender.

Before I realise it, her sleep takes me over too, and I only wake when something presses against my cock. When I open my eyes, those big black, mischievous ones look at me square — teasing my senses with her mischief and testing my self-control with her fingers.

"Good morning, sunshine," she says, giggling, her hand rubbing against my groin.

"Lisichka?" I say, my tone even because I'm seconds away from taking her here and making her scream the car to pieces. The only problem with that plan is I'd have to kill my men afterwards. There's no chance of their survival if they ever hear the moans that belong to me alone.

"What is it... master?"

The word is barely out, and it's like she's lit me on fire with a single breath. The next second she lunges for the car door, ready to sprint from me — but the chain snaps taut, yanking her back and sending her crashing down on top of me.

"Goddamn it! I forgot about this!" She dangles the chain in protest, pouting. "I had a good plan..."

Then she glances over her shoulder at me and bursts out laughing.

"Oh — I have a plan too. I'm going to make you scream until your beautiful mouth cannot make another sound."

My movements are slow, deliberate as I guide her out of the car, giving her the false sense that nothing will happen. The moment we're out, I lift her in one smooth motion and throw her over my shoulder. Three consecutive snaps reverberate across her arse so fast she doesn't yelp until the third strike lands — a final, sealing smack against my palm.

"Oh!" she gasps at me. "Elijah Dominion! You better put me down right now!" she yells.

She'll yell all right. Just let me get her to the bedroom on the plane and then she's mine.

My steps are slow as we move across the tarmac, my men behind me while the attendant staff greet us.

"Elijah!" she yells again, wiggling in my hold. "Down! Now!"

I let out a chuckle — she's adorable.

"I'll put you down, alright. Straight onto my cock, Lisichka." I say, then slap her cunt and she yells loud enough to draw everyone's eyes to her.

"Remember my words," I whisper as we're mere steps from the door. "You won't be able to walk after I finish with you today." I tilt her and bite her thigh hard. "I will break your pussy today and reward you with all my love."

With those words I set her down, pushing the door closed behind us with the heel of my foot. When the click registers, my hands are on her top and I rip it off in one motion. Her breasts spring free; her bra was nothing but a token of defiance, so I grunt and pull it away.

"Someone's in a hurry," she says, laughing. "You think I'll run away?"

I understand on a conscious level that she's teasing me — of course she is. But on a subconscious level it only sharpens the need to make her mine. Even though she's chained to me and there's no way she can escape, the fear still lingers at the back of my mind, and a slight tremor runs through my hand.

Our gazes meet, and she sees plainly what her words have done to me. As always, she deflects with jokes. I catch the split second when her mind sparks with something to make it all better.

"You might run away from me sooner than I'd run from you. I kick in my sleep," she continues, giving me puppy eyes.

I laugh and press down on her shoulder, guiding her to kneel before me. She's adorable — but I have a far better use for her lips right now.

"You're adorable, Lisichka," I murmur, caressing her cheek as she looks up at me. "Now suck me dry."

She doesn't wait for another prompt, doesn't pull a face, doesn't complain about being on her knees.

We both know the truth.

She may be the one kneeling, but I am the one at her feet.

The moment her soft fingers wrap around my cock and she strokes me through my pants, tormenting me further, a deep groan rips from my chest and I lean my head back.

Fuck — she's perfect. Everything she does is naturally pleasing to me. I like things a certain way, and most of the time when I say I like something I lie so people will leave me alone. With Lisichka, everything — absolutely everything — comes naturally: every movement, every touch, every word, even these ridiculous feelings.

Reality snaps back the moment her tongue teases the tip of my cock through my pants. I said I'd break her pussy, but clearly she'll break my mind first.

Fuck! I need these pants off! I need it now!

She lets out a soft laugh against the tip of my cock, and before I can react she takes the head into her mouth and sucks hard enough to tip me over the edge.

"You're mean," I laugh. "I'd call you mean... but you're perfect."

She laughs again, dragging my cock along her tongue before sucking hard once more.

"Fuuuck!" That's it. If there was any mercy left in me to go easy on her, it's gone. She did this to herself. I'll mark her today.

In mere seconds my top is off and my trousers hang at my ankles. When our eyes meet again there is no more me. Only her master come out to play.

The recognition in her gaze, her surrender to me, is a tiny movement at the corner of her eye. That is all the permission I need. She wants this as much as I want to give it to her.

I loop the chain around her neck — more a symbol than a restraint — then rest my palm at the base of her skull and guide her down onto me. For a split second I search her eyes for any hesitation; when she smiles around me I ease the rest of the way in and hold steady. Her throat tightens, a natural reflex, and the sensation of her closing around me is maddeningly exquisite. We press together — she gripping my hips, me anchoring her — both of us fighting not to let go until I lose myself in the moment.

I hold her there for a few more seconds, savouring the sight of her lips stretched around me, her eyes locked on mine, tears gathering in them. When I finally pull back, she barely has time to draw a breath before I guide her forward again, driving all the way in with each thrust. My pounding is relentless, deep, merciless, but her eager moan vibrates against me, letting me know she wants this as much as I do. I keep my rhythm, not giving her a chance to gag, just enjoy the maddening pleasure.

"You like that?" I growl, watching as a strand of drool slips from the corner of her mouth, her answer written across every inch of her face.

She nods and gives me a hard suck as I pull back. With the next thrust, I capture her again, holding her down on me, her lips stretched wide around my length. With every gag, I try to push deeper and deeper, even if I'm bottomed out and my balls rest on her chin. She takes all of me — she must take all of me. Everything I give her. Everything I am.

Her gaze locks on mine, and we both enjoy every gag and every added pressure to my thrusts. With every passing second, I feel the world blur at the edges. Every slick pull of her mouth, every desperate sound vibrating against me, her delicious gags, her willingness to suffocate on my cock... all of it! All of it! Strips away my sanity. It's too much — her messy devotion, her relentless hunger, the way she welcomes all of me without hesitation.

I'm losing myself in her, undone by the sight of her surrender and the sheer force of what we are together.

The second her eyes go red, I pinch her nose and take the remaining oxygen coming in. I want to see her reaction. I need to know it all with her. I need to see where our limit is.

If there had been any doubt in either of our minds, it's gone now. Instead of panicking, her jaw relaxes and her mouth opens for me just a fraction more, and I slide deeper. There's no stopping my release. My cum explodes out of me in a blinding, violent orgasm that takes us both. I let go of her nose as I pull back a little and then start thrusting fiercely into her as she cries out her pleasure, the sound shredding the world around us.

Ripples of cum shoot out of me like we haven't fucked in ages. As I work through my pleasure — thrusting, rubbing myself against her mouth — she circles her hands on my arse and anchors me to her. She takes me with an almost greedy hunger, demanding every last drop. Even when I'm ultra-sensitive it only sharpens the frenzy. Her cheeks are flushed, her breathing ragged, and the look on her, the eagerness in her movements make me let her do whatever she wants with me and my cock. Her face tells me she wants every last drop of my cum, and she'll do whatever it take to get it.

We are hers. I am hers. She can do with me whatever she pleases.

One thing I'll take from her... her freedom.

I say nothing as I lift her and throw her onto the bed. She is part of me — every dark piece of me as much as every unhinged part. She spreads her legs for me without a second's hesitation; when she lowers her fingers to her cunt and opens for me, I grunt, and she laughs. Her eyes don't even make that cute, half-closed motion before I slap her pussy twice, hard.

Her eyes shoot open and for a split second I see it — she can't believe I cut her orgasm short. When I hold her gaze, spread her wider and slap her twice more, she teeters on the edge of another orgasm, blood flushing hot through her cunt.

The corner of my mouth lifts at all the delicious things I'm planning for her tonight, but she has to give me her all. Today is the day I take it all from her.

I palm her pussy and make small circular motions over her clit with the heel of my hand; she answers with soft, pleading moans. When I see she's close, I lunge for her nipple — pinch hard, then pull.

A delicious squall of pain and pleasure explodes out of her, and what comes next will unmake her in the best possible way. I don't give her time to breathe, I drive into her in one brutal thrust, and it's all it takes for her to scream her orgasm, convulsing around me, gripping me with a force that it's surprising she's not strangling it off. She pulses and trembles, and I pound into her, the rhythm relentless.

When her spasms begin to subside, I ease my hand between her legs and rub my fingers in her cum. I slide two fingers inside her arse in one deliberate thrust, then press deeper as she parts for me—answering with ragged, needy sounds. She takes me greedily, every motion feeding the hunger between us. We lose ourselves together, raw and hungry, until nothing else exists but this.

She screams my name in a loud, rending moan, but I want more. I need more! More! More! More! Give me more!

I set a merciless, rhythmic tempo with my hips and fingers, driving until she teeters on the edge. Before she tips over again I pull out. The look on her face is pure heaven—confused and desperate, demanding and pleasing, aroused and mad.

The moment her eyes beg me, I'm done for. She can have my reality—not just my cock.

I reach over and grab one of the presents I brought her. From her position she can't see what I'm doing, but when I thrust into her pussy with all my force, in the same time as I press the vibrator, set to max, into her arse, she buckles, her back arching so hard for a split second I worry she might hurt herself.

"Fuuuuck!!!" she screams, the sound ripping through the place. "Iubire! Fuck!"

I can feel her gripping me so tight. Her moans and the rocking of her hips are all the indicators I need to start fucking the living daylights out of her.

It feels tighter with the vibrator lodged in her arse, but all I want is for her to lose her mind in pleasure. I start thrusting long and deep, rotating my hips on the way out, letting her feel the entirety of me. The vibrator sends little shocks along my shaft; surprisingly, it does something for me, too.

Keeping my rhythm soft and long, I give her time to adjust to the new sensations. When our eyes meet again she smiles — but it's her words that destroy me forever.

"More... master."

Her words aren't even finished when I start thrusting into her like a madman, my hand working the vibrator in time with my cock. She screams and spasms within seconds, but I give her no relief. I pound into her arse, and when I shift my grip on the vibrator I find higher settings. I crank it up and pinch her nipple hard; she screams with pleasure and I feel her cum slick across my shaft. My brain realises a beat too late there's more cum than usual, and when the wires connect and I see she's squirting, I completely lose my mind.

I need to drink her in! I need to have it all!

I drop to my knees — two fingers on her clit, three sliding inside to work her G-spot relentlessly.

"Fuck!" I yell, then lower my mouth and suck at her pussy, devouring every glistening bead of cum.

"Give me more! Give me more!" I bark, pressing and rolling her sweet spot. "Move! Give me more!"

She arches her back, answering my desperate need, and a geyser of cum bursts from her, splashing across my face. I lose my mind!

Shit!

I thought I knew what pleasure was, but this... Lisichka squirting on my face and into my mouth—there are no words for it. I drink it all. As the moment starts to slow and she spasms around my fingers, I latch onto her clit, pulling, sucking and nipping. When she tries to pull back I capture her clit in my greedy, demanding mouth. I reach for the vibrator and shove it into her arse on full blast, then roll my fingers against her G-spot and fuck her hard.

I told her I would break her pussy today — what I meant was I would break her reality.

Her moans are like nothing I've heard before, cries of agonising pure ecstasy. If I thought I knew how she sounded, looked, or felt when she lost herself in pleasure, I was wrong. What's before me is a free woman.

I suck and nip, rolling and groaning, and the moment I trap her G-spot between my fingers — roll, press, pull — she starts squirting. This time it's so violent it covers my entire chest. I don't relent with my fingers, but my mouth is too desperate for her, so I drink as much as I can as it pours out of her in wide, hot rivers.

Her moans and shakes are so loud and violent that anyone overhearing might think I'm hurting her, not giving her unimaginable pleasure. When she's finally spent and still, I start to suck and lick all the cum off her body— but when she doesn't move at all I look up and realise she's gone. She's passed out, spent from the intensity.

"Fuck!" I breathe. I didn't think this was possible, but she's out cold from pleasure. I grin and give her one long, indulgent lick as I withdraw the vibrator. It makes a small noise when it comes free, a sound I commit to memory, and already I'm hungry to play with her again.

My tongue is everywhere, on her, under her, desperate to drink it all. It's all mine. She is all mine.

Seeing how much I'd lost to the damn mattress, I think maybe I should have something to catch it for me, something I could keep and savour — because right now I want to set it on fire for stealing what's mine.

She stirs, and I realise she's come to. I rise and look down at her face. That look — the one she wears now — is the image I will carry to my grave.

She is happy.

"My love..." I say, my voice breaking. I don't even know what to say. I don't even know how to say it.

She smiles so small, so sincere. "I know," she says, and that is all — we both know. We've found our happiness in each other, in our purest form.

Her gaze travels down to my throbbing cock. When she licks her lips, the corner of my mouth lifts. I lean over her, kneeling with one knee on either side of her chest. I don't say a word — I lift my eyebrow, and that's all she needs. Her soft hands find me and she jerks me so hard, as hard as I fucked her, ready to break my cock off. I let her. I want her. I want this.

She spits on my cock and that's the last straw. I start thrusting into her hands and in seconds I explode so hard my sight goes white for a few beats. She doesn't ease up or make any attempt to slow down; she keeps devouring me, assaulting my senses until I groan and ripples of cum shoot out of me of their own accord. My reality narrows to her — my senses answer only to her. I shake my head in a desperate attempt to find myself again, but she's destroying my cock as thoroughly as I destroyed her pussy.

I look down my cum is everywhere. On her face, on her chest, on her neck. She reaches over with her tongue and slurps some from the corner of her mouth, and my cock twitches in approval.

She laughs as she jerks me again. It's painfully sensitive, but as always I melt in her hands.

When her fingers let go and she starts rubbing my cum into her skin, I forget how to breathe.

She smiles at my reaction and keeps rubbing my scent into her skin. Forget reality — forget everything. I feel breathless at the sight of her marking herself with my very essence.

"Breathe, master."

"Fuuuuuuck!" I yell, and my cock twitches in approval.

She smiles again, softer now. "Your scent was wearing off. We can't have that."

I thought I would take her freedom and chain her to me in every way I could imagine. But it's her who effortlessly breaks me. I'm going to break her today — until her entire body is drenched in my scent, just as I am drenched in hers.

Chapter Forty

Elijah

She regretted provoking me last night when she woke up this morning. I made good on my word and fucked her raw until she passed out several times, and when she came to, I was on her again. Her scent, her cum are the very reason I even consider eating anything. There will never be a day when I don't eat her. I couldn't care less if it's taboo or extreme. This craving for her cum owns me. Consumes me. So I do, and I have, and I most certainly will in the future. I'm completely and utterly addicted to her and everything that comes out of her.

I was planning to stop for a day in Cape Town before continuing on to Antarctica. But she forced my hand, made me fuck her the entire day on the plane, so I ended up texting Buddy to get everything ready. I gave him clear, specific instructions—what to do, what to buy, what to organise once we arrive.

Today is the 22nd of September. We're on our way to Antarctica, and by the time we arrive it'll be almost the 23rd — sunrise will be mere hours away. I told Buddy everything in detail and made it clear I will kill him and anyone involved in the most horrendous way possible if they fuck this up for me.

I am not asking my Queen to marry me. I am commanding her to marry me. There is no "would you" or "could you" or "will you." Even as the thought replays in my mind, I can feel something—some sensation, some feeling—building within me. It's so foreign, so intrusive, so unpleasant that I'm not even sure what it is.

"You okay?" Her soft voice pulls me back, and her studying gaze is as confused as I am about these feelings inside me.

"I'm well." I don't even know what to say.

"Did I break your cock? Are you mourning him?" she says, then explodes into a violent laugh at her own joke. I join in because I simply cannot help it. She's funny—hilarious, actually—in how she always keeps me on my toes, teasing or provoking me in some way.

"No. No cock-breakage, I'm afraid. You'll have to do better next time," I say, wrapping my arms around her.

The plane is about to land and the seatbelt signs flick on. I understand the sign is for our safety, but not even the possibility of a plane crash can wrench my life from my hands. In one move I pull her onto my lap and wrap my arms around her, securing her to me, then put the seatbelt around us both.

She searches my gaze and then shakes her head, a smile playing at her lips. Nothing escapes her, and she knows I'm having one of those moments where I simply cannot let go of her. I need to feel her on me at all costs to calm this hunger inside me.

I try to distract myself and look over at the team we brought with us. They're trusted men, but stupid as mules, compared to her and I. Lisichka doesn't know where we're going. She didn't ask, and I didn't tell. But these fools make it obvious we're headed somewhere cold, with all their gear on and whatnot.

Maybe I should leave one of them out in the cold and see how long it would take to freeze to death. My mind automatically starts mapping the details—colours, smells, the sensation of watching someone freeze, and I get completely lost in that possibility until I feel Lisichka wiggling in my lap.

I look up at her; she lowers her lips to mine and places the softest kiss.

"Who did you kill?" she whispers against my lips.

I smile and cradle the back of her head in a grip that leaves no room for escape. Does she think she can tease me with a soft smile when I want to devour her every second of every day? I crush my lips onto hers and press harder than I ever have before until my mouth aches from the pressure. When she softens in my arms I devour her, a kiss so ferocious lips, tongue, teeth. I bite and suck until I can feel myself getting so hard I'm about to lose my mind again. And I do. I fucking lose my mind again, because when she lets out a small moan and I pull back, she whispers, "More... master." I'm seconds away from killing every man who has the misfortune of being near her. But I know they are trusted man.

"I will remember this, Lisichka. You know I will. We're about to land, and when I come to collect for what you just said, remember you're chained to me — you'll never escape me."

She has the audacity to throw her head back and laugh so hard she shakes us both.

There you go — grown men shit themselves at just a look from me, and this woman laughs in my face for threatening her.

I glance around. None of my team are close enough to where we're seated to have heard any of it, but still, I don't like it.

"Stop it, my big bad wolf. Have some fun," she says as she turns and straddles me.

How could I possibly tell her that I've never had fun in my entire life until she walked into it? That no one, regardless of their power or wealth, has ever dared speak to me the way she does? More importantly, there has been nothing — absolutely nothing — in my entire life that has captivated my attention, my interest, my need, and overpowered me... until her.

She's fucking marrying me. That's the end of it.

As the thought screams in my mind, she wraps her arms around me, and now her core is pressing against my hard cock, her breasts crushed between us, her arms locked tight around me. I've noticed this about her. From time to time, she hugs me. I don't mean she just hugs me — she actually holds me as if I'm a part of her.

It's delirious, the sensation of her wrapped around me. So sincere. So clean. So profound. And every time she does it, all I can do is lose myself in her.

The plane lands and comes to a complete stop. The blistering cold is obvious now, and the wind's roar makes it clear harsh weather awaits us. She tries to pull back, but I don't let go; I want to enjoy this a little longer. She's an unpredictable little thing, and she's been more than docile since she killed that piece of shit.

I fear the moment she starts pushing back with all her might. She might not want to be here... or, even worse, she might not want to marry me.

That feeling explodes inside me at maximum volume, and I feel something shifting. I thought I knew what darkness was; pain I have mastered since I was little, manipulation is my true nature. But this feeling — the possibility that she might not want me as much as I want her — teaches me that all the pain I've suffered or inflicted on others is nothing compared to this.

This is real darkness. As dark as the outside of this plane.

"Calm, iubire scumpă," she whispers in my ear and then kisses my neck. "Whatever it is, you have me now."

You have me now. Her words are so soft, so true and kind — completely at odds with the killer she is. And it's magnificent.

I do have her. The feeling inside me subsides, and now we can get up, and I won't murder anyone around me.

We stand, and Buddy hands us the winter jackets suited for this weather. From the corner of my eye, I see her studying me, but she doesn't say a word. She takes the jacket and slips it on. I turn, making sure the hood is up and the fur covers most of her face as well. The jacket reaches down to her boots so that no part of her body is exposed to the hard elements.

We make our way to the entrance of the plane, and the moment the door opens, the wind is deafening, the complete darkness overwhelming. She tightens her fingers through mine and looks up at me.

"Siberia?"

I smile. Why in the hell would I take her to Siberia?

"Antarctica, my Queen."

"Antarctica?!" she says in a shocked voice. "Why?! Is your lab here?"

"No." I pull her close to me. "I'm not that cruel."

She gives me a side-eye at those words.

We quickly make our way to the waiting cars, and the moment we're inside I command the driver to crank the heat to maximum. I'm terrified she'll be cold, or worse, furious with me for bringing her here.

It's a completely out-of-the-box idea, but she'll understand in a moment.

My team pile into the remaining cars, and the next moment we're speeding down a path visible and known only to them. Buddy did well. He'll live another day.

Twenty minutes later the cars come to a complete stop. From my window I can see the base, but to the side a lit path catches my eye, and I know Buddy did really well. This will be as magnificent as she is.

I open the car door, and this time the wind sounds a little more manageable — or perhaps we're simply getting used to it. Either way, the cold hasn't faded. It reminds us exactly where we are, in this harsh environment.

"If you were planning to murder me, iubire, you're going through a lot of trouble getting rid of my body," she says as if it's just a simple comment, not a crack in my reality. If I weren't used to her teasing me, I'd have lost my mind right now. But I know her. I know how teasing and cheeky she is, so all I do in response is spank her hard.

"Oww! You have to kiss it better, you brute!"

I take her hand, pull her beside me, and we make our way to the side of the base. We walk a short distance, all the while enjoying the sound of the blistering wind, the smell of the ice, the crunch of snow beneath our boots.

It's surreal.

I never thought I would find someone like me — yet here I am.

I never imagined I would fall for someone — yet here I am.

I never believed I would give my life to someone else — yet here I am.

The path curves through the ice — narrow, glowing, deliberate.

I move just behind her, watching her take it all in, giving her the chance without me. The soft golden lights I had embedded in the ground reflect off the walls, illuminating every step as if the world itself were guiding her to this moment. To me.

"Look," I murmur, pointing toward the horizon.

The first hint of light cracks open the darkness — a soft, bladed glow on the edge of the ice. It slices through the night like it's furious at being forgotten.

"It's starting," I say. "The sun's taking its time, but it's coming."

She turns toward me, her breath fogging in the cold. I take her hand.

"Even here," I tell her, "where the world sleeps for months... light still finds its way back."

We walk deeper into the tunnel until the ceiling disappears. A dome of open sky yawns above us, tinged with the fragile light of a sun not yet risen but already promising more.

She gasps.

The red roses I had flown in rise from the ice, blooming from walls sculpted into thrones of glass. Light dances on their petals, refracting like fire trapped in crystal.

I let her look. Let her feel.

Then I step in front of her, memorising this moment — the look on her face at what I've created for her. Here, the wind is only a whisper. The perfume of the roses mingles with the sharp scent of ice, and the one true drumming power is the rhythm of my heart.

"They say darkness always needs the light," I whisper. "But what they don't say... is that sometimes, two creatures made of shadows can still burn brighter than the sun."

I lower myself to my knees before her, wrap my arms around her, and rest my head against her middle. I need a moment. I need *this* moment. I need to remember it for the rest of my days — what I have created for her, what I am willing to give her, before anything else happens.

Once she rests her hands around my head, cradling me, I feel loved. I feel cherished.

I look up at her, and the look on her face mirrors my own f*eelings.*

"Look up, my Queen," I encourage her once more. The sky is transforming from absolute darkness into rays of light.

"We are both made of darkness, but you brought light into my life."

Her eyes meet mine again, and the truth is there. We both know this is our truth.

"You are marrying me, Lisichka," I command, but my voice cracks with emotion for the first time in my life. "I could not exist without you."

She cups my face, and I curse that I can't feel her skin. It's the stupid jacket sleeves between us. She smiles wider, as if she can read my mind.

"You are marrying me."

She starts laughing again and tilts her head back from the force of it. No one, and I mean no one, would ever dare laugh at me. But her... she can do anything to me. I am completely lost in her, completely at her mercy.

"It didn't escape me that you didn't ask," she says once our eyes meet again. "But all the same, I will marry you."

The words aren't even out of her mouth before I move. I jump so fast and I'm on her that she loses her balance, and we both end up on the floor while I devour her. This consuming need to have more of her, to have all of her, to breathe in her existence, is finally going to come true. She is mine. She willingly gave herself to me, and I will take all of her.

The freeze registers finally and I break apart, but she's flushed and smiling at me. She loved this as much as I did.

"Iubire, quick. Turn around."

I do. I lower myself on the ground beside her and look up at the sky. Rainbows of red, orange, and yellow fight for dominance against the darkness, and we are here to witness it all. It's extraordinary. Magnificent in its truest form.

"Three days."

"Three days?" she turns to me.

"The wedding is in three days."

Epilogue 1

There is so much more...

Epilogue 2

Indeed!
This is just the beginning...

Afterword

Hello dear reader,

I want to extend my heartfelt gratitude for reading this series. Elijah and Monica have lived in my head for years, demanding their story be told. They are at the centre of my universe, and you'll be seeing more of them to come. I hope you loved The Weight of Dark Love as much as I loved bringing these characters to life.

If you enjoyed it, I'd truly appreciate it if you could leave a review. Every single review makes a huge difference in helping my books reach more readers. Your support means the world to me!

For more behind-the-scenes content, exclusive surprises, and early access to additional chapters, visit www.karinavega.com and sign up for my newsletter to stay updated on all my latest releases.

For your free bonus chapter click here. or visit my website.

See you in the next one ;)

From my heart to yours,
Karina V.

Background story

Hello dear reader,

I love giving you the background story of how I created my books. Let me share my secret from the beginning. Elijah and Monica are at the centre of it all. They are bold, they are loud, and they unsettled me so deeply in my own skin that I could no longer ignore them — I had to start writing.

When I finally decided to bring my characters to life, one image kept replaying in my mind: a luxurious SUV parked in front of a florist shop. That split second of contact changed everything. I knew my characters were powerful, but I didn't yet realise *how* powerful.

I began writing *The Path to Dark Love* (Book 1) in parallel with *The Weight of Dark Love* (Book 3), but soon I realised Monica and Elijah were consuming me. After eight chapters, I had to pause Book 3 to focus solely on Book 1.

When I returned to it, Monica rejected some of the earlier chapters, they no longer felt like her. She demanded changes until I used my author's "superpower" and deleted two full chapters. Only then did she relent, and we agreed the story was finally hers again.

As the book unfolded, something unexpected happened: **I fell in love with Elijah**. Truly, completely. I knew from the beginning that Monica and Elijah were the heart of my universe — because of that florist shop image, and because of all the side stories branching from them — but I never expected to fall for my own creation like I have. I find it both hilarious and humbling

At its core, this story was born from a universal need: **self-acceptance.**

It took me almost 40 years to learn this lesson for myself — that I should love and accept myself in my truest form. To not expect, demand, or break myself to fit others' expectations. To be my own best friend. To be kind to myself.

I hope, dear reader, that you learn this too — if not from my books, then from your own experiences. We are all just trying our best. No one has it all figured out. We all struggle in our own ways.

Elijah and Monica's story is dark, unhinged, and obsessive, but it is also about truth without apology. I hope, as you walk through their world, you discover a piece of ***your own acceptance reflected back at you.***

From my heart to yours,

Karina V.

... may you learn to embrace it.

Also By

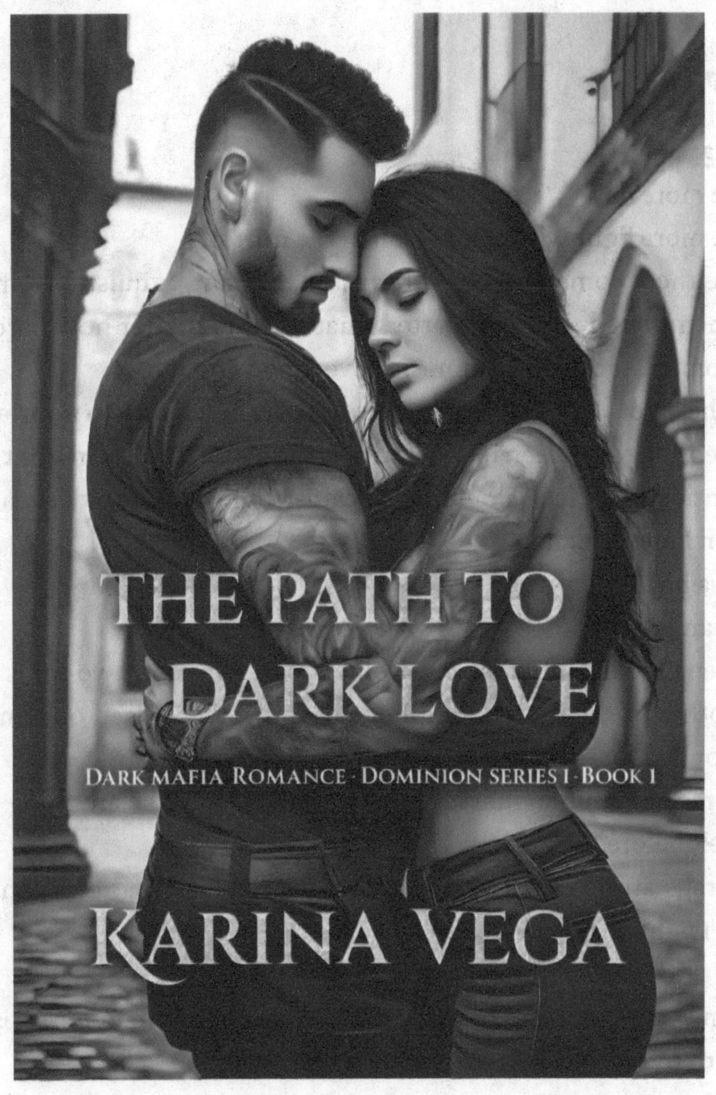

The Path to Dark Love

What would happen if you could read someone else's thoughts?

Blurb:

Angela:

One more day.

One more fight with the person in the mirror.

I see them come and go — beautiful, elegant, exquisite women — and then there is me. No matter what I do, no matter how hard I try, the woman staring back at me is never good enough.

It's hard to accept that, regardless of how much I try to improve.

Accepting the person in the mirror is the hardest battle in front of me.

Wanting more feels pointless — catastrophically stupid, even.

Then I met a man.

Not a boy. Not a guy.

A man.

When I looked into his ocean-blue eyes, it was as if two souls found each other in the midst of millions of souls, recognised one another, and bonded for eternity.

There is an unimaginable pull towards him, unlike anything I have ever felt before.

It drags at me relentlessly, ignoring logic, fear, and every internal battle I fight to stay in control.

But there is something there.

I can't quite name it, but I feel it — an edge to him. A darkness just beneath the surface.

And even so...

I don't think I can let go.

Dominic:

How can I ever be enough when I am always too much.

Too intense. Too honest. Too direct.

How can I be enough when my own parents did not want me.

Then I met an angel, and somehow, somewhere in this universe, everything went quiet.

With her, there is only silence.

All the noise in my head — every racing thought, every brutal edge — is silenced in an instant.

I know my life and my actions make me unworthy of this woman.

But none of that matters now, because she is mine.

I knew it the moment I saw her.

Soon, she will know it as well.

I will not stop until she gives herself to me willingly.

Angela is everything I have ever wanted and more. Her strength. Her vulnerability. Her fire.

All of it completes me in ways I never thought possible.

Maybe one day she will learn to love my darkness too.

But until that day, I will make her love me more than reality itself.

Chapter 1

Dominic

It's one of those days where you start questioning all your decisions, not just for the day but for the past month, maybe even the entire year. We just finished a "session," and instead of breaking, the idiot decided to keep his mouth shut for two solid hours. What the hell is wrong with these people? I mean, if we captured you and started torturing you, it wasn't rocket science. You talk. You tell us what we want to know. Who in their right mind thinks it's a good idea to hold out just to piss me off, knowing full well it was going to end with their death anyway?

Seriously, who takes that route? Like I said, absolute idiots.

Now I'm in the car, on my way to Barrow, and all I can think about is how I want to bring the bastard back to life just so I can kill him again. But slower this time, much slower, for wasting my precious time. I almost feel like drafting an email, a critical email, to these idiots, outlining some basic ground rules for torture. You know, just common sense stuff. That thought actually makes me chuckle, and I can feel the darkness in my mind easing a little. Hell, it might even be funny. Imagine sending that out:

subject: A Guide to Torture Etiquette for all the mafias.

"Dear idiots,

Please be so kind as to stop wasting my time when I have you in for "questioning".

You are already mine to do as I please, so you could save yourself some pain and me some time by spilling your guts and answering my questions quickly.

It is entirely up to you if you need me to be kind/not so kind/mental on your arse.

See you soon,

Dominic."

"Right! What is it this time? Package, letter, something else?" Elijah said with a straight face, he is my boss and like a father to me. Elijah's presence commands attention the moment you see him. His features are chiseled, giving him an air of stoic elegance. His eyes seem to hold untold depths of wisdom and experience, their mere existence enough to send a shiver down your spine.

An undeniable aura of intimidation surrounds him, an unspoken power that seems to emanate from his very being. Even without uttering a word, Elijah exudes a quiet confidence that demands respect. His closed eyes, rather than hindering his perception, seem to heighten his awareness as if he sees more with them shut than most do with their eyes wide open. Did he know I made another joke with his eyes closed?

"Email," I replied with one word. It might be a storm in my mind, but outside, I always joke. Elijah enjoys my company because I am quieter about the negative, and when I do speak, it's funny most of the time, or at least I think it's funny. In my 12 years working for him, I have never seen Elijah laughing out loud, he seems incapable of emotions like the rest of us. Yet, despite his apparent emotional detachment, Elijah has a depth that belies his stoic exterior. His silence speaks volumes, each unspoken word pregnant with meaning. It is as if he exists on a plane beyond the reach of mortal emotions, his very presence a reminder of the transient nature of human feeling.

"I just think they're idiots", I say with amusement on my lips. "How stupid can someone be to make us skin him alive? What the fuck is wrong with these idiots? We've already got him. Where did Bogdan hire this person? How can someone be this stupid?"

"Ah! That's a lot of questions for little result". Elijah says, not even bothering to open his eyes to acknowledge the storm of annoyance in me, signaling the discussion is over.

I get it, I do! There is nothing I would not do for Elijah and my brothers, but if I were captured, I'd annoy my captors with my jokes until they killed me faster.

Loyalty and respect! Under Elijah's guidance, I have become who I am today. Throughout our journey together, he's consistently shown me unwavering loyalty and treated me with the utmost respect. I would give my life for him and my brothers without a second hesitation. For Elijah, we are not merely dismissed as insignificant beings, soldiers that can be disposed of and replaced at any moment. Instead, he embraces us as his own, nurturing us and training us to become the best version of ourselves.

Loyalty and respect, till death!

I stare out of the tinted window of our SUV as we stop at the light, and next to us, a little green Volkswagen Beetle pulls up. It's blasting “Can't Stop the Feeling!” loud enough to rattle the frame, and inside, there's a girl singing completely off-key, dancing like her life depends on it. What the actual fuck?

And just like that, I forget how to breathe.

I sit there, stunned, staring at this ugly-arse green Beetle, covered in ugly-arse purple flowers, blasting an ugly-arse pop song... and yet inside is an angel who just knocked the wind out of me. My mind goes dead quiet. Completely silent.

What the hell just happened?

“Do you want to follow her?” Elijah's voice cuts through the silence. I didn't even notice him open his eyes. Silence. Complete and utter silence.

“Right,” he says knowingly, as if fully aware that my mind has short-circuited and I've forgotten how to breathe, let alone communicate.

"Vasile, follow the Beetle with the terrible music," Elijah instructs our driver, his tone as calm as ever. "And please, let's not scare the poor girl. We're just observing, right, Dominic?"

I can't respond. I've lost all connection to reality, to my surroundings, everything is consumed by the girl and her ugly car. So I just nod, barely acknowledging his words, signaling I won't engage.

She stopped in front of a flower shop with green and purple flowers in its design and logo. Right, that makes more sense now, maybe the girl doesn't have ugly-as-fuck taste in things, maybe her boss is a moron with zero taste, and she is suffering in silence like me. Yes, I'll accept this option as I look at my angel.

I reach for the car door, and the air inside shifts immediately. I can feel it, the tension, the silent disapproval from Elijah. His deep voice slices through the haze in my mind like a whip. "I think we should leave the girl alone. She's not from our world, Dominic. She wouldn't understand what we do."

His words hit me hard, cutting through the intensity of my desire and making me feel as though my very will to live has been stripped away. I can't breathe. I need to see her, to talk to her, even if just for a moment.

"Yes, boss," I manage to say, my voice strained, fighting the desperation in my chest. "But I was thinking... the Barrow could use some more flowers to brighten up the place."

The moment the words leave my mouth, I realise how utterly ridiculous I sound. Flowers? Really? It's the stupidest thing I've ever said. But before my mind can scramble to recover with a joke or something to defuse the awkwardness, my body moves on instinct, drawn to her like a magnet. I'm out of the car, pulled by an invisible force, every fiber of my being screams to get to that flower shop, to get to her.

The next thing I realise is that I am in the shop, not even knowing if I closed the car door with the speed I ran out of there, and this smell of green things and flowers hits me. My next hit is an overwhelming variety of colours and textures, like what the fuck, it's like information overload!

"Hi, can I help you with anything?" An woman in her mid-40s smiles at me from behind the counter. Her face radiates calmness, and now that I take her in she's an older version of my angel.

"Thank you. I'm browsing for a bit and will let you know." My sentence is cut short as my angel comes in from the back room, shivering, and an immense urge to go and comfort her overwhelms me. What the actual fuck! Since when is it "MY" angel and for me to "COMFORT" someone? What the actual fuck is happening to my mind and body? Less than 30 minutes ago, I was skinning someone alive, and now I feel like I can't breathe because of MY angel. I think I am losing my mind. I must be losing my mind. Am I imagining things? I turn and look at the SUV where Elijah is, and I take comfort in knowing that this is real, even if my mind is in absolute panic and I feel overwhelmed by the floods of emotions.

"The delivery went well, mum. They loved the colour scheme I used this week, and they asked if I could make an arrangement for his home and deliver it later today." What the fuck? Who is he that is about to die, and where is his home so I can burn it down? I am pretending to look at some ugly, hell-long flowers that I think I could use as a whip if I am short on other torture tools while listening to their discussion. This man will die today, and his home will be in ashes by tomorrow morning. How dare he ask for my angel to deliver flowers to his home?

"I'm sure he loved the arrangement last time you delivered" the older lady says. "Did he give you a budget or theme?"

"Not really. He said to just make something that I am happy with."

Fuck, that is a good line! "Excuse me, could you help me, please?" I turn and make a point to look at my angel so I don't end upspeaking to the older lady. The moment our eyes connect, my mind goes silent again. Silence!

My angel has this otherworldly grace, something I can't quite put into words. When she's around, it's like everything slows down, like the whole world holds its breath. Just being around her, there's this calm that seems to pull everything in, making the world go quiet.

Her features, sculpted as if by divine hands, exude another worldly beauty that could captivate anyone and bring any man to his knees. Even her movements are graceful, as every gesture has a purpose, meant to enchant me. Her words, spoken with a voice like the gentle whisper of the wind, penetrate my mind and soul as if they've found their home there.

Even without wings, there's something about her that feels...angelic, like she's a bright light cutting through the shadows in my life. It's like she was made to fit into a part of me I didn't even know was empty. But then it hits me Elijah was right. She wouldn't understand. She's too pure for someone like me.

"How can I help you?" She looks straight into my eyes, and I realise that her eyes are almost black, and I can feel my body being pulled by hers. I instinctively think I might hurt her or taint her with my darkness if I get too close. When she smiles, I'm scared I'll jump on her and pound, but then I hear my phone ping and know Elijah just texted me to leave. Just this one time! Fuck me I deserve this one time to be this close to an angel! Just once!

"Angela, I will arrange these flowers outside if you need me." The older woman looked at me while speaking to my angel. How unusual.

Angela, what a name.

"I am not the best with flowers, so I will need all your assistance and guidance with this," I say, returning her smile. She looks taken aback but quickly recovers and smiles again, keeping her tone friendly but professional. She continues, "I noticed you looking at Gladiolus. Would you like something along those lines?" The mere thought of it makes me laugh inside, imagining whipping someone to death with a fucking long flower. My brothers would forever laugh at me.

"Not quite, but thank you for noticing. I am a blank canvas, feel free to suggest anything that comes to mind." I say, trying fucking hard to sound casual like her. At least I am speaking, the words are fucking coming out. I look over my shoulder, and the old lady is arranging some flowers outside. The next moment, Elijah rolls down his window, and she looks at him and smiles. His face is blank as usual, but his eyes. What was that? It disappeared as fast as it was there, and he rolled the window back, giving him his much-loved privacy.

"Can you give me some information about who these flowers might be for? Or a type of flower that she likes or that you like? Or any information?" I am pulled back to Angela as if she were my gravity. How is she doing this? Is she "MY GRAVITY" now? I need to leave! Fuck me, this might truly have been the most stupid thing I've ever done in my life!

I think of the only fucking flower I actually know to name as I take my phone out of my pocket, trying to seem calm and collected. "I like roses." Gladiolus, what a shit name for a shit flower. Maybe we should track down who named this awful flower and whip them with it.

"Great! Any preference with the colour?"

"What flowers do you like?" I realise I am saying it out loud as I see her surprised face. "If it is something that you can share, of course."

She takes a deep breath and cleanses her hands on the apron, and that's when I realise she is nervous. Interesting! I might be making a fucking life mistake here, but at least I am not alone in it. She is nervous! She is with me in this fucked up situation. I got you, my angel!

"I love these yellow and orange roses. They are named Monica, the colour is a bit strange for some, if I am honest, but what is amazing about this rose is its perfume," she says with a shy smile, picking up some ugly-looking roses and shoving them in my face to smell.

"I like it! How many should we put in an arrangement if I am trying to impress someone?" I say, lifting the corner of my mouth with a seductive smile. As she starts to blush, I realise she picked up on my vibe, and I am most definitely not the only one in this situation.

"Perhaps around 30. How about I start the arrangement and see how we go? Can you let me know a budget that I can't exceed?" she says with a melodic voice, carefully avoiding eye contact. Her voice, her presence, her everything, her entire being is messing with my head. As I glance down and notice her more than generous breasts, I suddenly feel like a teenager again, getting hard at the speed of light.

Alright! Alright! Calm the fuck down, boy, we might scare her, and we might lose our angel. The thought takes me by surprise because until this moment, I was sure I wouldn't see this girl again, and I am just indulging in a bit of harmless fun.

"No limit, please have fun with it and make it as beautiful as you can," I say with a full smile on my face. It might be blood money, but it is still money, and she does not need to know it's blood money. I am paying with a card, for fuck's sake, so there is most definitely no traces of blood. Let her have fun with it. I started reading the text from Elijah and almost burst out laughing.

Elijah

Hey, Romeo. Make sure you keep your cool and be discreet about asking for her number. All the death threats flooding your mind, calm them the fuck down. She is not yours yet. Don't scare her if you are into her. Make sure you are into her before you do something stupid.

I quickly type a reply to mess with him a little. Shit, this is the most he's spoken to me in one go in a very long time. This might be serious, after all.

Dominic

I need Hunter to come with me later to deliver an "arrangement" to some fucker that thinks my angel needs to do home delivery.

Elijah

My angel?

Well, shit!

Dominic, don't start something that can only end one way.

Get back in the car.

Dominic

She is making an arrangement for me, and then we will leave and not come back. I will be there in a few minutes.

I look again at the car and can feel his presence and forceful gaze. I notice the older woman is still outside, and then I look at the car again, and I can feel that the gaze is not on me but on her.

I turn to look at Angela, memorising every movement of her beautiful body. The way her delicate hands cradle the flowers, the precise concentration in her eyes, and the deliberate way she avoids looking at me all captivates me. The silence between us grows heavy, thick with unspoken tension. She finally breaks it, her voice curious yet professional, attempting to make small talk.

“Do you work around here? I’ve never seen you before... or am I mistaken?” She asks, her eyes flickering up for just a moment before quickly returning to the flowers in her hands.

"No, I can't recall being in this shop before. It is a cute place you have here. Is it yours?" I say, patting myself on the back for sounding all kind and professional.

"It's my mum's shop," she says, her voice soft but steady. "The lady outside. I just help with deliveries and sometimes in the shop. I'm still studying, and this helps with the bills."

Before I can fully process her words, an unfamiliar feeling stirs deep inside me. It's like a dormant force has awoken, an instinctual need to unravel every mystery that surrounds her. I crave to know more, to understand everything that makes her who she is. And more than that, a fierce urge rises within me, a need to protect her, to shelter her with strength so relentless it could rival a thousand tsunamis.

"What do you study? If you don't mind telling me." I play the innocent as I pretend to be on my phone.

"Criminal law. I absolutely love it. The psychology of it fascinates me, especially the cause-and-effect element." I feel sucker punched! Fuck me! Out of all the women in the world and all the professions in the fucking world, she fucking had to be into criminal law? Wait, she did not say she loves it because of putting bad guys away, she said she loved the psychology of it. What the fuck does that mean?

"Interesting," I say with a smile. "What made you study this?" I look at the car and can feel Elijah's fury coming to life and radiating toward me. I'm fucked!

"I think we are all different in our own way. I believe, as I said, in the cause-and-effect element of life. Also, I take a lot of comfort in law, knowing where the limit is. What do you think?" She gives me the biggest smile I have ever received in my entire life, and the response is clear as I look into her eyes. "Beautiful!" She blushes a deep shade of red and looks away for a moment, breaking our connection. Silence! Just fucking silence!

"Do you need a vase, or are you happy to take them as is?" it's then that I look at the flowers and notice they are actually not that bad. My brothers would still laugh their arses off to see me with flowers, but they are actually nice, except for the ugly-as-fuck colour.

"I think I will take the vase as well, thank you," I say, trying to figure out how to pass the flowers to her without coming across as a creepy imbecile. Maybe I should email myself a highly important email on how not to be a creepy imbecile because, clearly, I might need some strong pointers.

"I'm just going to the back to clean up the fridge, Angela. Could you please come and help me once you are done with the gentlemen?" the old lady says as she walks past me toward the back.

"Sure, Mum, I am almost done. It comes to $480, thank you. Would that be card or cash today?" my angel says, giving me a very cold and professional smile. I don't care for it! I want the smile with the blush and the melody of her symphonic warm voice.

Blood money! Blood money! She is an angel, and you are touching her with your blood money.

What the fuck?! Is that my conscience? I thought I killed that fucker long ago, why would my insides scream at me that my money is bloody? Is a fucking card! There is no fucking blood on the card! I don't care for this conscience or this fucking voice in my head.

She is mine now!

My angel!

My fucking angel!

Ping! I hear my phone go off.

Elijah

She is not yours! Calm down, Dominic.

I hate how well he knows to read me. She is mine! She and he just don't know it yet!

"Card, thank you."

"Do you have one of those little cards to write a message?"

"Yes, of course. They are behind you. Please take whatever you like, it's on the house." She says with a shy smile again, now that her mum is out of sight. Oh! So the old lady is the problem? She can be removed very easily. Death by flowers! I almost burst into laughter at that thought! Where was that fucking long and awful flower again?

"That won't be necessary. Please charge me $600 and include a card as well. No need to wait while I think of something to write. Feel free to join your mum. Thank you, Angela." The moment her name leaves my mouth, she physically recoils as if I'd struck her. My voice had been calm, professional, hadn't it? Did I mess it up that fast?

I search her eyes, looking for the truth, and that's when I notice it, a faint blush creeping down her neck. She likes me back. I can sense it now, simmering just beneath the surface. The tension breaks as she lets out a soft laugh, an angelic sound that feels like it shouldn't even exist in this world. That sound, combined with her graceful movements, completely washes over me, leaving my body numb in the best possible way.

Elijah

Get in the car. I can feel you are making bad decisions by the second.

"Thank you again, Angela. You were very helpful," I say with a smile on my face.

"Not a problem at all! See you next time," she says, turning and walking toward the back door, giving me a perfect view of her arse. My brain short-circuits instantly. Okay, she's not allowed to wear clothes. Wait, what? That doesn't even make sense! In a matter of seconds, my thoughts spiral into chaos at the sight of her.

Oh, fuck! I want to bite that arse, mark it all over until she can't sit for days. I want to trail my mouth over her legs, her arse, bite, lick, suck, and claim her until she smells and tastes like me. What is it about this woman that makes me lose my mind without her even trying? I've never been on my knees for anyone, yet here I am, undone. Calm down, Dominic. Calm the hell down. If Elijah steps out of the car, all hell will break loose, and you won't get the girl.

No! Not a girl. She is not a girl. She is an angel.

What should I put on the fucking card? What should I say and not sound like an idiot? Fuck! Perhaps the silence that she makes in my mind may not be the best because I cannot write two sentences while

I am looking at the card. I'll just settle on honesty when all else fades away.

"Thank you for existing, Angela."

***

The Strength of Dark Love

What if your childhood trauma would try to define who you are?

Blurb:

Sofia

What they did to me? What they took from me? It's beyond words.

I hate men. All of them!

Except for my dad and Uncle Buddy. But the rest? They're all the same.

I promised myself at five years old, no man would ever hurt me again. Every one of them with a dick is a threat, and I'll destroy anyone who tries to hurt me. I won't be a victim again. No man will ever have power over me again.

What happened to me can never be erased. That's why I can't let anyone in. I won't!

I wish I could be attracted to women. It would make things so much easier. But then he walked in, this cocky, sunburnt Australian fool and everything I thought I'd buried came crashing back to the surface.

The first time I saw him? It was like someone knocked the wind out of me. I couldn't think. I couldn't breathe. In that moment, every defence I'd built around myself shattered, and I hated him for it.

How am I supposed to keep my distance when every day he's right there, breaking down my walls with that stupid grin, making me want what I swore I'd never let myself have?

Hunter

God, I love her! I've loved her in secret like a fool for two years.

How the mighty have fallen. Look at the big, scary SASR man trembling with desire over a little woman who doesn't even spare him a glance.

Sometimes, I swear I can feel it, maybe she loves me too. Maybe I'm delusional. Maybe I've finally lost my mind. But damn it, I love her with everything I am.

When I joined Elijah's team, I didn't expect much. I just wanted to lay low for a while, to escape the mess I'd made of my life. The world is full of fucked-up people, and I've seen the worst of them. My reality was falling apart.

Then I walked into the Security room, and there she was a goddess, staring me down like I was something stuck to the bottom of her shoe. Her eyes, sharp as knives, cut right through me. She barely said two words, but the second she took my hand, I felt it. Her hand trembled, and in that moment, I knew. She felt it, too. She was as affected by me as I was by her.

I want her so much! I need her! I crave her! But there's something between us, something like an invisible wall of concrete. Every time I think I'm breaking through, she shoves me right back on my ass tenfold.

Chapter 1

Hunter

God, I hate babysitting Dominic. I'm tired as hell, but I still make my way to the Barrow Building. I've got a few things to check on, but let's be real, I need to check on my sugar cube.

God, I miss her.

I haven't slept properly in 72 hours, not with everything Dominic's put me through. Got him drunk off his ass, but of course, the bastard sobered up and made a run for the door. I had to handcuff him to a support beam just to make sure he wouldn't disappear while I caught a few seconds of sleep.

I'm glad his woman took the leash off him. Now he can leave me the hell alone. He's pathetic, wearing his heart on his sleeve like that. What an idiot!

Who are you kidding? You could've stayed home, had your meetings online, but no, you came in, just to see her. Who's the pathetic one?

That thought knocks me back a bit because I know it's true. At least Dominic got his girl, made it happen. And here I am, working with Sofia for years, drooling over her like a horny teenager.

The first time I saw her... She gave me the coldest look I've ever gotten, like I didn't even exist. Like I was dirt under her shoe.

Fuck, that memory still stings. She's a goddess, all fire and ice. From her flawless skin to those ruthless, beautiful eyes. The way she talks, the way she moves, she owns every room she steps into. It doesn't matter who's in it or how big they are, she's always the alpha. The only ones above her are Elijah and Buddy, and that's it.

I walk into the Security Room, fire up all my monitoring software, and get on with it. Two hours in, and I'm still working, but there's no sign of my sugar cube.

Fucking hell, woman, where are you?

Another half hour passes, and now I'm beyond pissed. I log into the facial recognition software, and sure enough, I find her on the first floor, in an office in the East Wing.

What the hell are you doing there?

I watch her for what feels like hours. Damn, this woman is mesmerising. The number of times I've imagined my cock between those reality-shattering lips should be illegal. And the amount of times I've pissed her off to get her to fight me, just to catch a hint of her intoxicating scent, is ridiculous, but it works.

It took me months to figure out how to get her to touch me, and after that, I learned her fighting moves. Every time she throws her arms around my neck, her body pressed against mine, I swear it's the only thing keeping me going. Now, I get my regular dose of her like clockwork.

Sometimes, I swear she loves me back. I can see it when she trembles during our fights. But every time I back off or even try to be decent, she goes full psycho on me, and that monster inside her comes out. I don't know what the hell is going on, and I definitely haven't figured out how to make her even notice me.

I know she's not seeing anyone. I know because I've been following her for two years. Since day two on the job with Elijah. And I don't care. I'll stalk her for the rest of my life if I have to, but let's be real, I'd much rather be buried inside her than jerking off to her image on a monitor.

It doesn't matter how much I want her. It doesn't matter that I've studied her more than any assignment I had in the SASR. I've tried so many ways to get close, but nothing works. There's something there, something I can't see that's keeping her from me. And until I find it and neutralize it, this fire burning inside me won't be satisfied.

The problem is, she's smart like hell. If people think I'm a genius with computers, they haven't met my sugar cube. She's the best of the best.

It's funny, really, how small and delicate she looks at first glance, totally at odds with the fire boiling under the surface. But my sugar cube could put any man on his ass and make any demon fall to his knees. I know she put me on my ass and knees, and I would happily be there for the rest of my life as long as she is mine.

I'm lost in yet another fantasy of fucking the living daylights out of her when I spot something out of the corner of my eye on one of the security monitors. A guy power-walking out of the main entrance. He's trying hard not to stand out, but he's moving faster than the crowd around him.

I turn to study his body language as he makes his way to a car across the street, and that's when I feel it. The ground beneath me shakes. I know I've fucked up...

"Fucking hell, Sofia!" I yell, not caring who hears me, as the sound of the bomb ripples through the building. The next second, I'm flying down the emergency stairs, my heart pounding, desperate to get to level one and find her.

"Fuck, I didn't even start the evacuation protocol." I yank my phone out and punch in the P1 Emergency Evacuation code, then shove it back in my pocket. I don't need to check if it worked the loud P1 notification on my phone confirms just how badly I've fucked up.

My phone starts ringing, and I know it's Elijah. I know he wants a full report, but I don't care. I don't give a fuck. I need to get to Sofia and get her out, no matter the cost. No matter Elijah's wrath, no matter if he kills me for this.

When I push open the doors to level one, I barge past people scrambling to get out, dust covering everything. People are terrified, in shock, disoriented, and flashbacks of my deployments paralyze me for a second. The smell of the bomb mixed with the dust registers in my mind, snapping me back. My training kicks in, and I start helping people around me. I lock the door open to help people escape the building faster.

My phone rings again, and this time, it's Buddy. I sigh, relieved. This conversation will be easier than the one with Elijah.

"There was a bomb," I say, my voice sharp and firm.

"Yeah, we figured that out from the footage. Why are you on level one?"

"I came to get Sofia. She's here, in the East Wing..."

"Hunter, the bomb was in the East Wing." Buddy cuts me off, urgency clear in his tone.

Buddy's words hit me like a punch to the gut. A deep nausea rises in me. I can't lose her. I can't fucking lose her.

"How do you know?" I try to keep my voice level to not give away the absolute panic that is within me at the possibility of losing Sofia.

"We've been watching the cameras. The question is, why haven't you?"

"I ran to get Sofia," I say, my words clipped as I hang up and head straight for the East Wing. I know I'll probably be killed for this, but I don't care. I have to find my sugar cube.

The sight before me could be lifted straight from a war zone. Part of the exterior wall is gone, with debris scattered everywhere. The thick scent of dust, bomb residue, and blood fills the air, blending with the grim sight of torn body parts strewn about. People died on my watch because I wasn't paying attention.

I keep running, pushing through the wreckage, until I reach the area where I last saw Sofia on the monitors. She's nowhere in sight.

"Sofia! Sofia!" I scream, my voice frantic as I search through the destruction. "Sofia!" My voice cracks, sounding foreign to me, like a wounded animal crying out for its mate.

"I'm here..." Her voice is faint, trailing off before I can even locate where it's coming from.

"Cupcake, where are you?" I spin, desperately searching for any sign of her. "Please, cupcake, talk to me."

"One of these days..." Her voice is so weak, it takes me a second to realise it's coming from beneath a massive piece of collapsed concrete, somehow pinned to a desk. She's buried somewhere in the debris. "...I'm going to cut your balls off, you..." She breaks into a violent coughing fit. "you stupid motherfucker," she finishes, as sharp as she can manage in her condition. "Now get me out!"

"Hang on, I think there's a huge concrete slab on top of you. Are you injured? Can you move at all?" My voice is steady, hiding the absolute panic coursing through my veins.

"I'm not hurt... I don't think I am, at least."

"Did you lose consciousness?" I keep her talking, needing to know she's still with me as I assess the situation and try to figure out how the hell to move this thing off her.

"Yeah... I think I did. Now get me out!"

I finally find her and kneel next to Sofia, my heart hammering in my chest as I scan the wreckage pinning her down. The slab of concrete looks like it weighs a ton, and I have no clue how the hell I'm going to move it. But I have to. I fucking have to.

"Hang tight, cupcake," I say, forcing my voice to stay steady. "I'm going to try and get this off you. Tell me if anything hurts when I move it."

I can barely hear my own voice over the pounding in my ears, panic clawing at my insides. She coughs, dust swirling around her, making her look even smaller under that giant piece of debris. Her beautiful three-piece suit she is wearing is now shredded and dirty, but somehow, she still looks pristine.

"Fucking move it, jackass," she snaps, trying to sound sharp, but I can hear the crack of panic in her voice. "We need to get these fuckers!"

I press my shoulder against the slab and push. Hard. My muscles scream, but the damn thing barely moves. My boots slip in the rubble beneath me. I shove harder, my teeth grinding together as I strain against it, feeling it shift. It's just enough for Sofia to wiggle her shoulders free.

"There you go... just a little more..." I mutter, breathless.

She tries to move, but her legs are still trapped. Shit. It's not enough.

"I'm still stuck," she grits out.

I step back, glancing around the room, searching for anything to use as leverage. My eyes lock on a metal rod sticking out from the debris pile. I yank it free, my hands slick with sweat and dust. I jam it under the concrete, positioning myself to try again.

"You're insane if you think that's going to work," Sofia mutters, her voice weaker this time.

"I've done crazier things, cupcake. Just trust me."

I throw my weight onto the rod, feeling my muscles scream in protest, but the slab starts to shift, inch by inch. Just enough. Almost there...

Then, without warning, the rod snaps with a sickening crack, sending debris crashing down. I barely have time to throw myself over Sofia before something jagged slams into my back. The pain is instant, like fire searing through me.

"Hunter!" Sofia screams, panic clear in her voice.

I grit my teeth, biting back a groan as I try to keep my body braced over hers. Every breath feels like knives stabbing into my ribs, but I don't care. I'm fine. I don't even have the strength to lie convincingly, but I do it anyway. "I'm fine," I manage, my voice strained.

"You're hurt," she says, her voice cracking.

Doesn't matter. Nothing else matters except getting her out. I push through the pain, using my free arm to shove the remaining debris off her legs. My vision blurs, but I force myself to keep going, ignoring the agony coursing through my body.

"Stop," Sofia pleads. "You're making it worse."

"I'm getting you out," I growl, using the last of my strength to shove the rubble off her. With a final push, it gives way, and I collapse onto the floor beside her, gasping for breath. My whole body feels like it's on fire, but I don't care. I got her out. That's all that matters.

Sofia slowly starts to stand, her hands trembling as she leans over me. "You idiot!" She yells straight into my face. "Why didn't you wait for help?"

I chuckle, though it hurts like hell. "Couldn't risk losing you, cupcake." My eyelids feel heavy, but I force them open, trying to focus on her face. "You okay?"

"I'm fine," she says, her eyes scanning me, filled with worry. "But you're not." She holds my gaze, and the look on her face, something I've never seen before, stirs something deep inside me.

I slowly stand, every movement sending sharp pain through my ribs. Definitely broken. It'll hurt like hell for a while.

But I got her out. She's safe.

You know what? Fuck it!

One second, I'm holding her gaze, and the next, I'm kissing the living hell out of her. The kiss is fire and ice, just like her, deep, passionate, and completely out of control. And I know, even if I kissed her every day for the rest of my life, it wouldn't be enough.

Fuck, she tastes amazing!

"That's it, Sofia," I growl against her lips. "From now on, no more games. You're mine. I'll fight you if I have to, but I'm never letting you out of my sight again."

In that moment, I make the decision. This is it! I'm never letting her go, and she will have to deal with it or fight me 'til death.

Stay Connected

You can find more about me on:

Website – www.karinavega.com

You can stay connected to me through:

Facebook page – Author Karina Vega

Facebook group – Karina Vega's Lit Lounge & Book Nook

Instagram – authorkarinavega

TikTok – AuthorKarinaVega

YouTube channel – KarinaVegaAuthor